NEVER FORGIVE YOU

NEVER FORGIVE YOU

HILLY BARMBY

This edition produced in Great Britain in 2024

by Hobeck Books Limited, 24 Brookside Business Park, Stone, Staffordshire ST15 0RZ

www.hobeck.net

Copyright © Hilly Barmby 2024

This book is entirely a work of fiction. The names, characters and incidents portrayed in this novel are the work of the author's imagination. Any resemblance to actual persons (living or dead), events or localities is entirely coincidental.

Hilly Barmby has asserted her right under the Copyright, Design and Patents Act 1988 to be identified as the author of this work.

All rights reserved. No parts of this book may be used or reproduced by any means, graphic, electronic, or mechanical, including photocopying, recording, taping or by any information storage retrieval system without the written permission of the copyright holder.

A CIP catalogue for this book is available from the British Library.

ISBN 978-1-915-817-39-6 (pbk)

ISBN 978-1-915-817-38-9 (ebook)

Cover design by Jayne Mapp Design

Printed and bound in Great Britain

Are you a thriller seeker?

Hobeck Books is an independent publisher of crime, thrillers and suspense fiction and we have one aim – to bring you the books you want to read.

For more details about our books, our authors and our plans, plus the chance to download free novellas, sign up for our newsletter at **www.hobeck.net**.

You can also find us on Twitter **@hobeckbooks** or on Facebook **www.facebook.com/hobeckbooks10**.

To my partner Malk, always so supportive, who also lives and works in his own box (he's a musician), while I live and work in mine. We meet for coffee in the garden.

Prologue

How could you all have done that? You killed him. You stood and stared as he died and did nothing. We know who we are, and we know who you are. We will not forget, and we will never forgive you.

ONE

Hetty

AWKWARD

UNCLE ARCHIBALD, or Archie, as he now preferred, had been waiting for them at the train station at Le Puy, drinking a black coffee and puffing on a cigarette. Having never met him before, Hetty noted he had dark circles and a sagging look about him, with shoulders bowed and head lowered. Maybe he always looked like that, but as his daughter Isabel was getting married this week, Hetty doubted it. This was the reason they were all travel weary and a bit cantankerous. A French wedding in the countryside. Archie tossed the still-glowing cigarette into the bushes and flipped the empty coffee cup into a waiting bin, already overflowing with rubbish. It bounced on the edge, wobbled and fell off. He didn't bother to pick it up.

They walked over, dragging their suitcases behind them. It had been a long journey from Brighton to here in the Central Massif in France, and not just in time. Hetty sometimes wondered if her boyfriend, Davey, and his twin sisters, Ailsa and Jules, got on at all. So much unsaid *weirdness* in the air, covered by a patina of well-bred politeness. She couldn't work out why and Davey was less than forthcoming.

'It's just family stuff, you know...' he'd said, but she didn't know and that was kind of the point. From the way he said that, she wasn't sure if he knew either.

Now, Davey slipped his arm around her shoulders, bent down to her and whispered, 'Behold, the father of the bride. I bet he'll be glad when it's all done and dusted.'

'Not sure,' Ailsa said, 'if I'm looking forward to seeing the old place or not.' Hetty noted that she glanced at Jules. She found that an odd thing to say. Surely, they must all be so excited to be back here?

Davey made some sort of tutting sound. 'Bit late as there's Uncle Archibald now.' He waved. 'And he's still driving that old Citroën.' Hetty stared at the car. Rounded and low-slung. Painted a fifties olive green. She did wonder if it scraped the ground on occasion. She and Davey had bicycles at home in Brighton, as parking was non-existent and the buses and trains ran on time. So why bother with a car?

Jules strode off, and Hetty heard her say to her uncle, 'I thought you'd given up?' as she leaned in for a hug. She eyed the cigarette butt still smouldering beneath a shrub. Hetty thought that although Ailsa might be the outgoing twin, reeling in new friends as if they were plump trout on the line and often saying stuff without thinking about it beforehand (or maybe she did think beforehand and decided to say it anyway), it was Jules who she viewed as someone she'd like to spend time with, an ally in the MacGregor clan she was now part of. Mind you, Jules was a psychologist, at least in her final years of training, and Hetty wasn't sure if she was always making judgements about them. You should mind your 'Ps' and 'Qs' in front of a psychologist in case they worked out you were a serial killer before you did. That was a bit unnerving.

Archie made a grunting sound. 'You try giving up smoking

before your darling daughter's wedding.' His smile was lopsided. He might be topping fifty, but he was still a handsome man. Rangy, sandy-haired and dressed in that inimitable shabby-chic style the uber-rich seemed to pull off without a thought. She could see where Davey got it from. 'I promise to stop this filthy habit when they leave for their honeymoon. And not a moment before.' He twisted and scooped Ailsa into his arms. 'It's good to see you lot. It's been far too long. Eight years. I suppose it got a bit staid and boring for you all in the end, eh?' Hetty noticed his eye twitched.

Jules took a deep breath and then moved away from them, fiddling at her bags.

Ailsa swept her long, golden hair from her face and said, 'Yeah. The usual teenage angst and the horrors of Brexit.' She glanced again at Jules and stepped back. 'Has Aunt Romilly lost the plot yet?'

'She will if you call her aunt. You're all old enough to call us Archie and Romi. I'd like to say you all look wonderful. So grown-up.'

'That's probably because we are.'

'Romi has planned a little party for tonight. To welcome you all back and to have a little bit of close family time—'

'You mean,' said Davey, 'before the hordes arrive?'

Jules came over and leaned against Davey. 'Will Jean-Jacques be there?'

'I believe he'll be arriving much later. We may well miss him tonight.'

'His loss, then.' Ailsa motioned at the car. 'Will we all fit in that?'

'No,' said Archie, 'that's why I booked a taxi. It's waiting with a driver over there. You'll have to call dibs on it, or me.' He nodded across the parking lot and then waved at Davey. 'Come on then, Davey. Introduce me to your lovely girlfriend.' He let go of Ailsa and pulled Davey and Hetty into a vice-like hug. Speaking into her hair, he said, 'It's good to know that Davey is settled now. All we need to do,' he turned and grinned at the twins, 'is get these two a matching pair of nice boys.'

Hetty couldn't fail to notice that Jules blanched and stamped to the car. 'I'm bagging us the Citroën. Davey? Can you and Hetty go in the taxi?' She didn't wait for an answer but, leaving her suitcase by the boot, tugged the passenger door open and slumped in. Hetty secretly wondered if Jules was gay. Maybe a 'nice boy' wasn't on her agenda.

'Moody or what?' said Ailsa, shrugging her shoulders.

'It's the first time since...' Davey stared at Ailsa with a peculiar look on his face. 'I mean, we never quite got to the bottom of it all, did we? What happened? She seemed quite upset, you know, when it all went a bit weird.'

Ailsa rolled her eyes. 'That was years ago, and we were all just kids. It had nothing to do with us.' Appearing uncomfortable, her eyes slid sideways too fast. She shouted across the parking lot, 'And thanks for assuming you're in the front. I obviously love being in the back.'

'Whatever!' came the reply.

'I bet she's just tired,' said Hetty.

'Join the club.' Archie made a face and then smirked as if he'd been a naughty little boy that had been caught out. 'I should warn you it's like a military campaign back at the house—'

'Is it all going to plan?' Davey scrunched his eyes shut. 'Sorry, didn't mean to interrupt you.'

'If the plans include mayhem and madness, then I'd say yes, brilliantly.' Archie flapped his hand at the car. 'I suppose we'd better get off, although I was enjoying being out of the fray, if just for a moment.'

'God! That bad?' Davey tugged his suitcase to the boot of the waiting taxi. He said something in French to the driver, and Hetty felt embarrassed. Basic schoolgirl French was her level, and most of that was forgotten or mispronounced. Davey and the twins were fluent, not only because of spending every summer out here with their half-French family but because they had all attended the best schools. And, to top it all, they all spoke Swedish.

Hetty had been with Davey for over a year and moved in with him less than six months ago. The longest relationship she'd managed so far. She hadn't yet met Eva, his Swedish mum, or James, his Scottish dad. She'd waved at them and chatted on Facebook when Davey called them every week. There had been a promise of a visit, but they were still in Sweden, as James had had a stroke the month before. It had been touch and go for a while. She remembered their last conversation about the wedding.

'We're going to have to decline the invitation.' James' face was drawn and pale on the screen. 'We're absolutely gutted.'

Eva's head bobbed into view. 'Davey? You and the girls will have to do the honours in our stead.' Hetty noted that Eva had that bright, brittle smile of someone who was trying not to show how concerned she was.

'We'll do you both proud,' Davey said. 'Don't you worry.'

James nodded. 'I know you will. Well, have a toast for us.' He blew out the side of his mouth. 'Not even allowed a snifter of whiskey at the moment. Life is decidedly boring.'

'Don't fret, Dad.' Davey indicated himself and Hetty. 'We will video it all, and you can watch it live.'

'You won't miss a thing,' interjected Hetty.

Eva shook her head. 'Such a shame we couldn't make it there to see you all, but as you say, if you film it, it'll feel like we're there with you.'

When Davey closed his laptop, his face betrayed his fear. 'He doesn't look good. Maybe we should go and visit them?'

'It's too close to the wedding. Let's sort something after.' Hetty leaned in and kissed his cheek. 'Okay?'

Davey's cousin Isabel was marrying an eminent French MP. Well, of course she was. There would be no oiks here to sully the reputation of the MacGregor family. Oh, apart from her. Ho-hum!

Hetty bit her lower lip. She wondered if she was considered 'inferior' to Davey and his family? Although a weird undercurrent swirled around them all when they met up with Ailsa and Jules, she wasn't sure if it was directed at her. Luckily, it wasn't often. The MacGregors were moneyed and educated at the best schools. She'd gone to a grubby, run-down comprehensive with buildings and equipment from the 1950s. Still, she had worked harder than anyone to achieve her grades against the odds. Respectable grades. The library had been her escape, falling into the pages of books to sweep her away to another place, another life that wasn't her own. No, she shouldn't think about that now.

Mind you, that last bit of conversation was a bit cryptic, wasn't it? Something must have happened eight years ago, and that's why none of them had returned until now. So, what was it? She hefted her suitcase into the boot, alongside Davey's, and inched the heavy holdall off her shoulder. Squeezing it in the gap, she rubbed at her neck.

'I don't know what I've got in there, but it weighs a tonne.'

'Shouldn't have brought the kitchen sink, then,' said Davey as he *thunked* the boot shut.

'I didn't know what I'd need.' And wasn't that the truth. Not being part of the 'inner circle', she had no idea what might be required. Davey had mumbled something about cocktail dresses. Where the hell was she supposed to get hold of a cocktail dress? She would look a right frump in front of his wealthy relatives in her second-hand frock. Oh, well. Chin up.

'I know. I'm only joking.' He bent down and kissed the tip of her nose. 'Don't worry,' he whispered, 'it's going to be great.'

Hetty wasn't so sure. Davey had never experienced what it was like to be poor, make do, and scrabble for what you could get. And neither had his family. She had to be careful not to curtsey and tug her forelock.

Cruising along in the back of the taxi from the main town of Le Puy, Hetty breathed in the dusty smells of a tired summer turning to autumn, imprinting the rich colours on the back of her eyelids and allowing the fragile sun to kiss the skin of her bare, freckle-sprinkled arm, dangling out of the open window. Having never been abroad, at the ripe old age of twenty-two she wanted to preserve this all etched on her mind to keep for later. She'd need it when she returned to her reality. Three years older, Davey acted like he was *so* experienced in life that he was now jaded. It was all an act. At least, she hoped it was.

Hetty spotted the *house* as they wound down the picturesque lane across the valley from it. Imposing, it appeared to strobe through the densely packed trees, standing alone in a sea of wildflower meadows and sun-dried swathes of grass. Gently rolling hills and clumps of interwoven oak, beech and chestnuts surrounded it, with a black-green pine forest as a backdrop to highlight its golden stone walls.

'You didn't tell me it was a blinkin' chateau!' Hetty swivelled to stare at Davey. 'I know your family are wealthy but come on...' It was meant as a joke but boy, was *it big*!

'Look,' said Davey, 'it's not a chateau. It's more of a provincial house. Anyway, most of it is rented out in the summer months. As I told you, the family only has the top and ground floors. The four flats in between are normally booked up now.'

'Yes, but you told me it was usually rented to their fashionable, upmarket friends. That's not quite running an Airbnb, is it?' Hetty stared out at the house. 'That's having space to put your mates up. And, no matter which bit they've got, to me, it looks massive.' Gabled and turreted, with two tall chimneys at each end of the grey slate roof. Four stories high, and the windows peeking out in the attic that might or might not have a few children locked up in there. Symmetrical and balanced. A reflection of the MacGregor family. The Clan. It was posh, all right. Hetty glanced at the driver. Was he local? Did he view the family as interlopers? 'So, your aunt and uncle are kind of like the Lord and Lady of the manor here, then?' Could he speak English? Was she sticking her size six *pied* in it?

Davey wrinkled his nose, and frown lines creased his forehead. She knew he didn't enjoy discussing his privileged background. 'We don't like to think of it like that—'

'They are, really.' She waved out the window. 'Your uncle is a high-ranking judge, and your aunt owns a chateau—'

'Runs a guesthouse, you mean. Listen, Hetty, I don't want to argue before we've even stepped foot in the place.'

'All I'm saying is, this is your childhood playground. I had a patch of tarmac and boys trying to sell me fags from the age of seven.' Hetty gave him the 'whale eye'. 'And that was on a good day.'

'Lucky you.' He turned and laughed at her. 'I would have given my right arm for a patch of tarmac and some fags. Listen, we're probably all a bit jittery. A French wedding is something else, and I can't even imagine how Isabel is right now. She'll want everything perfect—'

'Of course, it's her wedding.'

'I hope it's not a nightmare. There are so many things that could go wrong.' Davey tapped a rhythm out on his knee.

'Something always goes wrong at a wedding. It's par for the course or whatever that stupid saying is.' Hetty reached out to touch him, yet he continued to stare ahead. 'Just as long as it's not us that's the cause of it.'

He glanced sideways at her. 'You mean with our big mouths?'

'Always putting our foot in it.'

He sniggered. 'Game on!' Taking a deep breath, he waggled his head. A slight bob. 'It won't be you putting your foot in it. It will most likely be me. I haven't seen them in over eight years, and it's going to be strange.'

'They're still your family, no matter what.'

TWO

Ailsa

THAT LITTLE GINGER MOUSE

You could always tell when you were in France. The smells gave it away. Scents you didn't encounter in England, except if you visited an old inn or expensive hotel. Especially here, stepping down from the train into the French countryside. Knowing that in less than half an hour, they would return to that big house and their childhood roots. All those memories. *That terrible secret.* Although it was a warm day – after all, they were in central France, and the weather was so much more clement here than in southern England – she shivered as if a cold hand had trailed down her neck.

'Not sure,' Ailsa said, 'if I'm looking forward to seeing the old place or not.'

Her brother Davey turned and stared across the station car park, squinting against the sun's glare. 'Bit late as there's Uncle Archibald now.' He held up a hand and waved. 'And he's still driving that old Citroën.'

Jules was the first to move, and Ailsa watched as her sister was swept into the arms of their uncle, who appeared well-worn, creased even, like he needed a good iron. Was that due to time passing or maybe the stress of a wedding? Or maybe, as she knew, something else entirely? She heard Jules admonish him for smoking. Closing her eyes, she wondered how long she could hold out before she had to slip away for a much-needed cigarette. Having given up for nearly five years, she was ashamed to admit she'd started again. There were mitigating circumstances. There always were, but she felt she would be perceived as weak, and she couldn't let that word enter her vocabulary.

Davey slung his arm around Hetty's shoulders as if she needed to be protected.

Ailsa wanted to know why this girl was even here with them. She was not one of them. Davey's new girl was a little mouse. A very ginger little mouse. Davey had reprimanded Ailsa when she called her 'ginger', but that's precisely what she was. She was a ginger! The last persecuted minority left on this earth, or so she'd been told. It wasn't even the sheer redness of the girl; it was that she was so common. She worked in a shop, for God's sake! And she wasn't going to start on her accent. Ailsa knew enough about her brother that if she got stuck in against this Hetty girl, he would dig his heels in harder. It was best to allow it to run its course and let him get bored, although she was disconcerted that it had been over a year now. After all, wasn't she simply a distraction? His bit of rough? It couldn't be real, could it? Whatever happened to that lovely young thing he'd been with before Hetty? Elizabeth? She was far more suitable.

Ailsa stared about her. Had it changed that much? Eight years ago, they had driven away from the house along this road. Eight years was a long time in anyone's books, but that time differential from the age of fifteen until now made it way more massive. Because of what had happened that hot and clammy afternoon. Because of what they'd *done*. Receiving the invitation to Isabel's wedding was a shock. She knew it was always going to happen, though she thought it would be later, at a time when they'd made up and were friends again. When there wasn't this ghastly wedge between them all.

She and Jules were a year and a couple of months younger than Davey. In fact, judging by the timelines, their poor mum had barely had time to catch her breath before she was pregnant again and this time with twins. At twenty-five, her cousin Isabel was nigh on the same age as Davey, and Pierre was a few months younger than them. A neat little package. Ready-made friends, and they'd been a unit from the start. Or, at least, they believed they had been until that day.

And she knew all Isabel had ever wanted since she was a kid was marriage and babies. And money, of course, but then who didn't want that? Twenty-five was an acceptable age to settle down into the delights of matrimony. Her husband-to-be was a government minister and would keep her in the style of living she believed Isabel wanted to become accustomed to. Jean-Jacques, or J.J. as he preferred. As long as the babies didn't appear too soon. Ailsa shuddered at the thought of pushing a rugby ball-sized being, squalling and covered in the most grotesque gunk, out of her. And then to have it latch itself to you, sucking you dry. Ugh! She was not up for any of that. Having her hard-won body ruined. What was the point of all that time down the gym, to have it go to pot after having a baby? No. Babies were not for her, and she wished Isabel all the best and hoped she'd never be asked to babysit. Ever.

Now, Davey and Jules were another consideration. Poor Davey had no idea why there was a certain frostiness between them all. He'd believed the lies they'd been told and Jules, obviously upset and bewildered, had accepted it all, too. It had been so easy for Ailsa to manipulate their parents when they'd got back to England after that final summer. Even Jules seemed loath to return here, and thank God for that! The excuse was that they were growing up and, also, that Brexit had thrown a spanner in the works. The real reason would destroy them.

Ailsa closed her eyes for a moment. She mustn't get bogged down in the past. It was, after all, the past, and no amount of wishing would ever change that. Let sleeping dogs lie. Isn't that what they say? In case one rears up and bites them.

Jules had bagged the front seat in Archie's car, and that rankled, as now she was expected to sit in the back, to be forced to lean at an awkward angle to hear the conversation from the front. That was not cool. Although Jules was her twin, identical twin, they had drifted in those intervening years. But that wasn't surprising, was it? Maybe this wedding could cement them all back together, as the last time they had been here, they had been fractured into a million pieces.

2016 - Ailsa

Ailsa was so bored! They'd arrived a week ago at the French house. The last few days of June were slipping past them in a haze of sticky evenings, sweaty faces and itching mosquito bites.

From the moment they'd arrived, their mum and dad had ensconced themselves with Aunt Romi and Uncle Archie in the salon drinking red wine, where intermittent shouting could be heard behind the closed door. As far as Ailsa could gather, they weren't shouting at each other (that was what Isabel had told her). They were shouting *with* each other. Ailsa wasn't sure what the difference was.

'It's about this Brexit thing,' explained Isabel in French, shaking her head. As she was the eldest of the girls at nearly seventeen, it was apparent that she viewed them all as children. Ailsa found it annoying, even if they were. 'From what I can work out, neither your lot nor mine can believe it actually happened.' They were in Isabel's bedroom. She was sitting at her dressing table and talking to Ailsa in the mirror, wrapped in a bath towel, her long dark hair dripping across her shoulder.

'Who cares. It's all boring politics,' replied Ailsa, also in French. They always spoke French while they were here.

'Yeah, though I think it's important. We're okay, as we're French citizens, but you're all English, well, British—'

'So?' Ailsa was sprawled on Isabel's bed, flicking through a recent edition of *Vogue*.

'It means you're no longer a European—'

'And?'

'You might not be able to come here anymore. You're not one of us!'

'Don't be stupid! Of course we can. Why wouldn't we?' Ailsa felt offended. She tossed the magazine aside. Not one of us? *What did that mean?*

'Because you'll be third-class citizens. Like an African or whatever. They'd better make a deal, or it'll be curtains for you lot.'

'What a load of rubbish.' If only she could flounce off in a melodramatic way, but Isabel probably wouldn't even notice. Or care. Time to change the subject, as Isabel often made her feel as if she knew nothing about the world around her. Isabel was right.

'Isabel? Where's Jules?' Picking up the discarded magazine, she used it to fan herself and wiped the sweat from her upper lip. These attic rooms were stifling, and her aunt and uncle hadn't installed air-conditioning, saying it 'would ruin the look of the place'. Jeez! They'd rather boil to death up here than put up a few modern air-con units? What was up with that?

'Off taking close-up photos of old trees and weird bugs, using her super-duper new camera your lot got her for her, I mean, your birthday.'

'Eugh! Nasty. I can't stand creepy crawlies. Why she didn't get the latest iPhone as I did beats me. She's still using that knackered old one from years ago.'

'Yeah, she's a funny one, all right. But you must admit the camera's cool. It takes great shots.'

'So does my iPhone, and it's an eighth of the size.' Ailsa dropped the magazine and lay back, staring at the flaking ceiling. 'I mean, what's up with her? She's being quite a pain in the bum at the moment.'

'From what I can see, Jules is doing everything she can to not be like you.'

Irritation welled up as if Ailsa had eaten something nasty. They were twins, sure, although their mum had never done the 'twin thing'. Even as toddlers, they'd had their own clothes, their separate styles. They might be genetically identical, but they weren't identical, not by a long shot. Now they were galloping up to sixteen, and Jules was going out of her way to somehow prove she was not Ailsa's *mini-me*. Toulouse, the MacGregor's ginger cat, was curled up on the bed beside her. She tickled his tummy as he purred.

'Don't encourage him,' Isabel eyed her in the mirror. Maman would go crazy if she knew we brought him up here, after what he did.'

'What did he do?'

'He knocked off some bit of glass that Maman said cost the earth and was irreplaceable. I mean, she was livid.'

'Naughty kitty.' Ailsa tickled him some more. 'Listen. It's not my fault I'm the outgoing twin!'

'Isn't it?' Isabel was trying out a new colour of lipstick. 'Too dark, do you think?'

'No, it looks good on you.'

Ailsa had mugged up on it. There were so many online theses on this subject, so close to her heart. As one article put it: How can one identical twin be a wallflower (Jules), and yet the other is showing off at the party (that would be her)? They'd studied mice to show all sorts of weird stuff, although Ailsa wasn't sure that counted. The next thing she read that intrigued her was that it was thought some twins turned out differently due to the behaviour around them, say if one twin was treated in another way by friends, teachers or even their parents. It appeared that all twins start out with very similar personalities, but as time goes by, they can drift apart. That was the same for all siblings. Just look at Isabel and Pierre. He used to follow her around like a little puppy, desperate to please and get a pat on the head, but now he was fifteen, he was metamorphosing into a complete *twat*.

'Do you think me and Jules are treated differently?'

'Don't you mean "Jules and me"?'

'Whatever. Do you?'

'Of course. You're two different people.' She stopped and peered over her shoulder. 'Why?'

'Just something I read online. It's not my fault she's not more like me.'

'And that's a bad thing?'

'Yeah?'

'And if she was more like you, wouldn't that make it so you have less time in the limelight? Maybe she'd have more friends on Facebook than you? Maybe, she'd be the one pitying you?'

'That's never going to happen.' Ailsa could hear the anger in her voice. Ouch! Isabel's last comment hurt.

'No. So be careful what you wish for, dear cousin. Jules being different to you helps you.'

There was one thing in her reading, though, that stood out. A chance event. A feedback loop. If one twin has an experience that makes her less extrovert, she will meet more introverted friends and vice versa. This will inevitably make one twin more extroverted and the other more introverted. Small changes in behaviour can lead to larger ones. It can even resculpt the brain. Ailsa shuddered as images of scalpels dripping blood filled her mind. It had grown more noticeable recently. Okay, she understood that Jules needed to establish her individual identity and get out from under Ailsa's massive shadow, but really! Wearing grubby dungarees and no make-up? Crawling around in the undergrowth, looking for her perfect shot and being covered in ants and dirt. Except, now it felt like there was something off. She couldn't blame it on the creepy crawlies.

'The thing is, Jules is acting more like she's hiding something, and that isn't on.'

'What do you think she's hiding?' Isabel stared at her, her eyeliner pencil suspended before her face. 'A boyfriend you don't know about?'

'A boyfriend...' That was one thing that had never crossed Ailsa's mind. *She* didn't have a boyfriend, so it meant that Jules couldn't have one either. But what if she did? And who was it?

Sisters shared and twins more so. What was Jules up to? Was there more than she was letting on? Isabel had thrown that comment out, not thinking as usual, though it was now stuck in Ailsa's head. A secret boyfriend? Before her? Not in this reality. Inquiring minds had to find out. After all, they were nearly the same person, so it wouldn't be snooping, would it? And she had to know.

'Ails?' Isabel swivelled in her chair. 'You know I was joking, right?'

'What if it isn't a joke?'

'Then we find out and, depending on who it is, stop it.'

'Stop it?'

'She's more of a kid than we are. We have to protect her.' As Isabel leaned back in to admire herself in the mirror, she added, 'And the family.'

That was one thing Ailsa definitely hadn't thought of. What would her mum and dad do if they discovered Jules was with a boy?

'She always has her phone on her, so it'll be tricky to get hold of, but if we can—'

'We can see what she's up to.' Isabel smiled like a shark at Ailsa in the mirror before blowing her a red kiss. 'Then we have to get it off her, don't we?'

THREE

Hetty

SCHOOLGIRL FRENCH

A CHAIN across the track that led to the chateau had been left curled by the side of the road like a sleeping snake, and there seemed to be a lot of through traffic. The track was wide enough for one car, and there were a lot of scary manoeuvrings as vehicles tried to pass each other. To Hetty's left, a massive white marquee was being erected in a lower field. Men ferried tables and chairs down a set of stone steps and stacked them in piles under the dome. Beyond that, she spied a meandering river overhung by trees, afternoon sunshine spangling as it splashed its way along. Talk about idyllic!

Hetty craned out of the side window as they finally crunched slowly up a wide gravel driveway and slid to a stop behind the Citroën. The high, double front door painted a soft light blue was open and a young woman bounded out, waving her arms and shrieking something unintelligible in French. Was she still in her pyjamas? Ailsa and Jules scrabbled out of the car and fell into her arms. Two golden heads against one dark.

'That's Isabel,' said Davey. 'Bridezilla herself!' He rolled his eyes. 'Only joking. She's lovely. Come on, I'm gagging for a coffee.' Without waiting for her, Davey flung the taxi door open and ran to his sisters and cousin.

Clambering out, Hetty wrestled both cases and the bag from the taxi's boot. The driver stood and stared around him momentarily, watching as she struggled with the cases, his arms braced across his chest. Maybe her intuition was correct. Perhaps the locals didn't like this foreign family lording it over them. Or he wasn't being paid enough to bother with niceties. The man raised his eyebrows at her, shrugged and then took off in a spurt of small stones. Looking upwards, the house seemed to go on forever, and, on either side, she could spy manicured, formal gardens. Davey was surrounded by his family, and Hetty was left alone, standing at the edge of something she didn't feel welcome to enter, a forcefield she had to fight her way through.

'Hetty? I'm so sorry. I didn't mean to leave you like that.' It was as if Davey suddenly remembered he had a girlfriend. He beckoned her over, and the girls opened up from their embraces to stare at her. 'This is my cousin, Isabel.' He beamed at the young woman in front of him. Hazel-eyed and olive-skinned, she was the opposite of Davey and his blue-eyed, brightly blonde sisters. Hetty hoped she wasn't blushing, which always made her freckles burn even brighter. She smarted at remembering the first words she'd heard Ailsa say when he introduced her. 'You're dating a ginger?' Oh, the scorn in her voice. It was obvious she didn't think she'd been heard in the noise from the pub, but Davey had reddened, and she'd never been sure if it was through anger or shame. Still, a year later and they were still together, so they must be doing something right. She dragged the two cases and her bag towards the group.

'Hey, Hetty, I'll do that.' Davey darted forward and helped her.

It was as if a cloud had crossed his face, although the skies above were a wash of blue. Had he seen something, or was he remembering something from before?

Isabel must have noticed as she stopped and stared up at him with a curious look. *'Tu vas bien?'*

'Oui, ça va.' He wiped his face. Turning to Isabel, he said, 'Why wouldn't I be?'

Hetty couldn't help but note that Jules also appeared to be distracted. She supposed the intervening years must alter how you view a place, especially if something had changed. Davey and the twins used to come here every year as kids. Their uncle Archie and his French wife Romilly lived here in this grand, ostentatious house through the long summer months and then retired to their flat in the town for the winter. Hetty already knew their flat was nothing like the doll's-house sized place she and Davey rented. Mind you, she was happy living in a tiny box in bustling Brighton. The countryside frightened her.

Davey had told her, 'You can get our flat in the living room alone.'

'How nice,' Hetty had said, wondering if any of the family had ever experienced hardship of any form. And she didn't mean being unable to buy the latest fashion accessory because they'd used up all their pocket money on all the other stuff they couldn't live without. Had any of them ever felt so hungry they'd scavenged through bins to find food? She thought not, and truthfully, she wouldn't wish that on anyone.

What was weird was that they abruptly stopped coming here as they hit sixteen or so. And now, Hetty had the burning desire to find out *why*.

'Why haven't you visited since then?' she'd asked, but Davey waved her off.

'I suppose we grew up. I mean,' and he always looked despondent when he spoke of this time, 'we hung out with our cousins for years before that. We didn't need to do it anymore. At least, Jules and Ailsa made it plain they didn't want to come here as they both had better things to do. I would have liked to come back again, but it just didn't happen.' He shrugged and smiled down at her. 'You know, beautiful as it is there, it can get pretty boring when you get into your teens. What is there to do for kids stuck out in the wilds?'

Hetty now scanned around her, remembering his words. What indeed? Apart from walking across those flower-strewn meadows, swimming in that river with a tiny beach, with trees offering shade and privacy. Swinging on that tyre strung high above the deepest part of the river. Yeah, what, indeed?

Then she remembered the final part of what he'd said. 'And then, we sort of all fell out that last time. Everyone was grouchy, even Uncle Archie, so I reasoned we'd got to that point and needed a break from each other.'

So that must be why they were all a bit stilted. They still needed to sort it out. This would be the time to work out their differences.

'*Ravi de vous rencontrer*,' Isabel said, snapping Hetty back to the now, and then Isabel slapped a hand over her mouth. 'Oh, I'm sorry. I meant I am pleased to meet you.' Hetty blushed further at the thought that Isabel naturally assumed she couldn't speak French. Even if she couldn't.

'Lovely to meet you too,' nodded Hetty. 'Congratulations. I'm really looking forward to experiencing a French wedding.'

'Then you are in for a treat.' Isabel waved around them. 'I am having a traditional wedding, and many things are different from your English ones.'

'Great,' said Hetty.

Davey waggled his eyebrows at her and winked. 'No expense spared, I'm sure.'

'Of course not,' said Jules. 'We are talking about Isabel's wedding. Only the best will do.'

'There's nothing wrong with that,' said Archie, sounding slightly defensive. 'We want the best for our little girl.'

'Coffee?' said Davey. 'We've been travelling for hours, and I need a restorative.' He glanced at his watch. 'It's nearly lunchtime. Have we got stuff in, or do we need to nip to Mrs Always Open?'

'Mrs who?' said Hetty.

'No one,' said Isabel, glancing at her father.

Davey continued, 'It's our nickname for the woman in the village who has a small shop in her back room. She stocks a bit of everything and seemingly never closes. As she lives there, all you do is tap on the door, and she lets you in.'

'It's bizarre,' said Jules, 'browsing for stuff when her son is in the next room watching telly.' Her body shuddered as if she'd walked into a cold fog, and she stared at the ground. 'How old would he be now? Seventeen, maybe?'

'Who cares?' Isabel made a gallic gesture. 'We don't go to the village anymore since—' She stopped and shook her head. 'Mum and Dad have enough supplies in, I think, to feed an army.' Listening to her, Hetty would never have believed she was French by birth. Not a trace of an accent. *And since what?*

A spasm flitted across Jules' face. Had anyone else seen it? Was it her place to ask her if she was okay? Probably not.

'If it's a restorative you want,' said Archie, laying a hand on Davey's shoulder, 'I'd suggest we have a brandy with our coffee. I find it mellows the rest of the day.'

'Sounds good to me.'

Hetty followed them all into the main entranceway and stopped. It was nearly as big as their whole home in Brighton. All it contained was a vast number of posh wellingtons and walking boots under a mammoth, slim table against one wall, an ornate coat rack big enough for that aforementioned army and boxes piled high, blocking the centre. An electric chandelier hung from the centre of the ceiling, and sconces were set into two alcoves. It was all painted a sorbet lemon with white woodwork details. In front of her was another door, which she presumed was a lower-floor bathroom or maybe a gigantic cupboard, and a broad set of stairs rose to the left. How many flights were there to get to the top?

'Sorry about the mess,' said Archie, fluttering a hand around, 'but all this is from the caterers. It'll be in situ soon enough, and until then, we pretend it isn't here.'

'We'll leave our cases by the table and haul them up after lunch,' said Davey.

Ailsa stretched. 'Still haven't fitted a lift yet?'

'You should be so lucky,' said Archie, heading through a door to their right.

'Well, yes,' Jules nodded, 'I think that was the point?' She shrugged and then, turning to Hetty, rolled her eyes. 'I think that went right over his head.'

Hetty nodded back at her. Peering around, she saw that Archie had entered the living room, though, at first glance, it wasn't like any living room she'd seen.

'Lucky for us,' said Ailsa, 'no bookings were taken for this month. So we can have a flat to ourselves and not have to rough it in a hotel in Le Puy.'

'Who's in the other flats?' Hetty squinted upwards. There was a strange thumping sound coming from above.

'My fiancé's mum and dad are in one,' said Isabel, 'and his brother and sister in the other. The fourth flat is undergoing repairs.'

The strange sound was a young man padding down the

stairs in his socks. 'Oy, cuz,' said a deep voice, 'there are some great hotels in Le Puy. Don't you knock our esteemed town. We are the home of the green Puy lentils, after all.' He hauled the twins into his arms, and there seemed to be a lot of kissing of this cheek and kissing of that cheek.

'Cousin Pierre,' said Davey, slapping the young man on his back. 'Wouldn't have recognised you if I'd passed you in the street. Can't believe you're taller than me now. You used to be a little shrimp.'

'Cousin Davey,' said Pierre. 'I would always be able to recognise you, as you haven't changed a bit.'

There was a moment when Hetty was unsure if they would hug or punch each other. She was relieved when they shook hands.

'Eight years is a long time, no?' said Pierre. He cocked his head to one side and gazed at Hetty. 'And who is this gorgeous young thing?' He smiled at Hetty and held out his hand. As she did the same, he took hold of her hand, bent over at the waist, and kissed it.

'*Enchanté, mademoiselle.*'

'Right. Thanks. I'm Hetty.'

'You are very pretty, Hetty.'

'Oh. Um, thanks again.' She cleared her throat. 'So, Puy lentils?'

Pierre laughed. 'Yes, they are delicious, but we are better known for our statue of the Virgin Mary. She is gigantic and is perched on a massive volcanic rock, but you know what she is most famous for?' His luminous eyes stared into hers. 'The man who designed her and had her built threw himself from her crown after he realised the baby Jesus was on the wrong side. Can you imagine?'

'Not really, no,' said Hetty. 'That's awful. It matters which side Jesus is on?'

'*Bien sûr*. It was an affront to God himself.' He shrugged. 'It was a long time ago. Maybe if we have a free day, we can go up inside the Virgin and look out over the town.'

'How big is this statue?' She tried not to snigger. Go up inside the virgin?

'It is sixteen metres high, and you can walk a staircase leading to a ladder, and then you have to climb to reach her crown. On windy days it can be quite something.'

'If I go, I'd prefer a nice calm day,' said Hetty, who could barely stand on the bottom rung of a ladder without feeling faint.

'We shall see what we can do, then.' Pierre nodded and walked into the living room after his father. 'Is Dad making coffee?'

Hetty tried to catch Davey's eye, but he was whispering with Ailsa and Isabel. Jules must have followed Archie. Hetty decided to check out what she'd glimpsed. It did not disappoint.

'Wow!' She sucked on her teeth. The first thing that hit her was the fireplace. It was nearly big enough to stand upright in and had metal bits sticking out that Hetty presumed would be necessary if you needed to roast a whole boar or hang a witch's cauldron. Some weird stick that looked like the bough of a tree was hanging off the thick wooden mantelpiece. She wondered what it was for. A gigantic, tarnished mirror was hung above the mantel, reflecting a large vase of roses. What was it with wealthy people? They could afford to have a brand new one, all clean and shiny, but no, they had to have the one that looked like it should be stuck at the back of a second-hand charity shop. Looking down, the floor was parquet wood, polished although worn. The walls were a soft duck-egg green. Cut wood was stacked down the side of the fireplace, and the remains of a fire still had a tendril of smoke drifting up the chimney. What could only be termed the biggest table she'd ever seen in her life was still dwarfed by two deep, plump settees with scattered cushions. High-backed easy chairs were placed near the fire. Other heavy, dark wood furniture and paintings of sombre-faced men and women dominated the room.

Hetty ran her hand over the surface of the table. Although it was warped in places and stained, it exuded not only age but love. There was a sense of a family who had sat at this table for generations, celebrating, or eating alone, maybe quarrelling (but gently), laughing... Hetty wondered what that might be like. Her family had eaten off plastic trays on their laps in front of the T.V. Engrossed in some long-running soap (if they were lucky and knew her dad was down the pub, but always with an ear listening out). A tiny respite. It was when *he* returned that the fear set in. Did this lot have any skeletons in their giant closets? Were any mad aunts hidden in the attic? Any children locked in the basement? She shouldn't have read all the horror and psychological thriller books she did, but it felt like coming home. That she understood this, knew the ending, as she'd lived it. And wasn't that a truly horrifying thought? Was she like the square peg being bashed into the round hole? She hoped not, but it sure felt like it.

FOUR

Ailsa

SLIGHTED

WELL, the little ginger mouse was all-agog on entering the *salon*. Ailsa bet she'd never seen the like in her sheltered little life of two up, two down. Davey had confided that she hadn't even been abroad before. Fancy that. Twenty-two and never travelled further than the Dartford Tunnel. Or some such hole.

Bustling sounds were coming from the kitchen, and then her aunt was calling them as she swept into the salon. '*Mes chéris!*'

'Romi!' Ailsa held out her hands to the woman. Eight years had changed them all, it appeared. Romi had been wafer thin, elegantly bony in the style of Wallace Simpson, but now she had plumped out. It was all well and good saying someone has a bit of meat on them, though not when they were waddling like a duck!

She felt herself enveloped. 'Ah, my beautiful nieces.' Romi nodded over her shoulder at Jules, standing in the kitchen staring back at them. 'You are all grown-up now.' She pulled apart and dabbed at her eyes. 'I am so sorry we missed all this. One moment you were kids, and the next, here you are, beautiful young women.'

'You're looking very well,' Ailsa lied. Well, what could she say except 'you've let yourself go a bit'? 'It's great to be back here, and you just need to let us know what you want us to do to help.'

Romi flicked her hand around the room. 'We have people in to sort it out. That's what we pay them for. All we need is to ensure we are gorgeous on the day.' She peered over Ailsa's shoulder. 'Davey? Oh my, haven't you grown into such a handsome young man?'

'Romi,' said Davey, and Ailsa noted that he looked like a shy boy. 'It's weird to call you by your first name now.'

'Don't worry about it. You'll get used to it quickly. Oh, it is so good to see you. It has been far too long, and we are still unsure why...'

'I've gone over that, my love,' said Archie. 'They grew up, and things, erm, changed, but the main thing is, they are all here again. We need to make the most of them in case it takes another eight years for them to return.'

'Don't say that.' Isabel wiped her brow theatrically. 'I'll be an old lady by then. Well over thirty!'

'And up to your eyeballs,' said Jules, 'in dirty nappies and squalling kids.'

'Oh, no, no, no!' Isabel waved an admonishing finger at Jules, 'that is why you employ a *nounou*!'

Hetty found her voice to ask, 'What is a *nounou*?'

'A nanny.' Isabel shrugged her shoulders. 'I will still have my career, so I'll need someone to look after the kids.'

Ailsa saw something flit over Hetty's face. Had Isabel hit a nerve? What could that be?

'Hetty, I presume?' Untangling herself, Romi side-stepped around Davey and went to embrace Hetty. 'The twins didn't mention how pretty you are. I would like to wish you welcome to our home. You must make yourself at home too. And if you need anything, let me know.'

'That's very kind of you.' Hetty smiled at Romi. Ailsa thought about what Romi had just said. That Hetty was pretty? Really? She supposed in an unkempt terrier sort of way.

Ailsa ambled over to where Jules stood, aware of the memories piling up around her. How many breakfasts had they cooked together in this kitchen? Mixing hot chocolate drinks, dunking croissants slathered in butter on the 'French' mornings, frying bacon and making large mugs of tea on the 'English' ones. Did the family still tramp down the lane to the local farmer in the mornings to fetch the milk? So early that the dawn had barely cracked, and mist curled in the dank undergrowth of the forests. Dodging the cow pats as they headed into the stable to watch the big old cow be milked by, now what was his name? Oh yes, M. Leclère, his head against the cow's quivering flank, the splish splash of the squirts of milk hitting the metal pail. Then the milk would be transferred into a carrying pitcher with a screw-on lid. It would have to be boiled thoroughly, although they always sipped some before they got it home. Warm and creamy, straight from the cow. Unpasteurised, it could have given them all some god-awful stomach bug or parasite, but they didn't think about stuff like that when they were kids.

And the mushrooms? Picking the wild mushrooms that lived in the mulch and old leaves under the bushes and trees of the forest on the hill above them. It was not so much about eating them; although fried in a bit of butter and olive oil, they were delicious. It was more the creeping out in the early hours of the morning as if they were hunting a shy animal hiding in the shadows. Seeing who had managed to pick the most, careful of any that could be poisonous, and then the final part, sitting at the huge table, picking out the blades of grass or tendrils of weeds.

Someone always got a bit of something they didn't bargain for. It was as if Romi read her mind.

'Darlings?' she called across the rooms. 'We decided to go out mushrooming tomorrow, just like we always used to. Won't that be fabulous?' She motioned at Hetty. 'It is a very French thing to do and is something we used to do all the time as a family. I hope you have stout shoes with you?'

Hetty nodded, looking a little confused. Ailsa couldn't help but sneer. Maybe she thought mushrooms came ready-made in polystyrene trays? Like all the people who didn't realise a cut of meat at the butcher used to be a whole, living animal. Ignorance was such bliss, wasn't it?

'How early are we talking here?' Davey wagged a finger as he escorted Hetty into the kitchen. Her eyes were still wide as she gawped about her. 'Remember, we've got a little family reunion tonight.'

'That's why,' interjected Archie, as he put two giant coffee percolators onto the hob to boil, 'the wedding is the day after—'

'You mean,' Pierre slung his arm over his dad's shoulders, 'tomorrow we can be sick in the bushes with impunity?'

'That wasn't quite how I'd put it, but yes, I suppose so. What we don't want is a colossal hang-over on the actual day.'

'I presume,' drawled Jules, 'you've already had your...' She scratched her head. 'Oh yes, your *enterrement de vie de jeune fille?*'

Davey looked over at Hetty. 'That means her hen do.'

Isabel stared at Jules. 'Of course. We had the weekend in Paris, and it was divine.' She twirled a lock of her long brown hair. 'We didn't invite you as we weren't even sure you were coming to the wedding.' She pouted. 'After all, it's been eight years since we last saw each other.'

'You could have asked anyway...' said Jules.

'And would you have come?'

'Maybe, but now we'll never know, will we?'

Ailsa heard the words. There had been a hen night in Paris. And they had not been invited. They were family, *and they had not been invited*. That stung. Okay, they had some issues between them all, yet surely as adults, they could work through them. Paris? She knew it would have started with a staged kidnapping, the bride to be whisked away for a night of revelry in some high-class hotel. Traditional and expensive. She was tempted to storm from the room, but she held back. There was a possibility there might be more secrets divulged, but weren't there also secrets that must never come out? They should be careful.

Davey stepped in. 'And talking of which, where is the man himself?'

'He's in Lyon,' said Isabel, 'sorting out some last government business.'

'Everyone for coffee?" said Jules, as she gathered tiny cups and saucers from an imposing dresser.

'I'll open a bottle of wine for lunch', said Archie, 'to celebrate our family finally being together after too long a gap.'

'Not all of us,' said Jules, and her voice was quiet. She visibly shuddered. 'I mean, I wish Mum and Dad could be here, too.'

'Of course, we all do, *ma chérie*.' Romi pulled Jules into a hug. It appeared to Ailsa that Jules clung to her like she used to do with their mum. If only she could read the look on Jules' face. What was up with her? After all, the news they'd received this morning was heartening.

'Listen,' said Ailsa, 'Mum told us Dad is off the critical list and is responding well.'

'I know, although I am allowed to be worried.'

'No need to be. Can't keep a MacGregor down,' Archie filled each tiny cup with a slosh of coffee and then offered everyone a splash of a quality brandy in their coffee. They all accepted.

'I know he's strong,' said Davey, sipping his coffee, 'but this has knocked him for six. And he's pissed off he's missing the wedding. Mmm, nice brandy.'

'Ah!' Isabel twirled around the room, 'We'll take so many photos and videos for them they'll believe they were here.'

'Yeah,' Davey nodded. 'I'm going to do a Facebook Messenger call for them. Then they can cry along with the rest of us.'

'Technology!' Archie handed out the rest of the cups and directed them to the milk and sugar he'd placed on the counter. 'It's amazing. I suppose, sometime in the near future, we won't have to go anywhere, just watch life on our screens—'

'Don't we already?' said Jules. 'And let's not forget all the emojis we'll need to put against them to make us relevant.'

'That sounds a bit heavy.' Romi yanked open the door of the American-style fridge freezer. It was one of those that had the plumbed-in water and ice dispenser. That must have set them back a couple of grand at least. 'We have cold cuts of meat and cheese for lunch. There are salads and cold drinks in here. Shall we put it all on the table, and then you can help yourselves?'

'I'll get the plates and cutlery,' said Isabel. 'Pierre? Clear all that stuff off the table.'

'Okay.' Pierre nodded and gathered the magazines and clutter off the table to dump them on one of the sofas instead. Everyone lined up to be handed a plate to place on the table.

Ailsa smiled at Jules. 'Just like old times, eh?'

'Yeah, sure,' said Jules.

2016 – Ailsa

Their parents had been so caught up in the whole stupid Brexit crap that this year's barbeque was well late. In fact, Ailsa had overheard a conversation in the salon that made her start to worry. Passing by to head up the stairs, she stopped to listen. It wasn't eavesdropping, as they had left the door open... slightly.

'Do we even need to do a barbeque this year?' This was Uncle Archie. 'What I mean is, the kids are not little anymore. Do they still want this?'

'Who, exactly,' said Aunt Romi, 'are we doing the barbeque for? Them or us? It keeps us in with the villagers. We all have a wonderful time, don't we? And anyway, everyone loves a barbeque no matter how old.'

'Yes, but I worry about the influence of the undesirables—'

'Influence on whom?'

'Our kids.'

'Then don't,' said her father, James, 'invite them this year.'

Uncle Archie snorted. 'Like that's an option. I rather think it's all of them or none. You know how the village sticks together.'

'Can't you do it subtly?' her dad said.

'The boys,' said her mum, Eva, 'are good boys.'

'Really, Eva?' Uncle Archie sounded annoyed. 'Is that what you think? I would have thought, with your background, you'd agree wholeheartedly with me.'

'I manage to differentiate between groups and individuals.'

'Come on now,' said Aunt Romi. 'Stop arguing—'

'Not to mention,' and now Uncle Archie sounded angry, 'it costs us a fortune—'

'Phooey!' Aunt Romi must have stood and walked into the kitchen, as her voice receded. 'Offset against keeping goodwill in our community, it's nothing.'

'Okay, okay.' Uncle Archie now appeared resigned. 'We'll have the barbeque this year and then have to think about it. We still have no idea of the ramifications of Brexit.'

'You think,' drawled her dad, 'that Project Fear might actually be right?'

'I think Project Fear doesn't know the half of it.'

'The government,' said her mum slowly, 'has promised us they will ensure it's not a hard Brexit. It won't impact us.'

'Hmm,' said Uncle Archie. 'I don't think your esteemed government is looking out for the people of Britain.'

'The proof is in the pudding,' said her mum. 'We'll have to wait and see what happens.'

'At least you can always move the family back to Sweden, Eva,' said Aunt Romi.

Hiding outside the salon door, Ailsa shook her head, her hair standing on end. Move back to Sweden? Not in this lifetime! They all had their friends in England. She and Jules were taking their GCSEs next year, and Davey would be in Year 12, taking his 'A' level options. They couldn't move away and especially not to Sweden. It might be a lovely place to visit for a month (maximum), but not to live there. It was cold, grey and boring as hell! And don't even mention the pickled herrings! Should she say anything to the others? Davey was going out with a girl in his class. Monica or Veronica or something. She seemed nice enough. He wouldn't be happy to be forced to move. Jules, well, Jules might be okay taking photos of wild, bleak landscapes, although perhaps it was too cold for the bugs she loved. Oh, this was not good.

As she ran tearfully up the stairs to her room, she passed the

Devereaux family coming out of their flat. They had stayed at the house every year since Ailsa could remember and were dear friends of Aunt Romi.

'Are you all right?' Madame Devereaux held out a hand as she swept past them.

'I'm fine, thank you, Madame.' Oh, how mortifying. The Devereaux family were the pinnacle of French High Society, and they had seen her bawling like a little baby.

Chapter Five

HERE YOU ALL ARE AGAIN. *Do you remember what you did that hot and sweaty summer afternoon? That day when the flies and midges buzzed around in slow motion, heat mirages danced out across the sunburnt meadows and eyes were blinded by the arc of the sun. I do. I saw what you did. I remember your words, the sheer disdain in your voices. How you weighed up a life against yours and found his wanting. He was cattle, only there to do your bidding, and when he was found to be worthless, you put that bolt gun against his head and fired the bolt to stun him. And then you slaughtered him. And I'm not speaking metaphorically, now am I?*

I remember, and I will not forgive you. And neither will she.

SIX

Hetty

JUST LIKE OLD TIMES?

It was always going to be tricky meeting Davey's family. They had so much to catch up on, so many memories to re-hash and laugh over. They would bond again after so many years through their shared experiences, and she would lurk bashfully on the fringes. Initially, Hetty had been anxious, although she knew she shouldn't be. If she felt inferior, whose fault was that? Hers and hers alone. No one should have the power to make a person feel shit about themselves solely through the accident of birth. That was a reflection on them. And she'd worked hard on losing her London accent, had learned to enunciate her words, taught herself to be someone different to who she was before. She was well-read, clever, despite the odds that had been stacked against her. A shiny new person scrabbling to get out of her chrysalis. And Davey must never know, find out...

Okay, she was not the same class as these people, but both Archie and Romi had welcomed her. They seemed to be sweet and down to earth. Hetty let a breath out. Isabel was excited by her wedding plans and cousins' arrival, so Hetty didn't feel slighted. Pierre was, well, he was a bit strange, but hey. He hadn't been horrible to her. It was Ailsa that was the cause of her main worries. It always felt like Ailsa was simply waiting for the time Hetty wasn't there anymore. She got the nasty feeling Ailsa couldn't be bothered to invest any time or effort into their relationship because she believed that very soon Hetty would be gone. Hetty didn't want to explore this, wondering if that was how Davey operated. Maybe Ailsa had seen so many girls come and go with him that it wasn't worth the trouble.

In fact, Hetty barely knew anything about his past life and loves. When they'd met, it was like they implicitly agreed it to be ground zero. They lived for the now. But then, what did he know of her previous incarnation? Zilch, and she wanted, no, needed it to stay that way. Meeting his parents wasn't on the cards any time soon, especially after the stroke had left his dad bedridden in Stockholm, and when Davey asked after her family, she was vague to the point of being nebulous. He didn't push, and she was thankful. He'd only opened up about his French connections when the wedding invite had plopped through the letterbox.

'Well, I never!' was all he'd said. It had taken a lot of subtle winkling for him to show her the card and to explain what it meant. It was a weird brown card with a pretty pattern on the front. The details were printed in copperplate script inside.

'Are you up for this?' He squinted at her as if she was suddenly out of focus.

'Am I invited? I know it says, 'Plus 1', but what I mean is, do you want me to go?' This was the crux, wasn't it? They were celebrating their first year together, yet if he said no, he didn't want her to go with him, what would that say about their relationship? Not a lot.

'Of course I want you to go.' It had taken a bit longer than she hoped, yet at least he'd said yes. 'Although,' he cupped her face and bent down to stare into her eyes, 'it'll be quite a full-on thing. A French wedding is something else.'

'You think I won't be able to cope, or I'll show you up?'

'It's not like that, Hetty, and you shouldn't say such stuff. You will never show me up. I'm not a classist pig, and I hoped I'd proven that to you.' He sounded exasperated. 'We are living together, we share everything, we've met each other's families... at least, you've met some of mine.' He rubbed his face. 'And as I said, it all went a bit weird when we left the place that last time.'

'So it's not me?'

'No. You know I don't look down on you. You're the most talented, strong-minded and sharpest person I've ever met.'

'Sorry. It's—'

'Ailsa?' He made a funny face. 'She thinks everyone is inferior. Don't worry about her. How many times have we met up with her and Jules? I can count on one hand alone. She may be my sister, but you can't choose family. You're sort of lumped with them, for good or for bad. You can choose the other people around you, and I choose you. So, if we're going, you'll have to buckle up!'

'Buckle up, buttercup!' Hetty grinned up at him. Lumped with his family for good or for bad. Wasn't that the truth?

Feeling like she should keep up with the conversation, Hetty caught the last bit from Isabel, something about a noonoo...

'Sorry, what's a noonoo?' Of course. A nanny. Silly Hetty. What world was she living in? Or, more to the point, what world were they in? No stinky nappies for these types of women. She caught the way Ailsa looked over at her and practically rolled her eyes. A career? Isabel was what they termed an 'influencer'. Someone who promotes a go-getter way of life.

And earns a mint from it. The fact she was already minted didn't seem to come into it. She promoted the life she was already living. She obviously just wanted more of it and also made so many others want this too, people who couldn't ever afford this existence yet who believed they deserved it somehow. Hetty didn't know what to think. Wouldn't Isabel have time in her busy 'schedule' to be a proper mum to her kids? How bizarre. For the same reason, albeit a polar one, Hetty had barely seen her own mum. Two, sometimes three jobs took her out of the house from before the sun came up to late evening. When she came home from school, Hetty had done all the chores and made a scraped-together dinner for her and her brother, Paul. Put him to bed and waited until her exhausted mum came home. She'd often find her still slumped on the tatty sofa in her work clothes the following day. They'd subsisted minimally. Three jobs just to keep a roof over their heads and food on the table. They'd never been on Benefit Street, her mum being too proud by half. And her dad? Now banged up for a heinous crime. He was ill. Hetty suspected now it was mental as well as physical, not that it changed the outcome. There was no coming back from what he did. He'd worked when he could but was often in and out of the hospital, maybe feeling less of a man because he couldn't support his family. That was no excuse. And he drank. And then the fists came out... and worse, judging by the sounds she'd heard growing up. As a little kid, she never connected the dots until... Well, now she knew what those sounds were, and the lump in her throat threatened tears. She had to push it all down, that indigestion, that dull ache in the chest and gut caused by a heady mixture of loathing, pity and fear. Was there any love left? Would she be able to recognise it if she saw it? Had her background of abuse made her unable to love another person? Did she genuinely love Davey? Woah! She had to get off this line of thought. Be here, in the present.

And yet Romi had been so kind to her. Told her to make herself at home. Did she mean that, or was she merely being polite? Did it include raiding the cupboards for biscuits? Were there any custard creams to be found? She hoped so, as she was starving. And what was with this mushrooming lark? Clambering about on the hills above the house and grubbing around in the dirt didn't sound like fun to her. And before the sun had even come up? What was with that? And as Pierre had pointed out, it was the morning after they were having a little party to celebrate as a family. Though it appeared the bridegroom would be conspicuously absent. Not that she was looking forward to this weird French ritual, (especially as she was leery of forests), as she didn't feel she was 'one of the family'. Yet. Although this was possibly the best time to start to bond with them, as she hoped she would be in their lives for a long time to come. That was one good reason to be careful what she drank. Wouldn't that be the cherry on top if she got drunk, fell over and showed her knickers? And then joined Pierre throwing up under the bushes the next morning. Now they were talking about filming the wedding for Davey's parents stuck in Sweden. She didn't need to make a fool of herself in front of them, even if it was remotely.

'And let's not forget,' said Jules, 'all the emojis we'll need to put against them to make us relevant.' She'd drifted from the kitchen and now stood by Hetty's elbow. They watched as Pierre grabbed stuff off the table only to dump it on the sofa.

'Don't let Ailsa get to you, Hetty.' Jules stared at her. Hetty was mesmerised by how deeply blue her eyes were, more lapis lazuli in intensity, whereas Davey had eyes the colour of an early morning sky.

'I'm okay. Thanks.'

'Of course, you are. We all are.' She raised an eyebrow. 'It's what is expected, isn't it?'

Hetty realised this was not a question. 'I suppose so.'

'Come on, let's grab a coffee.' Jules held out her hand, and Hetty gratefully took it and was led back into the kitchen. Clocking the scowl that zipped over Ailsa's face, Hetty decided she would ignore her and, following Jules, she took in how magnificent this kitchen was. The whole place might have been built a hundred years ago or whatever, but it was all mod-cons in here. That fridge-freezer was to die for and probably cost more than she earned in two months. There was a coffee machine that should have George Clooney leaning on it and a micro-wave that looked like you needed a degree in engineering to be able to operate. Hang on, why was Archie using these old coffee percolators? Was it because he didn't know how to use all this stuff, either? Another smaller table was in the centre of the long kitchen, and a shiny AGA range cooker had a vast, brushed copper extractor winging above it. The AGA was a vivid turquoise, and Hetty had the urge to lick it; it looked so yummy. Half the walls were tiled with white tiles, painted with lilac flower motifs, and shelves lining the walls had the most striking copper pans and jugs she had ever clapped eyes on. Underfoot were warm terracotta tiles. White-painted French windows reaching the ceiling were open, and Hetty caught a glimpse of the beautifully tended garden outside. It was a wonderful mixture of modern and timeworn.

The cups and saucers were all different colours and weeny. Barely a mouthful, though at least they'd been mention of lunch. And that slosh of brandy from Archie settled her stomach. Thank God for that, as Hetty was getting to the point of wanting to chew on the rather posh tea towels draped over the oven handle. Breakfast seemed like a million years ago, and as plates were hauled from the massive interior of the fridge, Hetty overheard Ailsa say to Jules, 'Just like old times, eh?'

'Yeah, sure.'

Judging by the look on Jules' face, Hetty got the feeling that it really wasn't.

'This is what I miss,' said Davey, reaching for another slice of cheese. 'Proper French lunches, where you start late and finish even later. And you have time to chat without feeling you're on a perennial time limit.'

'Gives you time to digest properly, too.' Archie loosened his belt.

'I'd like to get used to that,' said Hetty and then wished she'd kept her mouth shut.

'Oh yes,' drawled Ailsa, 'you work in a shop, don't you?'

'It's a brilliant shop,' said Davey. 'A mad emporium of crazy stuff—'

'You mean a second-hand shop?' said Ailsa. 'With second-hand stuff in it.'

'It's a great job, Ailsa, with amazing people,' said Hetty. 'As you've never seen this place, please don't judge it.' She felt the heat rise up her neck, not helped by a strong coffee and two glasses of a delicious red wine. She knew she must be glowing, but she ploughed on. 'It pays my half of the rent and keeps me fed.'

'Well said, Hetty.' Jules turned to her sister. 'Not everyone has had the advantages we've had.' Dearest God! Her eyes were like lasers. 'Anyway, buying second-hand,' continued Jules, lazily reaching for the bottle of wine and topping up Hetty first, 'is that it's a step towards saving this poor old world of ours. In case you didn't know, Ailsa, all that designer stuff you buy for extortionate prices is made by slave workers living in abhorrent conditions. Most of them are children and women.'

'I don't need you to preach at me, dearest sister mine!' Ailsa tweaked the bottle over, but it was empty. 'Any chance of another bottle, Archie?' She waved it under his nose.

'Feel free to open another bottle. The corkscrew is on the kitchen table.' He thought for a moment. 'As long as you don't end up in a state, like that last barbeque—' He stuttered, 'I mean, um...' It was as if he knew the moment the words had slipped from his mouth what effect they'd have and tried to drag them back in. It was too late. Jules shifted in her seat as if it had suddenly stuck a spring into her bum. Davey made a grab for his glass and nearly knocked it over, and Ailsa, well, she went very still, a golden-haired statue poised in the room. What had happened?

Romi stirred. 'That barbeque? Oh yes, you were all so drunk you could barely stand. So naughty. I seem to remember none of you felt that clever in the morning, eh?'

'No. We didn't.' Pierre waved his hand around. 'But we were stupid kids, and now we're all grown up, so I'll open another bottle.'

'Thinking about it,' said Archie, 'maybe we've all had enough. We're going to start again in a few hours.'

'Oh, Dad. You can't offer and then whip it away—'

'Come on now.' Davey held up his hand like a referee. 'Enough. I think it's time to clear the table, get the cases upstairs, and maybe have a little nap. I think we're all pretty knackered.'

Pierre grunted. 'Okay. I can clear this, and as we keep saying, we have to be bright-eyed and bushy-tailed for our party tonight.'

'Thank you very much,' said Hetty. 'I also need to get my

stuff hung up.' She tagged after Davey and then looked up apprehensively at the sheer number of stairs that faced them.

'Yep,' Davey nodded, 'I wish they'd got that lift sorted too. Come on, we'll definitely need a nap after this.'

'So, I gather you all got drunk at your last barbeque?' Soft voices burbled from the salon. They were sharing one of the flats with the twins (as the fourth flat was being overhauled), and Hetty hoped she and Davey could get in and sorted before the twins came up.

'We got absolutely hammered but someone else took the fall for it. I don't really want to talk about it, Hetty, as it's a long and pretty strange story.'

'Oh. Okay.' She'd seen him drunk a few times. Drinking to excess was never an issue. A long and strange story? She clamped her eyes shut and counted to ten. Stop looking for a mystery. She wasn't in a book, and she wasn't an amateur detective. Working in a wonderful and colourful second-hand emporium was her only claim to fame. And her paintings, which she sold in a local art gallery in Brighton. She'd asked Davey not to mention that she painted, as it was her thing, and she didn't want to be judged.

'Are you coming, Hetty?'

Four sets of staircases wound up to the flats. A tufty ginger cat sat sentinel at the top of the first staircase. Suddenly, it streaked past them down the stairs, making Hetty jump.

'Ah,' said Davey. 'Toulouse is still alive then. He was at least a couple of years old when we were last here.'

'Toulouse? Great name, but God! I thought it was a stuffed toy.' Hetty looked down in time to see a flash of orange as it shot across the hall. 'When does Isabel's fiancé's family arrive?' She had to stop halfway up and cling to the banister to catch her breath.

'I presume tomorrow. We'll have the place to ourselves for a bit.'

'And you don't know what's he called? J.J.? You don't know him from before?'

'No. It'll be interesting to meet him. See who has captured the Ice Queen's heart.'

'Ice Queen?'

'Yeah. Isabel used to be worse than Ailsa...' He glanced back down the staircase. 'By that, I mean picky.' He made a face at her. 'No boy was good enough for either of them.'

They were on the third floor, below the attic space that comprised the family's bedrooms and bathroom. Hetty was profoundly pleased they were not under the rafters (as she'd read far too many horror books and knew that all would not end well if they had to stay up there...), but they were still having to share with the twins. Not ideal, but at least they had a bedroom to themselves. The twins were in a room with two single beds, and she and Davey had a double. The shared bathroom, lounge and small kitchenette separated the two bedrooms.

'Can we just lie down and worry about showers and unpacking in a bit?' Hetty blew out the side of her mouth. 'I'm beat!'

'Of course. I'll set the alarm on my phone.'

When the alarm woke them, Hetty was in that state where she felt she either had slept for too long or needed more sleep. Groggy and headachy. Their cases were still unopened, so they hauled themselves from the warm bed and sorted their belongings into the heavy-looking dark wood wardrobes and chests of drawers. The walls were papered in faded pink and green flower motifs, and the rose-coloured carpet was thick and fluffy.

'It's so pretty here.' Hetty breathed deeply. 'Like we've stepped back in time.' She pointed at the fireplace. 'Does that work? Do you know how to light a real fire?'

'I'm a man, aren't I?' Davey put on his mock frowning face, 'Ergo, I can light a fire. Man is born with the inherent knowledge of fire making...'

'If you tell me that woman is born with the inherent knowledge of cooking and cleaning, I will thump you one!'

He leered at her.

'Let's see if the bathroom is free. You know what the twins are like—' He stopped and looked down. 'No, you don't, do you?'

'No. I don't.'

Bounding out, she heard Davey checking where the twins were. 'It's okay', he called through the doorway, 'they're both out now. Do you want a shower first?'

'Yeah, then I'll have time to put my face on.'

As she was applying the last touches of make-up in front of the giant mirror on the dresser in the bedroom, she glanced up in time to see Davey saunter in, a towel loose around his waist. She stopped and pursed her lips together, watching for his reaction.

She blew him a kiss in the mirror. 'Can't we just go back to bed?'

'I wish.' He winked at her. 'Don't worry, we'll have plenty of time later.' He slipped into his clothes. 'You look gorgeous, by the way.' He kissed the top of her head.

'Thanks. So do you.' Hetty paused. 'Is this dress really okay? It's just I haven't got anything much to wear, and I need my best dress for the wedding.'

'Listen, Hetty. If you wore a bin bag, you would still be the most beautiful woman in any room.'

'Don't make me blush. You know how my freckles go berserk when I blush.'

'I love your berserker freckles. Long may they berserk! Love you, Miss Hetty.'

'Love you, too, Mr Davey.'

'I love you more.'

SEVEN

Ailsa

HEALTH, WEALTH AND HAPPINESS

AFTER FRESHENING UP, the family met back in the salon. As Davey came in, leading Hetty, Ailsa stifled a giggle. What on earth was the little ginger mouse wearing? Ailsa wanted to 'tut' but held it in. It was probably something she'd picked up in her fabulous Emporium. It wasn't even something from Marks and Sparks. Good God! Couldn't the girl even afford a dress from there? What must Davey be thinking? He should be ashamed to be seen out with her in that, but he was looking at her as if she was the only person in the room.

'You look lovely, Hetty.' It was amazing how easily the lies slipped off the tongue. But then, she'd brought lying to a whole new level, hadn't she? Ailsa squirmed from the thoughts nipping at her like hyenas around a fresh kill. Best not to go there.

'Thanks.' Hetty blushed crimson. 'You all look gorgeous.'

'Come and sit next to me,' called Jules, patting a space beside her on one of the massive sofas. 'Davey?' She waved a hand at him, 'there's a bottle of champers open in the fridge. Get Hetty a glass, and you can top mine up while you're at it.'

Ailsa glanced down at the empty glass in her own hand.

Thanks for that. She was sitting on one of the easy chairs, as she'd been worried the 'mouse' might end up next to her.

'Why yes, my commandant!' Davey saluted Jules, and passing Isabel, he bent down to kiss her cheek. 'Good evening, soon-to-be Madame MacGregor-D'Aramitz.'

'Isabel MacGregor-D'Aramitz. Hmm,' she looked like she was rolling the name around in her mouth, 'it has a nice ring to it.'

'Talking of which,' said Romi, 'have you shown everyone your ring yet? I know you took it off earlier.' Romi looked like the perfect proud parent. 'Show everyone, darling. It's quite beautiful.'

'All right, then.' Isabel couldn't hide the smirk as she circled the room, hand outstretched, ring clearly visible. Her cousins made the requisite noises of 'oooh' and 'aaaah'.

Ailsa plastered a smile across her face as she looked at the chunk of diamond on Isabel's ring finger. That certainly wasn't diamante, now was it? Being a French member of parliament might be fairly lucrative, but she knew his family wealth came from stockbroking. She wondered if he had a viable brother.

Archie had been bent over in front of the fireplace for what seemed like hours now. There was a lot of huffing and puffing and breaking of twigs.

'I'm not winning here,' he grunted, straightening and rubbing small circles in his lower back. 'Anyone else want a go?'

'Is the kindling dry?' Pierre placed his glass on the table and knelt by a smouldering heap of twigs and small boughs of wood. He rolled a few pages from a newspaper and stuffed them under the twigs. Re-arranging the pile, he carefully lit it and then, standing, hooked the strange bough off the mantel, stuck one end in the fire and blew down it until his face went red.

Jules laughed. 'I'd forgotten what that was for. It's brilliant. I might have to take one back with me—'

'To your flat in Birmingham?' Ailsa raised her left eyebrow. 'Didn't think you had real fires there.'

'How would you know? You've never been.' Jules also raised her left eyebrow. 'And I live in Manchester, remember?'

'I don't remember because you never invited me.'

'Hey, come on.' Davey returned with the frosted black bottle of champagne and poured some for Jules. He carried two glasses in his other hand and poured a liberal amount into them. He handed Hetty one and placed his on the coffee table in front of the sofa where Isabel and Romi sat. 'This is a party for Isabel, who we haven't seen in years, and we're here to celebrate her getting hitched to one of the most eligible bachelors in France. And as far as I can see,' Davey eyed the ring, 'one of the richest.' He raised his glass. 'To Isabel and her soon-to-be hubby, J.J.' He took a swig. 'And again, where is Monsieur Elusive?'

'Still in Lyon, I presume. I believe he's coming back later tonight.' Isabel made an impatient gesture, and Ailsa had an image in her mind she shouldn't have. Was Monsieur D'Aramitz having a last fling before his nuptials? It was a very French thing to do. Was Isabel pondering this and coming to the same conclusion? Did she mind, as long as that ring was on her finger and the man said 'I do' the day after tomorrow? For richer, for poorer meant for richer and even richer. Poor Isabel.

'Ta-da!' Pierre waved at the blazing fire in the hearth. 'Sorry, did I miss a toast?' He raised his glass. 'To my beautiful sister, Isabel. May you have every happiness in your life.'

'Hear, hear,' shouted Archie. 'Need to open another bottle. Watch out, everyone, for flying corks!'

'I think you've had enough already,' said Romi. 'You need to slow down.'

Archie shook his head. 'I'm only just getting started, my love. When your only daughter is getting hitched, then it's a prerequisite you celebrate in style.'

'Bushes, here we come,' laughed Pierre, waving his own glass.

Ailsa followed him to the kitchen. 'If you can't beat them, join them.'

The night had progressed well. Now they were more relaxed; shoulders had lowered, and drawn lines on tired, worried faces had been wiped away. Music was playing softly in the background. An iPod and a small speaker were enough for a bit of ambience without drowning them all out.

'Pierre?' said Davey, 'I seem to remember you were into Techno when you were a kid. What do you listen to now?'

'I hope,' interjected Ailsa, 'you've grown out of all that ghastly noise. You can never call that music—'

Pierre narrowed his eyes at Ailsa. 'Sorry to inform you, my dear cousin, I still love that noise. Would you like me to put a bit on for you now?'

'Very kind,' said Ailsa, 'but no. Whatever this is now will do nicely. We can hear ourselves over the top of it.'

'What?' chided Davey, 'Not into a bit of banging music, Ailsa?'

'As I said, you can't call that music—'

'And what do you listen to now?' Pierre leaned forward. 'Chamber music? A lovely string quartet?'

Romi tutted. 'Classical music means just that. Classical!'

'Each to their own,' said Davey. He swivelled to Isabel. 'Have you got a wedding singer for the big day?'

'Ugh, no!' Isabel held up her hand. 'We have an orchestra—'

'A full orchestra?' Jules nearly spat her wine across herself. 'Sorry.' She dabbed at her mouth. 'Seriously? A whole orchestra? Will there be space for your guests?'

Archie popped the cork on another bottle. 'Have you not seen how big that marquee is? Even with the orchestra, there will be plenty of space for all of us. Is anyone ready for a spot of supper? Thought I'd get the cheese and pickles out.'

'Sounds good. Lunch seemed an age ago.' Ailsa nodded at him. 'How many are coming?' There was a soupçon of jealousy. She might not want that wedding ring, or at least, she'd like a big rock like that, just not a man that went with it, although it would be lovely to have a lavish, expensive party.

'A hundred guests.' Romi levered herself off the sofa to help Archie manoeuvre plates of cold food onto the table. 'As it's not in town, we decided all our guests can come to every part of the wedding after the civil ceremony at the *mairie*. We've laid on coaches to ferry those not staying with us back to Le Puy the next day. I assume we will still be dancing until dawn?' Romi smiled indulgently at Isabel. 'We thought one hundred was a reasonable number.'

Ailsa tried to calculate how much that was costing. There were no budget weddings in this family. One hundred thousand? Probably a lot more.

'It's such a shame your mum and dad can't be with us,' said Romi. She'd circled this a few times, and Ailsa wondered if she was drunk.

Having filled a plate, Archie was now slumped in one of the wing-backed chairs in front of the fire, picking at his food. 'They'd have had a ball with J.J.'s parents. Such lovely people.'

'Of course, only the best for us,' drawled Jules.

'I'm sorry, darling? I don't understand.' Romi leaned over the table to place another bowl and squinted at Jules.

'Oh, simply a casual observation.' She flicked a glance at Hetty, who was sitting by her side.

Ailsa scowled. Why was Jules so bloody obtuse all the time. 'Isabel, are you going for the whole French affair for the wedding? I mean, have you got the *dragées* for all your guests?'

'Sorry? What are *dragées*?' Hetty piped up.

'They are gifts of pastel-coloured sugared almonds that are given to every guest,' said Davey. 'There are five of them and, now let me see, each one symbolises...' He counted off on his fingers. 'Health, wealth, happiness, longevity and fertility.'

'It's traditional,' said Isabel. 'Of course we have them.'

Let's see. Wealth? Isabel certainly had that. Health. A big tick there. Happiness? Still trying to figure it out. Longevity and fertility were in the lap of the gods. And they weren't always the happy bunnies they were cracked up to be.

'And we need to mention the wedding cake.' Jules swivelled to look directly at Hetty. 'The French don't have wedding cakes, well, not as we know them. Instead, they have what is called a croquembouche – essentially a pyramid of vanilla cream-filled balls of yumminess. This custom stems from the Middle Ages when wedding guests would each bring a small cake to the wedding to be piled high.'

'What a wonderful tradition.' Hetty grinned at Jules. 'So, they're like a pile of profiteroles?'

'Exactly that.' Jules waved at Romi with a frown. 'I'm presuming you're having one?'

'Of course. Hetty?' Romi leaned forward. 'French weddings are quite different to English ones. We'll be off to *la mairie*,' Romi waved her hand, 'sorry, the town hall for the civil wedding and then back home for the, oh, we always say, the 'real' wedding afterwards.'

'Will it be held in that gorgeous little church I saw in the village?' asked Hetty.

'Why no, dear.' Romi's face creased in puzzlement. 'Isabel decided she'd prefer the ceremony to be held here.' She pouted. 'I couldn't seem to budge her on that one. I would have loved to have had it there, although we rarely, if ever, go there nowadays. I'm not really sure why.'

'I didn't need all that ostentatious religious stuff. That's all it was.' Isabel hauled herself out of her seat and grabbed a bottle. 'Anyone for a top-up?'

'It's still a shame. We never go to the village anymore since—'

'Leave it, Maman!' Isabel pouted. 'I've got a headache, and we have to get up early tomorrow. In fact, I'm going to bed.'

'What happened to that top-up?' said Ailsa. So, the village was out of bounds? And why was that? Was the family no longer welcome? Had something happened while they'd been hiding in England?

Isabel put the bottle back on the table and stamped from the room. It seemed the evening was over.

2016 - Ailsa

Ailsa now couldn't work out if Jules was acting strangely or if she was imagining she was. What was that experiment they'd done in science? You can change what happens to something by simply observing it. The simple act of observation can alter the outcome.

Isabel told her they must take turns watching Jules and try to be surreptitious. 'She mustn't cotton on we're following her.'

Isabel and Ailsa were tucked down the side of the house, peering out, shielding their eyes from the heat of the midday sun.

'Oh, bum!' whispered Ailsa. 'There are the Devereaux. They're bound to ask what we're doing—'

'Well,' Isabel placed her hands on her hips, 'we're not going to tell them we're spying on your sister, now are we?'

'No. Don't be stupid...' Ailsa could see the look passing over Isabel's face. Never call her stupid.

'It's a beautiful day, isn't it?' called Isabel gaily, waving like mad at the family as they passed. 'A bit too hot for us at the moment.'

'Indeed,' called Monsieur Devereaux, 'fair young ladies like yourselves should be wary of the sun. It plays havoc with one's skin.'

Madame Devereaux inclined her head to stare at them. 'We are off to the city for lunch. Isabel? Perhaps you can remind your dear maman that we invited her tonight to play bridge? At eight?'

'I will do my best to remember, Madame.' Isabel smiled her best smile at her.

'Have fun, my dears, but as my husband said, keep out of the sun, or you will look like you are common working people.'

'We will.' Isabel gave one final wave. Turning to Ailsa, she asked, 'Have we lost Jules?'

'No, she's just down there.' Ailsa pointed.

'Oh, good.'

'Where is she going?' Ailsa watched her sister as she threaded her way through the wildflower meadow and headed for the river. 'How many more bugs does she need to photograph? I mean, seriously?'

'She wants to be an entomologist when she's older—'

'A what?'

'Bug-hunter. Except paid to do it. I suppose like David Attenborough.'

'Does he do bugs? I thought he was big game?'

'I think if it moves, he does it.' Isabel pointed. 'Look. Is there someone else there under the trees?'

Ailsa squinted. 'I think so... but who is it? Davey? Pierre?'

'Davey went straight out this morning with Pierre somewhere down by the river, so yeah, probably.'

'Mucking about as only boys can.' Ailsa sighed. It was hard being so grown-up when she was surrounded by kids. Davey might be a year older, yet he was still immature and seemed even more stupid when he was around his younger cousin. Shouldn't it be the other way around?'

'If we follow her now, she'll see us—'

'We could just be meeting up with the boys?'

'Okay. Come on then.'

The sun was hot on her face and the glare was beginning to give her a headache. As they neared the small beach at the river's edge, they looked around them. No one.

'Where did they go?' Isabel kicked off her sandals and waded into the river to peer up and downstream. 'Nope. Can't see anyone.'

'I'll call her.' Ailsa whipped out her phone and dialled Jules. There was the faint sound of a phone ringing in the distance, but the call wasn't answered. Strange. A crashing sound came from in front of them as Davey and Pierre ran through the brush under the trees and splashed into the water. Their trainers were slung over their shoulders.

'Watch it!' Isabel kicked water at them. 'Were you just with Jules?'

'No,' Davey wiped his face on his T-shirt, 'we haven't seen her since breakfast. Wow. It's getting hot now.'

'That's odd...' Isabel turned to Ailsa, who shook her head. They should keep it to themselves until they knew what was going on.

'What are you guys up to?' Ailsa looked over to where she'd heard Jules' phone ringing.

'We were thinking of going into the village to get some fags,' said Davey, wading up to the gravelly area where Ailsa stood. Sitting on a jutting rock, he brushed his feet and put his trainers on.

'Mum and Dad would kill you if they knew you smoked.' Ailsa nudged her brother with her foot. 'It's not cool, you know, and you shouldn't encourage Pierre, who, as we all know, is dumb enough to do whatever you tell him.'

'I'm not dumb! And I don't just do what he tells me to. I have a mind of my own, you know.' Pierre's face scrunched up. 'Anyway, you lot are the stupid ones.'

'How's that, then?' Isabel raised a perfectly plucked eyebrow at him.

'Stuck indoors painting your faces and talking about boys all the time.'

'In case you hadn't noticed, we're out now.' Ailsa stared at Davey. 'Listen, pick us up a can of Coke, will you?'

'Why don't you come with us?' Davey followed her gaze. 'Something going on you're not telling us about?'

'No. Of course not. We... just don't want to go to the village right now.'

'Okay. See you back at the house. And make sure you pay for it. I'm sick of shelling out for you.'

'Wow! It's only a can of Coke. Don't bother, then.' Ailsa

pulled off her sandals and made her way across the river. At its deepest, it reached above her knees and wet the hem of her shorts. Oddly, a small bridge was about a hundred yards up, but they never bothered to use it. They just got wet and complained about the horrible gravel stuck between their toes. 'Come on, Izzy.'

'Er, I'd rather go to the village...' Isabel looked a little sheepish. As well she might. 'I'll get you a Coke. You just, you know...'

Ailsa rolled her eyes. 'Go on then. Abandon me.' Pushing through the bushes, branches and leaves, she found a large tree root and put her shoes back on. What a cow. Isabel was the one who'd said they should follow Jules, and now, when it came to the crunch, she had bottled it and wimped out. Ailsa wondered if she was being stupid for carrying on when a cold can of Coke and a sun bed in the secret garden could be hers. But no. Jules had snuck off into the forest with someone who obviously wasn't Davey or Pierre. So, who was it? And there must be a reason she hadn't answered her phone. What if it had been an emergency? What if it was the other way around? What if Jules was in trouble, and that was why she couldn't answer her phone? The decision was made. She'd have to go and search for her. *Shit, shit, shit!*

There was also a distinct possibility of being bitten to death by the humongous mosquitoes hanging about out here in the woods. Was it worth it? Probably not, although there was still a nag in the back of her mind. Then, after clambering up steep inclines, getting caught and scratched by rogue branches and grabbing brambles, Ailsa conceded defeat. Wherever Jules was, it wasn't anywhere near her. She tried to call her a couple more times and then gave up, as her battery was dangerously low, and the remaining bit might have to be used if she got into a difficult situation.

Like now. Where the hell was she? Having been so intent

on getting to where she believed she'd heard Jules' phone, she hadn't been paying attention. The forest was dim and claustrophobic, with trees towering above her and no visible eyeline to see where she was. Her heart began to race, pulsing out of her chest, and her breathing was ragged. Up or down? Up, she might be able to see some landmarks to guide her. Down would surely lead back to the river and, eventually, the house. Why hadn't she gone with Izzy? She could be sipping ice-cold Coke and sunbathing in one of the recliners in the secluded lower garden with a tinkling fountain and pretty, glowing fairy lights slowly coming on as the sun set. Now, red welts from brambles crisscrossed her arms and legs, and her nails were broken and filthy. She must look a real sight. Wiping at her nose, she vowed not to cry.

'*Jules!*' She should have just asked her what was going on instead of playing Miss Marple. 'Where are you?' Ah, hell! Now she was crying. At least, lost as she was, no one could see her snivelling. Thankfully the sun didn't set until late, but she didn't relish stumbling about in the dark in this forest. She'd heard too many awful tales sitting around the fire in the salon as her aunt and uncle regaled them with the terrible things that had happened to other people here. Was she going to be one of those 'others'? Would there be stories about her as families sat around their fires and whispered about the dark things in the forest? Good God! She'd managed to frighten herself half to death. Shaking herself and setting her shoulders back, she counted down from ten, wiped her nose again and set off purposefully, well, somewhere.

'Bollox, bollox, bollox!'

It took another hour before she realised she recognised where she was. A way off from the house and closer to the village. It was a backtrack, barely passable in a car, though used by the villagers to bypass some of the main roads. It meant another long trek ahead of her, but at least home was in sight. Talking of which... She slowed and held her hands across her eyes to screen them from the relentless sun. Who was that ahead of her? *Elias?* The wild gypsy boy from the village. Hang on, she'd been told she wasn't allowed to say that anymore by her social studies teacher at school. What was the pc version? Oh yeah. Traveller. Sure, they'd all played together as kids, but they were growing up now, and she was beginning to learn things she had never understood before. Listening to her aunt and uncle, she knew those days might be coming to an end. Something about him being an 'undesirable', although that wasn't exactly true. He was fit and actually handsome in a scruffy sort of way, but he was still a dirty gypsy, though... A ghastly thought was forming in her mind. Oh no! It couldn't be... could it? Pierre and Davey were still mates with him. Did they know anything? Would they tell her?

'Ergh!' She wanted to slap her forehead a few times. Wake up. If they knew, they would put a stop to it no matter how friendly they were.

EIGHT

Hetty
THE CITY GIRL

DAVEY TOLD Hetty that his joke about 'Bridezilla' was exactly that. A joke.

'French weddings are usually ungendered, which means the onus isn't all on the bride.' He'd winked at her. 'Although I suspect Isabel might prefer that.'

'It's going to be a big affair, isn't it?' Hetty sighed loudly. 'Please don't let me make a fool of myself.'

'Listen.' Davey pulled her close. 'These weddings are all about having fun. Even though Isabel has that big rock on her finger, she probably won't wear it out much—'

'I bet! Someone might have it, quick as a flash!'

'I didn't mean that, but you're right. What I actually meant was, since the French Revolution—'

'Off with their heads!'

'Exactly. Since then, the French have been pretty reticent about flashing their wealth around. They're not into flashy shows of money.'

'Apart from erecting a massive marquee in your garden, with

caterers and an orchestra?' Hetty eyed Davey, who had the grace to look a little uncomfortable.

'Yeah,' Davey rubbed at the bridge of his nose. 'Apart from that.'

'Davey?' Hetty wondered if this was a good time to ask or if there would never be a good time. She jumped in. 'Something is going on you're not telling me—'

'Have you ever thought there might be a reason for that?'

'Okay...' She rubbed at her eyes. 'It's just there's this strange *thing* between you all. This 'falling out' business. It's disconcerting.'

'We didn't exactly fall out, more that we reacted to a bad situation that happened the last time we were all here.' Davey closed his eyes. 'Now can we get some sleep before that damn alarm goes off?' He switched off his bedside lamp, hauled the covers up to his ears and rolled over. Hetty lay awake in the terrifying dark for a while, listening to the strange noises outside, the wind whistling through cracks, parts of the old house creaking, wondering...

That *damn* alarm. It couldn't be time to get up. They'd only just that minute gone to bed.

Hetty rolled over and poked at Davey. 'Switch it off, please.'

He grunted, and she could hear him flapping at the phone on the side table. Another alarm sounded faintly through the wall.

'We can't miss this.' Davey sat up, and Hetty felt the bed springs boing. It was so dark in the room she couldn't see his silhouette. No light whatsoever flooded in through the window here to illuminate the room. It was never fully dark in their bedroom in Brighton, what with the streetlamps and the red, green and blue glowing dots on their alarm clocks and the small TV always left on standby. She'd never realised that dark could be, well, so dark.

Even though the pillow was a long sausage she had to share with Davey, and she'd thought she'd have to wrestle him for it all night, she'd eventually fallen asleep. But now, what were those awful sounds?

'Davey?' She reached out and caught hold of a bit of him, although she wasn't sure which bit. 'What the heck is that?'

'That's a combination of foxes and Scops owls. The owls are the ones making that odd *toot, toot* sound.'

'And the foxes are the ones making the ghastly screaming sounds?'

'They're just having a bit of fun.' The light pinged on, and Hetty shielded her eyes.

'Do we have to do this? It's still nighttime out there.'

Davey chuckled. 'What? Miss out on the one thing we always used to do as a family? I know it seems crazy to you, Hetty, but we did this together for years. It's as French as a croissant or a croque-monsieur. They'd be pretty pissed off if we don't make it.' He pursed his lips. 'In fact, I'll be pretty pissed off if we miss it.'

'Eugh! Okay.' Hetty scrabbled out of bed. 'Do we need to shower first, or can I get straight into my warm clothes?'

'A quick shower and then get dressed. I can hear Ailsa and Jules banging about next door.'

'Can we just let them get ready first?' Hetty didn't want to go out in her Primark pyjamas. Things like that made her vulnerable. She could imagine what snide thoughts Ailsa would have. Though she couldn't tell Davey that.

'I'll get myself sorted and let you know when they've gone. Okay?' Davey kissed the end of her nose before slipping out.

She could hear a spattering of French words as they greeted each other. Gathering her clothes and boots, she waited, pulling the duvet around her to keep warm. Boy, these old places had draughts like you wouldn't believe. She'd nearly dozed off again when Davey barged back in.

'Come on, sleepy head. Your turn in the shower.'

Hetty hauled herself unwillingly from the bed. The bathroom was steamy, and condensation trickled down the mirror. Damp towels coiled on the floor. Didn't any of them ever pick up after themselves? At least the water was hot. Drying herself quickly, she folded the towels and put them back on the rail before creeping carefully into their bedroom. Davey was dragging on jeans, boots, a thick sweater and a scarf. Hetty did the same.

'I think,' said Hetty, 'you're going to seriously owe me for this.'

'I hear you.' He blew her a kiss. 'Come on. The sooner we get out there, the sooner we can return to the warmth. I'll tell you, it'll be worth it. These girolles and chanterelles are to die for. Fresh off the mountainside, not squashed in some polystyrene tray, all sweaty and slimy.'

Reaching the bottom of the stairs, Hetty was aware of muted voices from the salon. As they walked in, Ailsa and Jules were alternately yawning or rolling their eyes at each other. Pierre was bent over in one of the easy chairs, tying boot laces and grunting noisily. Archie, testing out head torches, nearly blinded Hetty as she walked in, the sudden strobing light flashing at her.

'Oops! Sorry!' He quickly pressed the next button, and the light went off.

Romi was laying out food and plates in the kitchen. 'Eh?'

she called through. 'We are all prepared. Davey? You go with Hetty and show her the correct mushrooms. We do not want a *Calice de la mort* to slip in, now do we?'

'A what?' said Hetty. It was too early to try to figure out what they were saying.

'She's asking us to avoid picking any death cap mushrooms.' Davey pulled her close and kissed her cheek. 'It's in the name.'

'Extremely poisonous.' Jules shrugged. 'To the point of a horrible death if you muck it up and get it wrong.'

Hetty now didn't want to go. Maybe she could feign picking and then leave the proper, safe picking to the rest of the family. Talking of which, where was the bride herself?

As if on cue, Isabel could be heard trotting down the stairs, giggling lightly. A male voice followed her. She entered the salon with a flourish.

'We're not late, are we?'

A man walked in behind her. Tall, dark, distinguished. Expensive looking.

'Are we all here then?' His voice was deep and quite gravelly. 'Forgive my lateness last night, and I'm sorry to have missed the family reunion, but it is what it is. You must introduce me to the rest of the family.' The thing that struck Hetty was that he appeared to have an American accent.

'J.J.,' said Isabel, 'this is my eldest cousin Davey and his girl-friend, Hetty.'

Davey walked up to him and firmly shook his hand. '*Je suis très content de vous rencontrer.*'

'*C'est un plaisir de vous rencontrer aussi.*' J.J. cocked his head to stare at Hetty. '*Communiquons-nous en Anglais ou en Français?* English or French?'

'I'm really sorry,' stammered Hetty. 'English if you can.'
'Of course I can. I speak four languages fluently.'

Hetty nodded and then looked at the floor. Once she and Davey confirmed they would attend the wedding, Hetty had looked up Jean-Jacques D'Aramitz before they came out, so she'd know a bit about him. She kind of wished she hadn't. It seems he was an esteemed member of the National Rally (read National Front), the largest parliamentary opposition group in the French National Assembly. Anti-immigration, anti-Europe, advocate for the protection of French identity, of France leaving NATO's integrated command to distance itself from the American sphere of influence. Hetty had read that the party had been accused of promoting xenophobia and antisemitism. This was who Davey's cousin Isabel was marrying? It was going to be a long day... a long few days. Hetty wished she could teleport back home to the cosy flat she shared with Davey in Brighton. She wanted that simplicity.

'And these are my cousins, Ailsa and Juliette, but she prefers to be called Jules.'

'It is a pleasure to meet you both.' J.J. did a sharp bow. 'It is a terrible shame your dear maman and papa cannot be here with us. Obviously, Isabel and I wish them all the very best.'

'They'll be here, if only in a virtual world.' Davey waved his phone.

'Good to hear.' J.J. rummaged in a pocket and pulled out a box of Tic-Tacs. Throwing a couple in his mouth, he crunched them down. 'Fresh breath in the morning is sacrosanct for me, as I smoke cigars.'

'And for me,' said Isabel.

'And I have upstairs a box of cigars for myself and Archie. The Padron fiftieth anniversary. I hope you approve, Archie?'

He waved a hand upwards. 'Ready to toast the union of our esteemed families.'

'The Padron, eh?' said Archie, with a raised eyebrow. '*Alors, c'est parfait.*' He executed his own smart bow. 'Thank you, Jean-Jacques.'

'What's this Padron thing?' Pierre grinned.

Archie wagged a finger. 'It's a celebratory cigar—'

'That is an understatement,' said J.J.

'Quite frankly,' continued Archie, 'it's hard to imagine a more impressive cigar for a special occasion...' he wrinkled his forehead, 'oh, you know, like the wedding of your only daughter to the man she loves.' He laid his hand on his heart. 'I also have the last quarter of a bottle of Martell Cohiba Estuche in my study, and woe betide anyone who sneaks in for a snifter before the wedding.'

'Then you'd better keep the door to your study shut,' said Romi. 'You know what Toulouse is like. He'd knock that expensive bottle off the shelf just to spite you.'

'Noted,' said Archie.

'Oh,' J.J. nodded his head appreciatively, 'that's a lovely cognac, indeed.'

'Nice,' said Pierre, 'although I'm trying to quit both and lead a healthy lifestyle. I'm getting to the point where I prefer smoke to be outside of me. Talking of which...' The fire still had embers glowing from the night before. Pierre bent over and coaxed it alive, placing more small branches and logs on it. 'This should be roaring by the time we return.'

Hetty sincerely wished she could stay by that fire. Would they miss her if she kept entirely still? Pretend to be invisible? She didn't want to be responsible for poisoning anyone.

Romi wound a scarf around Archie's neck as if he was a child. It made Hetty smile. Donning woolly hats and taking little hand-held wicker baskets Romi gave them, complete with a tiny, very sharp knife, they put their head torches on, adjusted the light settings so no one would have an epileptic fit, and headed out of the enormous front door.

'You know the drill,' shouted Archie, 'Up and at 'em!'

There was a chill in the air as they exited the house. Hetty stood for a moment, her hand over the light from her torch, and gazed upwards. Above them, the sky was vast. The Milky Way was clearly visible, and brighter stars or planets winked at her. Some seemed to even pulse with a slight hint of blue or red. She blinked rapidly. Was that red-hued one Mars? Having lived all her life in London and then Brighton, she'd never seen a sky so clear. She could have stayed, staring at the sky forever, but the call had gone out...

Gaggling along like a line of baby ducks, they followed Archie around the side of the house and down a gravel path that crunched noisily underfoot. Under the low-level branches, the light receded, and all Hetty could see were the bobbing head-lamps of her companions.

'Lucky we are not going shooting,' said J.J., 'or we would have frightened every living thing off for miles.'

'Yeah, well,' said Davey, 'lucky for us mushrooms aren't scared of us—'

'But they are still hard to track down,' said Jules. 'Hiding in all that mulch.' Her head torch could be seen as she swung around. 'I wondered if we might be going to collect milk from the farm afterwards?'

It seemed to Hetty that there was a strange hum in the air.

'Er, no,' said Isabel. 'We don't go there anymore, you know...'

'No, I obviously don't know,' said Jules. Her voice was light though there was a weird tone to it. 'Why don't you go there anymore?'

'Hey,' said Davey, 'what's with that? We used to go there every day for fresh milk.'

'Now we don't.' Isabel shrugged. 'End of.'

'But why not?' Jules cocked her head to stare at Isabel. 'That's what I'd like to know.'

Isabel pouted. 'We just don't, so leave it, Jules.' Her torch swung away from them as she stamped off.

'I was only asking! Wow!' Jules tutted. 'It was a simple question. Sorry to have bothered you, Izzy. Won't do it again.' She also stomped into the darkness ahead.

'Is Juliette okay?' said Romi. 'She seems a little preoccupied.'

'I'm sure she's just tired,' said Davey. 'But you must admit, we would wonder why you don't go to the farm anymore. It was such a big part of our life here.'

'I really can't remember now. I suppose things change.' Romi shrugged. 'That stand of trees over there will be a good starting point, yes?' She waved at a shadowy mound in the distance, and Hetty inwardly groaned. Mist was curling about them, and more sounds in the darkness made her jump. And it was cold enough that her breath curled visibly every time she exhaled.

'Come on, city girl,' said Davey. 'I have to give you a crash course in mushroom etiquette.'

'Great,' said Hetty, tagging behind him, as the group drifted apart and was swallowed by the mist.

Having grovelled around in damp leaf litter, clambered over thick roots threatening to trip them or snag an ankle so it could be broken, Hetty heard Davey let out a deep sigh. Had he finally found one of these elusive bloody mushrooms? Davey held out this yellowy-orange mushroom that had a trumpet-shaped head. It was frilly and looked like it could be seen swimming at the bottom of the sea. Did they really swoon over these ugly-looking things? And eat them?

'This is a chanterelle. They taste wonderful and will not kill you.'

'That's good to know,' said Hetty. 'How many have you got?' In other words, could they go back to the house now?

'Not as many as we need.'

'Oh, great.' Could Davey detect the sarcasm in her voice? Obviously not.

They were now grubbing (and that was meant literally) around the roots of some other colossal tree looming above them. Her knees were wet, and she was sure bugs were crawling up her legs, so she'd tucked her trouser bottoms into her socks. As she sifted through the soggy twigs, leaves and pine needles, things still tickled across her hands. She didn't want to even think about worms...

Having filled half of the wicker basket, Hetty thought that might be enough, but oh no, off he went again. She hauled herself upright and yelped as something stuck around her face. A spider's web? Seriously? Visions of Shelob from Lord of the Rings leapt into her mind. Did they have ginormous spiders here? It was likely, considering the age of this forest. Batting it all off, she groaned and heard a chuckle close by.

'It is a bit much, isn't it?' said Jules, emerging from the trees, misty tendrils curling about her ankles. 'This may have been fun when we were kids, but now we have hangovers and need more sleep.'

'It's certainly an experience,' smiled Hetty. Looking up, she realised that fingers of weak light were finally clawing through the canopy high above them. Her stomach rumbled. 'There was no time for even a cup of tea this morning. I hope this is worth it. I'm starving.'

'Trust me, these wild mushrooms, straight from the ground, are delicious and fetch a high price in the local markets.' Hetty could see the glint of a smile. 'I think we'll be going back soon. I just heard Pierre throwing up in the bushes.'

'Charming. Mind you, we all packed away quite a bit last night.'

'They tell us champagne doesn't make us drunk, darling!'

'Tell that to Pierre.'

'Hey, Jules.' Davey trod carefully around the roots. 'Have you beaten us?' He waved the basket. 'Because all I'm saying here is I hope Romi and Archie have some more brekkie things in, as three mushrooms each on toast might be a bit lacking.'

'I've got a few, but I saw bacon in their gigantic fridge. I think we're all right.'

'Where are the others?' said Hetty. 'I can't hear them.'

Davey peered about him. 'The sound in this forest is deadened, especially with all this mist.'

'Please tell me we're not lost.' Hetty wiped a clump of damp hair from her forehead.

'Hetty! My love,' laughed Davey, 'you can see the treeline over there.' He pointed, and Hetty was relieved to see the trees thinning and the new daylight washing in.

She tuned to Jules. 'We watched that Netflix series on that girl who crash-landed in the Canadian wilderness. I don't think I would have survived for long—'

'Not true,' said Davey.

'I'd have been eaten by bears within minutes.' Hetty rolled her eyes. 'I'm a city girl, through and through.'

'You might be a city girl, but you're the most resourceful person I know. You'd have smashed it out of the park!'

'Ha!' Hetty smiled up at Davey. 'Maybe...' She nodded at Jules. 'You're in Manchester now, aren't you?'

'Yep. Trying to acquire the accent, as I think it sounds so cool.' Jules scuffed through the leaves. 'And, I need to mask this old plum-in-the-mouth accent I have. Posh doesn't fit up there.'

Davey frowned. 'Has anyone had a go then?'

'No, most people are friendly. It's more I notice that I stick out. I'd like to fit in.'

'How weird,' mused Hetty. 'I'm worried I'm too common for your family, and I don't fit in, and you'd like to be more common, so you fit in elsewhere.'

'I suppose that's life.' Jules held out her hand. 'Come on then, Miss Common, let's get breakfast. I could eat a horse.'

'I like horse, actually,' said Davey. 'Do you remember when we had it in a local restaurant?'

'You've eaten horse?' Hetty couldn't believe it.

'Have you eaten a cow? And pigs? And poor little fluffy lambs?'

Hetty hung her head. 'Yes.'

'Then don't judge.' He grinned. 'We're going to have a roast dog at the wedding. It's traditional at a French wedding—'

'Dog!' shrieked Hetty.

Davey laughed so much that he had to hang onto a tree. 'God, Hetty! You're so gullible, sometimes.'

'French onion soup.' Jules pulled Hetty along. 'That's what is traditional at a French wedding.' She wagged an admonishing finger. 'Not dog.'

'Thank goodness for that.'

'Ha, ha, ha!' Davey stumbled along behind them. 'Look, everyone is waiting for us.'

'What's so funny?' Archie waved to them.

'Just a silly joke.' Davey patted Hetty on the back. She

hoped they couldn't all see how much she was blushing in the weak early morning light. How embarrassing. Even contemplating they might eat dogs here. In France, for God's sake – the centre of the gastronomic world.

Archie nodded. 'It's getting light now, so we'll make our way back. We need to check through the mushrooms carefully.'

'We are having that bacon, aren't we?' Jules nudged him.

'We're having the whole shebang!' Archie put his arm across Jules' shoulder. 'I'm so happy the family is all together again. We missed you a lot.'

Romi flapped at him, 'Don't get me going, or I'll cry.'

'You cry at everything, my love.'

'Well, at least I'll have a reason this time. Anyway, it's the menopause. It plays havoc with one's emotions.'

'Ah, Maman', said Isabel, 'I thought we spoke about this. Please don't bring the menopause into this weekend.'

'It's part of life, darling!'

'It's not part of mine yet, and I want it to stay that way.'

'I think I might be hitting mine,' said Archie, throwing his arms wide.

'What?' said Pierre. 'The male menopause? Dearest God, Dad! You're not thinking of running off with the au-pair, are you?'

'Don't be a dick, Pierre. I meant I'm feeling like upgrading the poor old Citroën to something with a lot more pizzazz!'

Romi tutted and blew kisses at her son. 'He'll never do it. Archie loves that old car more than I think he loves me.'

'Not true, my darling wife.' Archie spun her in his arms. 'I love that old Citroën *as much* as I love you.'

Hetty again saw the massive gap between her upbringing and the experiences of the people around her. How wonderful to even have the chance to talk about things so personal and women-orientated as the menopause. And in front of men. Her family were all blushes and hushed whisperings. And if overheard, blue/green bruises and split lips. Davey's family were so much more unrestricted in their expressions, unshackled by crippling anxiety, sure of themselves. Hetty's mum had never given her the 'frank' talk. No mention of sex at all, in any context. Had she hoped she'd learn it by osmosis? That it was someone else's responsibility to inform her, maybe the school, a friend's mother, or whatever. That certainly didn't work and nearly left her with the proverbial 'bun in the oven'. She'd survived but not unscathed. That memory was chained inside a lead box at the bottom of her memory cupboard, a clear warning spray painted across the top. *Never open this.*

Her mother was lower working class scraping her way up through years of hard work to simply working class. They'd finally fled from her dad to a women's refuge after another brutal beating, although he still found them. Hetty would die happy if she never saw her bastard father again in this life or any other. She sent as much of her wages to her mum as she could afford, even if it meant scrimping.

And she couldn't even face what had happened to her brother Paul. Three years on, she still couldn't come to terms with it.

NINE

Ailsa

UNDER THE RUG

Dreams merged with memories in the night until Ailsa woke, sweating and shivering, in the dark of morning, so early that even the cockerels were still tucked up in their coops and snoring. Was she going down with some nasty lurgy? Had she slept at all, because it sure felt like she hadn't? Recollections of those last few days here back in 2016 impinged on her mind. Things she never wished to see again and thought she'd buried deep now reared up, as clear and horribly fresh as if it was yesterday.

Hearing Jules banging about and groaning, she waited until there was a lull and hauled herself out of the warm bed and into the chilled bathroom.

As she came out, she shivered melodramatically. 'Bloody hell, Jules! They could at least get a heater in the bathroom!'

'Cold is good for you. It forces your body to pump more blood through your heart, or so I've heard.'

'Great.' Ailsa dressed, dragging on her clothes as fast as she could, and searched for her fingerless gloves. 'Did you hear J.J. come in last night? He and Izzy made quite a racket coming up the stairs.'

'I thought I heard something but was too tired to bother with it.'

'I wonder what he's like?'

'We're about to find out.'

'Are you ready to face the family?'

'As ready as I'll ever be.'

Ailsa followed Jules down the stairs. She knew that the way it was all handled eight years ago had driven a wedge between them all. Was this the time to try and bring them all back together as a family? Mend the rift? The thing was, and this was the bit that scared her: how much did Jules know?

Ailsa's mind drifted as she entered the salon. At least it was warm in here. She registered the family discussing how not to kill themselves with the mushrooms and then heard Isabel's distinctive chuckle and the sound of a man. When Izzy bounded in, the cat with the cream, the man following her exuded wealth from every pore. No wonder her cousin wanted the wedding sooner rather than later. No way was she going to chance losing this man to someone else. Handsome, in a heavy-lidded, plump-lipped way that bordered on feminine. He was politeness personified, well-educated and obviously cultured. A catch in any woman's book. Even if he did smoke cigars. Oh, and he was a right-wing knob. Lovely!

Archie was playing with the head torches, and Ailsa shook her head at Romi, who shrugged. Ailsa was beginning to remember stuff from before as Romi wound a scarf around Archie's neck. She treated him more like a naughty boy, so he sometimes acted accordingly. It was strange how other things came into focus. Then the cry went up, and that was the signal to move.

Ailsa dragged on her jacket and followed everyone outside. It was beautiful, no doubt about that, but tinged with a terrible ache in her gut. There was a distinct possibility she shouldn't have come for the wedding, should never have returned here.

Clutching the mushroom basket and knife, trailing along behind Isabel and her hubby-to-be, Ailsa wondered why it felt like she had a twisted ball of rubber marinating in acid in her gut. Oh no! Her face went clammy and cold, and something hot spread out from her stomach. Clinging to a tree, she stopped and waited until they were out of sight before she threw up. Scuffling leaves over the small, steaming pile, she glanced about her, searching for something to wipe her nose and mouth on. How disgusting! She found a hanky in the side pocket of her jacket and blew her nose. She was never sick after drinking unless she'd had a skinful of hard spirits. Thinking back, had they cracked open the tequila? Not that she could remember, but that was often the point. A dark space in her head with no memories. No, she'd been perfect last night, practically an angel, all things considered. It must be guilt. She didn't want to do 'guilt'. She'd slunk out for a crafty cigarette partway through the evening, and that was all. Talking of which. With her back against the bole of a wickedly huge tree, she hunkered down, rummaged in her jacket pocket, and tugged out a slightly crumpled carton of Dunhill's. Elegant packaging and, according to them, free of all the nasty stuff in more common brands. Like hell. She sucked in a lungful of smoke and held it there momentarily, closing her eyes. Expensive for some but not for her. Her hands were shaking.

'Oh, that's so good.' The smoke dribbled out of her nose, and she puffed a small smoke ring into the cold air.

A shadow emerged from the trees. 'That's impressive, *cousine*.' Pierre slumped beside her and clicked his fingers.

'I take that to mean you would like one?' Ailsa tossed him the box and her lighter. 'I didn't know you still smoked. In fact, I thought you said yesterday you'd given up. Or are you just a token smoker?'

'Oh, I smoke, but I'm trying to cut down.' His smoke ring was way more impressive than hers. 'You'd think in this day and age we'd never do it, but I started properly after...' He took another drag of his cigarette.

'Yeah, round about when I did.' Ailsa shifted to find a more comfortable position, though she was straddling a large root, which might be difficult. 'Not surprising, really.'

'No. How has...?' Pierre nodded in the general direction they'd seen Jules walking.

'Quite frankly, I have no idea. We're not exactly best buds anymore.'

'That's a terrible shame, then. And she never—'

'No.' She took a drag of her cigarette. 'What about your lot?'

'Swept under the rug.'

Ailsa leaned in close and whispered, 'Did Romi ever find out?'

'No, and we need it to stay that way. *Capisci?*'

'Of course I understand. Izzy and I are the ones with the most to lose.'

'Possibly. But don't forget the part my dad played.' Pierre stubbed the butt out on the sole of his boot and then buried it in the leaves. 'We all lost something that day, cuz.' Blowing smoke out of his nose, he stared upwards.

'What's with no one going to the village anymore?'

'Ah!' Pierre shifted and scanned around them. 'We're not exactly welcome there. Bad blood.'

'Really? Why?'

'Because after... there were accusations thrown our way—'

'How? No one knew anything—'

'Maybe.' He shrugged. 'Not totally sure about that, but the family threatened us.'

'And?'

'We had to threaten them back.' Pierre leaned back against the tree trunk. 'Dad won, of course. He always does. Nothing was proved, and it all, you know, went away.' He sniffed loudly. 'Apart from it was made plain we should never visit the village again.'

Went away? Could something like that go away? It had certainly never left her. That image, those moments imprinted on the back of her eyelids, so when she closed her eyes, there they were, as fresh as the day it happened.

'Changing the subject, then. You got a girl yet?' She nudged him. 'Or maybe a boy?'

'I may have both.' He smirked at her, and she could still see the boy he'd been. Eight years. A skinny, gangly kid to a handsome young man. He'd have no difficulty in the love department. 'You?'

'A few flings but nothing serious. I can't seem to settle.' She followed what he'd done with the cigarette butt. 'We're not going to cause a forest wildfire, are we?'

'It's too damp. I'm sorry you weren't invited to the hen and stag parties. I tried, but I think it brought back too much stuff.'

'*Enterrement de vie de jeune fille...*' Ailsa stared through the trees at the low-lying mist. 'The burial of the life of a young girl. That wasn't at the hen do a few weeks ago. It was eight years ago in the barn. That's when our childhood died.'

'We shouldn't talk any more about it.' Pierre clasped her shoulder. 'It's dangerous. For all of us.' He clambered upright. 'Come on, we're seriously lacking in mushrooms.'

'What's J.J. like?'

'A prize prick!' Pierre sniggered. 'I hope no one heard that.'

'It's good to know. Is he a match for Isabel, though?'

'They both want money, prestige, the good things in life, though I have no idea if they're compatible. I mean, I don't know if they actually love each other or are in love with the thought of each other. If you see what I mean.'

'I get that. Well, she has a magnificent ring on her finger, and tomorrow she'll get the rest. Good on her.'

'Not for you, then? It's not like your mum and dad can't afford a lavish wedding for you both.'

'It's not about the money. I want it all. I want unconditional love, but I don't believe it exists.' Although maybe it did for some.

2016 – Ailsa

Footsore and tear-stained, Ailsa limped into the big house and listened. Voices drifted from the kitchen. It was now past four in the afternoon, and they would be having a snack of dark chocolate in a hunk of French bread. Traditional. Just the thing to tide them over until dinner at nine. She'd missed lunch, and it was as if her backbone was fused to her belly button. Is this what it felt like to be starving? She couldn't be seen in this state, so she crawled up the stairs, quickly showered and changed. Even though it was summer, she tugged out a long-sleeved top to hide the vicious scratches lacing her arms. When she arrived downstairs in the kitchen, Jules was sitting at the kitchen table, stuffing the last bit of bread into her mouth. Isabel eyed her but said nothing. All the worry and pain Ailsa had gone through, expecting to find Jules' mutilated body under a bush and here she was, acting as if nothing had happened. She could clump her one! Pierre and Davey were fighting over the last few chunks of chocolate.

'Hey,' said Ailsa, holding out her hand, 'save some for me.'

'You should have been here earlier, then.' Davey yanked the last two chunks from Pierre's resisting fingers and popped them in his mouth. Through a mouthful, he gestured at the fridge. 'Your Coke is in there.'

At least she'd got that. Cracking open the tin, she poured it into a glass. Her first swallow felt so good. She shouldn't have bothered following Jules. She should have just let her get what was coming. She'd missed an afternoon of lazing around, her lunch and even the tea-time snack. And for what?

'You look weird,' said Pierre. 'What's up?'

'Nothing. I'm fine.'

'You look like you've been crying—'

'Don't be ridiculous.' Ailsa felt quite bristly. 'I'm just hot and tired. I went for a magnificent walk,' she noted that Jules jolted and then hid it with a cough, 'and I lost track of time. I didn't have any lunch.' She stood and rummaged through the cupboards. 'What? No chocolate left at all?'

'You know tomorrow is the big shop.' Pierre grinned at her. 'We'll have cabbage soup tonight, without even the cabbage.' He chortled to himself as Ailsa stared at him with a stony face.

'That's called a bowl of hot water—'

'Yeah, right!' Pierre peered at the doorway. 'You know what Maman is like. Makes sure there's nothing left before we do the next big shop.'

'That's because she knows how wasteful we all are.' Jules stood and stretched. 'I'm off for a bath. All that grubbing around in the forest has made me quite itchy.'

'Well,' said Pierre slyly, 'if you go hunting for bugs and grubs, you will get grubby... Get it?'

'Oh, shut it. Pierre.' Jules flounced out of the kitchen.

Collaring Jules on the stairwell before dinner, Ailsa knew she had to be careful.

'Missed you today. We were all down by the river. I called you to see if you wanted to join us.'

'I know.' Jules' eyes slid away a little too soon. 'I was trying to get some shots of the most amazing spider webs.'

'I called you a couple more times afterwards.'

'Did you? Soz, and all that.' She trotted faster down the stairs. 'I must have been really engrossed.'

No shit, Sherlock. Was Jules getting something on with the local rough boy? She needed to talk to Isabel about this. Isabel was a good year older (give or take) than them. Okay, she and Jules were nearly sixteen, but that was it. Nearly. This boy Elias was older. Not by a lot, but enough. And he wasn't one of them. She bet he wanted more from Jules than she should be giving. She was a kid. They were all kids. Ailsa closed her eyes and prayed for a minute that they hadn't done anything they shouldn't have. Maybe she was jumping to conclusions, though it was pretty odd he'd been heading to the village down the back route at the same time as she'd been searching for Jules. She and Isabel had seen someone with her at the forest's edge. And Jules had arrived home before her. A coincidence? Nah!

TEN

Hetty
FAMILY

THE SUN CRESTED to their left as they descended the hill behind the house. First a glow, then a sliver, then a partial disc.

'It's so beautiful here,' whispered Hetty, more to herself, but Davey must have heard.

'It is very special.' As Hetty looked up at him, something wistful passed across his face.

'Is there something wrong, Davey?'

'Look,' he stopped walking and turned to her, 'when we were last here, there was a tragedy, leaving us all reeling. It hit all of us in different ways.'

'I'm so sorry. I shouldn't have pushed.'

'No, I should have given you a heads-up, especially as we've all been acting weirdly. Just know it's nothing to do with you.'

'Thanks.' That was good to hear. Usually sure of herself, she hated feeling paranoid. A tragedy. How sad. She wondered what it was... No, it was none of her business.

After sloughing off all their outdoor gear and changing back into normal shoes, left in the front lobby, everyone rushed for the kitchen, baskets aloft.

Pierre darted to the fireplace. 'Great. The fire's still going strong.' He hefted another mammoth log onto it.

There was a bustle in the kitchen like she'd never seen before. That saying 'all hands-on deck' was never more appropriate. Hetty watched as everyone seemed to know their place and job in the scheme of things. The mushrooms from each basket were placed in small mounds on the massive table in the salon. Ailsa, Pierre and Davey sat and carefully checked each and every mushroom, tugging off caught weeds and grass. The piles of mushrooms grew.

'What can I help with?' Hetty jigged about in the centre of the kitchen, feeling like she was getting in the way.

'You can watch the bacon,' said Romi, waving at a skillet the size of a bin lid on the hob of the AGA, where oil was sizzling. 'The bacon is in the fridge. Put as many rashers in as you can fit in. I think we have a ravenous horde on our hands.'

Hetty delved into the fridge and found a waxed packet of bacon with at least a zillion thick rashers inside. Using tongs she found hanging on a rack, she squeezed most of the bacon into the pan. Each piece spat hot oil at her. Another pan was placed next to it, and more oil and some butter were plopped in it.

'This is for the mushrooms,' said Romi, and yet another frying pan was wiggled onto a back plate. 'And this for the eggs.'

Hetty prayed she wasn't being asked to cook all of it alone. Flipping each slice of bacon, she watched over her shoulder as Archie sliced baguette after baguette into little rounds and dropped them into a long toaster. As they pinged out, he slathered butter on each one and placed them on a large serving platter until it was a cockled pyramid.

'I've put all the plates in the hot drawer.' Romi checked they were not getting too hot. 'How's it coming with the mushrooms? The bacon is nearly done.'

'Sorted.' Ailsa hurried in and scraped the mushrooms into the pan. More sizzling and spitting. With Romi cracking eggs by the dozen into the egg pan and Ailsa stirring the mushrooms and grating fresh black pepper, there seemed far too many arms and hands all over the place. Elbows clacked, and many 'sorries' were to be heard.

Hetty breathed a sigh of relief when Romi pushed her towards the table. 'We can start plating up. Hetty, darling, can you put three pieces of toast on each plate? Then we can start dishing. Pierre?' She raised her voice, but he was standing next to her. 'How's the coffee coming?'

'Fine. All in hand, so don't panic.' Hetty heard the percolator bubbling and hissing as she popped the toast onto the warmed plates.

'I'll take the coffee cups through,' said Jules. She started to ferry them to the table and then returned to fetch milk and sugar.

'Isabel?' Romi bellowed into the salon. 'Can you start helping, please?'

'I'm coming. You wouldn't believe it's my wedding tomorrow, and here I am, being used as the skivvy!' She flounced into the kitchen. 'Give me the bacon pan.'

'I can dish out the mushrooms,' said Archie. 'Why are there so many people in the kitchen? Get yourselves seated. Where's J.J.?'

Hetty peeped into the salon to see J.J. sitting in one of the easy chairs, flicking through a newspaper. Ah! She knew this. A man who wouldn't deign to do 'women's work'. He had probably been waited on all his life. Hetty wondered if Isabel would continue to do that or if she'd demand that he did his fair share. Mind you, what did this man earn a year? She guessed more than she'd make in a whole lifetime. She supposed he could afford to be a lazy dipshit and get a maid in.

'*À table!*' Romi shooed them out, and everyone fumbled to find a place to sit at the huge table. Cutlery and coffee cups were being handed round the group. Romi brought each plate out using oven gloves. 'The plates are hot, so be careful. Quickly now. We don't want it to get cold.'

Hetty glanced around her as they ate. This was so nice. A family eating at the table as a family. They spoke with their mouths full, so intent on getting to say what they wanted to say, they laughed, made jokes at each other's expense, and then laughed some more. A lump in her throat made her stop eating. She couldn't swallow. It wasn't that she wished she'd had a different background (it was what it was, and no wishing could change that). It was more that she'd had a longing, a hunger for something more. Something just like this. It took a moment for her to be able to finish her breakfast. If only Paul could be here, now, experiencing all this. And their mum. How incredible would that be?

'So, *ma chérie*,' Romi indicated Hetty, 'was it worth getting up in the dark and crawling about in the undergrowth? Or do you think we are mad?' She suddenly raked under the table. 'Toulouse? Oh, that damn cat! Always sneaking about. Watch out, everyone, the little thief is on the scrounge.' She straightened up. 'Sorry, Hetty. Are we mad, then?'

Hetty licked her lips. 'Mmm...The mushrooms were to die for. I'm a convert.'

'Good,' said Archie, waggling his eyebrows, 'then you don't mind if we do it all again tomorrow before the wedding...'

Hetty stared at him. 'Um...'

'It was a joke, Hetty.' Romi rolled her eyes at Archie. 'My husband is an evil man.'

'I'd still be up for it.'

'Then you're the only one,' said Isabel. 'There is tradition, and then there is going completely overboard. As it's my wedding tomorrow, someone else can stack the dishwasher. I'm going up to check last-minute details.'

'What can be left to check?' Romi blew out the side of her mouth. 'We have left nothing to chance.' Turning to Jules and Ailsa, she held out her hands. 'We have been planning this wedding for months.'

'What she's saying,' drawled Archie, 'is it's all locked up tighter than a nun's—'

'Dad!' Isabel slapped at her forehead. 'Really? Lower the tone, why don't you?'

'I'm Scottish, my love.' He made a face at her. 'I say it as it is.'

'Well,' huffed Isabel, 'you don't need to say it like that!' She pushed from the table. 'J.J.?' She tripped as the cat shot out from under the table and wound around her ankles. 'Someone, please throw the stupid cat out! *J.J.?* Are you coming up?'

'I will be up in a minute.' J.J. snapped the paper, as if he was annoyed at the interruption. 'I wish to finish my paper by the fire.'

'Yeah,' said Pierre, gathering plates, 'it's your last day of freedom. Make the most of it.' Although he was mocking J.J., Hetty felt he meant it.

J.J. moved to the wing-backed easy chair and settled in with his paper over his knees. He didn't look up.

Romi waved about her. 'The people we've hired to lay out the marquee will be here at ten. They will place the tables and chairs ready for the main event tomorrow afternoon. They're already stacked down there. We also have the company coming that will erect the arch for the symbolic service and, again, put out the chairs for the guests. The caterers will be here mid-day and will be parked up in the lower field. They will ferry the courses up as and when needed—'

'What?' said Pierre, 'On scooters?'

'They have little vans, *mon cher*. They know what the layout is here.' Romi tutted under her breath. 'Pierre, as a witness, you need to be prepared.' She nodded at him. 'And please, Pierre, no awful jokes or pranks. There is a time and a place for such stuff, but not at your sister's wedding.'

'What? Are you saying we can't have fun at the wedding? It's traditional to embarrass the couple as best you can.' He winked at his mother, who rolled her eyes and groaned.

'Then, please,' Romi wrung her hands, 'make it tasteful.'

'I fancy a walk.' Davey looked out of the window of their bedroom. 'I think I need to lose a few calories after that breakfast.' Turning to Hetty, he pointed. 'How about we take a wander to the church? I remember it's lovely there and a nice walk through the lanes.'

'I'd love that. I shouldn't have removed my 'stout shoes' or whatever Romi called them.'

'I think, in her parlance, it means anything that isn't a stiletto.'

'Well, she is French. She is expected to be sophisticated.' Hetty tied up her boots and slung a cardigan around her shoulders. It might be warm and sunny outside, yet you never knew.

At the top of the stairs, she stopped. 'We haven't forgotten anything, have we? I mean, I don't want to come back up if we have.'

'If we have, it remains forgotten,' Davey winked at her, 'as I don't want to either.'

Turning left from the main front door, they ambled along the gravel driveway and onto the main road. Not that you could call it main, as it was barely big enough to allow even medium-sized cars to squeeze past each other. There were passing places at intervals. Hedgerows of hawthorn entangled with dog roses buzzed with bees and the scent of autumnal flowers. Obscuring the fields they fenced off, it was only as they came to a gate or a gap that Hetty could see across and marvel at how it looked like a quilted bedspread.

'It is so pretty here—'

'Says the girl who is terrified of the countryside!'

'I could get used to it. I remember you were not so hot on the sounds of sirens when we first moved into our flat in Brighton.'

'That's because it sounded like we were in Beirut.'

'God! Such a country boy.'

'Some of us weren't brought up in the scary parts of London. Give me credit where credit is due—'

'Brighton is one of the nicest, most cosmopolitan places in England. It's not exactly gang warfare there or Mexican cartels...' But she'd known the seedy side of life when she lived in London. Being dirt poor in a great city isn't fun, especially where the one place you should feel safe, your home, is the most dangerous place you could be. Hetty shook her head as if it could fling out these thoughts.

'Are you okay, Hetty?' Davey's concerned face slipped into view.

'Yeah. I'm fine. Just looking forward to the wedding tomorrow.'

A car came around the bend far too fast for the space there was, and Davey had to push himself and Hetty back into the bushes. The hedges and trees had muffled the sound of its approach.

'Arsehole!' Davey waved his fist. 'What a stupid twat!'

'Ha!' Hetty laughed. 'If he didn't understand the words, I'm sure he understood your middle finger. Or does that mean something else here? I know some things we take for granted have completely different connotations in other countries.'

'No. Middle finger means middle finger here.' Holding her hand, Davey hugged the hedge until they could see the beginnings of the tiny village opening up ahead and a stone-humped back bridge straddling the river. As it was fairly wide, the river meandered slowly beneath them as they walked over. A low stone wall trailed alongside them into the village to their right, and to their left were two-storey houses with steep grey slated roofs, window boxes stuffed with bright and bobbing geraniums and the most vivid turquoise shutters. They carried on walking, passing a woman cleaning her doorstep.

'*Bonjour, Madame,*' called Davey with a wave. The woman's face creased into a frown, and she turned from them.

'Is that normal?' Hetty glanced back in time to see the woman glaring at them over her shoulder.

'Not really, no.' Davey looked a little shaken. 'Never had that response from anyone here before. The village has been coming to the barbeque Archie and Romi put on each summer for years. That was plain weird.'

'Maybe they don't recognise you?'

'Or maybe they do.' His mouth set in a hard line. Passing a small bar with a striped awning and tables outside, the inhabitants, drinking coffee or small glasses of what looked like brandy, all stopped what they were doing, even mid-conversation, to stare at them. No one waved or responded when Davey greeted them again.

'I don't understand.'

'Isabel said something about not wanting to visit the village. Do you think something has happened you don't know about?'

'Only...' Davey ran his fingers through his hair. 'No, I'm sure it can't be that.'

'What? Is it what you were talking about earlier? That thing from eight years ago?'

'I wish I knew. Come on. We're here to see the church, so we're bloody well going to see it.'

The church was Norman. All rounded arches and heavy-set stone blocks, with a short, squat bell tower. Through the tall main door, it was cool inside, and light streamed in through narrow windows.

'Why on earth wouldn't Isabel want to be married here?' Hetty whispered, waving her arms. 'It's gorgeous.'

The dark wood pews were simple and unadorned, and the central aisle led to the altar, covered in a gold embroidered cloth, with two ornate candle stick holders and tall candles and a cross placed in the centre. Behind the altar was a stained-glass window depicting something from the bible that Hetty didn't recognise. Coloured light flooded down on them as they approached as if swimming through a rainbow. Looking down, the paving slabs were worn by the passing of time and many feet.

'How beautiful,' whispered Hetty again.

'Shh.' A hiss came from someone sitting at the front in one of the pews. An old lady swivelled and pointed towards the door. '*Partez maintenant. Vous n'êtes pas le bienvenus ici.*'

'What did she say?' Whatever it was, it didn't sound friendly.

Davey held out his hand and reached for her shoulder. He appeared unsteady. 'She basically told us to bugger off. She says we're not welcome here.'

'What?' That came out louder than she wanted, and the old lady hissed again and pointed to the door. 'What is going on here, Davey? It feels like we've fallen into the storyline for *An American Werewolf in London*. You remember the part where all the old codgers don't want the Americans there?'

'Not really, but I get your point. We need to get back to the house and ask some questions.'

As they returned, all sorts of new things were being constructed outside the front of the house.

'Wow!' Hetty pointed. 'Whatever that is, it's gorgeous.'

'It's the arch for when the real wedding happens. The first bit is like a registery office wedding. The legal bit, then they'll return here, and we get something closer to the wedding we're more used to.'

'It sounds amazing.'

'It certainly is.'

Hetty snuggled into him. Would she experience anything like this one day?

'Oy.' Pierre was waving from round the side of the house. 'You two? Can you help me with something?'

'Sure.' Davey glanced down at Hetty and grinned. 'Two birds with one stone.'

As they caught up with Pierre, he led them down a winding path.

'Are we going to the secret garden?' asked Davey.

'Yeah, some wonderful wildflowers are growing inside, and I wanted to pick a few bouquets for tomorrow to place on the tables.' Pierre scratched at his nose. 'I'll leave them in water until the last moment. I hope they survive. I just want Isabel to be surrounded by beautiful things tomorrow.'

'Listen, Pierre?' Davey touched him lightly on the shoulder, so he stopped and turned, one hand on the wrought iron gate. Hetty could see weathered stone benches and a fountain, now dry, enclosed by tall hedges.

'What?'

'We've just been into the village and, well, let's say the welcome was decidedly frosty.' Davey grimaced. 'And I don't think it was because they thought I was a dumb tourist. It was as if they actually recognised me.'

Hetty watched Pierre's face blanche. He cocked his head. 'Yeah, well, we don't go to the village often. I think Isabel mentioned that?'

'Okay, but why not? We used to love hanging out there—'

'Not anymore.' Pierre turned back to the gate and unlatched it.

'But why?' Davey glanced at Hetty and raised an eyebrow. 'We used to host the biggest barbeque in the area for them. They loved it—'

'Like I said, not anymore. Listen, there's a bit of bad blood between the people in the village and us. That's the way it goes, sometimes.'

'Bad blood? Why? Because of what happened?'

'Can we not talk about this now, Davey? It's not really the time and is kind of complicated and not very nice.'

'Really?'

'Yes, really. Come and help me pick some flowers for Izzy, and please don't bring this up with anyone else. It wasn't a good time for any of us, and I don't want anything to ruin Isabel's day tomorrow.'

'Understood.' Davey nearly saluted.

The thing is, Hetty didn't understand. Not one jot of it.

Half an hour later, holding armfuls of the prettiest flowers

Hetty had ever seen, with a scent that made you believe you were in heaven, she walked back towards the house, all theories of bad blood replaced with thoughts about tomorrow. The wedding!

Chapter Eleven

We've been thinking for a long time, yes, a very long time, about how to get you back, give you a taste of your own medicine, so to speak. We've been mulling over ideas. Shall we do this, or shall we do that? What we mean is we have so many courses of action open to us, especially here, that it's like being kids set free in a sweetie shop, able to grab anything we want, and all of them are delicious. Literally.

TWELVE

Ailsa

SCARY MUSHROOMS?

A PICTURE-PERFECT MORNING dawned bright and fair on the day of the wedding. Ailsa was convinced that if it hadn't, Isabel would have had something to say about it.

J.J.'s parents and his brother and sister had arrived late last night and gone quickly to their apartment with barely a greeting. Yes, it was late, but a moment for introductions would have been nice. They all appeared to have their noses in the air as they bustled up the stairs, leaving Pierre and Davey to drag their myriad bags up behind them. She noted that J.J. didn't deign to help. What a prick. A thought occurred that she found disquieting. Was this how the little ginger mouse felt with them? *With her?* She flung that thought right out.

Early morning, they all collided in the kitchen, and her opinion of J.J.s family slid ever lower. So that's where he got his manners from. *Vieux riche.* Old money. Refined and well-bred. Snotty. Long, long noses to look down. Well, sod them. She was here to have fun.

. . .

After a stilted breakfast, everyone retired to their rooms to get ready, to look their best, and to shine.

Ailsa loved the pomp and ceremony of a French wedding. Yesterday had been about close family. Mushrooming at dawn, breakfast all together around the table. Sharing food and sharing love. Or something like that. Now it was Isabel's big day, and the rest of the family would arrive. They would be important, the old friends and the new, a life Ailsa hadn't seen for eight years. Her dad had expected that she and Jules would be asked to be the witnesses, the equivalent of a bridesmaid, perhaps more significant, but the request never came. Instead, Isabel had chosen two girls she'd met at college.

'Jules? Who are these girls, again?' Ailsa stared at herself in the mirror. A short cocktail dress of fuchsia and baby blue that cinched in at the waist and accentuated all her assets. Heels not too high, as there were always cobblestones in French towns out to trip the unwary.

'Two girls she met at college.' Jules sounded bored.

Ailsa pouted. 'It should have been us. We're family.' She might be here to have fun, yet there was still a bad case of indigestion over what she perceived to be a slight on Isabel's behalf. Maybe not so much for Jules. It was harder on Ailsa. After all they'd been through, she should have been by Isabel's side today.

'We haven't been family for eight years.'

'Blood is thicker and all that…' She frowned over at Jules.

'Like I said, not for eight years.' Jules sucked on her bottom lip. 'We haven't been in her life for nearly a third of it.'

Ailsa wanted to retort: whose fault is that, then? But she kept her lips sealed tight. No need to rock an already unsteady boat. She stared at herself again. Hair and make-up styled simply, as who wants to outdo the bride on her big day? She needed to look good, though. Show she wasn't bothered, even if she was.

Dabbing on a deep pink lipstick, she turned to Jules. 'What do you think?' Jules was painting her toenails a rich ruby red. A sudden memory stirred of being in Isabel's bedroom all those years ago, her applying her lipstick as they discussed what to do about Jules. It made her shiver.

'You look gorgeous, as always.' Jules didn't look up as she spoke.

'What are you wearing?'

Jules sighed. 'I was thinking of my work dungarees. Do you think Isabel would appreciate that?'

'I'm sure she'd be chuffed—'

'You know that was a joke, right?' Jules waggled her toes. 'I'm in the deep blue chiffon number hanging in the wardrobe.'

Ailsa peered inside. 'Nice. I wonder what the little ginger mouse is wearing?'

'You know,' said Jules, and there was an edge to her voice, 'you can be a right *bitch*, sometimes.' Now she did look up, and her eyes were practically neon.

'Only sometimes? I must be slipping.' Ailsa waited. 'Come on, Jules. That was my little joke.'

'It may be a joke to you, but I'm sure it's not to her. She's not stupid. She has eyes and ears, and you don't hide the fact you don't like her. I mean, what has that poor girl ever done to you except be with Davey?' She closed her eyes at that, and Ailsa felt her heart constrict, feeling that this conversation was too close for comfort.

'Come on, I'll be nicer to her. Okay? I only meant it as a joke.'

'Ha, ha.' Jules looked up at her and gave her a crooked smile. It was better than nothing.

. . .

The arch where the second ceremony was to happen was constructed at a right angle to the main frontage of the house. Climbing roses had been trained around an ornate metal structure. The roses were in bloom, and their heady scent wafted in the air. Chairs had been arranged, with two red velvet ones placed at the front for the bride and groom. Only close family and guests were usually invited to this, but didn't Romi say they had a hundred guests coming? Not exactly intimate. This would be followed by a small cocktail reception, or *vin d'honneur*, where champagne would flow like water...

Ailsa nudged Jules as they exited the house. 'That is truly beautiful, isn't it? No plastic flowers here.'

'It shouldn't matter if they were. If you love someone, you can marry them in a dirty alley—'

'Seriously? Dear God, Jules. First the dungarees, now this? You do my head in sometimes. I don't think wanting it to be nice on your wedding day is asking too much, is it?'

'No. Of course not.' Jules' smile was a slit. 'I was just trying to get the point across.'

'Noted.'

The journey to *la mairie* was such fun. Ailsa had forgotten what French weddings were all about. How many of her rich and spoilt English friends had tied the knot to the tune of thousands of pounds and acted like she-monsters (she wouldn't deign to use the word Bridezilla, but it amounted to the same), and then the stress of the day, the sheer amount of build-up practically ruined the whole affair. Not here. Not now. And no big hats.

Archie drove the twins and Pierre to the town hall, and Romi went with Davey and Hetty. J.J. was driving Isabel, as this wasn't the important part. He could happily see her before the ceremony. The big one, the one that mattered, was this afternoon. New friends, childhood friends and other more distant relations had stayed in town and would meet them at the town hall with bags of flower petals and shouts of joy. French weddings were noisy events.

Parking in a municipal parking area near the town hall, they met outside the imposing building, waving at and kissing friends and family now crowding outside. Ailsa had to admit the little ginger mouse had scrubbed up quite nicely. A fitted green, knee-length dress that highlighted her mane of red curly hair, now caught back into a barrette, a few tendrils escaping prettily. Stylish low heels.

'*Bonjour, bonjour,*' Ailsa sang gaily, eyeing the people swirling around them. A quick head count. About thirty, then. Were there any eligible handsome bachelors here? Maybe one or two contenders. Some people she recognised and kissed, with exclamations about lost time, and some she merely kissed.

The family were called in by an officious little man and directed to the *Salles des Mariages*. This was now getting real. It was a bit of a bundle squeezing in. The parents, the witnesses and the bride and groom waited expectantly until they were all seated. Ailsa spotted J.J.s younger brother and sister. Unfortunately, the younger brother was precisely that. Young. Anyway, although he must be loaded, did she want to get entangled in the same family as her cousin? Probably not.

Once everyone had filed in, shuffled about and quietened, J.J. walked in on his mother's arm. Head held high, dressed and coiffured to within an inch of her life, she looked polished and sophisticated. The rest of the wedding party trotted in gaily behind them, and finally, Isabel, looking radiant on Archie's arm. Having delivered their prizes, the parents and the rest of the party sat down in the front aisle.

The room where the first ceremony was to be held was austere and obviously normally functioned as an auditorium. It was pretty echoey, with large, frosted glass windows that let in a lot of light. The chairs were laid out in rows. A desk on a raised platform served the mayor as he pulled out his notes. Voices drifted in from the street outside, as it was customary for the doors to be left open in case anyone wanted to pop in and object to the wedding. Mind you, who would dare?

As witnesses for the bride, two young women Ailsa didn't recognise stood on Isabel's left side, and J.J.'s sister and brother stood on his right. It was their job to bear witness that neither of them had any impediment, like already being married, that would get in the way of this marriage. Quite frankly, if Ailsa had been a witness, how would she know if Isabel had married before this? They last spoke over eight years ago. Anything could have happened. Isabel's witnesses were flushed and twittery, taking quick 'selfies' before the ceremony kicked off. How gauche!

Isabel gazed at J.J. like he was the breath in her lungs. He, on the other hand, looked like he was bored and would prefer to be anywhere else but here. Maybe that was his perennial resting 'bitch' face. What had Pierre called him? A 'prick'? She wished Isabel the best of luck.

Davey messaged their mum and dad in Sweden and started to film the affair. He moved the phone around, and Jules and Ailsa waved.

'Here's Hetty.' Davey held the phone up to her face, and she did a little wave too.

'Hi, lovely to see you.'

'It's lovely to see you too. We wish with all our hearts we could be there with you all.'

'You are,' said Davey. 'We won't let you miss a thing.' He swung the phone to the front, where Isabel and J.J. were preparing themselves. J.J. took out his tiny box of Tic-Tacs and threw a few into his mouth. Ailsa smiled. How considerate – he would say his simple vows with minty fresh breath.

Luckily, the ceremony was short, barely half an hour. Ailsa watched with amusement as the wedding party stepped back from the mayor when he began his speech about the 'sanctity of marriage'. Good God! Could the man spray fervent spit in his admonishing to be a 'good and faithful wife'? Ailsa waited for him to wag his finger at J.J., but of course, that would never happen. Perhaps that was why Ailsa had low hopes for marriage. Before you even managed to get out of the stall, it was rigged against you. Having been asked if they were ready for the challenge, Isabel and J.J. said simply, *'Oui.'* And that was that. They were officially married.

'How beautiful.' Ailsa could hear her mother talking from the speakerphone.

'Are you crying, Mum?' laughed Jules.

'Of course, my darlings. This is such a happy day.'

'Give them our heartiest congratulations,' said her dad. Ailsa couldn't help noting how frail he looked, how shrunken. It frightened her. She didn't like signs of mortality.

'We will,' she said, feeling tears prickle but not due to the festivities in hand.

When all the books had been signed and dated, and the bride and groom had kissed, the congregation erupted, shouting their congratulations. Except it was disconcerting when J.J. abruptly clutched at his stomach and whispered to the mayor. When the mayor pointed, J.J. rushed out of the room.

'Is he alright?' Ailsa tugged on Romi's arm as they stood to be with Isabel.

'Isabel told me he felt a little unwell this morning.' Romi shrugged but still appeared worried. 'I think the excitement of the day has caught up with him.'

Knowing what she did of the man, Ailsa doubted it was excitement.

'What's happening?' It was their father's voice. 'What's up with J.J?'

'I'm sure it's fine...' Davey glanced down at Hetty.

'It's not the scary mushrooms, is it?' she whispered.

Ailsa butted in. 'Don't be ridiculous. Of course, it's not the mushrooms—'

'What?' said their father. 'Please tell me you didn't go out mushrooming the day before the wedding?'

'It's fine, Dad.' Ailsa felt uncomfortable, as she'd been one of the three who'd examined them. 'We checked them carefully.'

'Dearest Lord!' said their mum, 'that was a big risk just before something so important.'

'At least,' Pierre was trying not to laugh, 'you got the marriage out of the way first, Izzy. If he pops his clogs now, you'll inherit everything.'

'*Fuck you*, Pierre!' Isabel was practically hissing. 'That's a horrible thing to say.'

'Sorry, sorry...' He held up his hands. 'It was just a joke. Come on, Izzy. You know I can't help being naughty—'

'There's being naughty, and then there's jinxing it. So cut it out. And anyway,' her voice lowered, 'we signed a Prenup—'

'What? Seriously? Are you saying you don't get anything?'

Isabel's jaw was grinding. 'No. It all reverts to his family. Now could you shut up about this?'

'What is wrong with you, Pierre?' Romi looked like she wanted to smack him. 'Fancy saying such a terrible thing!'

'It was just a stupid joke—'

'Yes. It was,' said Davey. 'Particularly stupid.'

Ailsa patted Isabel's shoulder, raising goosebumps. 'Your darling brother is a knob.'

'Don't I know it?' Isabel let her breath out with a whoosh. 'It's just J.J. was pretty sick this morning. I simply want the wedding to go perfectly.'

'It will. Don't worry.'

Movement by her shoulder heralded J.J.'s return. '*Je pense que mon estomac est trop sensible aujourd'hui.*' He grimaced, his face a strange olive green. 'Let's get back. I believe a glass of champagne will settle my stomach.'

As the happy couple exited the town hall after picking up their wedding certificate, and the crowds were throwing flower petals and rice over them, a loud clattering made them all jump. A lemon-yellow Citroën 2 CV drew up at the kerb, trailing old tin cans and small saucepans on long coloured ties, with bows and ribbons flapping.

Isabel waved everyone quiet and shouted in French about 'the broom' car. Ailsa wanted to roll her eyes, but she laughed and cheered with the rest of them. Isabel always had to make a big show of it all, as she and J.J. clambered into the back of the car. With a toot-toot of the horn, they screeched off up the road, the cans bouncing and the wedding party yelling.

'Did you see all that?' Davey squinted into his phone.

'Wonderful,' said his dad.

'Trust Isabel,' said his mum, 'to steal the broom car.'

'Listen,' Davey looked about him, 'I've got to go as we need to get back to the house. I'll get in contact again in a bit. Love you.' The phone went back in his pocket.

'Hang on?' Ailsa looked about her. 'Who will drive J.J.'s car back?'

'Why,' said Pierre, rattling a set of car keys in his hand, 'that'll be me. Who else wants to come with me in J.J.'s very posh and expensive car?' He waved over at Davey. 'You coming, cuz?'

'It will be a squash—'

'Don't worry,' said Jules, 'I can go back with *Tante Romi*.'

'No worries.' Pierre winked. 'It's a seven-seater.' He turned to Romi and Archie. 'That okay with you guys?'

'Sure, just drive carefully.' Archie took hold of Romi's arm. 'Are you up for the next stage in the proceedings, my love?'

'Can't wait.'

'Follow me, you lot.' Pierre scooted ahead, with Ailsa, Jules, Davey and Hetty trotting behind. In the municipal car park, they stopped in front of a sleek-looking car. 'Look what we're going home in.' Pressing a button on the key fob, lights flashed. Taking a step closer, Ailsa saw it was a BMW. An X7, no less. Rather yummy, a luxury ride.

'It goes like the clappers—'

'Pierre?' said Jules. 'I think we can all agree we'd like to get back to the house in one piece and not end up rolled on the roof in a ditch.' She raised an eyebrow at him. 'Or worse. We don't want any deaths and funerals at this wedding—' It was as if she'd realised what she'd said. Her eyebrows were now scrunched together. 'Oh!'

'You're such a party pooper.' Pierre rolled his eyes, seemingly oblivious. 'Get in, and I'll drive like my dad—'

'No,' said Ailsa, 'you drive like *our* dad. I seem to remember your dad drives like a maniac, too.'

'Okay. Look, they're already halfway home.' He pointed, and they could see the little yellow car cresting the nearest hill and a faint clanking in the distance.

2016 – Ailsa

'Elias?' Isabel's face drained of colour. 'No, no. Come on, Ails, you're kidding, right?'

Ailsa knew that her cousin was desperately hoping she was wrong, as she was herself. 'Look. I'm only telling you what I saw.'

'She can't be dating that gypsy boy. Surely she knows that's a big no-no? I mean, come on. He's a nobody, and she's, well, she's somebody.' Isabel rubbed at her face. 'His family are notorious in this area. Sticky fingers in every pie. If there's something bad happening, they're bound to be at the centre of it.'

'Yes, but we know Elias. I mean, we've known him for years. He's not like his family—'

'How do you know? Same tree and all that.'

'I'm hoping I got it wrong—'

'Oh God!' Isabel started to pace the room, 'She wouldn't do the dirty, would she?'

'Shag him? Of course not. Why can't we just ask her?' That awful thought had been lingering at the back of Ailsa's mind. She knew Jules was doing everything she could to be the opposite of her, but would that include having sex with the local bad boy? She knew they both had kissed a boy (not the same one), and Ailsa had let a boy touch her boob. It wasn't particularly nice as it was in the back of the cinema, and she'd been wedged against the arm of the seat. Still, she'd felt very grown-up and told Jules all about it. Was she now upstaging her? *Would she be that stupid?*

'Because we know how she'll react if we say anything to her. She'll want to be with him more than ever. We'd push them together.'

Ailsa had been so wrapped up in her thoughts that she'd practically forgotten the question. 'Then what do we do?' *Push them together.* That was an understatement. Jules would cling to Elias like a limpet just to piss Ailsa off.

Isabel continued, 'We have to get to him. Tell him to leave her alone, that it's not going to work—'

'Maybe we can ask my dad—'

'Oh hell, no. Can you imagine what'd happen if he got involved in all this? He'd kill Elias if he even suspected anything like this was happening.'

'What about your dad? He's a judge, isn't he? Can't he threaten him? You know, on the quiet?'

'Maybe, but I don't think it's a good idea. Let's work out what to do. We'll see if we can break them up.'

'What like spread stories about him, so she hears? That sort of thing?'

'Exactly that sort of thing.' Isabel paced the room and then shook her head. 'Maybe we need to be more proactive, as it might take way too long.' She sighed. 'Let me think about it, will you?'

'Do we tell Davey? Pierre?'

'No. Only if we need to. They might go overboard.'

'But they've been friends with him for years—'

'Not real friends, just friends *here*.'

'I don't understand—'

'If they met him anywhere but here, do you really think

they'd be seen dead with a guy like Elias? Or his brother, for that matter.'

'Seriously? They wouldn't be friends?'

'Of course not. They'd be ashamed to even acknowledge him outside of here.'

'We've known them both for ages since we were little kids. They're part of our lives—'

'Only here.' Isabel rolled her eyes for emphasis. 'We do what we want here because it doesn't matter. This is a bubble. Our real world is outside. Now, do you get it?'

'I think so.' Ailsa thought for a moment. 'Do you mean we can sort of play-act here? Is that what you mean?'

'Yeah, I think you've got it. Anyway, we need to find out for sure if Jules is with Elias, don't we?'

'Then I need to get hold of her phone. See if there's anything on it.'

THIRTEEN

Hetty

BIG FAT GYPSY WEDDING

Outside the town hall, Hetty watched as more people joined the throng, congratulating the happy couple and greeting old friends. J.J.'s family had arrived late the night before. Aloof was the word that sprung to mind. Or just plain rude. Hetty didn't care as long as she wasn't placed next to any of them at the reception.

The dress code was informal, compared to an English wedding, and she felt better about her choice of dress. She'd saved her best dress for the next part of the wedding. A small man finally rushed from the entrance and called them in. There was a surge as the family arranged themselves. There were fewer people here than she had expected, but she remembered that Davey had told her the wedding would be in stages. This was close friends and family. She'd also found out that work colleagues were rarely, if ever, invited to weddings. Now, what did that say? This building was austere, cold not only in temperature but in ambience. A registry office, she supposed. No frills or decorations. The rest of the week, the place must be used for boring committee meetings and town hall business.

The ceremony was thankfully short and completely incomprehensible. She sat next to Davey, and he translated in whispers as best he could until she shushed him. Heads had turned, and eyes were slitted.

'That's fine,' she whispered. 'I can get the gist of it all.'

She greeted his mum and dad on the phone, where Davey was filming the ceremony. Every so often, Davey would spin the phone to show them the congregation. The twins chatted with their parents, but mostly eyes were on the happy couple.

After they had bent over the book to sign as witnesses, the people around her yelled fit to bust. She tentatively made some sounds. She was as disconcerted as everyone else when J.J. hurtled out of the room, clutching his stomach. Oh God! He hadn't got food poisoning, had he? What had they all eaten that morning? Muesli? Toast? That couldn't be it. Maybe it was nerves. When he returned, he didn't look good, sort of green-hued and a bit sweaty.

Hetty turned to Davey. 'Do you think he's all right?'

'I have no idea. I hope so. I also hope it isn't catching. I don't want what he might have.'

'It couldn't be food poisoning, could it?' Hetty was thinking of death head mushrooms or whatever they were called.

A concerned burbling came from the phone as Ailsa and Jules discussed the mushroom hunting the day before.

Davey stared at Hetty. 'It can't be the mushrooms. We checked them all. Nothing slipped by...' He pursed his lips. 'At least it hadn't better...'

'It's probably just nerves,' said Hetty.

'Yes, you're right. Nerves.' Davey peered about. 'Listen, I've got to go as we need to get back to the house. I'll get in contact again in a bit. Love you.'

They waved and blew kisses until the screen went dark.

'Come on.' Hetty tugged on his arm. 'Looks like people are on the move.'

Outside, there was a shower of pink petals over the newlyweds, and the odd crunch underfoot of something she presumed was rice. As an old 2CV clanged and clattered up to the kerb, tin cans and various kitchen utensils hanging on strings behind it, Isabel shouted something in French, and then she and J.J. leapt into the back, to the raucous yelling of the wedding party and passing cars honking horns. The little car was an eye-watering shade of yellow.

'That car is called the broom car,' explained Davey, leaning down to shout in her ear, 'and it's meant to go behind the wedding procession to ensure no one gets lost. I suppose it's meant to sweep them up. It's been commandeered.' He laughed and hugged Hetty. 'Isabel never follows the rules.' Hetty wondered if any of them did.

'We're going back in J.J.s car.' Davey winked. 'A bit of style.'

Then they were off, trying to keep up with Pierre and his long legs, trailing after Ailsa and Jules and aware of trip hazards, of which there were many. The posh car J.J. had driven to the venue was in the car park.

'Pierre's going to drive us back to the house,' said Davey, opening the door for Hetty, who had noted that Ailsa had pushed to get in the front passenger seat next to Pierre. The rear of the car was spacious and smelled of new leather as she hitched up her dress and slid into the middle. Davey was to her right, and Jules thumped beside her on the left.

'I can't wait for a glass of champagne,' said Jules.

'I can't wait for a fag,' said Pierre. 'In fact, sorry, guys. I need one now. I'll open all the windows. Ailsa, can you light one for me? Have one yourself?' He rummaged in his jacket pocket and flipped a pack of cigarettes and a lighter into Ailsa's lap. Starting the engine, the car purred out of the parking lot, and Pierre moved them into the traffic leading out of the town.

'Ailsa? Are you smoking now?' Davey leaned forward. 'I thought you'd given up?'

Ailsa lit the two cigarettes and handed one back to Pierre. 'I did. Things got on top of me, and I just had one a few weeks back. I thought I could handle it, but they crept back in.'

'They always do.' Davey sounded exasperated. 'You worked so hard to quit, Ails. What a terrible shame—'

'Don't you judge me, Davey MacGregor!' Ailsa twisted around in her seat and glared at Davey. 'You have no idea what's going on in my life right now—'

'And whose fault is that? We barely meet up nowadays, just a quick chat on WhatsApp occasionally.'

'It takes two to tango.' There was a hiss in her voice.

'Sorry,' Pierre waved a hand but thankfully kept his eyes on the winding road ahead. 'I didn't realise you were trying to keep it a secret. That memo got lost, I'm afraid.'

'Not a secret.' Ailsa blew smoke out of the window. 'Just didn't need or want the judgy comments.'

'Look,' said Davey, 'I'm sorry. I wasn't judging. I'm disappointed—

'Ooh, not judgy in the slightest—'

'I can't win, can I?' Davey ran his finger through his hair. 'I was trying to be supportive. I know how hard you fought to stop smoking. And that's all I'll say on the matter.'

'Okay.' Jules held up her hands. 'Enough said. Let's get back and have that glass of bubbly. I think we all need it.'

. . .

'This is the point, Hetty,' said Davey, as they drew up on the gravel outside the house, 'where everyone goes to change for the next festivities.'

'Is this when Isabel will wear her bridal gown?'

'They don't do the whole meringue or mermaid thing here, thank God,' said Jules, opening the side door. 'It's way simpler—'

'You mean sophisticated?' Ailsa leaned over the back of the seat. 'No *My Big Fat Gypsy Wedding* here.' Her eyes practically glinted, and then they flicked to Jules, who seemed frozen, one hand on the half-open door and the other on the back of Pierre's seat. Ailsa made a strange sound and held her hand out to Jules through the gap between the seats, but Jules kicked her way out of the car. What had just happened? Hetty wondered if that was a jibe aimed at her. Did Ailsa consider *her* to be a gypsy? There was nothing wrong in that, but it was the way she said it, the sheer contempt in her voice. But then it seemed to have affected Jules way more than it should have.

'God!' Davey grimaced at Ailsa. 'Can't you just shut it for a moment?'

'*Fuck you.*' Ailsa nearly fell as she struggled from her seat.

Hetty's cheeks were burning as she climbed out of the car. Jules came to her side and took her elbow. Her blue eyes were like flints. 'Us commoners need to stick together, eh?' She smiled gently to show it was not an insult and made a face at Ailsa, who was striding away from them. 'She's such a snob. Don't worry about her. In fact,' Jules turned Hetty around to face her, 'don't worry about any of them. They're not worth it.' Her tone was unnerving.

'Thanks, Jules. I appreciate that.' She sighed and watched as Pierre harangued Davey over something, both growling in French, incomprehensible words. 'I do sometimes feel out of my depth.' Were they arguing over what Ailsa had said?

'No need to. Just be yourself and don't try to change to fit in. You're a lovely person, Hetty. You don't need their approval.' She nodded. 'Come on, race you to the shower.'

In their bedroom, Davey changed into a dark charcoal grey three-piece suit but left his crisp light blue shirt open at the neck.

'Don't you need a tie?'

'No ties, bow ties or top hats. Maybe a snazzy waistcoat.' He bent down and kissed the tip of her nose. 'Love you, Miss Hetty.'

'Love you, too, Mr Davey.'

'I love you more.'

Hetty nodded and slipped on her dress. Her hair was still damp from the shower, and tendrils were curling about her like the head of Medusa. She only had the three dresses with her, and she'd used up the green one for the morning session. 'Is this okay? I'm not going to make an awful faux pas, am I?'

'You look utterly gorgeous.' Davey pulled her over to the full-length mirror. 'See?'

Hetty gazed at her reflection. 'Are you sure my dress doesn't look like it's made from a set of curtains from a high street bargain store?'

Davey chuckled and then shook his head. 'You do make me laugh. Listen, the dress is gorgeous, you are gorgeous, and today, even I am particularly gorgeous.' He pouted at her. 'Am I not?'

'Very pretty, indeed.'

'It's going to be a great day, Hetty. And I really think Jules has taken a shine to you. That's a big thing, as recently she hasn't liked anyone.'

'I hope so, as I really like her, too.'

. . .

The whole thing was a fairy tale come true for Hetty. No need to go to Disneyland, as it seemed to have come to them. The chateau (or posh provincial house, as Davey preferred to call it) as the backdrop, the rose arch, with its spreading scent, the elegant chairs in lines in front of the small wooden podium, where the couple would say their vows. Another smaller white marquee had been set up at the end of the house. Waiters in black trousers and white shirts, with white aprons around their waists, hovered. Hetty spied the distinctive shape of champagne bottles and, by the looks of it, plates and plates of aperitifs and *hors d'oeuvres* on a long table with a snowy-white cloth. Glasses glinted as the afternoon sun slanted in. Hetty could do with a glass or two about now. And she prayed to a God she didn't believe in that her stomach wouldn't rumble part way through the ceremony. It had ways of betraying her at the most inopportune moments.

Hetty glanced behind them. Crunching up the gravel were more people dressed in their best. The rest of the wedding group, who had been only invited to the afternoon celebrations. The second ceremony, the small cocktail party, the reception dinner in the grand marquee on the grounds, and, finally, dancing in the barn. One of the lower fields had been put over for parking. Figures in high-vis jackets waved and directed the cars crawling down the lane. The caterers had a humongous vehicle parked there, with a series of small cars to ferry the food and drink to the marquee. A track had been cut through for them, and numerous waiters were busily doing something. Organised and efficient. That's what money could get you.

Hetty thought back to a particular wedding she'd attended when she was fifteen. Her cousin Nicola, barely a few months older, had got up the duff with some bloke she'd met at a nightclub. Snuck in, pretending to be eighteen. Plied with drink and then, well, she couldn't quite remember what happened next, but the end result was a baby. *Surprise!* She was a kid. A rushed affair when she hit her sixteenth birthday, as her parents threatened the man in question with the police. Hetty never wrapped her head around it. An underage girl had been given far too much to drink by an older man and then raped by this man (or men – as Nicola confided, she thought there might have been others...). He swore it was consensual. What? She was fifteen and very drunk. How could that be consensual? In Hetty's mind, they should have gone straight to the police, not into the arms of matrimony. Strict Catholics meant no termination. But they also didn't want shame brought on their family. So, he married her, and she gave birth to a bouncing baby boy and lived happily ever after. Except she didn't. Her son was sickly, and there were complications with the delivery. Another baby arrived far too soon after the first. That bubbly girl became old overnight, frail and brittle. Hetty heard the gossip. Her bloke was off shagging anything in a tight skirt he could get his sleazy hands on. And he drank. And he hit her. How were the women of her family ever going to break the chains that bound them to this life? By slinking off in the middle of the night, clutching minimal belongings as if they were thieves and then hiding in plain sight while their incensed menfolk hunted for them. And pled for forgiveness. She had to dislodge these worrisome thoughts, and concentrate on what was happening now, not get lost in the past. The only moment in time that mattered was this moment, and she shouldn't miss it. In truth, this might be the only real French wedding she would attend in her lifetime, and she wanted to remember every minute.

Davey contacted his parents and filmed about him. It was the closest they could be if they couldn't be here in person.

Isabel and J.J. sat in the traditional red velvet chairs while friends and family settled in their places. Close family at the front and lesser mortals ranging to the back. The dress code was casually elegant. Isabel's dress was ephemeral, light and airy, her hair swept up into a chignon, white flowers entwined and a silver necklace with something sparkly on it dangling low into her cleavage. Was that a diamond? Hetty corrected herself. Another diamond? Gadzooks!

J.J. was refinement itself in his costly looking suit. Again, no tie, but an embroidered waistcoat that must have come from a designer outfit Hetty probably couldn't pronounce correctly.

'Wow!' she breathed quietly, 'don't they look amazing?'

Davey grinned down at her. 'Are you enjoying yourself, Miss Hetty?'

'It's all perfect, thank you, Mr Davey.'

As it was all in French and Hetty wanted to avoid upsetting the group by having Davey translate it in loud whispers, she barely got the gist of what was said. Although she noticed that J.J. wiped at his brow often, and he was still a little green-hued.

This next bit, she understood. *'Vive les jeunes mariés!'* If there had been hats, they would be flying.

Hetty was shaken out of her self-indulgent fug when J.J. rushed into the house. Not again. How awful to have the squits on your wedding day. Poor bloke and poor Isabel. Maybe a romantic first night as man and wife would be off the cards now. Isabel looked quite bemused. His parents were remonstrating with Archie.

'That's really not good.' Davey sucked on his teeth. 'I know we made a joke about the mushrooms... but...'

His dad lunged into view. 'When did you say you had the mushrooms?'

'Yesterday morning—'

'Oh, Lord!' His dad disappeared out of the shot. They could hear him talking to Davey's mum. 'He should get seen by a doctor. Mushroom poisoning can be very serious, even fatal.'

'We checked them.' Davey scowled. 'The same as we've always done.'

'Still,' said his dad, 'better to be safe, not sorry.'

Isabel waved all the protestations down and shouted something.

'What did she say?' Hetty craned over the shoulder of the person in front of her.

Davey leaned down. 'Just for us to continue with the small cocktail reception or *vin d'honneur*. She said we'd take the photos when J.J. comes back out. Dicky stomach but not catching. Says she!' He searched around him. 'Ah! Great. *Lookee* there. The waiters are coming with the champagne. Mum? Dad? Got to go again but will catch up for the reception.'

Hetty watched as the waiters glided across the gravel towards the group, holding laden trays of glasses aloft with just one hand, splayed fingers stretched. She'd always marvelled at how easy waiters like these made it look.

'If I tried to do that,' she sniggered, 'I'd probably upend it all over the groom's mother.'

'As would we all,' said Davey, winking and taking two glasses smoothly. 'Looks like she could do with a dunking.'

'Don't be mean, Davey.'

'Yeah, well. She hasn't even said hello to us, the other side of the family. I can see why Ailsa is hacked off right now.'

'She might be anxious or shy—'

'Or, like most of them, she might be a stuck-up cow. We are only the hoi polloi to them.'

Hetty readjusted that statement in her head. If Davey and his side of the family were the hoi polloi, what did that make her? Handed a glass of champagne, she asked, 'Do we wait for a toast or just neck it?' She squinted at the people around her. No one knew what to do, some sipping and then looking guilty, others waiting and trying to catch each other's eyes.

'*Vive les jeunes mariés!*' Pierre raised his glass. 'Long live the newlyweds!'

'*Vive les jeunes mariés!*'

'*Vive les jeunes mariés!*'

Except one half of the newlyweds was splurging in the bathroom. It was getting surreal. She hoped it wouldn't turn into one of her favourite horror movies.

Hetty had a terrible thought. 'We're not expected to play any games tonight after the reception?'

'A quick game of pétanque, maybe. Why?'

Hetty shivered. 'You remember that film we saw? *Ready or not...*'

Davey laughed loudly. 'Christ, Hetty! What an over-active imagination you have. Sometimes you scare me.'

'Yes, but you must admit, it's all a bit weird?'

'Old J.J. has got a stomach upset. It's probably nerves, and that's it. No one is getting hunted by a maniacal family. At least, not by my maniacal family.'

A string quartet set up in the corner of the smaller marquee began to play. Focus on that, she scolded herself. Perhaps reading too many thrillers messed with your mind. She should stick to holiday romances for a while.

'That's so lovely.' Hetty closed her eyes to listen, aware of the burbling of voices that threatened to drown out the music. It occurred to her that the skills of these musicians were phenomenal, and yet here they were, playing earnestly while barely anyone (well, except her) was listening. How did that make them feel? Was it par for the course and thanks for the pay cheque, or did they ask themselves if it was worth it?

'A bit of grub, oh lovely lady?' Davey held out his elbow, but Jules ran up and grabbed his other arm. 'You been filming for Mum and Dad?'

'Yeah. I wish they were here. What an absolute bummer.'

'He couldn't risk it. I know Mum had to shout him down as he would have been on a plane regardless.'

'I can imagine. He's a tough old bird—'

'Not at the moment, he's not.' Hetty could see that Jules was struggling with her emotions. She laid a hand on her arm. Jules patted it. 'I'm okay, Hetty. Thank you.'

Hetty motioned to where she'd seen J.J. run. 'What's up with J.J.?'

'No idea,' said Jules, 'though I hope he bucks up soon.'

'I'm sure he'll be fine.' Davey led them to the marquee, where waiters were ready to hand a small plate to anyone passing. 'Oh, those look scrumptious.'

'I'm starving,' said Hetty.

'Save some space for later.' Jules nudged Hetty. 'You know we have at least four courses after this.'

'Yes,' said Davey, 'spread over hours and hours.' He heaped food onto the small plate, but Hetty felt she should be more circumspect. At least four courses? Maybe they meant one course was a quail's egg, and the next, three artfully arranged green beans and some tiny blob of posh sauce swirled next to it. What was it called? Haute cuisine? More like a rip-off. She piled some delicious whatsits on her plate and hoped no octopus was in any of it. Sidling off to free up the space for more guests, they ate and drank in companionable silence in the shade of the house, leaning against the wall. A window ledge allowed them to cockle their drinks. Draining her glass, Jules waved at a waiter who brought a tray.

'*Laissez-nous juste le plateau, s'il vous plaît,*' she said, smiling with crocodile teeth as the waiter placed the tray on the sill.

'Is that allowed?' Davey grabbed another glass. 'If we're not careful, we'll be pissed before we even take the photos.'

'I don't want to accidentally show my knickers!' Hetty eyed the glass of golden bubbles in her hand.

'I'm sorry? What?' Jules couldn't keep the laughter out of her voice.

'It's kind of like an in-joke.' Davey chucked Hetty under her chin. 'It translates to not wanting to get so drunk, she falls over and shows her knickers to everyone.'

'Well, there's something to aim for.' Jules squinted across to where Isabel, Romi and Archie talked to J.J.'s family. There was a lot of arm waving.

'Do you think he's okay? What if this is serious?' Hetty reached for another glass, swearing it would be her last until dinner, but a commotion stopped her. J.J. had returned.

'Looks like the photos are back on,' said Davey.

'At least we'll be more relaxed.' Jules swigged the last of her glass. 'Normally, we all end up looking like we're a member of the Munster family.'

'Jules!' Davy shook his head. 'You're worse than Pierre, sometimes. And he's pretty bad.'

'Oh!' Jules placed her hand against her cheek and looked coquettishly at him. 'Thanks for the accolade.'

'We need to be over there now.' Davey pointed, as Romi and Archie were waving frantically at them and shouting.

It was the usual rugby scrum until the photographer assembled them how he thought fit. Formal was the word Hetty would use. Stiff and posed, with fixed smiles. Hetty was tucked between Davey and Jules. Those couple of glasses of champagne had quelled the butterflies that had been fluttering in her stomach. The photographer directed people in or out of the shot until their little part was over. Retrieving their glasses, Hetty stood by Davey and Jules and watched as Isabel and J.J. stood with her parents, and then his, and then all of them together. Glancing surreptitiously up at Davey, Hetty wondered if she'd ever have anything like this. With him. Or with anyone. This was not her life; it was far too glamorous, but she'd like to think it could be. Then again, would she ever be accepted for who she was, or would she have to change to fit in? Become a chameleon. She doubted she could take the working class, council house girl out of her, no matter how many fancy dresses or elocution lessons she had.

'This is the stage,' whispered Davey, 'where the bride and groom sneak off somewhere to take their own photos.'

'They have to sneak off?' Hetty held out her hands. 'Why? Are they going to be taking dodgy shots of each other then?'

'Who knows?' Jules raised an eyebrow. 'The photos are just for them. We never get to see them unless they want us to.'

'How strange.'

'I believe we are meant to be mingling,' said Jules, poking Davey. 'Kissing ancient, whiskered aunties and batting off lecherous old uncles with roving hands—'

'God!' laughed Hetty. 'You must have been to all of my family's weddings.'

'Well,' Davey inclined his head, 'you don't get to choose your family.' He eyed Jules as he said it.

Jules looked down at the ground. 'More's the pity, sometimes. Come on. Duty calls.'

As twilight crept across the fields towards them, strings of lights pinged on. They were hung everywhere. The place became more romantic, if that was possible. Golden puddles of light held the deepening night at bay. Groups chatted, drifted apart, and joined others. Voices were initially muted, but the volume rose as the bottles of champagne were drunk. There was much back slapping and gesturing and many exclamations as they caught up.

Again, tagging behind Davey and Jules, Hetty smiled and kissed the many relatives and old friends Davey introduced her to. Wishing she'd eaten a few more of those delicious *hors d'oeuvres*, as her stomach was making weird sounds, she was relieved when Jules tugged her around. What time was it? Nearly nine? No wonder her stomach was complaining, as she normally ate dinner well before eight back home in Brighton.

'They're getting us sorted for the reception dinner. I presume we're all on the same table...'

'If not,' said Davey, 'I'll shuffle all the name tags around so we are.'

A pathway was lit with shimmering bulbs and led them from the stone steps below the house to the large marquee. The path had been cleared, though it was still tricky in heels.

'Have you got your gift, Davey?' As they entered, Jules pulled an envelope from her clutch bag and placed it in a large wooden box on a plinth.

'Yeah, I've got it. A nice round number, but I'm sure it's a drop in the ocean for them.' The envelope lay on top of Jules' one.

'So,' Hetty frowned, 'no catalogue of gifts to choose from or wedding list. Everyone gives them money?'

'Yep. 'Davey nodded. 'It's meant to cover the cost of us actually being at their wedding. So couples who might be a bit stretched financially aren't bankrupted by their own wedding. It makes sense. Anything left over can go towards a luxury item.'

'Not that they need any more luxury items,' said Jules.

'How come no workmates are invited?' Hetty followed along behind them. 'I find that very odd.'

'It's peculiarly French.' Jules was peering at the name tags on the large, central table. 'A wedding is for old friends and family. A work colleague has to be a really close friend to be invited. I suppose it's so you can keep your private life separate from work.'

Hetty knew if she got married and neglected to invite the people she worked with, her name would be mud, and she'd probably find a sharp knife sticking out from between her shoulder blades. They were family and, in some cases, closer than family. As Davey had said, you can't pick your family, but you can choose your friends wisely.

Under the dome of the marquee, all the tables were round, so there was no 'head' of the table. The full orchestra was at the back, on a stage, waiting quietly. They were in evening dress, with their instruments ready, barely a cough heard or shuffling of bums. There was a dance area inside the ring of tables. The marquee had been decorated with garlands of flowers and ribbons and artfully draped swathes of white material. Dotted around on tall plinths were fat church candles in glass hurricane jars. The chairs were white, the tablecloths snowy white, and pastel-coloured flowers in wreaths of deep green leaves were placed in the centre of each table, with candles in jars casting a soft glow. The wildflowers they had picked with Pierre the day before were entwined with the flower shop arrangements. It made them more personal. Each place setting had two plates, cutlery, flutes and wine glasses, and a baby pink napkin that looked like an origami expert had folded it. There were little pastel-coloured boxes with each guest's name written neatly on the lid. They must be the sugared almonds they'd spoken about.

'We're not on the main table with the bride and groom,' said Davey. 'That'll seriously piss Ailsa off.'

'Where are we then?' Hetty looked about them. Hopefully, not by the main entrance where the wind could whistle in. As it had been so warm throughout the day, she hadn't bothered with a cardigan, but now the temperature was noticeably dropping.

'I'm quite cold. Have I got time to nip back to our room to grab my cardi?'

'They've got garden heaters. That should be enough, and anyway, it's about to kick off. You don't want to be slinking in halfway through, do you?'

Hetty nodded and wrapped her thin arms around herself. She hoped they'd light the heaters soon.

'Here we are.... hmmm.' Jules was at the next closest table. Glancing about her, she shifted two cards and two little boxes around. 'That's better, or you'd have had my delightful sister all evening.'

Hetty didn't want to show how relieved she felt, but it must have been obvious, as Jules sniggered. 'I completely understand.'

They sat down, and waiters glided in on silent feet and with expressionless faces to fill fluted glasses with champagne. Ailsa tottered in, a weird expression on her face and a very visible sigh of relief when she saw where she'd been placed. Obviously she didn't want to be seated next to the 'oik'. Glad the feeling was mutual. Was Ailsa already drunk? Mind you, was that *de rigueur* at a French wedding? It certainly had been at every wedding Hetty had been to in England.

When all the seats were filled, the voices were hushed. There was an expectant hum in the air. The last to enter were the bride and groom, waving at their adoring audience like they were royalty, at which point the orchestra got into full flow. Everyone stood up and started to cheer and wave their napkins. On a table at the front was a champagne tower. A waiter carefully poured bottle after bottle, and Hetty watched, mesmerised, as the champagne filled all the lower glasses in the pyramid from the top glass. His hand didn't even shake.

'That's so cool.' Hetty nodded.

The filled glasses were handed to immediate family (including them), and then the happy couple sat in their places at the large central table with their parents and their brothers and sister. And the two female witnesses. A strange, medieval-looking receptacle was handed to them. Silver, ornate, more shaped like a bowl with two handles.

'What's that?' whispered Hetty.

'That is the wedding cup. It's been engraved with their names and the wedding date.'

Isabel and J.J. took a handle each and drank from the cup. Another cheer went up. Toasts of all kinds followed until it was time for their witnesses. Now, what did Davey call them? Oh yes, the *témons*, to regale the wedding group with stories about the happy couple and, more importantly, tales to embarrass them and make them blush. A screen had been set up behind the main table, and photos of the bride and groom beamed onto it. All the requisite naked baby pictures, the missing teeth pictures, the godawful hairdo and make-up pictures. J.J.'s sister recited a poem, and a few people wiped at furtive tears. To show willingness, Hetty laughed when everyone laughed, and clapped when they did, careful to stop just before the others.

When Pierre stood up, Hetty saw Romi close her eyes. Was Pierre so mischievous that his mother believed he'd say something dreadful at his sister's wedding? It looked like it, as after regaling them with his first story, there were gasps of shock, and a few women tutted. True to form then, and Hetty smiled. There was a young man not beset by insecurities. Maybe being privileged gave you a sense of entitlement that swept all that away. Mind you, if she ever got married, she would have loved to have her brother there, making a knob of himself, causing the ancient aunties to roll their eyes. But that was never going to happen. Paul was dead. And whose fault was that?

J.J.'s brother must have said something hilarious, as even Davey nearly rolled off his chair through laughing so hard. Hetty felt it then. The only person here who couldn't make head nor tail of what was going on. The dumb English girl from a council estate. Straight As in all her exams meant nothing here. Attended a comprehensive? Pah! Must be thick as pig shit! For all this splendour, Hetty wished she was at home, curled in a blanket on the sofa, watching Netflix. Possibly, being forced out of your comfort zone wasn't all it was cracked up to be.

FOURTEEN

Ailsa

THE TITANIC UNDER THEIR FEET

AILSA HAD to admit it was a beautiful ceremony. (Apart from when J.J. ran off, but then you can't have everything.) And the whole place had scrubbed up nicely. Mind you, the scent of so many roses was beginning to be a little cloying. There was a touch of an elderly aunt or grandmother about it, and she didn't do 'old'.

When J.J. reappeared, the call to come for the photos went out. She'd been practising her poses and expressions in the mirror. She had to be able to hold a pose long enough that it looked natural. She was sick of Jules' throw-away remarks that they always looked like the Munster Family... or was it the Addams family? Whichever, it wasn't a compliment. At least she knew she had a fabulous figure, unlike one of the porky girls Isabel had chosen as her witness. Damn. She mustn't get hooked up on that. Isabel had made new friends in those intervening years, as they all had, so why was she acting like a jealous ex-lover? Why? Because she'd been there for all her life, was the one who'd sorted out the terrible 'mistake', had stood by her, lied and covered up for her...

'Get a grip.' It was a whisper.

She'd done the rounds of the friends and family she vaguely recognised. Listened to the same questions and repeated the same answers over and over again...

'It's been such a long time. You look great for your age. What are you up to now, dear?'

'I'm a web designer.' It was as if she'd spoken in Klingon.

'That's nice. Married yet? Kids?'

'No. Not yet, because I'm concentrating on my career. As a web designer.'

'Well, there's still time, but don't leave it too late, eh?'

'Maybe I don't want a husband and kids?' She'd raised her eyebrow playfully at first until it got stale.

'Of course you do. It's what every woman wants. You obviously haven't met the right young man so far.' And then the clincher. 'Don't leave it too long. Time is of the essence. You don't want to be an *old* mother, now, do you?'

'I'm doing very well on my own.'

'It's so nice to have a hobby until you find the right one.' They'd pat her like she was a dog and walk off. This was lucky, as the raising of the eyebrow would be replaced quite soon with a deft backhander to the cheek. *Shut up, you stupid old bitches!* That's what she longed to shout in their sanctimonious old faces. We're not living in the bloody 1940s and don't have to depend on men for our happiness.

Grabbing two flutes of champagne, Ailsa scanned around her. Typical. There was Jules snuggled up with Davey and his mouse... oops! Hadn't she promised she'd try to be nicer to her? Well, that was before her inanely dull afternoon. When was the reception dinner going to start? She was ravenous, having spent a lot of calories controlling her urge to deck someone. Hugging the wall at the furthest point from all activity, she let the autumn evening air cool her and swigged her drinks in a very unladylike manner. Sod them. *Sod the lot of them.*

The window to her side was brightly lit. Peering in, she saw Archie and J.J. seated in comfy seats in what Archie termed his 'snug'. There was nothing snug about it except the name. A large room with a mahogany desk that could easily grace the oval office in the White House, walls lined from floor to ceiling with bookshelves and proper hardback books that she knew smelled of age and told of knowledge. A Turkish rug was on the dark wood floor, and the lights were shaded and soft. A squat, square decanter was set on the table, the warm lights in the room making the liquid inside glow a deep amber. Ah! She remembered what Archie had said yesterday. It was the dregs of some prohibitively expensive cognac (that was probably only meant for the boys). Both men twirled crystal cut glass tumblers, liberally filled with this deep golden liquid. And they held cigars. The box of those overpriced cigars was on the table next to the decanter. There was a haze of blueish smoke above their heads.

Pierre entered, and she could see them offer a cigar to him, but he waved them down and got himself a tumbler. He didn't touch the posh stuff but went to the drinks cabinet and chose what looked like a whiskey instead. What an *oik*, eh? Although she couldn't hear the words, she could easily guess what was said when he poured a huge slosh into his glass. Boys will be boys.

She felt like sauntering into the snug and taking a cigar from that box. She'd light it and suck that smoke into her mouth and then blow a smoke ring, to the shock and horror of these Dark-Age-minded men. A woman smoking a cigar? In their inner sanctum? *Quelle horreur!* Although maybe they wouldn't give a damn? Perhaps they'd welcome her in, offer her that fancy cigar? What did she know of these men?

Leaving the two empty glasses cockled on the windowsill, she crunched across the gravel. Earlier, the light had leached from the sky at a rate of knots and, now, the temperature was dropping. While it had been pleasantly warm during the day, with nighttime fast heading in, Ailsa weighed up the sheer number of stairs to get to her room and the cute little shrug hanging over the back of the chair or to rough it out and get chilly. Maybe she could bribe Pierre to go and find it for her?

Where was Isabel? There she was, laughing, her head thrown back and whitened teeth showing, the cat who had got the cream, with her two cronies. Who the hell were they anyway? It should have been her and Jules standing by her side as witnesses. What did these women really know about Isabel? Ailsa shook her head. They didn't know that she had killed someone, did they? Ailsa shook her head harder. Shut up. *Shut up*. Perhaps a coffee would be better rather than another glass of bubbly, delightful as it was, as she knew loose lips sink ships. *And they had the bloody Titanic under their feet.*

Thank God, she was on Davey's left-hand side, and Jules was next to the mouse. She giggled a bit but covered her mouth. She must be careful not to accidentally call her that out loud. The table was gloriously decked out. As was the whole marquee. So bloody romantic; it made her want to puke. Again, she was annoyed that they were on this secondary table while Isabel's two new friends were on the main bridal table with the parents and siblings. Sure that if their mum and dad had been here, they would have been on the main table, Ailsa had to squash her angst down into the deepest part of her. She plastered on a fake smile so bright, it would bedazzle even the devil himself.

'You alright, Ails?' Davey seemed to be peering at her. 'You look a bit weird.'

'I'm absolutely bloody fantastic. Why wouldn't I be?' She glanced at the main table, all those laughing faces, those little in-jokes, while Isabel's real family were here on the outside. Why hadn't Archie put his foot down and placed them on their table? After all, didn't she have dirt on him that would mire him down until he no longer existed? She felt a tingle of power. To have the knowledge that could destroy someone. Completely. Not that she would ever use it, as they were all complicit, yet it would wipe that smug look off his face.

Davey stared over and then back at her. Voice low, he said, 'We haven't been in their lives for nigh on eight years. We've had a pandemic in between, and I'm not sure we're through that yet. She moved on. In fact, I thought we all did.'

'Yeah, well. It still rankles.' To the left of her, a garden heater had been lit. So much for climate change. At least it was now warm. 'Thank God! The appetiser is finally coming.' Tweaking the menu off the table, she read it out loud. 'Heirloom tomatoes tarte Tatin, baked with goat cheese, caramelised onions and fennel. Sounds delicious.'

'What did you order for the entrée?' Davey looked over her shoulder. 'We chose the beef. I mean, come on. You can't come to France and not have the beef.'

'You can,' said Jules, 'if you are vegetarian, or rather pescatarian. As I am. So it's the Chilean sea bass for me.'

'You're a veggie now?' Davey turned to her. 'When did that happen?'

'When I watched a programme on how all the animals we eat that are farmed live the most horrendous lives, albeit quite short, and then are killed barbarically.' She sniffed. 'That's when.'

'Right.' Davey sucked on his bottom lip and must have been weighing up his next words. 'But,' he took the menu from Ailsa, 'grilled tournedos of beef, topped with caramelised onions and crispy yams, served with roast garlic smashed potatoes, and tarragon creamed spinach. I can't help myself.'

'I don't feel guilty,' said Ailsa, as a beautifully arranged plate was placed before her. 'It's them or us. A dog-eat-dog world.'

'No,' said Jules, 'you've never felt guilty for anything, have you, Ails?'

Ailsa didn't like the way Jules was looking at her. It made the tiny hairs on the nape of her neck rise. 'What's that supposed to mean?' Her fork was suspended in front of her, her appetite gone.

'Nothing. Don't worry about it.'

The food was delicious, but it was as though a few pinches of ash had been sprinkled over it all. Ailsa was now worrying at Jules' last comment as if it was a wobbly tooth. The salad of gorgonzola, lettuce and various arty bits and bobs came and was devoured, but again, Ailsa couldn't concentrate fully on it, eating mechanically with little enjoyment. Trust Jules to ruin this for her. What a bitch. By the time the slab of beef was slipped onto the tablecloth in front of her, with its reek of garlic and twiddles of crispy things, she nearly heaved. What the hell was the matter with her? Oh, no! She hadn't got what J.J. had?

'Excuse me.' Ailsa tottered from the table, stumbled up the bulb-lit path, stared at the stone steps, and then down at her high-heeled shoes. Should have worn her trainers. To her right was the row of porta-toilets ready for the wedding guests. There was no way she was going into one of those, as God alone knew what state they'd be in. She had to use the loo in the house.

Would she make it in time, or was it best to sneak into the bushes to her left? It was dark and secluded, but she wasn't sure if she might be sick, have awful diarrhoea or simply need a wee. And if anyone saw her with her knickers down? How humiliating. Taking a deep breath, she took the steps at a run, hoped she wouldn't crick an ankle, and then galloped to the downstairs toilet. Thank God there was no one in there or waiting outside. Slamming and locking the heavy door, she collapsed on the toilet. Wind. She had wind. Ailsa laughed a little hysterically, but hey. Too much champagne, a tight-fitting dress and rich food. Maybe that was all that was wrong with J.J. He needed to have a great big, fat fart, and all would be well. She laughed again.

'Er, my God!' She patted a dampened hand towel over her face and stared at herself in the baroque-style mirror on the wall. 'You need to get a grip.' Nodding as if her reflection in the mirror was another person, Ailsa ambled back to the marquee. Looking from the outside in, it was dreamlike, a shimmering mirage. Beautiful, but was it real? Stopping momentarily, she observed Isabel and J.J. Were they in love? She hoped so, for Isabel's sake, although it seemed a rather cold and impersonal type of love. Her gaze shifted to Davey and Hetty, heads close together, laughing and mucking around. Intimate and caring. Was that love, then? And then she thought about her and Jules. Where were their soul mates? Their better, other significant halves? Over the years, there had been no long-term boyfriend for either of them. Maybe Jules had a bloke she hadn't told them about back in Manchester, someone she didn't want to share with her family yet. They'd drifted slowly apart over the years. None of this identical twin thing. No matching hairstyles and clothes. How ghastly was that? They were so busy trying not to be like each other, they'd swung completely in the opposite direction,

She'd taken her shoes off in the bathroom to rub her toes and discovered two blisters, one on each heel. Oh, the sacrifices a woman makes to look perfect, the best version of herself. But why bother? Having appraised all the male guests under forty, she calculated there were four candidates worth looking at, except two of them appeared to be married. Would that stop her if the chance arose? Probably not.

Hanging onto her shoes, she walked back to the table barefoot. The beef was cold, and the tarragon creamed spinach looked, well, she didn't wish to think about what it reminded her of. Pushing the plate away from her, she studied the group around her until Davey nudged her.

'You don't seem to be yourself, Ails. What's up?'

'Don't go getting ideas in your head, Davey. I'm not jealous or hankering for a wedding like this. I'm just thinking about things.'

'Care to share?'

'No. Maybe later.' She eyed Jules, sitting on the other side of... Hetty. They seemed to be getting on. Was it a genuine friendship, or was Jules using Hetty as a slap in the face for her? Knowing Ailsa would view Hetty as beneath Davey (and not in the biblical sense, either). She was not in his league and wouldn't fit into his world. Except she did. Strange. Or maybe he now fitted into hers? That brought back a memory she didn't want to investigate. The words she hadn't understood then were becoming clearer, watching Davey and Hetty. Seeing how they interacted.

'They're bringing in the cake,' said Davey to Hetty.

'A croquembouche?' Hetty raised an eyebrow. 'Is that how you pronounce it?'

'Perfect,' said Davey.

'I wish I could,' said Ailsa, 'but I don't think I can eat another bite.'

The little ginger mouse tucked in, though. She should be the size of a house with that appetite. It was as if she'd never seen food before and had to eat whatever came her way. Again, a thought snuck in. Maybe Hetty had known hunger. Real hunger and not like that afternoon when she'd traipsed after Jules and missed her lunch. And wailed that she was starving. What did she really know about Davey's girlfriend? Nothing.

'I think it's that time,' said Jules, 'we desperate singles are meant to claw each other's eyes out...'

'I'm sorry, what?' Hetty looked as if a bucket of blood had been tossed over her.

'Isabel is going to throw the bouquet.' Ailsa eyed her. 'Are you going to try and catch it?' She threw a look at Davey, who stared back at her coldly. Woah! All kinds of expressions galloped across the mouse's face. Ailsa wondered what was going on in her vacuous little head. Contemplating marrying into the clan? She looked at Davey, who avoided her by pulling Hetty to her feet.

'Go for it,' he grinned.

Ailsa nearly fell off her chair. What! Encouraging her? Surely not. The mouse was now a delightful pink colour and obviously flustered.

'Come on, Hetty.' Jules stood up and took hold of her hand. 'If you're not in it, you can't win it.' She flashed a crooked smile at Ailsa as she pulled Hetty to where a gaggle of young women shuffled expectedly.

The hairs on the back of Ailsa's neck rose. She hated it

when Jules baited her. Was it on purpose, or didn't she think what she was doing might have an effect? It was as if Jules was rubbing her 'friendship' with Hetty in her face.

'*Est-ce-qu'on prêt, mesdames?*'

Ailsa realised she was too late to enter the fray, but then, did she want to? The significance of catching the bouquet was not lost on her. The waiting men, watching from behind, showed their fear. If one of the women grabbed that bunch of flowers, was it beholden of them to bend the knee and pop the question? A few now appeared a bit sweaty, as well they should. Ailsa sniggered, then stopped when she saw Davey frowning at her.

'Why can't you just enjoy yourself, Ails?' He gestured around them. 'I mean, it's beautiful, and we should be happy for Isabel, but you're acting more like the Grinch at Christmas—'

'What if Hetty catches the bouquet? What then?'

'You mean, will I ask her to marry me? Well, dear sister, that's between Hetty and me, now, isn't it?'

Isabel strung it out, but when the bouquet shot up and hit a strut, it changed course. And then the worst happened. You had to be joking! Ailsa couldn't believe it. Karma's a bitch, isn't it! Although it looked like the bouquet was heading straight for Jules, she fumbled with it, and then it sort of bounced and… Hetty caught it. *Fuck!* The odd thing was that she didn't look happy about it, and there was some sort of altercation between her and Jules. There was a definite grump when she sat down. Had Ailsa got it completely wrong? Surely Hetty should be gloating and doing some sort of moonwalk while shouting 'in yer face' or whatever. Now she appeared to be sulking.

The orchestra had taken a break during the reception dinner and was now assembling. There was the usual scraping of a bow and the toot of a flute as they tuned up again. The tradition was that the bride and her father would open the ball with a dance.

Archie escorted Isabel to the centre of the marquee. The music started, and off they went, twirling, feet flying and laughing in each other's arms. All eyes were riveted on them. It was like a scene from a film, choreographed and precise.

'They practised that for weeks,' said Pierre, dragging a chair from another table and landing with an 'oomph' next to her.

'It shows. Very impressive.'

'I wished you could have been on our table, except there wasn't enough room. Soz and all that.'

'I was initially a bit piqued, but it's okay.' Ailsa nodded at Davey and Jules. 'We've been out of the loop for too long. It's not like it was all going to go back to how it was overnight—'

'If ever,' said Pierre as he fumbled with a left-over fork, using it to tap on the table. But not in time to the music. Was that a sign of nerves? Were they all thinking the same? The last time they were all here, it was a mess. And then, it was like an unwritten agreement to never talk about what happened, to never broach the subject, to pretend it hadn't happened and to hide the memories in a box marked 'Do not open ever'. Although Ailsa wondered if the box had been unlocked and they were flying free.

2016 - Ailsa

Isabel had given Ailsa a tiny torch. Not bright enough to wake Jules up but bright enough that she wouldn't stub her toe or trip over any furniture in the dark. Jules' breathing had deepened and slowed, and as far as Ailsa could tell, she was facing towards the wall and away from the bedside table where her phone was. The bed *boinged* as Ailsa climbed out of it. She could always say she was off to the loo if Jules woke up now. Waiting a few moments, she crept up and, angling the light away from Jules' face, located the phone. Carefully tweaking it off, she tucked it under her arm and tip-toed to the door, which, being the last one to go to bed that night, she'd left slightly ajar.

'Have you got it?' Isabel was waiting in her room for her; a bedside lamp was the only illumination and she'd placed that on the floor. Shutting the door quietly, Ailsa sprang onto the bed next to Isabel. 'Can you get in?'

'Der!' Ailsa shrugged. 'I know all her passwords.' Her fingers flew over the screen, but then she stopped. 'Should we be doing this?' Running her fingers through her hair, she held out a hand. 'This is snooping, and it's not nice.'

'It's not snooping,' Isabel wagged a finger at her, 'it's looking after her. If there's nothing to find, it won't matter; if there is, we have to sort it. Okay?'

'I suppose so.' Ailsa drew in a deep breath and opened Jules' text messages. 'Oh, shit!'

'What? *What!*' Isabel snatched the phone from her hand and read the messages. '*Oh, shit!*'

Ailsa knuckled at her eyes. 'I think that means she's with him.'

'And then some!' Isabel thumped the bedclothes. Her voice rose. 'What the hell does she think she's doing?'

'Shh! You'll wake her up. You know,' Ailsa retrieved the phone and reread all the words between them. Private, intimate words, 'they sound like they're in love—'

'No, no, no!' Isabel lunged forward until their faces nearly touched. Ailsa could feel her hot breath on her cheek. 'This is wrong. Don't you ever go down the "they're in love" route. They're not. She's a kid, and we have to look after her. We must keep her safe. Can you imagine if your dad finds out? He'll go mental.' Isabel sighed. 'Not to mention my dad.' Rummaging on her own bedside table, she pulled over her phone.

'What are you doing?'

'I need to take photos of all these—'

'You can't do that. It's totally unfair. How would you like it if someone you trusted did that to you?'

'She can trust me to take care of her.' The phone made clicking noises as Isabel scrolled down. 'There. It's evidence. Just in case.'

'Evidence of what? You can't show anyone else her private stuff.' Ailsa's head felt like it was stuffed with unshelled walnuts, and her stomach hurt.

'If I need to, I will. You need to understand what's at stake here.'

'I know my sister will hate me forever if she finds out about this.'

'Maybe. For a bit, but she'll know it was for the best. In the end.'

'I need to get this back. I feel bad we've read these. It doesn't feel right, Izzy.'

'Would you feel better if Jules gets pregnant and Elias is the dad? Would that be better?'

Pregnant? Even that word made her feel dizzy, sick. 'No. Of course not, but—'

'No buts, Ails. Put the phone back and don't let on you know anything. All right?' Izzy shook her by the shoulder. 'All right?'

'Yes. Okay.'

The barbeque was on. All the arrangements had been made. The fourth of July. Auspicious in so many ways. Clouds marred the morning, and eyes were cast up to see if it would bucket down on their festivities this afternoon.

'Typical!' grumbled Ailsa's dad, James. 'It's not even a bank holiday in England—'

'Yes,' said Eva, her mum, 'but it is the equivalent.' She sighed loudly. 'It's not going to rain, and if it does, we shift it all to the barn.'

The enormous industrial-sized barbeques were already set up in their usual place. The meat had been delivered and all the handmade bowls of this and that were in the fridge. It was positively groaning with all the stuff crammed in it. Salads, sauce bottles and a million baguettes were placed on the main table, ready to be ferried down. Outdoor tables and chairs had been placed artfully around the field. A small stripy marquee was set up, with a long table, so the plates and bowls could be covered against the wind, bad weather and, very importantly, wasps. There were jugs of lemonade, cans of kiddie pop and adult drinks. Ailsa had never really thought about the cost of all this before now. It had always been part of her childhood here in France. None of this was free, now, was it?

The barn was set up. Fairy lights were strung from hooks in the wooden walls. Two sturdy trestle tables with red and white chequered tablecloths were set up down one side. The ladder to the hayloft was roped off, although some of the kids would sneak up there at some point in the night to snog or drink stolen wine. Or, more likely, both. Everyone knew not to lean on the rickety old railing, as it was riddled with woodworm. Aunt Romi had banged on about how it was a potential accident in the waiting and that Uncle Archie should get it replaced, but at the end of each summer, the old railing was still there, a bit more of it eaten by the bugs. During the evening, an adult would periodically go up to check who was doing what, and there would be squeals, shouts, wagging fingers and a lot of laughter. As yet, no one had had an accident.

Plastic-lined wooden barrels were waiting to be filled with ice, bottles and cans of beer. Row upon row of red and white wine lined the back wall. Glasses sparkled on the tables. Packets of finger snacks were in boxes, as if, after the barbeque, anyone could be hungry. It was amazing how you could still stuff down a handful of crisps or nuts sometime through the evening. The so-called stage (a raised platform that wobbled when the band was playing) was set up under the hayloft. Three microphones were placed at the front, for the singer and guitarists, with two prominent speakers at either side. A complete drum kit was at the back. Ailsa knew Davey and Pierre itched to be set free on it. Luckily, the owner of the drum kit had sworn he would commit murder if anyone touched his stuff. Luckily for the rest of them, that was.

The Devereaux family had gone to a hotel in Le Puy, stating that they couldn't be doing with the racket and sheer mayhem of the barbeque. They did the same every year, vacated their flat in the chateau, and Isabel whispered to Ailsa that it was because they couldn't bear to mingle with the 'commoners'.

'They are so snobby,' said Ailsa, putting on her best snooty-nosed face. Isabel didn't laugh.

'We only have the barbeque because we feel we have to, not because we want to. There's a difference. I'd rather be in a posh hotel in Le Puy than be here.'

Ailsa stared at her cousin. 'We always have loads of fun—'

'Of sorts, but it's a P.R. stunt. My parents want the locals to like them. They want them to believe we are integrated here.'

'And you're not?'

'My dad is a high court judge. This lot,' she indicated

towards the village, 'are peasants, growing tomatoes and apples—'

'What's wrong with that? I love tomatoes and apples.'

'Sure, but that doesn't mean we have to be besties with the farmers, does it?'

'I suppose not.' Ailsa thought about it. 'Aren't people supposed to get along, regardless of who they are and where they come from?'

'What planet are you living on?' Isabel's laughter followed her as she walked off.

A band named 'The ShitKickers' had been booked to play tonight. They were an Irish band who'd been touring around France. Uncle Archie had managed to persuade them, for a price, to play for them. Ailsa and the other kids had sniggered noisily at their name.

'Are we allowed to swear now?' Ailsa batted her eyelashes up at her father.

'No. Why?' He seemed genuinely puzzled.

'The ShitKickers?' She raised her eyebrows saucily.

'That's their name. There's a difference.' He pulled a face at her. 'Don't get ideas, Miss Cheeky.'

'Is the whole village coming?' It wasn't like they sent out invites. It was all done by word of mouth.

'Anyone who can walk here will no doubt come. Who is going to turn down free food and drink?' He motioned around them. 'I need to go and get stuff done, or there might not be a barbeque today.' He strode off. When he was out of earshot, Ailsa stood close to Isabel and whispered, 'Do you think Elias will come?'

'Why wouldn't he?' Isabel stared out of the main doors, now

propped open. 'He's come every year since we were all kids. There's no reason for him to stop coming now, is there?'

'Maybe.' Ailsa scuffed the hay underfoot and caught a wisp in her sandal. She bent to pull it out.

'Maybe,' Isabel looked directly into Ailsa's eyes, 'we need to be really on it tonight. We can't let this get out of hand. All right?'

'Yeah, all right.'

Isabel spotted Elias first. With strategic waggling of eyebrows, she managed to convey to Ailsa that she should get her arse up sharpish to where she was lounging against a tree. Grabbing a can of Coke as she passed, Ailsa loped up and looked in the direction Isabel indicated with her chin.

'Jules is with Elias down near the bridge.'

'So, what do we do? Sneak up on them? They'll see us coming a mile off.'

'No. We wait and see what they do.'

'What if they go off into the woods? Like that last time. We'd never see them. We'd be stuck here like a couple of twits.'

'Then we go down and, you know, sort of bump into them. We are allowed to be ambling about.'

'Okay.'

They set off, wandering towards the bridge, but were surprised when they saw Davey and Pierre running down towards them.

'We're meeting everyone by the bridge,' shouted Davey as they pounded up. 'We've snagged a couple of bottles of wine.' He waggled a bag that clanked at them. 'You coming, or are you going to rat on us?'

'You tell Dad anything, Izzy,' said Pierre, 'and I'll tell him about *you know what.*'

'Izzy?' Ailsa pulled her around, 'what is "you know what", and why don't I know about it?'

'Nothing, Ails, and as to you, Pierre, if you say one word, I will beat the living shit out of you.'

'Okay, okay! No need to get your knickers in a twist.' Pierre winked at her.

'What secrets are these then?' Davey had slowed and was getting closer.

'None of your business.' Isabel walked ahead of them.

Ailsa was disconcerted to learn that there were other secrets she knew nothing about. Why hadn't Izzy told her? If she had a secret, Izzy would be the first person she would tell over and above her own twin. She felt slighted, nearly turning back until Isabel called, 'Come on, slow coach. Catch up.'

Ailsa trotted to Izzy's side but purposely kept her head down. Izzy wasn't forgiven until she revealed what was going on. She was so caught up in wondering what Izzy was hiding that she nearly forgot why they were there in the first place. Jolting to a halt, she saw Jules with Elias sitting by the river's edge, tossing small pebbles into it as it meandered past. By Jules' side was Elias' younger brother, Mattias. How could there be anything untoward going on if Jules was with Elias and his brother? Especially as both boys jumped up and went to shake Davey and Pierre's hands. The bottles were tugged out of the bag, and Davey opened the first with a corkscrew that was usually tucked in one of the drawers in the kitchen. It wouldn't be missed.

'No cups, so we'll have to take turns to swig from the bottle.' He handed Elias the second bottle. 'You can open this one.'

Settling in a huddled group on the grassy bank, they shared

the wine. Initially, it made Ailsa scrunch her eyes shut for a moment and shudder, but after the second gulp, it tasted rather nice.

'It's getting hot.' She fanned at her face.

'I think that might be the wine,' said Elias. 'It has that effect.'

Isabel stood and yanked down her shorts, and stripped off her T-shirt. 'I'm going for a splash. Anyone want to join me?' She was in her tiny bikini, and it struck Ailsa how Izzy now had the body of an adult woman. Full breasts popped out of her bikini top, and her minuscule briefs barely contained her toned bum.

Ailsa watched the looks on the boys' faces, staring at Isabel as she swayed into the water. As if she was an iced lolly that needed to be licked.

'Oh wow! That's cold,' cooed Isabel, dribbling water over herself.

Ailsa knew something was happening, although she wasn't sure what it was. Peering at Davey, she saw him frown heavily.

'Last one in is a sissy,' shouted Jules, ripping off her shorts and leaping into the water. She caught a great handful of water and threw it over Isabel, who squealed noisily, far more than was warranted. The boys all dragged off their clothes and waded in. Ailsa was the last one in, but after Mattias had splashed her and she'd splashed Davey, and Pierre splashed everyone and then pushed over anyone within his reach, they were all laughing and yelling, and there wasn't anything to be worried about. Was there?

The barbeque was well underway when they all stumbled, damp and drunk, back up from the river.

'Act normally,' hissed Davey, and just those few words were

so funny, they all laughed, causing more than one startled or suspicious glance to be cast their way.

'You kids all right?' shouted Uncle Archie from where he was flipping burgers. A small queue waited patiently, plates held out and chatting.

'We're brilliant, thanks, Dad.' Pierre waved with a floppy hand.

Those few gulps of wine had gone to Ailsa's head. She needed more.

'Oy?' She motioned at Davey. 'Can you get us another bottle?'

'I'm sure between us, we can manage that.' He winked at her. 'Elias? Pierre? Where's Mattias?'

'No idea. I think he's with Juliette,' said Elias, waving back towards the river.

'Never mind. Come on, you are needed.' He beckoned them over, and they huddled. Ailsa could hear low voices but couldn't make out any words. Two dark heads against a bright golden one.

'Sorted,' she heard Elias say. They bobbed apart and walked towards the barn, where they knew the wine bottles were ready for the evening party. Ailsa drifted along behind.

'There you are.' Izzy caught up with her, making her jump. 'Lost you for a moment there. Had to nip for a wee.' Searching about her, she asked, 'Where's Jules?'

'Well, not with Elias, that's for sure, as he's up ahead with Davey and Pierre. They're going to nick some more bottles of wine.'

'Great. So where is Jules then?'

'Still with Mattias. Down there.' She nodded over her shoulder.

'Do you think we got it wrong?'

'Maybe. I don't know. Come on, let's see what the boys have nicked.'

'Our dads will kill them if they find out—'

'Easy. We don't let them know.' Ailsa pointed. 'Look. There they are, heading off to the secret garden.'

As they entered through the wrought iron gate, they heard laughing. Davey, Elias and Pierre were all brandishing their stolen loot. A bottle of red, a bottle of white and one that was jet black and frosted. Was that champagne?

'Where's the corkscrew?' Davey motioned at Elias. 'You had it last.

'Hang on.' Elias patted at his pockets. 'It's got to be here somewhere...'

'Please tell me you didn't drop it down by the river?' Davey waggled his bottle of red wine.

'Well, if I did,' Elias pulled a wicked-looking blade from his back pocket, 'we'll have to knock the top off the bottle with a knife, and that's messy.'

'We'd end up drinking shards of glass.' Isabel sat down on one of the stone benches. 'And that's one way to die horribly.'

'Good thing I found it then.' Elias pulled the corkscrew out and threw it to Davey. 'You do the honours on this one.'

Davey reached for the corkscrew. 'We'll have the posh bottle of champagne first before it gets too warm. I think we should hide the other two bottles in the bushes, just in case an angry dad comes by, you know?'

'Oh hell, yeah.' Elias grabbed the remaining bottles and tucked them under some low-level leafy shrub.

'There you are!' Jules pushed through the gate, Mattias one step behind her. 'Lost you for a bit there.'

'We're all here now,' said Isabel, 'so what are you waiting for, Davey?'

'Your wish is my command, my lady.' The outer metal mesh was torn off, and he wiggled the cork until it popped and sprayed Pierre, who was standing too close. Raising the bottle quickly, Davey gulped the drink down and choked. Holding the bottle out, he rasped, 'Next.'

Elias upended it, and he, too, gagged. Laughing and spluttering, the bottle was handed around them. Ailsa found the bottle quite heavy, and it was difficult to drink from, as frothing wine spilt down her chin and wet her T-shirt.

That bottle was quickly replaced with a bottle of red, then another white. Was it a chardonnay? It was yummy... except now Ailsa didn't feel particularly well. In fact, she was sure she was going to throw up. Getting unsteadily to her feet, she wobbled towards the gate and the enticing smell of grilled meat.

'I need something to eat.' Wrenching the gate open, she tottered in the direction of the barbeques.

'Wait for me,' shouted Isabel. 'I'm coming too.' Catching hold of Ailsa's elbow, they clung to each other as they navigated the bowls of creamy dips and crisps, the salads and finally, plates of crispy, meaty things that had been cooked earlier and were piled on a plate.

'This is exactly what I need.' Stuffing down a fat cheeseburger and a few chicken wings made Ailsa feel marginally better. After slugging back a Coke, it must have mixed like dropping indigestion tablets into fizzy drinks. Her stomach started to roil inside her.

'Listen, Izzy.' Was she slurring her words? 'I feel a bit weird, so I'm just going over by that tree for a minute. Okay?'

'Sure.' Isabel stuffed a massive piece of potato into her mouth and chewed with her mouth open. Her eyes were glazed. Oops! Had they overdone it?

Clinging to a tree away from the main group, Ailsa was sick.

The food had barely been in her stomach for more than a few minutes, and now it lay, chewed remnants, in a pile at her feet. Sweat slicked her clammy forehead as she wiped her hand across it.

'I'm never drinking again.' She spat and wiped her mouth and then peered about her. Had anyone seen this horrible display? No. Phew! Where was Izzy now? Just wandered off and left her? A great friend she was.

The villagers were drifting into the barn for the evening's revelries. A few people were still loitering by the barbeque grills or scouring along the bowls of dips and salads.

What was that sound? The band? Was it starting already? Squinting at her watch, Ailsa realised she'd lost track of time. Dusk was rolling in across the fields. It'd be dark soon. Where were the others? Wow, it was tricky to walk. Uncle Archie needed to cut the grass a bit. Wobbling up to the barn doors, Ailsa looked in. Villagers were in clumps, chatting or listening to the music being belted out. The ShitKickers were living up to their name. Was that called hard rock? Or punk? Ailsa wasn't sure if she liked it, but she watched in fascination as first one person and then the next began to sway or tap their feet. Next thing, there were swirls of people dancing. Oh no, were her mum and dad cavorting in front of the stage? How embarrassing.

Walking past a barrel of cans of beer in ice, Ailsa scooped one up and cracked it.

'I don't think you're meant to be drinking that, young lady!' Uncle Archie materialised by her side. Where the hell did he come from?

'It's my first, and I'm not a kid.'

'Your first, is it? Doesn't look like that to me.'

'Why's that then?'

'Possibly the fact you can't stand up straight, and you're slurring?'

'Am I?'

'Most assuredly. I presume all you young reprobates have been nicking the booze?'

'No!' Ailsa waved her can at him. 'Have you seen the others?'

'Not yet, but I think I'll be looking for them now.' He pointed out of the door. 'I think you should go to bed. You've had more than enough—'

'No—'

'Shall I call your parents over?'

'No.'

Uncle Archie prised the can from her gripping fingers. 'Go to bed. Now.'

'Eurgh!' Ailsa stamped off, vaguely aware there was something she was meant to be doing, but she couldn't remember what.

Movement caught her eye as two shadows slipped down the side of the barn.

FIFTEEN

Hetty

MORTIFIED

It was marvellous watching the different parts of this wedding, though all Hetty longed for was the reception dinner to start. She nearly swooned when a plate was finally placed in front of her. The food was unlike anything she had tasted before. She savoured each mouthful.

Davey had topped up her wine so much she was unsure how many glasses she'd drunk. She hated it when he did that. One, because it meant she lost count of what she'd drunk, and two, because she felt like she should be able to choose when she wanted another drink and not have it foisted on her. She knew he was only being kind, but she didn't want to make a complete twat of herself in front of his entire family. Mind you, both Ailsa and Jules were still holding out their glasses for more.

There had been a weird conversation between Jules and Ailsa about eating animals. Struggling with the whole 'eating meat' thing, she was always torn between never wanting to touch an animal product again and falling face-first into a rare steak Davey had cooked for her at home in Brighton. Then it was hard. A lovely lettuce leaf versus a bloody steak and chips? Hmm...

It was when Ailsa said 'I don't feel guilty. It's them or us. A dog-eat-dog world' and Jules responded that Ailsa had never felt guilty for anything in her life, and when she said, 'Nothing. Don't worry about it' that Hetty thought there was, indeed, something to worry about and was pleased it was not directed at her. It had never occurred to her that twins might not get on. All she'd ever seen were photos of twins dressed the same, same hairstyle, shoes and probably knickers. That was a bizarre thought in itself. Yet these two seemed to be spitting glass shards at each other with big smiles on their faces.

It was odd when Ailsa rushed from the table, leaving that expensive beef dish cooling on her plate. Hetty stopped eating for a moment. She wasn't ill, was she? Had she caught whatever J.J. had? Were they all going to get it? Especially considering the French tradition of kissing both cheeks. Were they all spreading something ghastly at a rate of knots? Another Covid variant? Was she feeling ill herself? No. Best not to waste that gorgeous grub, then.

'What do you make of our big, fat French wedding?' Davey grinned at her. 'Enjoying the show so far?'

'It's great.'

'Ostentatious enough for you?'

'It's beautiful, and it suits them.' Hetty picked up her glass and gulped a swig of wine, hoping he didn't interpret that to mean his family were ostentatious. Even if they were. The white wine from before had been changed into a red. When had that happened? Even the glasses had changed shape. That wasn't due to the mushrooms, was it? Was she now hallucinating? But of course not. It was simply a posh dinner with trained waiters who were invisible.

Davey leaned in close. 'I can't remember if I told you, but French weddings go on until sunrise. Then we all have breakfast and think about either going home or climbing into bed.'

'That's hours away. What are we supposed to do in between?'

'Dance. And drink and dance some more.' He waved over his shoulder. 'The barn is set up for all that. The orchestra can go home, and we have a band to replace them, playing stuff we can actually dance to.'

'I like what they've been playing. Have they finished now?'

'They're on a break. They'll start again when we have the father of the bride and the bride dance.'

'Fred Astaire and whatsherface?'

'Ginger Rogers?' Davey raised an eyebrow. 'I wouldn't put it past them. They're both very competitive, and I expect they will be perfect.'

At some point, coffee and cream were served to those who wanted it. Followed by a warm oozing chocolate soufflé in a teeny-tiny glass and a coffee almond ice cream bar. Hetty wriggled around and tried to hold her stomach in. Even though she'd made sure her dress was not too tight, having been forewarned by Davey that there would be a great deal of eating, and then more eating, her dress was stretched against her belly.

When Ailsa came back to the table, Hetty noticed she was barefoot. This certainly wasn't the terrain for spindly high heels, and a little wave of smugness swept over her, as she'd opted for comfort over elegance. Davey appeared concerned about his sister, although, as Hetty looked over at her, Ailsa's face betrayed nothing but contempt. What was that saying? In vino veritas? Well, there you go. She also felt an underlying niggle that Jules had befriended her to annoy Ailsa. If that was true, then neither of them was worth her time or effort.

Davey nudged her. 'They're bringing in the cake.'

What was it called again? 'A croquembouche? Is that how you pronounce it?'

'Perfect,' said Davey.

'You'll love it,' said Jules, 'so much nicer than the heavy English wedding cake. But only if you like cold custard. Many don't.'

'I wish I could,' said Ailsa, 'but I don't think I can eat another bite.'

Hetty didn't care if they thought she was a little piggy. She was bloomin' well going to have a piece... or a bobble of that cake. Why come all this way and not enjoy the whole shebang? And she was not disappointed. Light, fluffy and creamy with a drizzle of toffee. What was not to like? Except now, her insides were grumbling. She might well have overdone it.

'I think it's that time,' said Jules, 'we desperate singles are meant to claw each other's eyes out....'

'I'm sorry, what?' Hetty had a momentary vision of the recent horror film she'd watched with Davey. She might have joked about it earlier, but was it now coming true?

'Isabel is going to throw the bouquet,' Ailsa said. 'Are you going to try and catch it?'

Oh, if looks could kill. It was pretty transparent what Ailsa thought about that. It was all a load of rubbish, anyway. Feeling Davey pulling on her elbow, she was levered upright.

'Go for it.' He smiled at her, and Hetty was submerged in a wave of emotion. Taking a deep breath, she calmed herself. She mustn't read anything into this. Davey was having a laugh, that was all.

'Come on, Hetty.' Jules stood up and grabbed her hand. 'If you're not in it, you can't win it.' She stumbled behind Jules, and they pushed into the middle of all the excited women and girls.

A few cast coquettish glances over their shoulders at their boyfriends, who Hetty imagined must be waiting in trepidation.

'*Est-ce-qu'on prêt, mesdames?*'

Jules translated, 'Are we all ready? Are we, Hetty?' She leered wolfishly at Hetty.

'*C'est parti. Que la meilleure gagne!*' Turning her back, Isabel waited for a moment (to keep up the suspense) and then threw the bouquet over her head. Hetty watched as if in slow motion as it arced into the air, bounced off a strut holding the marquee up, changed trajectory and seemed to be hurtling towards her and Jules. Hetty was about to step out of its path, when Jules sort of jumped up and bumped the flowers, now shedding petals, which fell into Hetty's arms. Along with the cheers, there were a few disappointed mewls from the other women and some muttering under breaths.

'You could have easily caught it,' accused Hetty, holding out the bouquet to Jules. 'Why didn't you?'

'What? Are you saying I gave it to you? Not likely—'

'It looked like that.' Hetty glanced over to Davey, who appeared puzzled. 'I got this by default. It doesn't count.' She thrust the bunch of flowers back at Jules and went to sit down. Casting her eyes down, she found she couldn't look at Davey until he placed his hand under her chin and gently pulled her head up.

'What's the matter? I'm not going to fall to my knees because you caught the bouquet. If and when we feel it's right, then one of us can do that. Neither of us should be forced to do anything that isn't right for us yet. Okay?'

Hetty blinked away tears. 'Good. I'm not sure what happened there—'

'Jules happened. I suppose she thinks she's helping, but I'm not sure how.' He cocked his head and peered over her shoulder.

'Looks as if the orchestra is getting back. The father and daughter dance must be about to begin.'

On cue, Isabel wafted like a fairy princess onto the dance floor in the centre of the marquee. Standing still for a moment, they looked like statues, although the moment the music started, Archie and Isabel were swirling around, elegant and sure-footed.

Hetty suddenly had a horrible image in her head. Her father and her doing the same. He'd be drunk and falling over, his shirt hanging out, swearing at the people around them, waving his fist and challenging any stupid sod who got in his way. He could pick a fight with himself on occasion. And how would that make her feel? Embarrassed? Humiliated? Ashamed. Ashamed of her own father, her flesh and blood. It was hard to be forgiving after everything he'd done to her and her mum. Not to mention her brother. She'd changed her name by deed poll and moved as far from him as possible. But he took it out on her mother and brother, didn't he? Tears slid greasily down her cheeks, and she wiped them away, hoping no one had noticed. Don't go there. Not now, after sacrificing so much to get away. She wouldn't let him take that from her after he'd taken so much already. She was here to have fun, and she'd bloody well have fun.

Movement behind her and Jules saying, 'What's happening now?' made her swivel. There was a flash of white as Isabel ran to her husband's side, Archie trailing behind with his face creased into a frown. J.J. was doubled over, his arms wrapped around his middle, his face twisted in a rictus of pain.

Chapter Sixteen

A WEDDING IS *such a wonderful affair. The happy couple looking forward to spending the rest of their lives together. Sharing the joy of children and grandchildren. Accepting the wrinkles that appear, the bits that sag, the parts that won't bend as they did in your youth, the receding hairline, or the loss of teeth. Deafness and the dimming of vision. Did we mention sharing? Sharing a life lived together? That was what you stole.*

It's a beautiful day for a wedding, isn't it?

SEVENTEEN

Ailsa

UNWANTED MEMORIES

Jules swivelled around to look. 'What's happening now?'

'Oh, God! Is J.J. off again?' Davey picked up his glass and drank deeply. 'Here's to the not-so-happy couple.'

'No,' said Jules, 'this looks serious. I mean really serious.'

Ailsa twisted to see. J.J. doubled over. Isabel pulled from Archie and ran to him, trailing lace, grasping him around the waist, worried parents on both sides flapping hands and remonstrating. Then Ailsa heard the words shouted, 'Call an ambulance! Someone, please call an ambulance now!'

The orchestra stopped playing slowly until all that could be heard were a violin's final squeak and a double bass twang. And then the rise of voices.

'This is bad,' said Davey. 'You don't think it was the mushrooms, do you?'

'You all checked them,' said Jules, frowning. 'We've all done it for years and never got ill.'

'Could one have slipped by us? Jesus!' Davey rubbed his hand over his face. 'Have we accidentally poisoned the groom on his wedding day?' He turned to Hetty. 'This sounds like the premise to one of your thriller books you always read—'

'I hope not,' said Hetty, her eyes wide, 'as they never end well.'

Ailsa half stood. 'Should we go over to help? Offer support?'

'Sure,' Davey nodded and stood, 'but I don't know what we can do.'

'Can we offer to drive him to the hospital?' said Hetty.

Jules wagged a finger. 'We've all drunk way over the limit. I don't think that's a good idea.'

Davey jogged over to where the family were huddled around J.J., and Ailsa followed.

She heard Davey ask, 'What can we do to help?'

Romi looked up at him, her face a mask of fear. 'There's something terribly wrong with J.J. One of our guests has offered to drive him to the *Centre Hospitalier Sainte-Marie*. It is a bit further away than the local hospital, but it has better facilities. He hasn't drunk anything all day. It'll be faster than if we waited for an ambulance, as they said it might be up to half an hour before they can get here.'

Archie butted in. 'Isabel will go with him and his father and brother, and Romi and his mother and sister will get a taxi with me.'

Isabel was on her phone, asking for a taxi to be sent. Her hand was shaking. How bad was this?

'What can we do?' Jules looked ashen under the lights.

Archie said, 'You can keep the party going. I don't want our guests rattled. I'm sure there's a reasonable explanation. We'll get him checked over at the hospital and get back as soon as possible—'

'But the bride and groom won't be here—' Pierre held out his hands.

'Listen.' Archie waved at the diners. 'No need to cancel all of this. It's all been paid for, so make the most of it. It should all run like clockwork, with or without us. Remember, the barn is all kitted out for the evening stint. We have to go.' He hurried to Isabel's side to help J.J. along the track towards the house, parents and siblings in tow. They had to practically carry him up the stone steps. Ailsa could hear a car revving its engine in front of the house, and then it was gone. She could track it by the headlights bobbing through the trees as it hurtled onto the main road.

'So,' said Pierre, 'we carry on as if nothing has happened?'

'Looks like it,' said Davey. 'I think you need to let people know what's going on.'

Pierre looked down at his feet. 'Oh, joy.' Then he straightened and called for everyone's attention. The hubbub died down slowly until everyone was staring at Pierre.

Clearing his throat a couple of times, he said, '*Il y a eu une petite, hum, interruption dans les procédures mais J.J. et Isabel devraient être là dès que possible. La famille souhaite que vous vous amusiez autant que possible et que vous ne vous inquiétiez pas.*'

Faces were creased in puzzlement or worry.

'*Je vous assure que tout va bien.*' Pierre waved his hand. '*Continuez et amusez-vous. Les mariés ne vont pas tarder à retourner.*'

'What did he say?' said Hetty.

Jules answered her. 'He told them it's only an interruption and to continue to have fun until the family return.'

'And not to worry,' said Ailsa. 'I think that was the most important bit.' She stared at the looks on the guests' faces. They didn't seem to be convinced, and no wonder. Being rushed to hospital was a serious affair.

'In that case,' said Davey, 'Hetty? Fancy a spin out on the dance floor?'

'Not really,' said Hetty, but she took hold of his hand and they walked onto the dance floor.

'*S'il vous plaît?*' Davey gestured at the conductor, who made an elegant bow and then waved his baton. The orchestra squeaked into life.

Other couples were hanging about at the edges, waiting to see what was expected, but as soon as they saw Davey and Hetty, they swarmed out, and there was a mass of twining bodies.

'Pierre?' Ailsa tugged on his elbow. 'Is your phone charged?'

'Yes. You think this is serious?'

Jules shook her head. 'Come on, it could be anything. Probably appendicitis—'

'I hope so, but it's not great when you are whisked off to the hospital at your own wedding. No one does that lightly.' Pierre checked his phone. 'I'll let you all know if I hear anything. Okay?' He looked about him. 'Ailsa? Can you go up to the barn to check it's all going to plan?'

Ailsa nodded, although a trip to the barn was the last thing she needed right now. Having planned to retire to bed before the party moved up to there, she was disturbed at how she felt about it. The place where it had all happened. As a close family member, she was expected to do her part in this crisis, but all she wanted to do was run up the steps to the house and barricade herself in her bedroom under the fat quilt.

'Come on! Move!' It was a whisper, but she commanded her legs to walk. One step after the other. That was all it took until she reached for the handle on the barn door. The memories hit. Bright and brittle. The night of the barbeque and what came later. Had she ever confronted what they'd done? What Isabel had done? Or had she squashed it down so deep, it was like she had the weight of a black hole bearing down on her?

The same table was set out in the same place. Things don't change. A stage, like that last stage, set up, figures milling around getting mikes plugged in and placed, someone readjusting the speakers, a sound test blaring out that made them all start. Waiters chatting behind the table, smoking a crafty fag before the rest of the party lurched in. Already, couples were drifting through the door. Ailsa blinked a few times and kept her gaze averted from the hay loft. Billows of white material were arranged artistically from every strut, draped above their heads across the ceiling like puffs of clouds. Fairy lights and soft bulbs twinkled and shone, enough to be able to see without tripping over but sufficiently warm and soft to be romantic.

'Thought that we'd start to lead the charge up here,' said Davey, making her jump. 'You all right, Ails? You look like you've seen a ghost.'

That was an unfortunate thing to say. Clasping a hand over her mouth, Ailsa dashed for the barn door and the welcome cool and deep dark of the night outside. Stumbling further, she leaned over, a hand against the planked wall of the barn, and threw up.

'Woah! Ailsa! Are you okay?'

'Too much to drink.' What else could she say?

'Ha!' Davey patted her back. 'Do you remember that barbeque where we all got wasted? Boy, were we in trouble the next day.'

'I remember,' she said quietly, wiping her mouth. How could she forget, although she wished every day that she could?

'Dad was so mad, I thought he might give us a good hiding...' It was as if Davey was re-living the memory – it wouldn't take long to get to the conclusion. 'We got off lightly, all things considered.'

'Yes, we did.' Ailsa straightened. 'Come on, don't leave Hetty to the wolves in there all alone; they'll skin her alive or worse, practise their bad English on her, and I wouldn't wish that on anyone.' By being flippant, it would steer his mind away from that time. Davey knew nothing of those last few days here. How many times had she longed to tell him, to confess, but a tiny voice told her it would ruin her relationship with him for all time. And she couldn't bear to lose him.

2016 – Ailsa

Ah! Wasn't she supposed to be watching Jules and Elias? Turning, she followed the shadows that had snuck down the side of the barn. It was pretty brambly, and she tripped a few times, scraping her hand down the wooden planks and getting horrendous splinters. Those would hurt in the morning. Why was she going down here again? What if she was chasing two complete strangers? They wouldn't be happy if she popped out and caught them doing something naughty. Stopping, she covered her mouth to mask her sniggering. Light was spilling out up ahead. A window. An open window. She approached and stood on tiptoe, peering in. She was behind the stage and saw the drummer thrashing at his drums like a lunatic. It reverberated through the thin wooden walls and made her ribcage ache. Dancers were strutting their stuff out the front as the singer belted out his song. Could she climb through this window unnoticed? Rattling it, she managed to push it open a fair way, but it was too high, and then it got stuck. Anyway, she'd need something to stand on, and there weren't many stools out here. How else could she get in? Wasn't there a back entrance around the corner?

Patting further along the wall, Ailsa tripped and stumbled until she found the back door to the barn. It squeaked alarmingly as she tugged it open, but who would hear against the racket from within? Creeping in low, she looked about her. She was underneath the hayloft. Where were the others? Why was she doing this all alone? Kicking out at a bale of hay made her feel marginally better.

'Ails?' Davey reared out of one of the stables like a monster in a B-movie. Ailsa yelped and fell back.

'Sorry, sorry,' soothed Davey. 'Didn't mean to scare you. We wondered where you'd got to.' He pulled her upright, and then she saw Pierre, Isabel and Mattias sitting in the stall. They looked a bit weird to Ailsa.

'You all left me behind.' She wanted to kick that hay bale again.

'Didn't mean to.' Isabel waved her over. 'You disappeared behind a tree, and then Davey called me over, and I sort of forgot where you were.'

'Okay.' Ailsa slumped down beside her. 'Got anything more to drink?'

'Only this.' Isabel handed her a different-looking bottle.

'What is it? Wine?'

'Nah,' said Pierre, 'it's brandy. The good stuff. I bet my dad would go apeshit if he knew we'd swiped it.' He giggled, and Mattias giggled too.

'I bet he'd beat you,' said Mattias. 'I know my dad would.'

'Talking of which, where's Elias?' Davey twisted over his shoulder, 'and—'

'We're here.' Elias pushed through the door, tailed by Jules.

'Where the hell did you lot go to? We've been searching everywhere for you.' He sounded like he wanted to kick a hay bale. Ailsa knew how he felt.

'Couldn't have searched that hard.' Isabel was eyeing both Elias and, more significantly, Jules.

Hang on. Ailsa wondered if the two shadows had been Jules and Elias. Because if they were, then they should have got in here before her. The door was easy to find. They all knew where it was. So what had they been doing in between?

'Is that brandy?' Elias clicked his fingers at Davey. 'Hand it over. You lot look like you've had way too much already. You need to share.'

'Haven't touched a drop,' said Pierre, who then laughed so much he fell off his hay bale sideways and rolled around on the dirty floor.

Ailsa saw Elias give the bottle to Jules, who took a swig and handed it back. She made a face, but that wasn't what Ailsa noticed. Their fingers snaked around the bottle, entwined. Oh, and the way she looked up at him...

'Oy, give me some, bruv.' Mattias waved his hand until Elias, taking another gulp, passed it to him. A thought popped into Ailsa's mind. Did Mattias know about Jules and Elias? Her reverie was broken by Davey jumping up, tripping over, sprawling on the ground and then declaring, 'We need another bottle. Pierre? Are you with me?'

'Sure thing, cuz.' He stumbled after Davey.

A few moments later, there were noises outside their little sanctuary. Sort of shouting, a few bangs and lots of scuffling, and then a head poked around the edge of their hidey-hole.

'Dearest God!' Uncle Archie came into full view. 'What the hell have we got here?' Turning, he bellowed, 'James? Get over here quick!'

Elias gestured at Mattias, and swiftly, they were under Uncle Archie's arm and shoving each other out of the back door.

'Oy! You two come back here now!'

James, her dad, appeared. Well, he appeared extremely angry, in Ailsa's opinion. Dragging Davey and Pierre behind him, she watched as his face turned a funny red colour, and then, letting go of the boys, he pointed at her and Jules. 'Get your skinny little arses up to your rooms now.' He waited. 'I said now!'

Ailsa stood unsteadily, was about to protest, saw the look on his face and then grabbed Jules by the hand.

'Okay, okay. Don't get your pants in a twist—'

Davey snorkelled with laughter, turning to hiccups.

'*Get to your rooms now!*' It came out as a roar, making them all jump and cower. She'd never seen her dad so angry. Oops...

Boy, had they got a telling off the following day. They stood in a row as each parent told them what they thought of their drunken, thieving ways. It transpired the boys had been caught trying to extricate another bottle (or two) from the stash under the table in the barn.

'I hope you're all feeling really shit this morning,' said her dad.

'Yep,' said Davey,' his head in his hands. 'I think you can say that.'

Ailsa had been sick again and thought she'd heard unsavoury sounds coming from other bathrooms.

'Well,' said her mum, 'I hope you have all learned your lessons. Drinking to excess isn't so much fun in the morning, is it?'

'No, Mum,' mumbled Jules. Ailsa wondered if she felt worse

than Jules. Which would be saying something, as Jules was white and sweaty, with dark rings under her eyes.

Pierre raised his hand as if in school. 'I'd like to say that I will never, ever, ever drink again.'

'That's good to hear. I'll hold you to it,' said Uncle Archie, but Ailsa caught a smile as he said it.

'And don't think this is the last of it, either,' Aunt Romi tutted. 'You're not getting out of this lightly.'

Ailsa considered what the punishment might be. It wasn't going to be nice, now was it?

'What about Elias and Mattias?' Pierre obviously felt hard done by if they were the only ones to get it in the back of the neck.

'Their father knows.' Uncle Archie looked down at the floor. 'All things considered, you lot have been let off lightly.'

EIGHTEEN

Hetty

THE START OF THE STORY

'I DON'T KNOW how to dance like this, Davey.' Tears prickled. Making a fool of herself wasn't on her 'to-do' list.

'I know, love.' Davey pulled them through the dancers. 'It was to show the others it was all right to have fun.' He laughed. 'We can stop now.'

'Ah! Thank God for that. I trod on your foot quite a few times, didn't I?'

'Yep, a few times, but then I tripped you over quite a few times more. There's Pierre. We need to find out what we should be doing. I'm sure he's freaked out.'

'As we all are. I hope poor old J.J. is okay.'

They headed towards Pierre, who looked harassed as he spoke to various family members. They caught the last part of his conversation.

'—they'll get him tested, don't worry.'

Nodding and grumbling, the family members walked away.

'Tested?' Davey sucked on his bottom lip, a sure sign of anxiety. 'You mean for mushroom poisoning? Or Covid?'

Pierre ran his fingers through his hair. 'Word got out we

went mushrooming yesterday, and people are putting two and two together...' He shrugged.

'And getting five.' Davey patted his shoulder. 'Listen, we examined them all, and nothing got past us—'

'But what if something did?'

'Then they'll give him the correct antidote at the hospital, and he'll be fine.'

'And what if it's nothing to do with all that, and it's a horrible disease? Worse than Covid. We'll all have it.'

'Is anyone else feeling ill?'

'Ails looks rough—'

'I think that's drink. She's a bit mashed.' Davey swung to talk to Hetty. 'You're feeling okay, aren't you?'

'Apart from worried sick, I'm fine. Where's Jules?'

Pierre gazed around him. 'Dunno. I sent Ailsa up to the barn. Maybe we should be getting up there. It should be all prepped for the evening extravaganza—'

'Where the two most important people are missing—'

'We get through this. It's all we can do.' Pierre motioned over to the barn. 'Let's get up there and see what comes next.'

The barn was decked out so prettily. Shame Isabel and J.J. weren't here to enjoy it. Many more of the guests flocked in after them. Although there were constant questions, huddled groups and a few objections, most decided to continue as expected and headed for the drinks and snack tables. The dancing started as soon as the band came on stage. Some sort of eclectic middle eastern mix that was so easy to kick up your heels to.

'This is more like it,' said Hetty, jigging along with the music. 'This will take their minds off it all.'

'We need a glass of water,' said Davey. 'We need to be on the ball now. Wait here while I go and get us a couple of glasses.'

He skirted the crowd and disappeared under the hay loft. Hetty peered up. No hay was up there, so maybe it was used as storage. Shifting sideways, so she wasn't in anyone's way, she leaned against a wooden pillar and watched the dancing. There was a movement to her right, and she saw Ailsa scoot past her, covering her mouth, Davey trotting behind her. He was mouthing words, although she couldn't hear them above the din of the music. Was she rushing out to be sick? Hetty wasn't going to investigate.

'There you are.' Jules appeared at her shoulder. There was a strange expression on her face. 'Davey left you to fend for yourself again?'

'I think he followed Ailsa outside. She... looked a bit poorly.'

'As well she might.' Jules held out her hand. 'Come on, let's dance.'

'I feel funny dancing when we don't know what's up with J.J.'

'They'll get him sorted, I'm sure. No need to waste all this.' She waved around. 'Listen, Hetty. J.J. will be fine.'

'How do you know? I mean, they've carted him off to the hospital!'

'How do I know? Because it's his bloody wedding day, and he can't be anything but fine.' She looked quizzically at Hetty. 'Can he? I can't countenance there's anything really wrong, and I'm sure Archie will send a message through soon to tell us not to worry.'

'I hope so.'

'Come on.' Jules flung her arms into the air and wiggled into the middle of the dance floor. 'Until we know for sure what's happening, I'm going to pretend it's all okay and have fun.'

Glad that Jules was enjoying herself, Hetty was about to follow her when Davey arrived with two glasses of water in his hands.

'Sorry, got waylaid.' Handing her a drink, he took a big swallow of his own. Hetty realised that she was quite thirsty.

'Jules is over there dancing.' She pointed. 'She wanted me to join her.'

'We'll dance in a bit. I need a moment. It's amazing how all the memories come back.' He wiped his mouth with his sleeve. 'Some of them are not so good, you know?'

'No, because you've never shared any of this with me. So I don't know.' Was that harsh? Had he ever experienced anything nasty in his life? There were things she could tell him about her life that would make his hair go curly. Ooh, maybe he was about to tell her about this tragedy?

'Can we go somewhere a little quieter?' Was he finally about to divulge the details to her?

'Yeah, sure.'

Nodding the direction, he tugged her towards a door she hadn't seen, behind the stage and under the hay loft. There was a point where the music couldn't be any louder as they passed the speakers, her head thrumming and her ribcage rattling. Then they were behind them, and the noise lessened. Heading out of the door, he took a left, and Hetty tried to watch where she was going, scared of tripping over the roots and brambles that snagged her. Using his phone, he lit the way, alternately shining it in front so he could see and then quickly behind him, so Hetty didn't lose her footing.

'Slow down, Davey.'

He stopped a few feet away and gestured at a low but sizeable root. 'We can sit on this, and I'll tell you what happened the last year we were here.'

Aware her dress might have to be dry-cleaned, Hetty sat down gingerly, her back against the main bole of the tree. He straddled the root in front of her.

'When we were kids, we played with all the village kids. It was great. There was a boy in particular we all liked. His name was Elias, and he was basically up for anything. Pierre and I always hung out with him and his little brother. We used to go fishing up and down the river. Never caught much, and what we did, we threw back. Most of the villagers are farmers of some sort. We knew all their barns, played on their tractors, even tipped a few of their cows, you know, boy stuff—'

'Tipped cows?'

'Okay, tried to tip a few cows. You wouldn't believe how hard it is to shove a great big cow over, but we sure did try. They either faced us off, ran away or leaned back on us. It was funny, except one farmer caught us doing it. Elias told him it was all his idea and got us off the hook.' Davey looked down. 'Paid for it, too.'

'Is Elias here today?'

'No. And that's the point.'

It was as if a cold snap had descended on them. She wanted to avoid where this was heading. Weren't childhood friends always invited to your wedding? So where was he?

Davey stopped speaking and seemed lost in thought.

'And?'

'And there were loads of times me and Pierre did stupid stuff with him and Mattias, his brother, and it was always Elias who owned up. He protected us, and that wasn't all.' Davey finished off his glass of water. 'Shit. I could do with a proper drink. Do you mind if I nip back and grab us a bottle?'

'Yeah, go for it.'

Using the torch on his phone, Davey slipped down the side

of the barn, and the darkness closed in around Hetty. Now she was cold, with no giant garden heater and her cardigan left upstairs. Branches scraped across the barn's roof and set her teeth on edge. A city girl through and through, she'd rather be alone late at night at a tube station, waiting for a cancelled train than sit in the shadows at the edge of a wood.

Something happened years ago, something tricky. That's what Davey had said to her that first morning in the cold and dark.

Yeah, she knew all about that. Would she ever divulge what had happened to her? If he was coming clean about a troublesome past event, shouldn't she? How was she to explain she wasn't who she said she was? That her name, her life was a sham. No, she shook her head. Not a sham but false, nonetheless. And that other 'thing'. The one she couldn't bear to remember, or it would break her once again. The event that had cut her life into 'before' and 'after'. Her mother had tried to protect her, though it wasn't enough. She shouldn't blame her mother, beaten down to a wisp of the woman she was. But it was too late when her mother told her to run. It was far too late by then. And she thought, now, Paul had known what their father had done to her. Had her father sworn he'd find her, drag her back by her hair, do what he wanted to her because that was his right? Had Paul, faced with all the blood and fear that night, had he broken too? Snapped and shattered, drowning in his rage, it flooding out, so he chose to fight, knowing he could never win against the beast. Did he die knowing he'd saved their mum? Hetty hoped so. Tears slid down her cheeks. She hadn't gone to counselling. She couldn't. What? Air her dirty laundry? Bare her shredded soul to another human? Not likely. She'd decided the person she was before was dead and buried, along with her brother. She had to live as Hetty now. A bright, new, shiny person. Wiping the wetness from her face, she breathed in deeply. Let it go.

Someone was coming towards her, not creeping so much as crashing.

Starting up, she held her hands in front of her defensively. 'Davey?'

'Yeah, it's me. Archie called Pierre a minute ago. We need to go back in. Now.' His face looked like a wax mask in the torchlight.

He wasn't carrying a bottle, and Hetty felt her stomach drop to the floor. As they rushed into the barn, he turned and said, 'Pierre's gone to find Ailsa. We need to get Jules, too.'

'I'll find her.' Hetty pushed her way into the crowd of dancers and searched about her. How could there be this many people? It was more like being in the mosh pit at a concert. There she was. Hetty saw a flash of deep blue as Jules' skirt flared out as she spun. She seemed so happy. Was this all about to come crashing down?

'Heya, Hetty. Having fun? 'I want to carry on dancing all night—'

'Jules! I think something bad has happened.' Hetty swallowed, but the spit got caught in her throat. Taking a deep breath, she pulled Jules close and shouted in her ear. 'To J.J.'

A look of puzzlement flashed over Jules' face. 'I'm sure he's fine. Why do you think that?'

'Because Archie has called Pierre, and he seems in a right state.'

'Oh, shit. Okay, I'm coming.'

NINETEEN

Ailsa

BAD NEWS

KNOWING she'd admonished Davey to return and find his darling Hetty didn't lessen the sting when he did. He should be out here, all things considered, making sure his sister was okay. Leaning back against the planked wall of the barn, Ailsa relished the cool wind that flowed over her hot cheeks. She needed time to process what the actual *fuck* was going on. Were they now all amidst a bloody Covid outbreak? Or worse? Dengy fever or whatever it was called? Didn't all these things start with nausea, vomiting and horrible rashes? She scratched at her bare arms and then stopped. At this point, she was hoping J.J. had been poisoned by a rogue death's cap. Oh no, that was a bad, *bad* thing to say... Still, it was true.

'Ailsa?' Pierre staggered up, banging on the wall to keep his balance. 'You need to come in right now. Dad's called me.'

'What?' Ailsa stood and grabbed for the wall to hold herself up, her head spinning. 'What has he told you?'

'You need to come in. We need to hear this as a family. We need to be together.'

'Are you crying, Pierre?' Ailsa went to him. 'What's

happened? Tell me.' A cold chill fluttered through her. This wasn't good, was it?

Wiping snot and tears from his face, he nodded his head. 'Inside.'

A heavy weight threatened to crush her across her chest as Ailsa crept behind him. All she could hear was a soft sob drifting back to her. She couldn't tolerate what was going through her head. No, she must not jump to conclusions. After all, assumptions were the mother of all fuckups, weren't they?

On entering the barn, she spied Davey waving at them and Hetty dragging Jules out from the dancers. Mixed emotions ranged across their faces, shock, fear and panic being topmost.

'We need to go somewhere more private.' Pierre beckoned them back outside. 'The secret garden. We can talk there.'

'*Pierre?*' Oh Lord, was that one of their elderly second cousins? '*Avez-vous entendu quelque chose? Vous avez l'air très inquiets.*'

'*Non, je n'ai rien entendu. Je vous informerai quand j'en saurai plus.*' Pierre smiled shakily.

'Are you?' Ailsa grabbed hold of his elbow. 'Because you do know something, don't you. Are you going to tell them?'

'I suppose I have to at some point.'

Again, they followed in the dark. The old gate squeaked as he pushed it open. Fairy lights barely illuminated the place, but it was enough for them to find the stone benches and sit down. No one spoke, and the silence stretched on.

'Pierre?' Davey moved to lay a hand on his shoulder. 'You need to tell us what your dad said.'

Through stuttering words, Pierre said, 'He's dead. J.J. is dead.'

'*What?*' Davey took a step back. 'No, no, no! That can't be true. I mean, *what the fuck?*'

'Oh, God, no!' Jules put her head in her hands. 'Was it the bloody mushrooms?'

'No.' Pierre rocked on his feet. 'They tested him, and there was no trace. They couldn't work out what it was, and then he died. They couldn't do anything to help him.' Sobbing and holding his arms protectively around his chest, he sank onto the grass. 'I know I called him a *prick*, but I never wished him any harm. Isabel loved him. Oh God! Poor Isabel...' He fell heavily to his knees.

Jules crawled across the grass to rock him in her arms. 'I can't believe it. How did this happen? If it wasn't the mushrooms, what the hell was it?'

'Dead?' Ailsa felt like she was trying to swim out of a deep lake, and she'd been at the bottom. Her ears were ringing. 'He can't be dead.'

'Pierre?' Hetty asked. 'What did your dad say to do now?'

'He told me to stay put and try to act normally. Ha!' There was a note of hysteria in his voice. 'Yeah, like any of us will be able to act normally. The groom has died on his wedding day. Right. That's normal, isn't it?'

Davey grimaced. 'Are they coming back now? We can't be the ones to tell everyone.'

'Dad said he would be coming back as soon as possible, but he's leaving Isabel with J.J.s family... I suppose to sort out his... body.'

His body. Ailsa held a shaking hand over her mouth. How many times could she throw up? This was beyond awful. What was going through Isabel's mind? No, she couldn't think about that. It brought back too many memories.

2016 - Ailsa

A couple of days later, they all met up by the river's edge. They might have been moaning about 'how unfair' it all was until they saw Elias and Mattias.

Let off lightly. Yes, that'd be it. Ailsa saw how Elias and Mattias' dad had dealt with them. You don't call the police on your dad, now do you? But they should have.

'Gave us a proper beating.' Elias could hardly get the words past his swollen lips. His left eye had disappeared into folds of purple and ruby-red flesh. His arm was held stiffly in a makeshift sling.

Mattias hadn't fared any better. As he held a protective arm around his chest, Ailsa guessed he might have a broken rib. Or two.

'Have you been to the doctor?' Davey had the grace to appear sheepish. Stealing the drink had been all his idea in the first place.

'Don't be daft!' Elias laughed, although it sounded a bit strangled. 'Our family don't do doctors, hospitals—'

'And especially not the police.' Mattias cocked his head. 'For some weird reason or other.'

They all knew what that meant. Their family were not exactly the flavour of the month with the local police, or even of the year, for that matter. Sticky fingers in too many pies or whatever that saying was. Jules was quiet, head down. Ailsa wondered what she was thinking. Still a good idea to be with this boy with a father who could happily beat both his sons half to death? Or maybe that made him more alluring. Like wanting to rescue the kicked, bone-thin dog on a chain in someone's backyard that had never experienced a kind word or a pat on the head. Did Jules view Elias as if he was that dog? It wasn't like she didn't feel sorry for the brothers. She lived a life of pampered luxury (Elias' words, not hers), so what did she know (again, what he'd said to her another day)?

She did know that her family, on both sides, would do anything in their power to stop a relationship between their precious Jules and this wild boy. But how did she feel about it? About him? Undoubtedly handsome, not stupid by a long way (maybe ill-educated, although that wasn't his fault), kind, fierce when needed, and a loyal friend. Why wouldn't she want Jules to be with him? Because she had that voice in her head. A voice that came from the rest of her family. He's a gypsy. He's not one of us, and you can't trust him. Ever. Or was there an even more insidious reason? One she wouldn't, no, couldn't even admit to herself? Was it because she also liked Elias?

Having followed Jules for a couple of days, Ailsa finally spotted her acting all weird. She was about to give up when she spied Jules creeping into the old barn, so she had to follow her. She just had to! The fact she looked suspicious made it even more suspicious. Didn't it? She stopped at the barn door. Should she just walk in behind her, all innocent like? Breathing hard, Ailsa tried to move, but it was as if her feet had rooted to the dirt floor.

The sun was setting, and a smudge of purple and lilac was hovering over a luminous band of pink and yellow, a gilded lake that could be seen through the silhouettes of the trees on the hill above the river.

Sneaking up to one of the windows, she raised her head until she was peering over the sill. He was there. With her. Elias. And they had their arms wrapped around each other and were... kissing. Ailsa felt bile shoot up her throat, and she ducked down and hunkered under a nearby bush, trying to gain control. Had they heard her? Spitting as quietly as she could, she listened. No footsteps or raised voices. Back at the window, she scanned around the barn. Shadows filled every corner where the failing daylight couldn't penetrate. Hang on. There was movement. Two darker shadows were climbing up the ladder to the hayloft. They weren't going up there to play cards, now were they? Ailsa put her head in her hands. What should she do? Run in and yell at them to stop? That would go down like a lead balloon, and she'd push Jules closer to him, contrary as she was.

Where the hell was Isabel? She'd know what to do. Backtracking as fast as she dared, Ailsa texted through to Isabel. Her reply was swift to meet her in her bedroom. Although sporty, Ailsa sometimes cursed her uncle for not installing a lift. The Devereaux family were heading down the stairs as she pelted up them. Nearly colliding with the youngest son, who was hurtling down, she called her apology and pushed past them. They must be off out to dinner in the town. Usually, she'd stop to say hello and have a little catch-up. All of *Tante* Romi's friends who stayed in the flats were sophistication itself, and she loved to pretend she was one of them. Parisian. How stylish, coiffured and amazingly made up, with a perfume that hung about them like an aroma of extreme wealth. But not today. A little startled, they moved out of her way.

Isabel was waiting at her door. 'What the hell is so urgent—?'

'Jules is with...' Ailsa looked over her shoulder and pushed Isabel back into her room, kicking the door shut. 'She's with Elias. In the barn, no, I mean worse than that. They're in the hayloft—'

'You're kidding. No way!' Isabel scrunched her eyes shut, and her fists were balled. 'How stupid can she be?'

'What do we do?'

'Give me a minute.' Isabel opened her hands and stared at them. White half-moons were dug into her palms from her nails. 'We can't do anything tonight—'

'We can't just let it happen—'

'No, but we have to be careful. You know who his family is. They'd be right angsty if we muck it up for him.'

'Do you think he's only after her 'cos he thinks she's got money?'

'Well, der!'

'What if they're in love?'

'With her money. Don't get all gooey on me now. This is seriously bad news. Listen, I've got an idea. We've got to get hold of a burner phone. When's the next big shop in town?'

'It's the day after tomorrow, but I'm sure we can get your mum to go tomorrow. What do we need a burner for?' Ailsa could see what Isabel was thinking. 'You're going to contact him and pretend it's Jules. What if he knows it's not her?'

'I took photos of their texts, didn't I? If we work together, we can make a text sound like her.'

For Ailsa, it wasn't so much sounding like Jules. That was easy. It was more that what they were contemplating was just plain wrong.

TWENTY

Hetty

A BAD DREAM?

'You're all in shock.' Hetty stood up. 'I'm going back to the house, and I'm going to make us all a cup of tea—'

'Coffee,' said Pierre. 'I think I need a coffee.'

'Okay, I'll get prepped for whatever anyone wants.'

'We'll be up in a moment, Hetty.' Davey wiped a hand across his face. 'Thank you.'

Hetty pulled her phone from her clutch bag and switched on the torch. Walking and watching where she trod, she navigated to the big house. In the kitchen, she orientated herself, rummaging in cupboards and finding mugs, spoons and sugar. Milk was in the fridge. Coffee in a large tin with an Art Nouveau image on it. The lid was battered and difficult to yank off, but she managed it, and having cleaned out all the percolators, she filled them ready and placed a fat kettle onto the AGA hob. Peering into the gigantic fridge, she stared at the remains of the wedding cake. Only a few sticky toffee-covered balls of choux pastry remained on the platter. Hetty banged the door shut, making the fridge rattle.

She hadn't particularly liked the man (especially his political leanings), but to die like this, on his wedding day, of something ghastly, and worse, unknown. What the hell was it? A terrible thought occurred to her. Had she cursed this wedding by mentioning that horror film? Made a joke about none of her books or films ending well, ha, ha! Except it hadn't ended well at all. If it was anything like one of her books, his would not be the only death. Slapping the side of her face, she closed her eyes and whispered, 'Shut up. Just shut up.' None of this was her fault. And she was not in the middle of a horror novel, acting out a part. She was in the middle of a terrible tragedy... another terrible tragedy. Davey had been about to tell her what the last one was. Were they connected in any way?

'Hetty?' Davey had come into the kitchen so quietly, she hadn't heard him, and her hair stood on end.

'Bloody hell, Davey, you frightened me.' She clutched at her chest.

'Sorry.' With her arm around Pierre, Jules came creeping in after him, with Ailsa drifting behind.

'Who wants coffee, and who wants tea?' Hetty waved the percolator.

They mumbled what they wanted, and Hetty prepared their drinks. It was nice, in a rather horrible way, to feel useful.

'When's Archie going to get here?' Jules stirred from where she had her head on her arms, sprawled across the kitchen table. 'We can't do this alone, and people will start asking questions.'

'He'll be here when he can, I suppose.' Pierre grabbed his phone and scrolled up and down. 'No new messages, and no one has called.' Laying it on the table, he kept his fingers on it. 'They must be going through hell.'

A voice coming from the salon made them all jump. '*Vous êtes tous là.*' It was the elderly second cousin from before. Were the wedding guests now wondering what was going on? Archie had better hurry up, as Hetty could see it was too much for Pierre to have to explain.

Pierre stood and held the older man by the shoulders. '*Nous attendons le retour de Papa l'hôpital. Il nous expliquera tout à ce moment-là.*'

'*Est-ce que tout va bien?*' The second cousin's face creased into a deep frown. '*Y a-t-il d'autres informations sur Jean-Jacques?*' Even Hetty and her schoolgirl French could understand this. The guests were restless and needed an answer. But none of them would be prepared for the response they would be given.

A vehicle crunching to a stop outside the house roused them.

'Dad!' Pierre rushed past the old man and hurtled out.

'*Pouvez-vous nous laisser un moment, s'il vous plaît?*' Davey ushered the cousin out, saying over his shoulder, 'We need privacy for this.'

Voices were heard, and then Archie finally walked into the salon. If Hetty had thought he looked bowed before, it was nothing to how he appeared now. Shrunk in on himself, eyes and nose red, a haunted expression on his face. He slumped at the table after Pierre pulled out a chair for him.

'Dad?'

Archie groaned and rubbed at his eyes. 'They have no idea what killed him. We had to give a list of everything he ate, which will be matched with what we've all eaten. Just in case there's an overlap—'

'You mean, one of us might get sick and die?' Ailsa half rose from her chair.

'They're not saying that but must rule out every possibility.' He looked about him. 'Any chance of a coffee? I'll tell you hospital coffee leaves a lot to be desired.'

'I'll get another coffee on,' said Hetty. She listened as the family spoke in hushed tones.

'Thanks, Hetty, love.' Archie's hands trembled as he drank his coffee. 'The hospital and authorities have requested the full guest list in case it's an outbreak of something. We have to provide forwarding addresses for each one and ask them to self-isolate for a few days until they know what caused his death.'

'Dingy fever!' Ailsa's outburst made Hetty jump.

'I think you mean Dengue fever...' Davey put his cup down with a clatter. 'I don't think we have to worry about a disease from tropical places. Maybe it's a virulent mutation of the Coronavirus—'

'Then we're all buggered,' said Jules.

Archie took another big swallow. 'The police have been called—'

'Why?' Pierre held out his hands. 'They don't think it's suspicious, do they?'

'Well,' Archie raised an eyebrow, 'a perfectly fit young man dies horribly on his wedding day. No one else appears to be ill. What do you think?'

'Are we talking murder?' Ailsa shook her head.

'Christ!' Davey looked over to where Hetty was pouring top-ups of coffee for everyone. 'Hetty! You were right. We are in one of your thriller books.'

Hetty stopped and had to suck in a breath as if her throat had suddenly closed. Her head spun. Having convinced herself that this was simply a heart-breaking misfortune, she was disconcerted when Davey mentioned her thrillers. Having an overactive mind that always thought the worst (as that meant she could only go up from that vantage point), and having been living a horror story for most of her life, she had to keep repeating to herself that this could all be easily explained, and there was no cold-hearted murderer in their midst. But what if there was...?

'This is not funny, Davey.' Jules held out her cup for more.

'No. It's not. It's deadly serious, but we must face the fact that if the police think J.J. died suspiciously, we are the ones they'll be looking at. It's usually someone close to the... deceased.'

Hetty knew that for a fact. Her brother was testament to that.

Archie nodded. 'The police want to interview the immediate family.'

'What? We don't even know him. That's ridiculous.' Jules hooked a bottle of what looked like brandy off the counter and sloshed some into her cup. Waving the bottle, she said, 'Anyone?'

'Okay,' said Ailsa, 'it's obviously nothing to do with us. Like Jules said, Davey, Jules and I had never met him before yesterday. Hetty wouldn't know him from Adam, and Pierre; well, what reason would he have to want J.J. dead? None of this makes sense. Archie and Romi have just organised the most amazing wedding, so it's unlikely to be you two, and as to his own family, only they know what their relationship was like. I mean, they seemed amicable.'

'Then who would have it in for J.J.?' Davey looked around them. 'Someone he works with? A jealous business partner—'

'Maybe,' said Jules, 'an angry, jilted ex-girlfriend?'

Ailsa piped up. 'Perhaps he shafted someone in one of his deals?'

'Stop it, all of you. It's disrespectful.' Archie hauled himself upright and stumbled out of the kitchen. 'I need to tell the guests, and I have to do it now.'

. . .

Hetty cowered down behind Davey. They were huddled in the barn, listening to Archie's broken voice as he spoke of J.J.s death. At a wedding, the happy couple is expected to have a fairy tale ending and drive off into the night in their gold-plated carriage. No one expects to be told that the evil witch has poisoned the prince, and no magic kiss will revive him. Add to that the request to stay put until contacted by the authorities.

Archie shouted something in French, and there were loud grumblings and tearful faces.

'What did he tell them?' Hetty could feel the horror and fear like a mist in the air.

Archie turned to her. 'I've contacted the coach companies and explained what's happened. They will send out two coaches to pick up our guests and take them back to their hotels in town. I stated we'd let them know it's safe to leave their hotels when we are told.'

'What a shit show!' Davey blew out the side of his mouth. 'I can't believe this. When will we wake up and find this was only a bad dream?'

Hetty said in a soft voice, 'No one ever does unless it's a terrible script.'

'Thanks for that, Hetty.' Jules slugged the remainder of the brandy bottle.

Chapter Twenty-One

*O*H*, can you feel it now? Is a vice clamped around your heart, squeezing and tightening until you can't breathe? I'm watching you all from the shadows, where you put me. I can see your faces clearly. Poor Jean-Jacques. He's a shell now, only the husk of the man he was. At least you will have the privilege of burying him. You can say your goodbyes and weep over his body. What did you leave us? Lies and heartbreak. And nothing. Nothing at all. A void. Don't worry. We're not finished yet. Are we having fun?*

TWENTY-TWO

Ailsa

CAN'T GET ANY WORSE?

A SUSPICIOUS DEATH. Who would wish harm to J.J.? (Apart from every minority group that his political party persecuted and vilified... Oh, Lord! Had some disgruntled immigrant got in as a waiter and slipped him something nasty?) Frightened as she was of some sneaking virus that could already be infecting her, Ailsa was aware they might all be prime suspects in a murder case. Surely once the police interviewed them and discovered that none of them knew him, (and if she mentioned immigrants to put them onto another scent), that would be it, and they could return to England. And wouldn't that be a relief?

It was a mess, but that was expected. The coaches arrived, the drivers masked and looking apprehensive, spending ages manoeuvring so they could get back out. The stunned guests, many the worse for wear because of drink, were helped onto the first coach, which left, horrified faces pressed against the windows. The same retort was heard, over and over: 'how could this be?' It took a while until every member and friend of the family was rounded up and sent on their way. The second coach left, and they could see the taillights disappearing up the road across the valley. Had murder popped into anybody's mind yet? They had kept the police inquiry to themselves. No need, as Archie had said, to worry anyone unnecessarily. Needless to say, she could worry enough for all of them.

Archie spoke to the band, money passed hands, and they nodded, looking confused, and then packed up their gear. One drove their van to the barn, where they humped all the equipment over and arranged it in the back.

'So sorry for your loss,' said the lead singer as they slammed the doors shut and drove off.

When everyone had gone, Ailsa stared about her. Only the family were left. How could any of these people she loved so much be a murderer? The thought was preposterous. Although there was a murderer already in the family, wasn't there? Trailing into the salon, the family milled about, seemingly unsure what to do next.

'I'm shattered,' said Davey, slumping onto one of the sofas. 'Can we clear up what's left tomorrow? It's amazing how exhausting a death in the family is.' He closed his eyes briefly. 'That came out wrong, and I apologise. I'm just tired.'

'We all are,' nodded Archie. 'Go up to bed, all of you. We'll meet at breakfast to discuss where we go from here.'

'I want to go home,' said Ailsa. And she knew the others seconded her sentiment.

Having firmly believed things couldn't get any worse, of course, they did. Be careful a thought doesn't jinx everything.

Ailsa arrived in the kitchen the next morning to the spectacle of Archie hanging over the sink, being sick. What an awful noise. Scooting back, she put her hand over her mouth. All that time during the pandemic, they had masks in every pocket, but they'd become complacent. It was over, wasn't it? Yes, many thousands had died, though Ailsa was convinced (because she'd read this online) most had died because they were old, fat and unfit. Stands to reason, doesn't it? Whereas she was slim and worked out three times a week at her local gym. But faced with the mortality of J.J., who was young and toned, she was not so sure, and here was Archie, also fit and relatively young. Did he have the thing that killed J.J.? Or was this simply stress and too much to drink last night, on top of being shattered?

'Archie?' She mumbled past her hand, unwilling to expose herself further. 'Are you okay?'

He spat and wiped his mouth. 'I feel shit, Ails. I've got a bad feeling about this. Can you wake the others? I think I need to go to the hospital.'

'Where's Romi? Is she still at the hospital?'

'She drove back early this morning to pick up some fresh clothes for Izzy. I mean, dearest God! Poor Izzy was still in her wedding dress! They're there, trying to get things sorted.' He turned to her. 'Ailsa? Go wake the others now!'

Ailsa was up the stairs and wailing their names. *Oh God! Were they all going to die?* Nearly tripping at the top, she fell into Davey's open arms and slumped to the floor.

'What? What's happened?'

'Archie's now ill. *We're all going to die like J.J. did.*' She could hear the hysteria in her own voice.

'What?' Hetty ran out, pulling on a cardigan.

'You've got to be joking.' Jules came out after Hetty. 'This is such a clusterfuck!' She ran her fingers through her hair. 'We all need to go to the hospital now and get checked out. Where's Romi?'

'At the hospital.' Ailsa backed away from them. 'Supporting Izzy.'

'Does anyone else feel ill?' Hetty looked at them all.

'I feel like I have a colossal hangover.' Jules bit her bottom lip. 'At least I hope it's a hangover. Maybe that's what's wrong with Archie—'

'What's wrong with my dad?' Pierre had slipped down from the attic. He looked dishevelled, his hair stood on end, and it was apparent he'd slept in his clothes, as he was still wearing his suit from yesterday, albeit pretty crumpled.

'He's throwing up in the kitchen.' Ailsa nodded down the stairs. 'And it's not a hangover. It's bad.'

'Should we all go to the hospital?' Jules sat on the top step. 'It might be the best course. Just in case...'

'Look,' said Hetty, 'if Archie is ill, it couldn't have been murder, could it? Why would anyone want to hurt J.J. *and* his father-in-law? So it must be something else. At the moment, we're all fine. Maybe it was something only J.J. and Archie ate or touched?'

'We've been at a wedding!' Jules sounded exasperated. 'How the hell do we know what they might or might not have touched that the rest of us didn't? I'd say that was the proverbial needle in the haystack...' All the colour left her face. 'I know I might be clutching at straws here, but J.J. isn't here to tell us anything, and Archie is sick. As I said, we need to go to the hospital. We need to be in a safe environment.'

'Agreed,' said Davey. 'Although I still think Hetty might be onto something. We have to wrap our heads around what that might be.'

2016 – Ailsa

Of course, Isabel managed to browbeat her mum into taking them to town early the next day. Ailsa was a mass of nerves when they were once again ensconced in Isabel's bedroom waiting to go, the door closed.

'When are we going to do this? I mean,' Ailsa had a lump in her throat that she couldn't swallow, 'if we make an arrangement for tonight and they already have one sorted, he'll know there's something wrong—'

'No, we'll say she lost her phone and can't quite remember when she'd arranged to meet up with him. It'll work, trust me.'

'What if it doesn't? She'll never forgive us.'

'She'll thank us in time.'

Ailsa wasn't convinced. 'I can't believe you said that. You're so old, sometimes.'

'Well, she will. She'll see that being with a boy like Elias is dumb 'cause he's dumb. He's not in her league at all. Not in a million years.'

Ailsa bit down hard on her bottom lip. 'I know that.' But did she?

'And our families would put a stop to it anyway. Best for us to do it.'

'Tomorrow then? Get him to come to the hayloft for some reason?'

Isabel practically purred. 'Perfect.'

'How do we stop Jules from catching us with him?'

'We get her out of the picture.'

'But how?'

'I have an idea.' Pulling Ailsa close, Izzy whispered in her ear.

. . .

The trip to town was boring, but they'd volunteered, much to the surprise of their mothers. Jules was exempt, as she was off with her father taking photos in the forest. Yet more bugs, so at least they didn't have to deal with her. And as it was Friday, they knew that Elias would be working. If they were going to follow their plan through, it had to be the next day, as Elias worked every other Saturday. He would be off tomorrow.

They were in Carrefour, which seemed to have an eclectic range of goods, including various coffins propped at the supermarket's entrance.

Ailsa nodded at them as they walked past. 'That's creepy. I mean, if you're really old, that must do your head in.'

Aunt Romi looked perplexed. 'Death is part of life. No need to hide it in dark places. It's nice to be able to choose what you would like before you go.'

'That's plain weird.' Ailsa turned her face away.

Her mother tutted. 'Too English by half.' She grinned at Ailsa.

Ailsa rolled her eyes. 'Whose fault is that then? You didn't have to marry an Englishman, did you?' Her mother raised her eyebrows. 'Did you, Mum?'

'Does it matter? Remember, if I'd married someone else, you wouldn't be here.' She shook her head. 'And Dad's not English, he's Scottish and don't you forget it.'

'And you wouldn't have us,' agreed Aunt Romi.

The list of groceries was endless, and they piled it all into two mammoth shopping trolleys with a mind of their own. The fact that both trolleys rolled off in different directions to where they were being pushed was laughable. The more laden the trolleys, the more they bucked back.

'Maman?' Isabel laid her hand on her mother's arm. 'Do you

mind if Ails and I nip off to get something? We'll be quick, and then we can help load the car.'

'Fine, but don't be too long.'

Ailsa tagged after Isabel, who knew exactly where she was going. To the phone store.

'Listen, Izzy?' Ailsa had to be careful how she worded this. 'What was Pierre talking about at the barbeque?'

'What do you mean?' She had a hooded look in her eyes. What was she hiding?

'Come on. I'm your best friend. If I had any secrets, you'd be the first person I'd tell.'

'Read my lips. There's nothing to tell—'

'Then why did you get so shirty with Pierre?'

'Because he's an interfering little twat?'

'I know that, but—'

'Just leave it, Ails. Anyway, we're here, and we need to get this right.'

Ailsa glanced up at the mobile phone shop façade.

'The phone doesn't have to be expensive,' Isabel continued, 'it just needs to work.'

Choosing a phone for a ridiculously small amount of money (because its only use was as a phone), Isabel got it set up, paid for it and secreted it in an inside pocket of her bag. 'We'll chuck it somewhere no one can find it afterwards.'

'Okay,' nodded Ailsa. 'Look, we'd better get back to our mums, or they'll be narky.'

Having loaded the carrier bags into the boot of the car, Ailsa and Isabel settled in the back of the old Citroën while their mothers chatted quietly in the front seats.

'You two all right back there?' Ailsa's mum craned over the headrest of the seat. 'Awfully quiet. Normally you're chattering like sparrows.'

'Just a bit tired, Mum.' Ailsa did a theatrical yawn for effect.

'If a bit of shopping can wear you out, we may need to make your bedtimes a little earlier.

'No, Mum. Don't be ridiculous.'

'Ha! A joke, my love.'

They had to wait until Jules returned before they could carry out the next part of the plan.

'She's not always that careful with her stuff.' Isabel pointed to where Jules had dumped the camera on her bedside table. She'd taken the photo card out, presumably ready to upload to her computer. It was awfully near to the edge. 'It could easily be knocked off, and see how close that half-drunk mug of tea is.'

'Listen,' said Ailsa, 'she's downstairs making a sandwich with Dad. If we're going to do this, it has to be now.' She paused, aware her hands were shaking. 'How can we make this look like an accident?' She picked the camera up, conscious of not only how much it cost but what it meant to Jules. Could she do this to her own sister? 'She always closes the door, so that's an obstacle—'

'We use Toulouse—'

'The cat? You're going to blame this on the cat?'

'Why not? He's done it before. Got into our rooms and knocked stuff off. We'll say it was him.'

'He climbed four floors to get into your rooms? What is he? Supercat?'

'He's a cat. That's what they do. They sleep most of the time but love knocking stuff off things when awake. You've seen all the YouTube clips. It's an art form for them.' Isabel narrowed her eyes at her. 'I've already told you this. Weren't you listening to me?'

'Yeah, I was. Poor old Toulouse. He's not going to have a good day, is he? So what did he do that made your mum so mad?'

'He knocked off a very expensive René Lalique last year. I've never seen Maman so furious. It cost loads.' Isabel motioned at her. 'Are you waiting until Jules comes back up?'

Ailsa hesitated. Dropping the camera on the hardwood floor felt terrible. It'd been Jules' main birthday present, and she loved it. 'What if she can't get it fixed?'

'Give it here!' Isabel snatched it from her hand and let it fall. 'Your daddy dearest will simply buy her another one, won't he?' It landed with a crunch of plastic and metal. She tossed the photo card close to it. Using the base of the mug, she whacked the photo card. 'Just to make sure.' She winked at Ailsa, who wiped the sweat off her top lip. She didn't feel good about this.

Then Isabel tipped the cold tea over it and the broken camera, spattering it around before she dropped the mug. Shards of porcelain scattered across the floor. 'Ooops!' Isabel held her hand to her mouth. 'Bad Toulouse. We need to leave the door open, so it looks like he got in and messed up her stuff.'

'I think you might have gone a bit overboard, Izzy.'

'Whatever gets the job done, dear cousin.'

TWENTY-THREE

Hetty

BLAME?

'I've phoned the hospital,' said Archie, 'and they've advised all of you to remain here. If we do have something contagious, they don't want us to spread it. If anyone feels even slightly ill, then you are to come in, and we'll be put in an isolation ward. They're still set up from the first Covid outbreak.' He wiped a shaking hand over his face. 'Pierre? Can you drive me in and then come back home straight afterwards? No stopping for a MacDonalds on the way back, you hear me?' His attempt at a joke obviously wore him out, as he sagged on his chair.

Pierre looked stricken. 'Give us a hand, Davey. I need help getting Dad to the car. Ails? Can you drive it to the front of the house?' He flipped the keys to Ailsa, who scuttled out. Davey and Pierre got an arm around Archie's waist as they levered him upright.

A car could be heard outside, scrunching to a halt. But this was followed by a second vehicle.

Ailsa ducked back in. 'It's the police.'

'Okay,' said Jules, 'we knew they would be coming at some point. I bet they're here to simply remove us all from the mix.

I'm sure the hospital is working on what happened to J.J., and they'll have something ready for Archie—'

'If he's got the same thing...' Ailsa stepped aside as the boys half-carried Archie to the front door. Hetty and Jules followed, and then there were two police officers climbing from their car and watching the proceedings. They clarified they were *Officiers de la Police Judiciaire*. They had guns on their hips and icy stares. And masks.

They seemed perturbed by the fact that another family member was being manhandled out of the door. Davey explained that now Archie had been taken ill and was on his way to the hospital. Hetty saw their expressions change. What were they now thinking? That a murderer had been upgraded to a serial killer? Or were the masks a testament to them regarding this as a natural, if ghastly, outbreak of something? Nodding to the salon, they followed Jules, Davey and Hetty in.

'I speak English for you?' The lead policemen motioned around them.

'Yes, that would be better,' said Davey. 'Hetty, my girlfriend,' he pointed at her, 'doesn't speak French. But the rest of us do. So that should make it easier for you.'

'Sorry,' said Hetty.

'We need to know what you see or hear at the wedding?'

'We also,' said the other, 'need to find out what you all eat. If zis is a case of bad of the food, then it is very sad for you, but if it is somesing else...?' He let the words hang in the air.

It took a while, and a cup of strong coffee had to be made partway through the questions. Whoever was not being questioned sat outside, waiting for their turn. Each was asked individually, perched on the sofa, while the attending policeman jotted things down, a recorder lying on the table between them.

The masks didn't come off, and a safe distance was maintained between them.

When it came to Hetty's turn, she felt as guilty as sin. She could only imagine what they might be writing, as it was all being recorded. Maybe it was 'this one definitely looks guilty'.

The first question came. 'Describe, please, how you know Jean-Jacques D'Aramitz?'

'I've never even been to France before,' she bumbled. 'I only met J.J. the day before yesterday.'

'So, you have never meet any of ze French side of ze family before zis?'

'No.'

He cleared his throat. 'Obviously, I am not talking of your boyfriend here, but how well do you know ze, oh, what is ze word... *les jumeaux...*?'

'Twins?' said the other officer.

'Yes, twins. How well you know zem?'

'I've met them both a handful of times.'

'So not real well?'

'Not really, no.'

'Do you know of any problems of ze family or any reason why anyone might want Jean-Jacques dead?'

Hetty shook her head. 'As far as I know, they only met him the day before, too. The same for all of us.'

'Did you, er, *avez-vous senti...?*'

'You feel?' The other officer raised an eyebrow.

'Yes, you feel any bad in the family?'

Hetty gulped in a breath. 'We were all here for a wedding. It was meant to be a happy event—'

'Oh, please,' the officer waved his hand, 'please speak more slowly. You have a strange accent for us.'

'Sorry. I'm from London.' Hetty tried to slow her words and

pronounce them clearly. 'Everyone was expecting a marvellous day. Not that. Not death.' She wiped at her eyes. 'I'm sorry, but it's all very shocking, and the fact Archie is now ill... Well, you can imagine we are all a bit on edge.'

'Of course. I understand. Can you think of anysing only Jean-Jacques and Archie MacGregor perhaps have eat or drink? Somesing ze rest of you not have?'

'I don't know. I wasn't keeping tabs on whatever other people were eating and drinking.' Hetty pursed her lips. 'I must admit, I was too busy eating and drinking myself to notice. I've never been outside England before, and this was so amazing; I was pretty wrapped up in it all. I'm sorry.'

'Your first French wedding, eh?' The officer's eyes crinkled at the edges. Was he smiling at her behind his mask? 'Hopefully, not your last. Please tell us if you remember anysing that helps us with zis terrible time. You sink it not useful, but for us,' he indicated himself and his companion, 'it might be a, oh, *clef*?'

Again, the other officer knew the word and Hetty wondered why he wasn't the one asking the questions. 'A key.'

'*Oui*. A key to save Archibald MacGregor.'

'I'll help in any way I can.'

'*Merci*. You may go now.'

Hetty watched apprehensively as each of them went into the salon and came out looking stressed. Perhaps they were being grilled a lot more than she had been. After all, what did she know about anything here...? Except that the family were no longer welcome in the village. Bad blood. Could that 'bad blood' have blown up into full-blown murder? Hetty rolled her eyes. If it was 'the thing' from eight years ago, J.J. hadn't even been on the scene then. If it was recent, then had he pissed off someone enough for them to kill him? And where did Archie fit in all this? No. She had to stop. So prone to fantasising and getting lost in her books, she was missing the most crucial part here. If it was a virus, any one of them might be next, and if it was a type of food poisoning, then maybe she should be going through what she ate and drank now, before it was too late.

Backing hastily out of the door, the lead policemen barked something at Davey before getting back into their car and driving towards the main road.

'What did he say?' Hetty bit her lip, as her emotions were see-sawing.

'He said to remain in the house and to start compiling a list.'

'I have a pen and a notepad upstairs in my bag. Shall I go and get them?'

'That's a good idea.'

Back in the salon, Davey and Hetty sat on one sofa, the twins on the other.

'What questions did they ask you?' Ailsa nodded at Hetty.

'How well do I know you all, um, did I notice any angst between you all, and what did everyone eat. That was about it.' Hetty stared back. You?'

'About that.'

'Shouldn't Pierre be back by now?' Jules went to peer out of the window. 'It's been ages...'

'You don't think,' said Davey hesitantly, 'he's been taken ill too, do you?'

Hetty closed her eyes, just for a moment. 'If he has, that doesn't bode well for the rest of us.' Breathing deeply, she waggled the notepad. 'Let's start compiling that list.'

'I can see the car. It's Pierre. He's coming up the lane.' Jules rushed from the room, and Hetty could hear her shouting and the sound of wheels crunching across gravel. As Davey leapt up, Hetty followed him outside.

'Pierre!' Jules tugged him into an embrace before he was even out of the car. 'How is he? How's Archie?'

Hetty could see Pierre biting down on his lip. 'Not good. The doctors say he's following the same pattern as J.J.' He started to shake. 'Maman's now with him, but they told me to go home and wait. We're not to go back unless another of us gets ill. I can't believe this is happening!'

'Come inside.' Davey ushered him forward, but it was like his legs were made of wood. 'They'll work it out, Pierre.'

'They didn't work it out in time for J.J., did they?'

'They've had more time.'

Hetty asked, 'Shall I make us some breakfast? We might feel better if we have some food inside us?'

'I'll help.' Jules patted her way along the wall into the kitchen. Hetty watched her as she then stood immobile, gazing into space.

'You get some toast on, Jules, and I'll make us some coffee. I'll look for something more substantial in the fridge.' Rummaging around, she discovered more packs of bacon. Yes, that would do it. Make or break with a bacon sarnie. Voices burbled from the salon as she got the AGA heated up and found the big old skillet and some oil. The toaster *sproinged*, making both her and Jules jump. Jules put more bread in. But it was as though she wasn't seeing what she was doing. They were all looking inwards, weren't they? Contemplating mortality. The mortality of others, and especially their own. Hetty didn't want to die. She had to keep busy to stop her mind from going where it was trying to lead her.

. . .

The Women's Refuge four years before had not kept them safe, no matter what it said on the bloody tin. Her bastard dad had found them and dragged them back. The air was blue with his cussing, and then the floor, the walls and the kitchen cabinets were red with blood. He was forced to take her mum to the hospital, although not for humanitarian reasons. It was more that he didn't want her death at his door. Hetty had never seen her beaten like this. Such ferocity. He made it plain that leaving him was not an option, or they'd leave him for good.

'Six feet under,' he'd said. And they knew he meant it.

But when he turned his mad eyes on Hetty, her mum pulled her close one evening when he was down the pub.

'You have to run, love.'

'I can't leave you and Paul—'

'You can and you will. The beatings aren't the half of it. I don't want him to do to you what he does to me. Do you understand what I'm saying?'

Hetty hung her head. It was already too late. 'Yes, Mum.'

'Now,' her mum went to the cabinet and pulled it out, reaching down the back of it, 'I squirrelled some money away for just this. Here's an address for you. You're a smart girl, and you can work this out. You get as far from here as you can. Use a different name. Change it as fast as you can. You're nigh on eighteen. Nearly an adult. Don't come back here. If you can call us, do it from a phone box or from somewhere he can't trace you—'

'Mum!' Tears streamed down her face. 'I can't do this. I can't—'

'You have to. And one last thing. Don't find a man like him. Don't let this be the legacy of our family. Be careful who you pick in life. I love you so much, Becky'.

Her real name was Becky.

. . .

Paul. Three years ago. At seventeen, he was two years younger than Hetty and still lived at home with their mum. She was sure their mum had plans to send him off into the world like her, to hide, but neither of them made it that far. Hetty had run and kept on running for a year, barely surviving, changing her name to Hetty. Why not? What was one name compared to another? She phoned when she could and tried to work out how they could escape and come and live with her.

Her dad's anger at her 'betrayal' grew. Poor Paul. One beating too many when the belt had come off, and the buckle had nearly torn out his mother's eye, Paul fought back. Hetty knew all the gory, horrible details when it went to court. He was slight. Her dad was a bear of a man. Neither of them had inherited his brawn or his temperament. Paul didn't stand a chance. His body was discovered when a neighbour called the police. A terrible racket, they'd complained. Hetty supposed that a man beating a boy to death might be a bit noisy...

Her mum had been hospitalised, and Hetty had stood by her bedside, watching the fluids enter her, staring at the bandage around her face, the rising and falling of her chest, now bound to protect her broken ribs.

'She's lost her right eye, although we saved her left one.' The doctor spoke quietly.

'Thanks,' said Hetty. 'This was my fault, you know.'

'It wasn't.' The doctor laid a hand on her shoulder, but she started from him. She'd been touched before and not willingly. 'I'm sorry. I don't think anything would have stopped him at that point. You probably would be here in the hospital or...'

'In the morgue with my brother?'

'Yes.' He nodded. 'I don't believe you could have changed this outcome. You cannot and should not blame yourself.'

'Oh, I can.' Hetty kissed her mother on the bit of her cheek not bandaged. 'And I will.'

Due to the condition of her brother's body, it was thought best if it was a closed casket. Her father was in prison, awaiting his trial with no bail. But she wasn't taking any chances, slipping off with her fake name and life.

Then she met Davey MacGregor, and her life changed.

TWENTY-FOUR

Ailsa

SCHEMING

2016 - Ailsa

THE WAITING GAME. It was horrendous, having to pretend that everything was normal. To act, smile and say what was expected instead of second-guessing herself. Finally, Jules went upstairs. Isabel tensed and then relaxed. They both had to wait some more. Would she find it immediately?

'Dad? *Dad!*' Jules could be heard pounding down the stairs. Breathless, she bounded into the salon, waving something in her hand. 'The camera's been smashed.' Tears were streaming down her face. 'I don't know how it happened, but I went in just now and found it on the floor and it's all wet—'

'Slow down,' said their dad. 'Where did you put it? Could it have fallen off?' He scowled, and Ailsa felt a pang of guilt. The blame would eventually come back to Jules.

'It was on the bedside table. It couldn't have fallen off—'

'How could it be wet?'

'Well,' Jules scuffed the floor and wouldn't meet his eye, 'I left a half-drunk cup of tea next to it.'

'Oh, Jules. You know better than that. Was it at the back?' Their dad stared at her. 'I know you leave things all over the place and you're not always that careful—'

Ailsa winced as her father echoed what Isabel had said upstairs.

Jules' face scrunched and she looked like she might cry or maybe scream, *'That's not fair!'*

'Was the door open?' asked Aunt Romi.

'It was sort of open, but, but—' Jules held out her hands imploringly. 'I always close it behind me. I never leave it open.'

'Well,' said their mum, 'you must have left it open this time.'

'So what if she left it open?' Ailsa had to pretend to defend her sister. It was what she would have done normally (except she was the one that had done this to her). 'Why does that matter? I mean, it's not like anyone would risk sneaking up four flights of stairs to smash Jules' camera, is it?'

'Not any*one*.' Aunt Romi shook her head and wiped her brow. 'A cat. A very naughty cat. This can only be Toulouse. I thought we warned you to keep your doors closed for this very reason?'

'Your cat knocked the camera off?' Their mum closed her eyes for a moment. 'James? Can you look at it to see how badly it has been damaged? Perhaps we can get it on the insurance.'

Jules, her hand shaking, passed the camera to their dad. 'Can we fix it, Dad?' She handed over the photo card. 'I don't think this looks good.'

'Hmmm.' Their dad scrutinised it from every angle. 'I think the camera can be mended. It's more superficial damage, but the card looks buggered to me. Oops, sorry for swearing.'

'When?' The distraught tone of Jules' voice made Ailsa wince. It was like she'd hack-sawed Jules' arm off. Ailsa hated any feelings of guilt. She didn't do 'guilt', as it made her feel like she'd swallowed some lizards with suckered feet. Live lizards that now wanted to get back out.

'Can we Google a store that mends stuff like this?' Isabel was the consummate actor. It was like she'd suddenly had this idea and was trying to help. 'I'll look now.'

Ailsa knew she'd already done this and knew exactly where to direct them.

'Okay.' Isabel's deft fingers had flown over the face of her phone. 'There's a place in Clermont Ferrand, one in Lyon and one, um, in Montpellier.'

'They're all miles away!' Their dad rolled his eyes. 'It's Jules' fault for not keeping the door shut—'

'James!' said their mum. 'Don't be mean. I guess we weren't paying attention when we were warned about the cat.'

'I hate to say this,' said Isabel, shuffling about, 'but Toulouse can open doors. He jumps at the handle until it opens.'

'He does?' Their dad looked shocked, and then he drummed his fingers on the table. 'Really?' He stared at Uncle Archie.

'Unfortunately, yes.' Uncle Archie cleared his throat. 'Listen, if you can't get it on your insurance, we'll pay for it or get a replacement—'

'All my photos are on it!' Jules was beginning to wail. 'Everything I've taken since my birthday. I can't lose all that.'

'Tell me you've downloaded them all?' Isabel raised an eyebrow.

'No, I was going to... but, you know...' Jules slumped in her chair. 'That's why the card was out of the camera.'

'Oh, that's awful. Uncle James, you have to help her.' Isabel put on her best wheedling voice. 'After all, it wasn't her fault. It was Toulouse.'

Ailsa nearly laughed. What a great actress she'd make. She almost believed her lies.

'You won't lose anything, don't worry,' soothed their dad. 'There are ways of getting it all off for you. That's simply a just-in-case scenario. Okay?' He nodded at Uncle Archie. 'And thanks. It's appreciated.'

'Nothing will be open yet. You can drive to one of these places after lunch,' said Aunt Romi. 'I believe they are about the same distance from here.'

'Yeah,' groaned their dad. 'They're all miles away.'

'I'm sorry, Dad.' Jules wiped at the tears on her cheeks. 'You know I would never do anything like this on purpose.'

'I know, love. I simply wanted a quiet afternoon after our walk this morning. But I can have a quiet evening instead. We'll have a great time. Does anyone else want to come with us?'

'No, sorry. If you don't mind?' Although Ailsa knew it was for a good cause, the best cause, she still felt shitty as she thought about what they were going to do while Jules was out. What they were prepared to do.

Lunch was stilted, but they pushed through it with Isabel's help. Ailsa nibbled at her food, moved it around on the plate and then declared she'd eaten too much for breakfast and now wasn't hungry.

'Put it in a plastic box for later,' said her mum. 'Don't waste it. I bet you'll be looking for something else to eat in half an hour.'

Ailsa doubted it. She thought she might puke instead.

Just before Jules and her dad headed out, Isabel nipped to the downstairs bathroom and texted Elias using the number she'd taken from Jules' phone. When she returned, she nodded slightly at Ailsa and started to help her mum clear the table and load the dishwasher. Normal stuff. Ailsa also helped but was listening out for the squeak of the old front door to tell them Jules was gone.

'I told him,' whispered Isabel, 'to get here as fast as he could. I said it was urgent. I told him that she'd dropped her phone and had to buy a new one, so that's why the number is different.'

Glancing at her watch, Ailsa stopped. It was already nearing four. They should have at least two, maybe three hours to get this done before Jules and their dad came home. That should be enough, shouldn't it? Whatever 'it' was. Davey and Pierre had gone fishing and they rarely came back until it was starting to get dark, and soon, Aunt Romi and her mum would be in the back garden, cracking open a bottle of wine and gossiping fit to bust. They were a couple of right old lushes!

'Isabel, we need to go and, um, watch that programme we were talking about?'

'Oh yeah, I'd nearly forgotten. Maman?' Isabel made it look so easy. 'Do you need us for anything else?'

'No, my love. You two go and do what you need to do. Leave us old codgers yapping in here.'

'Thanks, Maman.' Isabel sauntered to catch up with Ailsa, but the moment they were out of the salon, they crept to the front door, and she pulled it oh so carefully.

'I have the knack of opening it quietly. Had to get out of here a few times without my parents knowing.' Closing it behind them, they ensured it was still partially ajar, so they could sneak back in after... Ailsa wasn't sure what they were going to do.

'What are you going to say to Elias?' They both ducked under the salon window and headed to the barn.

'I'm going to tell him the truth. Here. We'll hide here.' Isabel dragged her behind one of the animal stalls, and they crouched down. Holding her finger to her lips, Isabel shook her head.

Now they must wait in silence and see if Elias had been tricked. Minutes ticked on, and Ailsa shifted as a cramp began in her calf, but then she heard a soft sound. Quiet footsteps came into the barn.

'Juliette?' The footsteps crept closer. 'Juliette, are you here?'

There was movement, and Elias passed within a couple of feet of where they were hiding, but he was gazing upwards. The bruising on his face had lessened, though he still seemed to be limping a little, and his movements were stiff. Ailsa had a strange, momentary vision of the scene from Romeo and Juliet. Romeo searching for Juliet on that balcony. Then the ladder creaked as he climbed up to the hayloft.

'Juliette? Where are you? What's so urgent? I thought we were meeting tomorrow?' Ailsa could track his movements above them.

Isabel ducked out and headed for the ladder, Ailsa tagging along like a frightened puppy. The ladder creaked as Isabel started to climb, and they could hear Elias backtrack towards them.

'Juliette? What's going on?'

'Not Juliette. It's Ails and me. We'd like a word with you, Elias.'

TWENTY-FIVE

Ailsa

DIDN'T TELL

AILSA HATED TO SAY IT, but that bacon sandwich hit the spot. Licking her fingers, she nodded at Hetty. 'Thanks, Hetty. Appreciated.'

Hetty smiled tentatively at her. 'Shall I start writing out that list?' She reached beside her and pulled out a slim notepad and pen.

'I think we should,' said Pierre, glancing apprehensively at his phone. 'We need to find out anything they had that we didn't.'

'Who wants to go first?' Jules looked at each of them in turn. 'Davey? You're the eldest. Do you want to start?'

'Okay. So where do we start? I mean, *when*?'

I suppose,' murmured Ailsa, 'the morning when we first met J.J. He, as far as I know, didn't have anything the night before. Did he?' Everyone shrugged or looked at each other.

'I'll list the food and drink, etcetera,' said Hetty, 'and then put an initial against it of anyone who had it.'

'Yes, that'll work.' Jules nodded, but Ailsa could see by the set of her jaw that Jules was anxious. Of course she was. They all were.

Touching the tips of his fingers together, his eyes rolled sideways, Davey listed all the things he could remember eating and drinking, while Hetty scribbled it all down. They went around the room. New things came up, but many were dishes or the aperitifs they'd all sampled.

'Anything else?' said Hetty. 'Anything at all? That policeman said it could be something we'd normally dismiss, although it could be relevant and to put it down regardless.'

'God!' said Pierre, 'that's like trying to find that stupid needle in a haystack. Neither J.J. nor my dad are here to tell us if they did anything different to us. How the hell would we know?' He heaved himself upright. 'I need another coffee—'

'Is that a good idea?' Jules held out a warning hand. 'We've all had buckets already, and maybe it's not so good for our nerves.'

'Fuck it!' Pierre stamped into the kitchen. 'At this point, I really don't give a shit!'

'How is everyone feeling?' Hetty looked around the room.

'Worried stupid but no more than that.' Davey also looked about him. 'If this was a virus, surely someone else would be showing symptoms by now?' He rubbed a shaking hand over his face. 'Don't you think? So, we're back to what they might have had differently to us.' He stopped. 'Are you texting someone, Jules?'

'Yep. Sorry, it's important. Won't be a mo.'

'More important than finding out if something will kill us all?' Davey shook his head and looked around the room as if searching for support. '*Really?*'

'Yep.' Jules walked into the hallway, and Ailsa could hear low whispers. Then she walked back in. 'All done.'

'The only thing I saw,' said Hetty, 'was that J.J. popped those Tic-Tacs all the time. Maybe he had some sort of reaction to them? Maybe?' She shrugged. 'You should never give dogs chocolate made for humans as it makes them very sick and can kill them. Perhaps it was the same for J.J?'

'But that doesn't explain Archie, and anyway,' Davey frowned, lines crisscrossing his brow, 'are Tic-Tacs in any way dangerous?'

'I suppose not.'

It was like a white light burning in Ailsa's mind. 'Hang on.' She waved her hand. 'I saw both Archie and J.J. in the snug the day of the wedding. They were smoking those bloody great big cigars. I remember watching them through the window, feeling all miffed. Pierre?' She shouted into the kitchen, where she could hear clanking and banging. 'You saw your dad and J.J. smoking those cigars, didn't you?'

Pierre came back in quietly. 'You're right. They offered one to me, but I hate cigars. And anyway, I'm trying to give up smoking. I poured myself a whiskey instead.'

'Probably for the best,' said Jules. 'Smoking kills. Oh, and drinking.'

'So, what you're saying,' Hetty was breathless, 'is the only thing Archie and J.J. had that the rest of us didn't, was those cigars?'

'Looks like it.' Davey stood. 'They must still be in the snug—'

'Don't touch them!' Hetty wagged her finger at him. 'It might be something on the outside, a bacterium or something. Don't let it get onto your skin.'

'Oh, my God!' Ailsa felt her heart thump in her chest. 'This might be it. If there's something nasty on those cigars, then the rest of us might be okay.'

'Gee!' Pierre's eyes narrowed. 'Nothing like only looking out for yourself! Don't worry about Dad. I'm sure he'll be fine!'

'I didn't mean it like that, and you know it. I'm trying to say that they now have something to test. We need to get them to the police for them to check.'

'But very carefully.' Hetty motioned to the kitchen. 'Have you got a sturdy plastic bag or box or whatever we can put them in?'

Pierre rummaged, tugging out drawers and swearing under his breath. He came back with a tea towel and a reusable bag. 'Will these do?'

'They'll have to.'

'Listen.' Davey was halfway to the door. 'Is that a car?'

'Isabel?' Pierre shoved past Davey and raced to the front door. 'It is,' he called. 'It's Isabel.'

'Leave them for a minute,' said Ailsa. 'Let her come in when she's ready.'

It seemed like hours had passed before she heard footsteps in the entranceway. Isabel crept into the room.

'Oh, Izzy!' Ailsa held her hand over her mouth. The woman before her did not resemble the woman who had married J.J. yesterday. Her eyes were haunted and sunken, her skin sallow, and her slender shoulders bowed. 'I'm so sorry... I don't know what to say—'

'What can you say?' Isabel's voice was flat, detached, all emotion crushed out of her. Thank God she was no longer in her wedding dress. Ailsa didn't think she could bear to see her in her that. She was glad that Romi had taken a change of clothes in this morning. 'My love is dead. Snatched from me, and I don't understand how or why. And my dad is in hospital, and we don't know what has done this.'

'How is your mum?' Davey hovered close to Isabel but

didn't touch her. Maybe he thought she might shatter into a thousand pieces if he did.

'She's by his bed in the hospital, where I was last night with J.J.' She ran her fingers through her tangled hair. 'Until he died.'

'Izzy?' Pierre took hold of her shoulders. 'We think we know what caused... all this. The cigars. They're the only things we can think of that Dad and J.J. shared. They must be contaminated—'

'Oh, they're contaminated, all right. But they weren't the only things we doused.'

Isabel spun towards the voice. 'What? What did you say?'

Ailsa also turned. Jules was grinning. Literally, grinning from ear to ear. 'I said the cigars are contaminated. And the funny thing is, Hetty was kind of right about the Tic-Taks. It was one of the first things I thought of, except I found you can't inject them. Shame.'

'Thallium sulfate!' Hetty blurted.

'You're clever.' Jules clapped her hands together. 'Well done, Hetty, super-sleuth.'

TWENTY-SIX

Jules

THE TRUTH WILL OUT

2016 - Jules' story

'Your ever-loving sister and cousin are tailing you again.' Elias ducked back into the gloom of the tree line and waved Jules over the stream. 'We need to go.'

Jules grunted as she waded across, her sandals tucked under one arm and clutching her rucksack with the other. 'Maybe we should say something now? Get them off our backs?'

'They won't be happy—' Elias held out his hand to help her scramble up the bank.

'I'm nearly sixteen—'

'*Nearly* being the main word here.'

'Can I stay with you and your family until I am?' Having done up her sandals, she trudged behind him as they headed deeper into the forest. Elias knew every inch of the area.

'You mean not go home with them?' He turned so abruptly, she trod on the back of his trainer.

'Sorry,' she mumbled. 'Listen, your dad knows about us. I know he wasn't that happy to start with—'

'He was worried your dad or Archie MacGregor would mount his head on a plaque in the living room.'

'That is a possibility...' Jules caught hold of his arm and pulled him back. 'I love you. Your dad can see I do. And I think he even likes me!' She stuck her tongue out at him.

'Well, that's something,' he laughed, 'as he surely doesn't like me.'

'Your dad is a hard man and overdoes it, but he's preparing you for an even harder world. He knows what it's like out there.' She waved her hand around randomly. 'Especially for you lot.'

'You mean us gypos?'

'For you Romanis.'

'You really are so old sometimes, Juliette.' He bent down and kissed her gently.

'More like wise. That's how I like to think of myself.' She stared up at him. 'Do you think your dad will let me stay with you?'

'It wouldn't be safe with us, although we do have an extended family. We might be able to hide you with one of them, but remember your uncle is a high court judge, who probably has a few of the local police here in his pocket—'

'You don't really believe that, do you?'

'That's what my pa told me. Don't be naïve enough to think that doesn't happen. They all look after their own, Juliette.'

'Then we wait and get married as soon as we can. Deal?'

'Deal.' He blew out the side of his mouth. 'I knew I loved you from the first day I saw you—'

'When you pushed me over into the river?' She placed her hands on her hips. 'And made me cry? That day?'

'That day. I was trying to impress you.'

'Well, you certainly did. I was scared of you for ages—'

'Until you saw what a great guy I was?'

'Until I fell in love with you too.'

Peering over her shoulder, she felt his body tense. 'We should get a shift on. Izzy and Ailsa are by the river now.'

'Come on then. Race you to the top, slow coach!' Pelting up the slope, she used the branches to pull herself up and over obstructions, careful of the tangling brambles, but, as usual, he streaked past her, longer legs able to stride further, arms pumping. Fit as he was, she would never be able to beat him.

'Who are you calling slow coach?'

As they crested the hill, the trees thinned out to reveal a grassy patch dappled in sunshine, tall grasses waving in a slight breeze. They slowed down. The phone in Jules' bag rang, making them both jump.

'Ailsa?' Elias raised an eyebrow.

Tugging it out, Jules stared at the screen. 'Yep. Do I answer it?'

'No. She'll tell you to come back, and I thought today was our day? I'm not working for once, and we should make the most of it.' Holding out his hand, he caught hold of her free hand. 'We need to start planning how we will escape the clutches of the great MacGregor clan.'

'The great MacGregor clan do not own me. I can do what I want with my life. And I want to spend the rest of my life with you.'

'They won't be happy. Even my pa said they won't let you go without a fight.'

'Then they'll have that fight, won't they?' Stuffing the phone back into a side pocket of her rucksack, Jules towed him across the meadow.

. . .

A couple of days after the barbeque, Jules discovered her camera smashed on the floor. She couldn't believe it! How had the damn cat, Toulouse, managed to get into the room, choose her beautiful and costly camera and decide, out of everything, that was what he would select to knock off?

'That's what cats do,' her dad had remonstrated in the car. 'They're absolute...' He swallowed.

'You can swear, Dad. I'm nearly sixteen, and if you heard the village boys, you wouldn't bat an eyelid.'

'Well, I was going to say a particular word, but I'll amend it to *wanker*. Cats are absolute wankers. Okay?' He grinned at her and then focused back on the road. 'Also, which village boys are you referring to?'

'All of them.'

'I know you spend time with Elias and Mattias quite a lot—'

Jules tried not to show she was surprised at this. 'They're our mates. Davey and Pierre hang out with them all the time—'

'I know, but perhaps you should all be careful. Their family don't have the best reputation hereabouts.'

Swivelling to look at her dad, Jules narrowed her eyes. 'I don't worry about reputations, Dad. I go by how kind a person is.'

'Yes, yes. You're right. We shouldn't judge a book by its cover and all that.'

'Anyway, all I'm worried about today is can my work be saved—'

'The moral of this particular tale being?'

'Always back my work up regularly. I will from now on. It's just I can't lose the photos I've already taken. It's my best work.'

'We'll sort it, I'm sure.'

. . .

Returning quite late, the house seemed strangely quiet. As if all the inhabitants were hibernating deep underground.

'Where is everyone?' Her dad hung his jacket on the hanger and walked into the salon. 'Ah! Looks like the women have opened the wine and are enjoying the evening outside. I suppose the kids are in their rooms then. Fancy a bite to eat?'

Jules followed him in, spying her mum and Tante Romi through the kitchen doors, a bottle and glasses on the glass table outside in the cobbled courtyard. Soft voices drifted in. Jules wondered if they were still talking about Brexit. She understood that this decision to leave Europe would have a massive impact on many lives. She, unlike Ailsa, kept up with the news and tried her best to understand what was happening around her. She asked questions all the time until her dad joked she would make a great investigative journalist.

After a light supper, tucked in her room, aware of sounds that shouldn't be there, Jules tried calling Elias for the millionth time. Where the hell was he? She knew she shouldn't get exasperated, but it was tempting to throw her phone at the wall, although she didn't want to find out how her dad would react if she trotted downstairs to tell him the cat had now got her phone too.

Elias was frequently requested by his dad to do some dodgy deed or whatever. So that would explain it, but usually he managed to at least text her to let her know. Never any details, just he had to 'go and do something'. Mattias, his younger brother, was often out with him, so it was no good contacting him. Mattias adored her and had even started to flirt with her. She'd found it cute, although Elias had play-slapped his brother around.

'Not cool!' Although even Elias couldn't keep it up when Mattias was sniggering and snorkelling and sounding like a sink emptying of water.

After three days, she succumbed and rang Mattias.

'He's had a massive barny with Pa.' Mattias sounded shaky. 'He's gone to the city—'

'To the city?' Jules couldn't believe it. Gone without her?' 'Which city?'

'Does it matter? He's gone, and I don't know when he's coming back.'

'You're playing a prank on me, right?' Jules felt like a vice was tightening about her chest. She was having trouble breathing. 'Please, Mattias? Tell me this is a joke?'

'I'm not joking. I...I...' She heard him swallow loudly. 'I have to go.' There was a pause. 'I'm changing my phone, Juliette. You can't contact me anymore on this. I have your number, and I'll call you in a bit. I'll tell you what's going on then. Okay?' He waited. '*Okay?*'

'Yes, all right. But call me soon. I need to know what's happening.'

There was something wrong. Something terribly wrong. Had a fight with his dad? Yeah, sure, but that happened all the time. It was always a momentary thing like a flash in a hot pan. Then they were over it. What the hell could have happened to have pushed Elias away? To force him to leave for another city? She had to get to the bottom of it.

The other thing was that half her family were acting decidedly strange. Ailsa was brittle, Isabel sharp and scratchy, Pierre monosyllabic and doleful, and as to Uncle Archie, it was like he'd been poked with a very sharp stick. Quite a few times. Even her mum and dad noticed it and commented on it. Tante Romi was her usual buoyant self, so that was a relief.

And then came the news.

'Oh, my God!' Her dad walked into the kitchen, where they were all having French breakfast. Hot chocolate and croissants. 'I'm so sorry, my dears,' he said, sitting heavily at the table. 'I've heard some awful news. Now be prepared. I should tell you, as I don't want you to hear it from someone else.' He stopped and ran his fingers through his hair.

'What?' Isabel had gone quite white and was sat frozen, one hand suspended, dribbling raspberry jam. 'What is it?'

'Elias and Mattias' dad has had an accident. His car was found at the bottom of the ravine early this morning. He didn't survive.'

'What? Elias' dad is dead?' Jules half rose from the table. 'No, that can't be true—'

Uncle Archie tailed her dad in. 'I'm afraid it is. It transpires that Elias and his dad had a blazing row. His dad beat Elias, who then ran off. His dad went to one of the mountain village bars and got wasted. I mean absolutely blotto. He drove down but lost control and went over the edge.'

'How do you know all this?' Jules held out her hands to him.

'The other villagers confirmed they heard the fight. They said it was the worst one yet—'

Jules' whole body was shaking. 'And Mattias? Where is he now?'

'No one knows where he is. The police are out looking for him. He's a minor and needs to be found for his own safety. If you hear from Elias or Mattias, you must tell us? Okay?'

Jules looked around the kitchen. Ailsa stared at the tabletop, a green tinge to her face. Isabel put her croissant down and wiped her hands on a napkin. Pierre had his head in his hands.

Davey shook his head. 'We need to find both of them. What

if Elias doesn't know about his dad? That's terrible. What else can we do? We need to support them.'

'Yes, we do,' agreed her dad, 'but we have to find them first.'

'Or worse,' said Davey, obviously thinking it through. 'What if he blames himself for his dad's death?'

'Well,' said Uncle Archie, 'he did have a hand in it. The neighbours said the stuff they shouted at each other was appalling.' Snorting breath in through his nose, he rubbed at his chin. 'Yes, he'll probably feel really guilty. He may never come back here.'

'That's not fair!' Jules noted that both Pierre and Ailsa had jolted at her shout. They must be feeling it, too. 'No one can blame him. He has to come home. *He has to!'*

'No, he probably won't come back,' said Isabel, enunciating each word.

'What?' Jules sprang to her feet. 'Of course he'll come back here. It's not his fault his father chose to drink and drive. No one can blame him—'

'He'll blame himself.' Davey stood and pulled Jules into a hug. 'We know what he's like. Oh, poor Elias. This is going to be so hard for him.'

Jules wanted to slap them, scream at them. 'We're their friends. We have to do something to help them—'

'Have you their numbers? Maybe we can track them?' Uncle Archie came over to Jules and laid a comforting hand on her shoulder. A cold chill trickled down her neck. She squirmed away from him.

'I'll write down their numbers for you.' It didn't matter, did it? Elias wasn't answering, and Mattias had a new phone.

. . .

'You need to stop moping about.' That's what Isabel told her. 'You're all going back to England in a few days, and you're ruining it for the rest of us.'

They were in the kitchen, having finished their hot chocolate and croissant breakfasts.

'I'm sorry—' Jules couldn't understand why Isabel was so blasé about what had happened. She crashed the sticky crockery into the dishwasher and heard a mug crack. Had she broken it? Did she care?

'No need to be sorry,' Isabel shrugged, 'just sort it out—'

'I wasn't apologising for being upset. I was saying that maybe we should *all* be upset. Our friends have just experienced something terrible, and you don't seem at all bothered—'

'Why should I be? They weren't really my friends...' Isabel was drifting into the salon.

'We've known them for years. How can you say that?' Jules followed her like she was on a leash. She couldn't let this go.

'Quite easily. In fact, I think I just said it.' Isabel pouted at her. 'Come on, Jules. Shit happens—'

'Is that it?' Jules turned to see that Pierre had walked in, spotted them and was backtracking. 'Pierre? Oy, *Pierre!*'

Pierre shuffled his way over to them as if his feet were on the wrong way. 'What?'

'Have you heard from them?'

'No. I haven't.' He looked away from her and scuffed his feet.

'Don't you feel sad about Elias and Mattias? They've just lost their dad in a terrible accident. Aren't you worried about them?'

Pierre blinked rapidly, stuffed his hands into his pockets and hunched over. 'Yeah. Sure. You have to remember that their dad crashed his car 'cause he was drunk. He brought it on himself. But what can we do about it?' He glanced at Isabel.

'There's nothing we can do,' she said, 'and especially as it's none of our business—'

'What?' Jules was having trouble understanding why they were acting this way. 'They're our friends. You just don't turn your back on friends.'

'Like Pierre said. Their dad got what was coming—'

'That's a rotten thing to say—'

'Well, he did.'

Squaring up to Pierre, Jules stared at him. 'You and Davey have been mates with them since you were little kids. We should be out looking for them—'

'Just stop it, will you?' He turned and stomped out, calling over his shoulder, 'Leave it to the adults to sort.'

'Yeah,' said Isabel, 'I don't know why you're so upset about this, unless,' her voice changed, 'there's something you're not telling us?'

Jules ground her teeth together but kept silent.

'Come on, Jules. Let's have some fun before you go, eh?'

'Fun?' Jules snorted in through her nose. 'I don't think so.'

'You can't say I didn't try.' Isabel sighed and slipped into the hall. 'I'm off shopping with Mum and Ailsa. You're welcome to join us, but only if you can manage to lighten up a bit. You really are bringing us down.'

'I think I'll pass.' Jules pushed past her and yanked on the front door. It squeaked as it swung open.

'Hey?' Her father trotted down the stairs. 'You all right, kiddo?'

'Not really, no.' Jules wiped at the hot tears on her cheeks. 'I'm worried sick about Elias and Mattias, and no one seems to give a damn about them—'

'Oy, no swearing. And people do care, sweetheart. The authorities are doing all they can to find the boys.'

Uncle Archie tailed his brother down the stairs. He didn't look happy. 'Not nearly enough, in my opinion. We need to find Mattias... I mean the boys, as fast as possible.'

Jules stopped. 'When's their dad's funeral? Aren't we staying for that? You know? Show our respect and all that?'

'No.' Her dad shook his head. 'We have our flights booked, and it's too much of a faff to change them. Anyway, I'm sure the family would prefer it to be a private affair.'

I'm family, Jules wanted to shout. *I'm their family!*

'Anyway,' said Uncle Archie, 'whatever mess they're all in, they got into it. Let them get out of it. One way or another.' He patted Jules' shoulder as he passed her. 'Don't ever get involved with any of these... people. They're not like us. They're not dependable.'

'Archie?' said her father. 'That's a bit harsh, isn't it?'

'They are gypsies, James. What do you expect?'

Jules was flabbergasted, 'That's an awful thing to say! There's something not right about any of this—'

'You need to listen, young lady.' Uncle Archie swivelled and took a step towards her. 'They are not our people. They never were and never will be. Put these boys out of your mind. They are nothing but thieving scum—'

'*Fuck you!*' Jules slammed the door behind her as hard as she could, then ran across the meadow to the river. This was where she had often met Elias. *Please be here today.* Her father's strident calls followed her, but she chose to ignore them. If she was going to be told off for swearing, she might as well make it the best possible reason. Her uncle Archie was a complete *arse*! Panting, a stitch cramping in her side, Jules sank down onto the cool grass. Where was Elias? Why hadn't he contacted her? It didn't matter what the others might think. She knew he wouldn't take the blame for what his father had done. And even that didn't make sense. His dad would never drink and drive. Never. She knew the story about Elias' grandfather. Had she fallen down the rabbit hole like Alice? Was her white rabbit going to pop out, looking at his watch? Tears streamed down her face.

They should wait for the funeral. Elias would come back for that, wouldn't he? And why was Mattias now missing? There was something off about the whole thing. In the space of a few days, Pierre had turned into a slouching, monosyllabic teenager, Ailsa was creeping her out by being nice to her (God forbid!), and Isabel was even more catty than usual. Uncle Archie was lumbering about the place with a face like thunder as if he'd trodden on a nail or something. The only normal people were her mum and dad and her lovely Tante Romi, who was busy in the kitchen cooking and baking. Maybe she should take up baking? Take her mind off it all? Davey appeared to be as nonplussed by it all as much as she was. When she'd asked him what he thought, he told her that whatever it was, they'd see Elias and Mattias next year. They'd be able to find out then. But next year was exactly that. A whole year away. She couldn't wait that long. And although Davey said it was weird that Elias and Mattias' dad had been drinking and driving, he seemed to accept it and then move on. Moving on wasn't an option for her until she'd found out the truth. Time felt suspended, as if she'd got caught and was now floating inside in a giant bubble, unable to do anything.

Elias still hadn't called her by the time they arrived back in England. The glorious French summer swiftly became a chilly, blustery English autumn. She heard that neither Elias nor Mattias had attended their father's funeral. What the hell was she to make of that? What kind of trouble were they in that they couldn't pay their last respects to their father? Mattias had promised to call her, but the call never came. When she phoned him, she was told this number was disconnected. He'd told her that, but she had to try.

One morning, they were sat in Ailsa's bedroom. Their sixteenth birthday was in a couple of days and just for a moment, it felt like they were sisters again. 'Ails? What do you think happened to them?' Jules tried on her new birthday top. It looked great on her, but it might as well be a binbag for all she cared.

'You need to forget about them,' said Ailsa. She never met Jules' eye when they spoke about Elias and Mattias. Maybe she did feel something for them, if only pity.

'I can't.' Jules tossed the new top onto her bed. 'I really can't.'

'You should. I heard Mum and Dad saying we probably won't be going next year—'

'What? We're not going back to France?'

'They said that things have changed—'

'Brexit? Is that what you're saying?'

'Probably. Listen, I don't know for sure, so don't quote me on it.'

'Bloody brilliant!' Jules held her head in her hands. So, unless she managed to get there under her own steam, she wouldn't even be able to catch up with them this next summer. Maybe she should let it all go if she was the only one invested in this relationship. She must be an idiot. Wiping the wetness from her face, she vowed these would be her last tears for Elias. Anger welled up. He should have contacted her by now. *Sod him!*

. . .

Celebrating her sixteenth birthday felt flat. All her hopes and dreams were melting away like early morning mist. Had any of it been real? It was like being on a seesaw. One moment she knew Elias loved her, had loved her and would always love her. The next, she believed he'd used her, that she meant nothing to him, and all his words of a life together had been honeyed lies. Time passed, but her heart didn't mend. How could she trust anything ever again?

Then, after her seventeenth birthday, Mattias finally contacted her, and her world fell to dust and ruin. He sent her a film.

TWENTY-SEVEN

Ailsa

BETRAYAL FROM ALL SIDES

JULES WAS GRINNING. 'Oh, they're contaminated, all right. But they weren't the only things we doused.'

Isabel spun towards the voice. 'What? What did you say?'

Ailsa also turned. Jules was grinning. Literally, grinning from ear to ear. 'I said the cigars are contaminated. And the funny thing is, Hetty was kind of right about the Tic-Tacs. It was one of the first things I thought of, except I found you can't inject them. Shame.'

'Thallium!' Hetty blurted.

'You're clever.' Jules clapped her hands together. 'Well done, Hetty, super-sleuth.'

'I don't understand...' Isabel's voice was a mewl as she took a step towards Jules. 'What are you saying?'

'She's saying,' said Hetty quietly, 'she either poisoned J.J. and Archie, or she knows who did. Is that about right, Jules?'

'Correct again. Davey told me you loved your thrillers, though I never guessed that you'd be this good—'

'What the fuck!' Ailsa couldn't understand what was being

said. 'This isn't a fucking book. What the hell are you talking about?'

Davey's face had coloured. He looked as if he might explode. 'Christ Almighty! Did you poison J.J. and Archie? Deliberately?'

'Hell, yeah.' Jules did a little curtsey and a flourish of her hand as if she'd just come off stage. 'As Hetty sussed, a little thallium goes a long way.'

'Why?' Isabel lunged towards Jules and tried to grab her. 'Why did you do this? You murdered my husband.' Isabel's face was a mask of hate and rage. 'You fucking bitch!'

Jules shrugged her off. 'Why did I kill your husband? Because you killed mine.'

'What the fuck are you talking about?' Davey's hands were clenched in front of him.

'Oh, my God!' Pierre crumpled onto the sofa and put his head in his hands. 'Elias.'

'What has Elias to do with all this?' said Davey.

'Everything,' said Jules. 'They didn't tell you, did they? What they did that day. What Isabel did. How they covered it all up. The lengths they went to sweep it all under the carpet.'

There was silence for a few moments. Ailsa could hear the big old clock on the mantelpiece tick-ticking. Was she underwater? Her head was being compressed with so much pressure, and she couldn't breathe. She knew! *Jules knew!*

2016 – Ailsa

Ailsa clambered over onto the steadier wooden floor of the hayloft. Not good with heights or rickety old ladders, she clung to the railing at the edge. Now they were here, standing in front of Elias, she took in the size of him. They were little girls compared to him. His muscles bulged under his tight-fitting T-shirt, and what looked like a new tattoo curled from under his sleeve down his arm. This was a man before them, not a boy. He might already be battered, but he was still a man.

'What would you like to talk about?' He didn't smile.

'I'm sure you know.' Isabel stood with her hands on her hips, legs apart. Was she advertising a position in the army, because it sure looked like it? Ailsa suppressed a giggle. It must be nerves. Isabel gave her an evil glance.

Isabel continued, 'We know about you and Jules—'

'Ah! It was you who sent the message? The urgent thing is me, isn't it? You don't approve of me.' Folding his arms across his chest, he cocked his head, staring at them through his swollen eye.

'You're right. We don't approve of you. She's just a kid—'

'But,' Elias shifted a step forward, 'what if I told you we are in love? That we plan to marry? What would you say then?'

Isabel made a spluttering noise and clapped her hands together. 'Bravo! Well played. I think you are in love with her wealth—'

His eyes narrowed. 'You can't believe someone like Juliette can love someone like me? And that I can love, and I mean really love, her back. You have to make it about money, and do you know why? Because you people are so obsessed with money, you can't see anything else. You are driven by it.' He spat on the hay-strewn floor by her feet.

'She's my sister.' Ailsa moved to Isabel's side. 'All I want is the best for her—'

'And how do you know I'm not what is best for her?'

'Because you're...' Ailsa sucked on her lips.

'A gypsy? A vagabond, thieving, lying, cheating gypsy?' He smiled at them, but it didn't reach his eyes. 'That's what you're thinking, isn't it?' Wagging his finger, he bent down so his face was inches from Ailsa's. 'You can't ever believe we don't care about money. We don't need all the stuff *you lot* can't live without. We can be happy—'

'What?' Isabel laughed. 'Living off air? Eating cold baked beans from the can because you can't afford anything else?'

'If that's what it takes, yes. She's agreed to marry me—'

'No way!' Ailsa covered her mouth with her hands. 'That's never, ever going to happen.'

'She's sixteen in a few months. We're going to get married, and there's nothing you can do. We knew your family would want to stop it. That you would be an obstacle, but do you know what? We don't care. I've loved Juliette since the first day I saw her. We knew from that moment we were meant to be together—'

'Shut up, *just shut up!*' Ailsa put her hands over her ears. She couldn't bear to hear this. 'It's all lies. She'd never agree to marry you without telling me first. She just wouldn't!'

'She didn't tell you because you're such a snob. She told me you'd never understand as you couldn't see past your ancestry and superior genes. She said you'd view me like you would look at a cockroach.' He held out his hands. 'And here we are.'

'That's not true, I—' Ailsa struggled to breathe.

'Deny it then. Go on. Why can't I marry your sister?'

'She's too young for a start,' interrupted Isabel. 'Have you had sex with her? Because she's underage, and we'll do you for rape!'

'Whatever we have done is nothing to do with you—'

'You've had sex with my *sister*?' Ailsa had never believed it was possible, but a red mist blurred her vision. So that was what was meant: a rage that threatened to overwhelm her. Her fists bunched, and she ran at him, feeling her jaw clenched to the point where she might crush her own teeth. He sidestepped her, and she tripped and sprawled onto a hay bale, cricking her ankle as she fell.

'Ouch! That hurt!'

'I'm sorry, Ailsa. I didn't mean for you to fall like that.' She could see him bending down, hand outstretched to help her up, concern in his dark brown velvet eyes.

Isabel screamed, '*Fuck you, you filthy gypo!*'

Turning, tears blinding her eyes, Ailsa saw Isabel shove Elias. Watching as she caught him off-balance, he twisted to right himself, flailing his arms, and just as he regained his balance, Isabel took a step forward. It was as if it was in slow motion. Ailsa saw the look on her cousin's face as her hand shot out, clipping Elias on his shoulder. His expression changed from anger to shock as he crashed heavily into the railing. The wood gave way with a terrible cracking sound, and he suddenly wasn't there.

Panting, Ailsa dragged herself upright. 'Where did he go?' Pain throbbed up her calf from her ankle.

Isabel stood like a statue, her mouth slightly open and eyes wide. She was staring down.

'Isabel? Is he okay?' Why was it so quiet? Why wasn't Elias yelling or screaming or pleading... anything?

Shaking her head slowly, Isabel pointed. 'I don't think so.'

Ailsa limped to the broken railing, aware of sharp shards of wood, careful not to grab hold of it. She didn't want to look down, but she had to. Elias was lying in one of the stables below them. His neck was at a peculiar angle. And his shoulder was sticking out where a shoulder should not stick out. Ailsa wondered how that felt. His eyes were open.

'Why isn't he moving?' Ailsa swallowed though there was no spit in her mouth, only old ash. 'He should be moving. I mean, that must hurt.'

'Oh God!' Isabel lunged sideways and threw up. 'What have we done?'

'We?' Ailsa shook her head. 'I didn't shove him over there—'

'I was protecting you. He was going to attack you.'

'Was he?' Ailsa's head hurt. 'I thought I was attacking him.'

'You can't say that. Not ever.' Grabbing hold of Ailsa's arm, she gripped her tightly, digging her fingers into the soft part. 'This was self-defence. Do you understand me, Ailsa? Self-defence.'

Pulling from her, Ailsa stumbled to the ladder, nearly slipping as she grasped the rungs with sweating hands, her ankle throbbing. Peering over the cross-pieces of the stable, she crept to where Elias lay.

'He still isn't moving. He must be knocked out. Izzy, we have to get him to the hospital. Izzy?'

Isabel slumped to her knees by her side. 'I don't think anyone can help him. I think he's dead.' Her voice was flat.

'What?' Ailsa couldn't believe what Izzy was saying. 'No, no, you're wrong. He can't be dead.'

'Oh, I think he can be. I think he's broken his neck. When he fell...'

Ailsa heard the words, though different ones superimposed themselves over the top. *When you pushed him...*

'We need to call somebody. Izzy!' Ailsa grabbed her cousin by the shoulders. 'Who do we call?'

'My father.' It was as if Isabel was coming out of a trance. 'Dad will help us.'

'Yes, yes, of course. Hang on, he's a judge...' Ailsa pushed back as far as she could go until she hit the wall. It juddered with the force. 'He'll put us in jail, won't he? For murder!'

Isabel scooted in front of her, her face a mask of rage. 'Stop saying stuff like that. We didn't murder him; we were defending ourselves against him. He was going to... rape us. Yes, we tell my father that. We found him in the barn, and when we challenged him, he tried to attack us.'

'But he didn't.' Sobbing, Ailsa clung to her cousin. 'He didn't do that.'

'There's nothing we can do for him, but Ailsa? Do you want to spend the rest of your life in a French prison as a murderer?'

'I didn't do anything,' Ailsa wailed. 'You did it. You were the one who pushed him.'

'Listen to me, Ailsa. Get it through your thick head. You either back me up, or I tell my father that you were the one who pushed him. Who do you think he'll believe?'

Ailsa felt like she'd been doused in freezing water. Her hair stood on end, and her fingertips were like ice cubes.

'So what will it be?' Isabel's beautiful brown eyes seemed to be glowing orange in the half-light in the barn.

'He was going to attack us. Yes, that's right.' Ailsa nodded her head until she thought it might fall off.

'I'm going to get Dad. He'll sort this out.'

As Isabel headed out of the barn door, Ailsa saw a shadow at a side window. It was a shadow, but it moved strangely. Had someone seen them? Scuttling over, she peered through the grime-stained window, aware of thick cobwebs and waiting, patient fat spiders. It was partly open, warped to the point where it no longer shut. Was anyone there listening to them? She jumped when she saw movement, but it was only branches from the trees outside moving fitfully in a soft breeze. That must be it, as there was no one there.

Keeping her eyes from Elias' still form, her breathing came in fits and starts. She was here, alone with a dead body. She'd cried for weeks when her pet dog had died a couple of years ago. Why wasn't she crying now? Shock? Oh, hell yeah. Which was worse? That he was dead, completely dead, or if he suddenly woke up? Or came back to life like one of the Walking Dead? Beginning to shake, she turned to face him. He was still staring at the vaulted ceiling above them, a slightly puzzled look on his face, his mouth slack. He'd told them he was going to marry Jules, implying they'd already had sex. But what if they hadn't, and he'd been lying just to piss them off? In fact, what exactly had he said? That whatever they'd done was nothing to do with her? He hadn't said he'd had sex with Jules, had he? *Oh God!* He was now dead, and between her and Izzy, they'd killed him.

Footsteps scurried in. Please don't let it be Jules.

'We're here,' said Uncle Archie. 'Good God!' He pushed into the stall and bent over Elias, touching his fingers to his throat and shaking his head. 'Isabel told me what happened.'

'What can we do?' Ailsa was still shaking. 'Are we going to prison?'

Standing, he turned to her. He looked stupefied. 'This can't get out. Our name will be ruined if we have a big scandal on our hands.' He groaned. 'I'm a fucking high court judge, for Christ's sake!'

'You have to help us, Dad.' Isabel reached out to him. 'You know we can't go to the police. It'd ruin all our lives.'

'Don't I know it? Probably more than you ever could.' He swivelled to stare at Ailsa. 'You tell me, quickly, what happened.'

Ailsa glanced at Isabel, whose face was set like granite.

'We...' Ailsa had a lump of something sticky in her throat. She couldn't swallow properly. 'We saw him, Elias, in here, up in the loft,' she jerked her head upwards as if Uncle Archie didn't know where the stupid loft was, 'and we followed him up there, you know, to ask him what he was doing.' She tried to swallow again but nearly gagged. 'He went mental at us and... and he attacked us. We had to fight back. He, well, he slipped, and sort of tipped backwards through the railing—'

Isabel butted in, 'It broke like a matchstick—'

'Are you saying this is my fault?' Uncle Archie's face was deepening in colour. 'That the wood was rotten? Is that what you're saying?' He glowered at Isabel.

'I'm just saying,' Isabel panted, her eyes wide, 'he crashed through it like it wasn't even there. That's all I'm saying.'

Ailsa understood at that moment that Isabel was blackmailing her father. She was saying it was his fault that this boy had died. He should have mended the railing years before this. It might even be his fault, thinking about it. He must have assumed the same.

Uncle Archie snorted in air through his nose and let it out in a loud breath. 'I need you both to grasp what I'm about to say. Are you listening?'

'Yes.'

'Yes.'

'I am going to get the car. One of you will keep watch over... Elias, and the other will stand at the barn door. No one must come in. Do you understand me?'

Ailsa and Isabel nodded.

'Okay. I'll be as quick as I can...' He crouched, got his hands under Elias' arms and started to haul him across the barn floor.

'Then what?' Isabel bent down to stare into his face. 'Then what will you do?'

He stopped and looked intently at her. 'I will,' he rubbed a shaking hand over his eyes, 'dispose of... the body.' He continued to drag Elias closer towards the barn door.

'*What?*' Ailsa held out her hands. 'You can't do that. He's not a bag of rubbish—'

'Isn't he?' Uncle Archie stood and towered over them. 'You said he tried to attack you, that you defended yourself. He's a trash nobody. One less gypo to worry about.'

'That's not right.' Ailsa felt hot tears rolling down her cheeks. 'What about his family?'

'If we go to the police, whose family will be held accountable? Is that what you want? That your own family be dragged through the courts, and your family name be sullied because of an accident? An accident that this boy brought on himself?' Uncle Archie clenched his fists. 'Well, is it, Ailsa?'

'No,' she whispered. 'I don't want that.'

'Good. Now we have to hurry.' Trotting to the barn door, he slowed and then ambled out. It must all look normal. Ailsa realised 'normal' was never going to be the same again.

'I'll keep check,' said Ailsa, running after Uncle Archie before Isabel could object. She couldn't bear to be anywhere near his body... oh God... his body. They'd known Elias since they were all little kids. Swum with him in the river, played mad footie with him and all the village kids in the big field, eaten messy barbeques with him and his brother every summer, smoked her first fag with him when she was thirteen, the same as Jules and Isabel. Jules. She must never find out about this, about her part in it. What was her part?

Leaning heavily against one of the stable walls, Ailsa went over in her mind what had happened. She kept returning to what he'd said, or rather, what he hadn't said. There was an insinuation, or was there? He might have been goading them, and she'd fallen for it. Wanted to kill him but not really, not actually kill him. She'd gone for him first, but all he'd done was get out of her way. Yes, she'd fallen and hurt herself, but he never pushed her over. She tripped over all by herself. He'd tried to help her up after she fell. Oh God! The look in his eyes. Then Isabel shouted something; it wasn't pleasant. She'd seen Isabel run at him, thrust him backwards, and he was gone. No, that wasn't right. Ailsa re-ran it in her mind. Isabel could have pushed him the other way, but the angle she barged into him meant the only direction he could go was against the railing. He'd got his balance, and then... and then? Isabel had shoved him again. Hang on... Isabel knew the railing was rotted at that point. They all knew you should never hold onto it or put weight on it, as it could easily give way. She knew that! So what did that mean? Had Isabel done this on purpose? Did she mean for him to fall? Did she mean to kill him? It was too much. Ailsa wanted to run to her own mum and dad, confess it all, grovel in front of Jules and say she was sorry... beg for forgiveness, and now they were going to toss out Elias as if he was nothing, no, less than nothing. This was when Ailsa knew her life had altered beyond recognition.

TWENTY-EIGHT

Hetty

LACED WITH A LITTLE SOMETHING...

IT WAS like something clicked into place. Hetty had written out the list of foods and drinks, but there were so many crossovers; either they were all going to get sick... she couldn't face the next bit... and die, or there was something they were missing.

Davey pointed out that Jules was contacting someone; was it to say 'goodbye?' Who would Hetty herself want to say goodbye to? The only person she truly loved was in this room, and he might soon be beside her in the hospital. Could she rush to him, haul him into her arms, hug him until she'd squeezed all the air out of his lungs and tell him how much she loved him? And she did. Why did it always take a traumatic event to put things into perspective? They had to find whatever it was. She had to live. Twenty-two was far too young to die. Scanning around the room, they all looked tense. Were they all contemplating their own mortality?

Even when she mentioned the Tic-Tacs, she could hear how stupid that sounded, but when Ailsa remembered about the cigars, it didn't sound so dumb. Something popped up in her mind. An Agatha Christie tale. A story of poisoning. Poisoning a cigar. She'd looked this specific poison up because it intrigued her. Some part of her had wondered whether, if she'd known about it before, she'd have tried to find some to give to her father. A few cups of tea and Bob's your uncle. Dead as a dodo. No more monster. Except this is what many had thought, to the extent that this particular poison, originally used as a rat poison, had been commandeered by would-be assassins and murderers as their poison of choice. The authorities were forced to make it illegal, not that it stopped the more audacious. Its effects differed radically, depending on the dosage. Some got numb legs or burning extremities, though most got stomach cramps, sickness and horrendous shits. Just what J.J. had experienced. There had been a big kerfuffle over some Chinese girl recently trying to bump off her mother with the stuff. Was this her over-active mind going into hyper-drive, because that would mean a family member was a murderer?

Then Isabel came home. Though not all of her. She must have left a chunk of her on that hospital bed. Hetty wiped away tears. It wasn't her place to cry. She didn't wish to make a scene, though she knew what death was. How it tore a great hole, the shape of the person you'd lost, inside you. That hole never diminished. You simply built around it and tried not to fall in.

But then Jules said, 'Oh, they're contaminated all right.' And she knew, Hetty knew she'd been correct all along.

'Thallium!' Odourless and tasteless. When was she going to wake up? This dream was getting too much. Wake up. Wake up!

She heard Davey say, 'What has Elias to do with all this?'

Then Jules' reply, 'Everything. They didn't tell you, did they? What they did that day. What Isabel did. How they covered it all up. The lengths they went to sweep it all under the carpet.'

And Hetty felt relief sweep through her. Not because she now knew she wouldn't die but because Davey didn't know about this. He wasn't part of this, because if he had been, how would that make her feel about him?

Looking up, she saw a man stride into the room. The epitome of a tall, dark, handsome stranger.

'Mattias?' Isabel fell backwards and crumpled into the sofa. 'What are you doing here?'

'He has every right to be here,' said Jules. Her voice was so calm as she reached up, cupped his cheek and gently pulled him down to place a kiss on his lips. 'It was his brother you murdered.'

'Who told you that?' Isabel held a shaking hand over her mouth, her face in a hideous rictus. 'They're lying. I didn't do anything—'

'Shut up, Izzy!' Ailsa slapped at her cousin. 'Don't say another word!'

'You don't need to.' The man called Mattias smiled so sweetly at the two women huddled on the sofa. 'I have it all on film. Everything you did.' His English accent was perfect.

Hetty saw a look pass over Ailsa's face. 'You were outside the window—'

'*What?*' screeched Isabel.

'I thought it was just a shadow, the trees moving in the wind, but it was you.'

'No. I was already in the barn in the stall next to you. I saw you go and check the window. I filmed all you did, up close and personal. How you killed my brother.'

'What are you talking about?' Davey looked close to tears, his face blotchy. 'Elias wasn't murdered! He went to the city after... he...' Davey wiped at his nose. 'He's not dead. Is he?'

'I need to tell you all a story,' said Mattias.

TWENTY-NINE

Mattias

FROM THE HORSES' MOUTH

2016 - Mattias

'Mattias?' Elias leaned around his bedroom door. 'I've just got a text from Juliette, but there's something off with it.'

'Told you! Didn't I tell you?' Mattias scrambled off the bed and poked his brother. 'I told you they were suspicious.'

'I know you did. It's not like I'm oblivious. I noticed, too.'

'Yeah, if they were trying to be careful, they were pretty rubbish. I mean, as if we wouldn't notice them following you both or popping up where you were. They nearly caught you at the river.'

'I know, and I'm sure they heard Juliette's phone ringing in the forest. They must have wondered then.'

'Look, she's nearly sixteen. We used to be able to marry by then. It was traditional.'

'Not anymore, bro.' Elias raised an eyebrow. 'But we could if we ran away.'

Mattias felt shocked. 'Are you? Are you going to run away?'

'No. We're going to do it properly and wait.'

'Okay. So, what did this text say then?'

'It says to meet Juliette this afternoon in the barn. It's on another phone, as she,' Elias twiddled his fingers in the air, 'said she'd dropped her phone—'

'And you're sure it's not from her?'

'I know my Juliette, and this isn't her.'

'Why don't you call Juliette's phone and tell her what's happening?'

'I want to see what they have to say for themselves.'

'They'll tell you to stop seeing her. That's what they'll say.'

'And I'll tell them to mind their own business—'

'They won't like that,' said Mattias. 'Especially Isabel. You know what her family are like. All crocodile smiles and sausages and then wham – we're in the slammer for a petty misdemeanour.' He sniffed loudly to show his contempt. 'Because we're Romani.'

'I'm not stupid. I understand how these people work.'

'Don't go.' Mattias grimaced at his brother. It was like a cold shower had drenched him. 'It doesn't feel right—'

'Oh, God! Not one of your Gypsy Rose premonitions?'

'Don't joke! I've been right before. I really don't think you should meet them.'

'Okay, if you're worried, you can come with me—'

'They won't like that—'

'I meant skulking in the bushes, just in case.'

'Oh. Right. And I'll film whatever I see.' He grinned at Elias. 'Just in case...'

'Do you think they're in there?' Mattias motioned at the barn as they both crept up. 'Ready to leap out on you?' Mattias sniggered until Elias gave him 'the look'.

'Keep out of sight but make sure you hear everything, and if you can, at least get an audible copy. These girls are like foxes.'

'I will, don't worry.'

Mattias watched as Elias entered the barn, calling Juliette's name. He scooted to the side window to listen, his phone in his hand, but there was no way he could get anything through this. It was so filthy and covered in cobwebs. He didn't relish poking his hand through either, as he judged a recording from this distance would be fuzzy at best or just garbled noises. He could hear voices now. His ribs still ached from when their pa had belted them. He understood why. Being caught red-handed nicking from a high court judge wasn't a good move. Their pa had always warned them of what the repercussions could be. He didn't paint a pretty picture.

Jogging back to the barn door, he hunkered down and squinted in. The girls climbed the ladder to the hayloft, so he scrambled to an animal pen. Moving to a position where he had a good line of sight, he pulled out his phone and started filming.

Nothing could prepare him for what happened. There was a scuffle with Ailsa, and she tripped.

'Ouch! That hurt!' That couldn't be good. Elias didn't need to have any of the girls injured.

Then he heard Isabel roar, '*Fuck you, you filthy gypo!*' And she shoved him. Mattias saw Elias teetering and whirling his arms to get his balance. He nearly shouted, but Elias righted himself. Mattias didn't have time to draw a breath before he saw Isabel whack Elias hard on the shoulder. He jerked and was thrown off balance again, but this time, he couldn't save himself. Elias smashed through the railing, and Mattias heard a heavy *thump* as his brother landed on the ground below the hayloft. He was still filming, his breath coming in stutters. It was silent for a few moments. Why wasn't Elias filling the barn with the choicest swear words? Had he been knocked out? What should he do? He made to move and heard Ailsa clambering down the ladder, followed by Isabel. What were they going to do? He carried on filming. Words came to him from the next stall. He heard Isabel say something and then, 'This was self-defence. Do you understand me, Ailsa? Self-defence.'

No, no, it wasn't. Mattias had seen the look on Isabel's face as she shoved Elias. Glee. The bitch knew what she was doing.

'He still isn't moving. He must be knocked out. Izzy, we have to get him to the hospital. Izzy?'

Mattias was about to shriek at them to call that fucking ambulance when he heard Isabel say, 'I don't think anyone can help him. I think he's dead.'

Mattias heard the words. 'I think he's dead.' No... *no!* That couldn't be true. Elias couldn't be dead. Yet the feeling of dread that had enveloped him that morning when Elias told him of this meeting came back. Elias might joke about it, but he knew when bad things were about to happen.

'What? No, no, you're wrong. He can't be dead.'

'Oh, I think he can be. I think he's broken his neck. When he fell...'

Oh God! Oh God! Oh God! Mattias' legs failed him, turned to rubber. He clung to the railing, white-knuckled. But still, he listened and recorded.

'We have to call somebody. Izzy! Who do we call?'

'My father. Dad will help us.'

It was like a burning flash of light that seared his mind. Isabel's father. The judge. Yes, he'd help, wouldn't he? He'd help them. There would be no help for Elias. Oh, my brother,

Mattias wiped the tears from his face and stared at the phone. I will get you justice.

Mattias ducked back low as Ailsa scurried to peer out of the window he'd been looking through earlier. It was only the wind in the trees, but he saw the fear on her face. Yes, let them feel fear. Something ice cold and sharp clamped itself around his heart.

Footsteps could be heard entering the barn. Mattias kept low and hidden, not wanting to risk being spotted.

'We're here,' said Archie MacGregor. 'Good God! Isabel told me what happened.'

Mattias burned with a cold fury. The lies they were spinning about Elias. And how they were frightened for themselves, with no thought of what evil they had done. Mattias glanced about him. There was a discarded pitchfork in the corner, leaning against the wall. Could he grab it? Run out to them, screaming, and spear them through their black hearts? And how would that help Elias? He'd probably end up lying next to his brother. Wiping the snot from his face, Mattias carried on filming, his hand shaking.

MacGregor was talking again. 'I am going to get the car. One of you will keep watch over... Elias and the other will stand at the barn door. No one must come in. Do you understand me?'

'Okay. I'll be as quick as I can...'

Mattias listened. Oh God! MacGregor must be dragging Elias across the floor like a fucking sack of potatoes!

'Then what?' Isabel was insistent. 'Then what will you do?'

'I will dispose of... the body.'

Dispose of the body? That was his brother. Again, Mattias longed to erupt from where he was hiding, rip MacGregor's face off, kick him until he screamed, and mash his face into the floor until he had no face left. But he remained still. If he did anything now, the full weight of the law would be against him. He understood that as he understood what would happen to him, a gypsy boy from the roughest family accusing a high court judge.

'*What?*' Ailsa sounded distraught. At least she had some decency left in her. 'You can't do that. He's not a bag of rubbish—'

'Isn't he?' MacGregor was close, his voice a snarl. Mattias had to unclench his fists. His nails had cut half-moons into his palms, which now trickled blood. 'You said,' continued MacGregor, 'he tried to attack you, that you defended yourself. He's a trash nobody. One less gypo to worry about.'

'That's not right.' Was Ailsa sobbing? 'What about his family?'

'If we go to the police, whose family will be held accountable? Is that what you want? That your own family be dragged through the courts, your family name be sullied because of an accident? An accident that this boy brought on himself? Well, is it, Ailsa?'

'No,' she whispered. 'I don't want that.'

'Good. Now we have to hurry.' MacGregor walked out of the barn. Mattias had to drag in a breath, then the next, blood pounding in his temples, white lights at the edge of his vision. He mustn't pass out now. He must follow this through to the end, and then he would bring a world of pain to their door. The MacGregors would pay dearly for this.

'I'll keep watch,' said Ailsa. Through slats, Mattias could see her clinging to the wall of the next pen.

. . .

A car crunched up the gravel drive and stopped close to the main entrance.

'Quickly now, girls,' said MacGregor, 'I need your help. The boot is open, but I can't do this by myself.'

Do this? *Do this?* Bundle his brother into the boot of his car? Mattias continued to film through a crack. Peering at the image on his phone, it was just enough to show what was happening outside.

'You both need to take his legs—'

Mattias heard Ailsa wail. 'I can't do this. It's not fair—'

'Shut up and do it,' hissed Isabel. 'We have to do it now, or we'll get caught—'

Another voice joined in. 'Get caught doing what? *Oh shit!*'

'Pierre?' MacGregor slapped at his head. 'Fuck!'

'Is that Elias?' Pierre's hands flew to his mouth. 'What the hell is going on?' He bent down. 'Oh, my God! *Is he dead?*'

'Listen,' said MacGregor, holding his hand out, 'I don't have time to explain this, but you need to help us get... Elias into the boot of the car—'

'I have to do what?' Pierre stepped backwards so fast he tripped and sprawled. 'No way. I'm not doing that.'

'We have to get rid of... the evidence.'

'Evidence?' Pierre's voice was rising. 'That's Elias—'

'Was Elias,' said Isabel. 'Where's Davey?'

'Up in his room watching YouTube vids.'

'Listen, Pierre,' said MacGregor. 'He attacked your sister and Ailsa. They defended themselves. It was an accident, a terrible accident, but surely you can see this would ruin the family? Our family? We can't do anything for him now—'

'You can...' Pierre's hands were shaking as he pointed. 'You can go to the police and tell them what happened.'

'No, son. We can't. This is the only way.'

'No, no. We can't do this. I mean, what are you going to do? Bury his body in the forest or something?' It must have dawned on Pierre that this was precisely what his father was going to do. 'Oh, God! Dad, no. Please, no!'

Mattias rammed his hand into his mouth and bit down. He had to stifle the sobs threatening to erupt. They had made up their story about Elias, and now he could see they were beginning to believe their own lies. Planting the seeds: he had brought this on himself; he was going to try and rape these two girls; he deserved to die. They had only defended themselves, after all. That would be the tale they would tell. They would make Elias' name mud and make people think Elias was a monster.

'Help me, Pierre, or at least help this family.'

'This is so wrong.' Pierre stumbled back towards Elias' body and heaved at a leg. Ailsa took the other one, and MacGregor got his hands under Elias' armpits. Together they manhandled Elias out of the barn. Isabel stood and watched.

Mattias heard the awful sound as his brother's body *thunked* into the boot.

'Get back in the house. Do you understand me?' MacGregor's voice wavered slightly. 'I need you all composed by the time James and Jules return. And don't say anything to Davey or the others.' There was silence for a moment. MacGregor's voice cracked. 'Do you all *fucking* understand me?'

'Yes,' they mumbled.

Mattias saw their shadows receding as MacGregor revved the car's engine. He crept forward, aware of every sound, ready to duck back in. Hunkering low, he peered out. Pierre, Ailsa and Isabel were walking to the house, casting apprehensive looks over their shoulders as they followed the car's route.

Mattias filmed the car speeding away. It was heading down towards the deep forest tracks. He slumped against the barn door, no longer able to hold it in. Clamping his hand over his mouth, he let the tears flow and allowed the great sobs that clawed up his throat to be free. That *bitch* Isabel had killed his brother. He knew she'd pushed him on purpose that second time. She meant to kill him. It was then he thought of Juliette.

THIRTY

Ailsa

CHECKMATE

'You were in the barn?' Ailsa couldn't swallow, and it felt like some spit had caught in her throat. 'You filmed it all?'

'I did.' Mattias sat on the arm of the sofa. 'We know you were browbeaten into going along with it, and you didn't, really, have a choice.' He turned to Isabel. 'It's this *bitch* I have a beef with. And what sweet revenge it is.'

'What's that supposed to mean?' Isabel rose out of the sofa, but Jules wagged her finger. 'Nah-ah! You're not going to bully your way out of this.'

'Oh, God! Jules?' Ailsa put her head in her hands. 'Did you see the film?'

'Yes. Mattias showed me the film. I...' Jules looked down and folded her hands in her lap. 'I've struggled for years. I hated you, Ailsa, because you went along with it. Because you changed your story, though I know how – oh how can I put this? – persuasive Isabel can be.'

'You're mad,' said Isabel, her voice shaking, 'if you think you can get away with this. You've murdered my husband and attempted to murder my dad. You're both going to go to prison for a very long time—'

'Well, dear cousin,' it was like there was a purr in Jules' voice, 'we can chat through the bars, can't we? I mean, if we go down,' she indicated herself and Mattias, 'then you'll be going down too.'

And me! Ailsa couldn't face it. She might have been a minor, but she was sure she'd go to prison too, for perverting the course of justice, accessory to a heinous crime. After all these years, she'd believed they'd got away with it. She'd had to fight her demons, burn the images from her mind, and try to convince herself it had happened the way Isabel had said. Turn into as much of a bitch as Isabel. Now their 'house of cards' was crashing down.

'All these years,' Pierre looked from Ailsa to Isabel, 'you lied to me and have been lying ever since. You told me he'd tried to attack you. You made it sound like he deserved it.'

'Oh, he did.' Isabel's mouth was razor thin.

'Fuck you,' said Mattias. 'I wanted to throttle you with my bare hands.' He made the motion of wrapping his hands around her throat. The look on his face was terrifying. A calm sort of madness. 'The only reason you're still breathing is that Juliette wants you alive.'

'Um?' Hetty raised her hand tentatively. 'Shouldn't we alert the hospital about, you know, the thallium poisoning? There is an easy antidote if they can get hold of it.'

'There's an antidote?' Pierre grabbed for his phone. 'We have to tell the hospital—'

'Hold your horses,' said Jules. 'And what will you tell them? If you incriminate us, we'll incriminate you, too.'

Pierre looked as if he might explode. 'But we have to let them know. Dad's life is on the line!'

'He has a little longer,' said Jules. 'Well, maybe. It depends on how much of that expensive cognac he swilled, doesn't it? I gathered that J.J. really liked to knock it back. That rather gorgeous bottle of Martell Cohiba Estuche. How bloody pretentious. Costs nearly five hundred euros, you know! One stupid bottle.'

'It was in the cognac?' Hetty looked puzzled. 'Not in the cigars?'

'Oh no. It was in the cigars as well. But having read up on it, we weren't sure if the poison would remain in the ash, as the temperature of a burning cigar might not be hot enough to carry it through the smoke. We had to hedge our bets.'

It was as if Davey had finally surfaced. He faced Isabel. 'You killed Elias?' His voice rasped. 'You decided he wasn't one of us, and you had to eliminate him? Is that what happened? Because I'll tell you, Elias was the best of us. And you, Pierre?' Davey rounded on him. 'How could you ever believe Elias would try to do anything like that? Rape Ailsa and Isabel? Seriously? You knew he was the biggest hearted of us all. You knew what he did to save us each time we did some stupid things, how he always took the fall for us!' He was beginning to shout. 'We were told he'd left, gone to the city as he couldn't bear his dad beating him anymore. That after his dad died, he couldn't face coming back here. Because he felt responsible... I don't understand. We were told he was doing all right in the city—'

'Davey,' said Mattias quietly, 'you accepted that, didn't you? Though did you ever ask where he'd gone? Did you ever think of finding his phone number to call him? Or his address, so you could meet up for a chat to talk about the good old days? Eight years is a long time, my friend.'

Davey closed his eyes and wiped at his nose. 'No. I didn't.'

'No. You didn't.' Mattias shook his head. 'It was so easy,

wasn't it? Just to let him go. We were only diversions for you when you came out here. Not real friends.'

'I'm sorry, Mattias. I did love Elias, but I suppose I just let it all slip away once I got back to England.'

Jules stood up. 'I loved Elias with all my heart and soul. I'd always loved him, and he loved me. You stole that from me, Isabel, because you thought he wasn't worthy of a MacGregor. You weighed him up and found him wanting. You couldn't bear the thought of having *gypsy* scum sully the bloodline, could you?'

'No. I was looking out for you. You should be thanking me—'

'Thanking you? You're one whacko, Isabel!'

Davey rose from his seat. 'And you, Jules. Dearest God, you poisoned J.J.? You killed him to get back at Isabel?'

'Ain't that the truth!'

'Is this funny to you? You've murdered a man you didn't even know—'

'Oh, I think we knew him. He was a right-wing nut job who went out of his way to make life unbearably hard for the Romani people and the other so-called undesirables. Proposing this law and that law that cut every freedom left in their society. Whereas Isabel murdered a man she didn't know.' Jules cocked her head and stared at Davey. 'You knew him, though, didn't you, Davey? You knew what kind of man he was.' She laid her hand gently on his shoulder. 'What did you say about him? He was the best of us. And he was. Isabel stole him from me, from Mattias and his dad. At least she'll have somewhere to go, something to cry over. Where is Elias? Buried abandoned and in an unknown place deep in the forest. Archie did that, and that's why we chose to lace his posh cognac. We knew he'd have a drink with J.J. Elias is alone somewhere out there. Do you have any idea how that makes us feel? Do you know what we've been doing for the last five years? I've been coming out here to visit Mattias, and we've been searching for Elias. We've gone up and down every track for miles. We want to bring him home. Give him a proper burial with his friends and family there to grieve him.'

'I'm so sorry.' Davey slumped back into his chair. 'I can't wrap my head around any of this.' He swivelled to Ailsa. 'I know you felt like you couldn't go up against Isabel and Archie, but I wish to God you'd told me. It's awful, finding out like this.'

Ailsa had known that this time might come. When she had to confess her sin to her brother, but it didn't make it easier. She'd rehearsed this so many times, but the words got tangled, and she couldn't remember what she'd practised for so long.

Finally, she said, 'I thought I'd lose you, Davey. I thought you'd hate me, and I couldn't bear that.'

'I can't hate you.' Davey pulled her into a tight hug. 'I can never hate you. You were a kid, and you were manipulated—'

'Manipulated, is it?' Isabel visibly twitched. 'I'd say I saved this family from ruin. None of you would be where you are today if Jules had married Elias.'

'It wasn't your decision.' The rage in Jules' voice was palpable. 'And look where your decision has got us, eh?' She laughed. 'Your decision got your hubby in the morgue—'

'Christ! Jules!' Pierre stumbled into the kitchen. 'Just stop it, please.' There was a banging and clanking as he rummaged for something. He returned, clutching a half-empty bottle of wine. Ailsa had a momentary image of the wine they'd nicked the night of the barbeque all those years ago. Tears prickled in her eyes. That night when they were still kids.

2016 - Ailsa

Ailsa found herself stumbling after Isabel and Pierre like she was drunk again. She wished she was.

'Wait for me.'

Isabel turned, and her face was white and pinched. Grabbing hold of Pierre's elbow, she propelled him back to where Ailsa was now swaying. 'Now you listen to me. I need you to remember what will happen to us, *to our family*, if anyone finds out about this.'

'I still don't understand,' said Pierre. 'It was an accident, wasn't it? And you said he'd tried to... attack you?'

'Yes. He did, didn't he, Ails?'

Ailsa could only scrunch her eyes shut and hope that was enough to persuade Pierre. She couldn't risk her voice in case the truth popped out. Because she clearly remembered that Elias hadn't tried anything with them, and she clearly remembered that Isabel had given him an extra shove just as he regained his balance. On purpose. What had she screamed at him? Something about him being '*a filthy gypo*'? And now he was dead.

Pierre's leg was jiggling. 'What do we tell the others?'

'Nothing. You heard Dad. We get ourselves cleaned up, and we keep our mouths shut. Dad will sort it.'

'What about Jules? You know she's always liked Elias—'

'Like I just said,' hissed Isabel, her eyes narrowed to slits, 'you say nothing.'

'And Davey?' Pierre looked as if he was being buffeted by high winds. His skinny body was shaking and shuddering, his thin arms wrapped around himself. 'He's really good friends with Elias. He'll wonder what is going on, too.'

'Nothing.' Isabel turned and stamped back to the house.

'Come on. Jules and your dad will be back soon. We must get past our mums and get upstairs without them seeing us.'

Ailsa and Pierre trotted to catch up with her.

Pierre looked down at her. 'Was that what really happened, Ails?'

Ailsa couldn't look him in the eye. 'It was just as Izzy said.'

They managed to open the front door with no squeaks to alert Aunt Romi or her mum and creep up the stairs to their rooms. Ailsa rushed into the bedroom and shut the door, wedging a chair against it. No locks were allowed, so this was the only way she could ensure privacy. She didn't need any more lectures from Izzy. She craved space and some time to process, think through her options and plan what she might have to say to Jules. No, she didn't need to say anything to her, as she wasn't meant to know anything in the first place. What a truly ghastly mess. What would have happened if she'd contradicted Izzy? Told Uncle Archie exactly what she'd seen? Would she and Izzy be in a cell in the local police station, hand-cuffed to the bars? She could barely think about it. It was for the best, then. Jules would wonder where he was... not to mention his family... poor little Mattias. This would hit him hard, as he adored his big brother. Ailsa felt the tears well up. But she reasoned that Isabel and Uncle Archie must know best.

Two days later, Jules was acting very strangely, but Ailsa reckoned that none of them were acting normally. She must have phoned Elias and not received an answer. Mattias must be next, but what did he know? That Elias never came home that night. Or the next. Strange though not unheard of. She wondered what he'd told Jules, because they must be worried.

'Act normal!' Isabel was back to hissing again, and Ailsa wanted to thump her one.

'I'm trying,' she hissed back. They were halfway up the stairs, one peering up towards the bedrooms, the other leaning over the bannisters to scan the entranceway below.

'Find out what she's been told.'

'You find out.'

'You're her bloody twin sister. Ask her.'

'What has your dad said?'

'He's acting all weird too. He got a phone call yesterday, and you should have seen his face—'

'Like he'd seen a ghost?' Ailsa raised an eyebrow and glared at her cousin.

'Sort of. He looked frightened, and then he looked angry.'

'So you ask him what's going on. I'd really like to know if I'm going to a French prison for a long time.'

'Don't be ridiculous. You're acting like a child—'

'Probably because I am still a child?'

'That's not what you told me last week.'

'Last week, I hadn't been a witness to a murder—'

'Murder? What? *What the hell are you saying?*'

'I saw what you did, Izzy. You pushed him on purpose—'

'I didn't. He was going to attack us. I tried to defend myself. I don't need you saying stuff like that, Ailsa. You watch that mouth of yours.'

'Or what?'

'Like I told you. I'll say you pushed him. And you know they'll always believe me over you.'

'I hate you. You can be such a *bitch*.'

'Takes one to know one.'

'Do you feel any remorse for what you did?'

'Remorse?' The sneer on her face was ugly. 'For a boy like

Elias? Not ever. Like Dad said, "he's a trash nobody. One less gypo to worry about." And he's right.'

If she had to act normally, she should pretend to find out what was bothering Jules. Even if she already knew. Collaring Jules in her bedroom, she asked, 'What's up, Jules?' She smiled, but it physically hurt. 'You seem a bit off.'

'Everything's fine.' Jules went back to reading her Kindle.

'No. It's not. I can read you, well, like a Kindle.' She motioned at it.

'Ha, ha!' Jules looked up at her. 'Funny. I... well, I've just had some news I wasn't expecting. That's all.'

'Bad news? Is it something to do with school?' Ailsa prayed Jules wouldn't tell her anything. She didn't know if she could maintain the façade or if she'd break down and howl the truth to her.

'No. Nothing like that. It's personal, and by that, I mean I don't want you doing your best to try and get it out of me. It's to do with me and not you. Do you understand what I'm saying, Ailsa, as sometimes I think you regard me as your pet project?'

'I'm sorry.' Could Jules see the relief spreading through her? Did it show on her face? But then Jules would interpret it to mean she, Ailsa, was glad she didn't have to get involved, you know, being the ultimate selfish sister that she was.

She mumbled, 'I don't mean to do that. I only want to say I'm here if you need me.'

'Okay,' Jules smiled hesitantly, 'thanks, and I appreciate it. Look, we're back off to England in a few days. I'm kinda looking forward to being home.' Something passed over her face. It was fleeting, but Ailsa saw such sadness she could hear her own heart cracking. She'd done this to her sister. She longed to tell her the truth, but that would break everything between them.

'Me too. Not sure if I can stomach any more of Tante Romi's cabbage soup—'

'Without any cabbage in it!' They both giggled.

Oh God! It was going to be okay. Jules couldn't be that upset about the fact Elias seemed to have disappeared. And that realisation made her go cold. If there hadn't been that much between them, then his death was about as senseless as you could get.

When she heard Izzy's little throaty chuckle, which before had seemed so inviting, she walked quickly in the opposite direction to avoid her. These last few days were going to be long ones. Pierre took himself off into the woods for hours on end. Ailsa got it. He needed time to process what he'd been told and what he'd seen. No one should ever have to bundle the body of a friend into the boot of a car. Especially a kid, seeing the dead body of another kid, a boy he knew and liked, thrown away like a black bin bag of trash. Every night, before she went to sleep, even when she closed her eyes, she could see Elias' eyes open but unseeing. There were moments when she woke with a start and saw a figure standing in the corner of the room. But it was only the curtains. Where was he? Slowly, oh so slowly, she began to ask herself what his family must be thinking. They would have no body to bury, no grave to visit, and no reason to grieve because they didn't know he was dead. Maybe in time, they'd work out he would never be coming home, yet still, they wouldn't know for sure. How would that feel? She tried to project those feelings as if it was about Davey, and then she found herself sobbing her guts out on her bed, stuffing the duvet into her mouth to stop the screams trying to escape from inside, crawling up her throat, prising open her mouth.

'I'm so sorry,' she wailed over and over again. *'I'm so sorry!'*

. . .

'What's up with your dad?' Ailsa tagged Isabel into the secret garden. It was where they met to catch up, secure and hidden. Secret being the operative word here. 'He's acting like a bear with a sore head.'

'I think it has something to do with that phone call. He's been really off since then.'

'Haven't you asked him?'

'I tried, but he said he didn't want to hear anything more about it. You know, the "thing".' Isabel waggled her eyebrows and grinned at her.

Ailsa wanted to slap her. 'That "thing",' she did the obligatory bunny ears, 'was a person, a person we knew and liked. I've been thinking about this. Have you thought how you'd feel if Pierre suddenly disappeared – poof – and you had no idea what had happened to him?'

Isabel shifted on the stone bench as if she was uncomfortable. 'No. Because that would never happen.'

'How do you know?'

'He'd never be dumb enough to get himself into a situation he couldn't get out of.'

'I don't think Elias ever thought there was any situation he couldn't get out of. Until he met you.' Ouch. Ailsa could see that hit home.

'I'm not going through this again, Ails. What happened, happened. End of. Now we have to move on, get over it.' She smiled slyly at Ailsa. 'Jules doesn't seem that bothered, does she?'

'Maybe. Maybe not. She doesn't talk to me much these days.'

'Well, water under the bridge and all that.'

'Do you dream?'

'Do I what? Why?'

'I do. I dream of him. I see his face every night before I go to sleep. That's if I can sleep.'

'Boo-hoo. Poor little sensitive Ails. No, I sleep like a baby. No problems there.'

THIRTY-ONE

Ailsa

SECRETS

'Maybe,' said Mattias, 'this is the point where we tell you something. We're married. We have been married for three years, so sorry, but I think your bloodline, Isabel, is well and truly sullied!' He waved his arms. '*Surprise!*'

'Married?' Ailsa stirred. 'You're married?' She wiped at her eyes. 'Oh, I wish you could have told me. I wish I could have been there.'

Jules made a derisive sound. 'I didn't, all things considered, think you'd want to come.'

Davey began to laugh, but it sounded more hysterical than happy. 'Holy Mary, Mother of God! That's the cherry on top, that is. Well, I suppose congratulations are in order.' His shoulders heaved as he stifled a sob. 'A week ago, I believed we were slightly dysfunctional, but I thought, hey, most families aren't perfect. Now, I seem to have woken up to find my family are not who I thought they were. That two of them have happily killed people. My family are a bunch of murderers. Brilliant! Where's Elias, then?' Davey ran his fingers through his hair, although he looked like he'd rather rip it all out. 'Where did Archie bury him? We need to find him.'

'What we need to do is we need to call the hospital and the police.' Pierre looked distraught. 'We can sort out all the other bits later, but we need to save my dad!'

'It's called Prussian Blue.' Hetty said. 'The antidote. Just thought I'd put that out there...'

'What the fuck is the matter with you all?' Pierre was shrieking now. *'My father is dying, and we have to get him the fucking antidote!'*

'Your father is dying,' said Mattias, and the calmness in his voice was more frightening than if he'd roared, 'whereas my father is dead.'

'We know that,' said Davey. 'We were all very sorry to hear about it. About the accident—'

'Ah, yes,' said Mattias. 'The famous accident. Where you all "knew" my pa went mad at us after the barbeque. You remember how he beat us, eh, Davey?'

Davey swallowed loudly and nodded.

'And then it came out that Elias and Pa had a massive row. That Elias had stormed off, saying he wouldn't stand for it anymore. He left for the city, and it didn't seem to matter to anyone which city.' Mattias looked down. His fists were clenched and white-knuckled. 'The police told everyone my pa got so drunk, somewhere up in the mountains, again, it didn't really matter in which bar; that was never disclosed, was it? Just that he was drunk, driving down the mountain recklessly, speeding and dangerous, and he went over the edge into the ravine. The consensus was he could have caused an accident, the stupid, ignorant man.'

Ailsa could see his jaw grinding.

'Oh, I think,' said Jules, 'you need to hear the next part of the story.' She glanced up at Mattias.

'We knew better, except who would listen to us? The police? No. They were the ones who killed him. To protect this *putain* family.'

THIRTY-TWO

Mattias

THE WITNESS

2016 - Mattias' story

IT TOOK A WHILE, though, at some point, Mattias found himself back home in his bedroom. He'd tried to follow the route the car took for as long as he could. But he knew the direction, and there were only a few tracks from where he lost sight of the vehicle. He put his phone onto charge and curled up on his bed, the duvet pulled over his head, and he cried until he thought he had no more moisture left inside him. Until he must be a husk, dried out, empty.

What should he do? He couldn't go to the police, as he knew they would 'lose' the evidence or accuse Elias and Mattias of doing something they shouldn't have. It was so easy to pin stuff on people like them. It had happened for years, and it wouldn't change now.

Clambering from the embrace of his duvet, he wiped the snot and tears from his face. Powering up the laptop, he plugged in the phone and downloaded the film. Then he sent another copy to himself via email. He'd watched far too many cop shows to risk only having this one copy. As yet, he didn't know how he could use it, but should he find a way, he needed to know he had access to it. He wanted to talk to his ma, but she'd been dead for five years. He missed her so much, the quiet voice of reason, most often the only one of them who could calm their pa. She'd have known what to do about this. Making a decision, he headed out to the churchyard. Her gravestone was scrubbed, and the area around was weedless. Fairly fresh flowers were in a jar.

'Ma? Oh God, Ma!' He hunched over the headstone, encircling it with his arms, feeling its chill touching his sweaty face. 'He's gone, Ma. They took him, and I don't know where.' He sniffed loudly. 'What do I do? Please tell me what to do.' He breathed what he'd witnessed. Hot words against the cold stone.

'Please help me, Ma.'

Much as he wished for it, there was no voice on the wind, no whisper in his ear, no sound at all. He had to work this out for himself. Stumbling home, he thought of Juliette. What would he say to her? He couldn't tell her the truth. That would break her more. Sucking on his bottom lip, he pushed into his living room to be confronted by his father.

'What have you two devils been up to now?' His father stared hard at him. 'Come on now, boy. I can see it written all over your face.'

Decision made. 'Elias is dead. The MacGregors killed him. I filmed it all.'

'What? *What did you say?*' The look of shock on his father's face made him step back.

'Here, I'll show you. You're the adult. You tell me what to do. What I could have done.' Mattias started the clip, watching his father. He might have been a hard man, a brutish man, but Mattias knew he'd always loved Elias. His ways were meant to make his boys into men, albeit men like him. Tough love, he'd called it. Mattias saw his face change, the horror and then anger bloom across it.

'Should I have confronted them, Pa? Should I?'

His father was snorting in air through his nostrils like a frightened horse. 'No, son. You did the right thing...'

'What are we going to do?'

'Not go to the police, that's for sure. They would protect these bastards no matter what was thrown at them. They look after their own.'

'I thought they would. So what else?'

'Much as I would love to slip into that big old house of theirs and slit that little bitch's throat and then beat old Archie MacGregor's head in, this is not an option.'

'Why not? Sounds good to me.'

'Of course it does, but you have never taken a life—'

'I wrung that old rooster's neck—'

'Because he was injured, and anyway, that old bird tasted good, didn't he? We made use of his death and thanked the Lord for his sacrifice. It wasn't a senseless death...' He knuckled at his eyes, the closest Mattias had seen him cry since his ma died. 'Not only did that girl kill him, she told a pack of lies to the rest of them. She dragged our boy through the filth and mud.'

'Then we have to do something, Pa!'

'I know we do, son. First, we must pretend we know nothing about this and give ourselves time to grieve. If we do something in anger, it won't end well for us. They think we're stupid, but we'll show them. Yes, we'll show them.'

Mattias clenched his fists. 'What do I tell Juliette? She'll ring his phone when she doesn't hear from him, and then she'll ring me when she doesn't get an answer.

'You...' His pa paused and rubbed at his chin. 'You tell her you saw him this morning but haven't heard from him since then. You say that maybe I called him away to do something. Make up some shit about us off doing a dodgy deal somewhere. Keep it vague.' His pa turned, cupped his face and peered into his eyes. 'Can you do that, Mattias?'

Mattias didn't trust his voice, so he nodded.

'Good boy.'

'Now, is this the only copy you have?'

Mattias thought quickly. 'Yes, Pa. I only got back a bit ago. I went to tell Ma—'

'She'd have known what to do.' His pa sighed loudly. 'I'm glad she's not here to see this. It would've broken her heart in two.'

'It'll break Juliette's heart. She'll think he's abandoned her.'

'We'll let her know in time, but not now.' He kind of shuffled. 'I need you to give me your phone now, boy. It's for the best if I look after it. Put it somewhere safe, like.'

Mattias made a great show of handing the phone over slowly, reluctantly, although he knew he still had copies. Just in case.

The following day, his father walked into the kitchen where Mattias was boiling water for noodles. It was all he could stomach. His dad looked strange.

'Listen, son,' he said. 'I'm not sure if I've done a stupid thing or not.' He chewed a thumbnail, his eyes unfocused.

'What did you do?' Mattias waited. 'Pa?'

'I called Archie MacGregor and told him there was a witness, and what they'd all done to my son had been filmed—'

'You did what?' Mattias flung his hands into the air. 'Jesus Christ, Pa! You said we had to have time to calm down, so we didn't do anything stupid—'

'I know. I know. But...' He also raised his hands into the air and shrugged. 'I couldn't stop myself.'

'Did you say it was me?' Mattias was breathing hard. This wasn't good.

'Of course not. I told him I'd followed Elias and caught the whole thing.'

'And he believed you?' Mattias knew his father was crafty, everyone did, but he was not top of the list to ask for tech support. He was an old-fashioned dial phone sort of guy. Surely MacGregor would know it was him and not his pa who'd filmed it?

'He had no choice but to believe me.'

'Why did you do that? You've given our hand away.'

'I told him what really happened. I told him his daughter murdered my son—'

'*Holy shit!*' Mattias shook his head. 'Why? What good can that do?'

'I asked him for money—'

'Blackmailed him?' Mattias span around, his hands tangled in his hair. 'You've tried to blackmail a high court judge? Are you out of your fucking mind?'

'Oy, don't you swear at me, boy!'

'Really? Personally, I think this is the best time to swear.' Mattias wiped his nose. 'He'll come for you. He'll get one of his cronies in the police force to kill you. They'll make it look like an accident.'

'I told him, if anything happened to me, the film would be shown all over the internet. I told him it was my insurance.' His dad cocked his head and stared at him. 'Is that stupid enough for you?'

Mattias looked at the floor, at his dusty shoes. The laces on one shoe were trailing. He should be careful he didn't trip...

'And have you? Have you got it somewhere they can't find it? And please don't say it's in your sock drawer.'

His dad looked sheepish. 'I'm just stashing it there while I think of where it should go.'

'What did you ask for?'

'What do you think? Money, of course.'

'I meant how much?'

'One million euros.'

'Oh, you've got to be kidding me! Like he's got that lying around under the bed!'

'He gave me two hundred and fifty thousand euros. I've just met him.' Brandishing a plastic bag, his pa opened it, and Mattias peered in. 'This, obviously, isn't going into the sock drawer.'

'He'll come for you. For us.' Mattias wrapped his arms around himself, his fingers digging into his ribs. 'We need to run, Pa. We're going to be picked up and put in jail for something. They'll make something up, say we were selling hard drugs, that we stole this money from him—'

'But then the film will go out, and we'll be, what's that big word that means you get off?'

'Exonerated?'

'Yes. He's between a rock and a hard place, my boy.'

'I don't like this one bit, Pa.'

'That's why we are going into the forest today, and we are going to bury this money. Just in case.'

'And then what?'

'I will send you to my third cousin's great-aunt in Belgium.'

'No way. I'm not leaving you—'

'Just until this all dies down.'

'I'm not running. They killed Elias, and I want, no, I need to be here.'

'That's exactly why you can't be.' His pa pulled him into a tight hug. 'Go and pack only what you need. We're doing this now, and then I'll get you onto a train at Ardeche, as I think we shouldn't go too near Le Puy. I'll drive you there. It's just over sixty kilometres, so it shouldn't take long. Your great aunt Tasha will meet you at the station. She knows what to do.'

X marks the spot!

Why on earth had his pa gone straight down the route of blackmail? It was such a cliché for a start! The money was in cellophane, wrapped in plastic, and placed in a small waterproof bag. Having dug the hole under the large root of a massive oak, they stared solemnly at it. It was a place they both knew they'd never forget (as they'd joked about all the films where the money ended up lost or, worse, under a tonne of concrete that formed the floor of the new shopping mall). At least here, the forest was protected in a conservation area of natural beauty.

'This isn't in exchange for Elias' life,' said his father, his hands crossed before him. 'I want you to know that, Mattias. I have not bought your brother's life.'

'I know, Pa.' Mattias bit down on his lip. But it sure felt like it was.

'There was nothing either of us could do to save him.' His pa laid a meaty hand on his shoulder. 'But at least this can ensure you might have a chance at a different life.'

'What have you done with the phone, Pa?'

'It's safe, don't worry about that.'

'But are you?'

'Don't worry about me, boy. I can look after myself.'

. . .

Mattias rode the train from Ardeche, changing trains when needed. He had to keep his head clear and watch for danger, although all he wanted to do was bawl his eyes out. He had five thousand euros in his holdall. It should be enough for a while, especially if he got work. Going over all that had occurred in the last few weeks, he found he couldn't mourn his brother yet. Not properly.

Tante Tasha was everything a gypsy matriarch should be. Fierce, compassionate and protective to the nth degree.

A few days later, Mattias received a phone call from his father.

'There's another two hundred and fifty thousand euros in the same place, Mattias. That should set you up. Don't go looking for it for a while, you hear me. I promised I would spread the rumour Elias left for the city—'

'Which city?'

'Any city, what does it matter? I will say he needed to move on, find newer pastures or some such drivel.' He paused. 'People will believe that, won't they?'

'Say... say he got sick of you beating him.'

There was an audible sound of breath being sucked in. 'I should say that?'

'They'd believe that more.'

'Hmm.' His father must be smoking. 'All right. But Mattias? Whatever I did, I did out of love. You understand?'

'Yes, Pa. I know. Oh, and Pa? Please say hello to Ma for me?'

'I will do, but you know you can chat with her anytime. She's always with us.'

'Thanks, Pa. I'll see you soon, eh?'

'Bye, Mattias.' As the phone clicked dead, Mattias felt his hair rise on end. A cold sensation swept over him. It was the same as the day that Elias died. He knew then he would never see his father alive again.

The next call came in from his uncle Tobias.

'There's been a terrible accident, Mattias.'

'Pa?' The word stuck in his throat.

'Yes. His car went off the road and into one of the deep ravines. They found him this morning. The police said he must have been speeding, as he clipped the barrier and went over the edge. They said it happened last night. Which is strange, as I know your pa never liked to drive at night.' Mattias heard him swallow. 'I'm so sorry, Mattias. Are you in contact with Elias? He needs to know, but no one can seem to get hold of him.'

'Yes. I'll tell him.'

'Was your pa up to something? I got the feeling there was something off?'

Mattias laughed, although it sounded more like a bark. 'Come on, Pa was always up to something. I think that this time, the "something" finally caught up with him.' Resting his head against the wall didn't help. 'I'll call you back.' The MacGregors had now killed his brother and his father. Archie MacGregor was a high court judge. Romilly MacGregor moved in the very best circles of society. They were practically untouchable.

When his phone rang again, he expected it to be his uncle.

'Mattias? It's Juliette. I need to talk to you about Elias.'

THIRTY-THREE

Hetty

FORGIVENESS

HETTY MIGHT HAVE READ hundreds of thrillers in her relatively short life, but she'd never been in one before now. The accusations, the revelations, the sheer horror of it, except this was real life, with real people involved, not actors on a screen or characters in a book. And three men had died. So far. No one seemed to be listening to her, even though she knew that this stuff called Prussian Blue could save him.

They were still bickering over who'd done what to whom. It was hard to wrap her head around all the who, where and why's. Either all of them were going down the nick, or none of them. The fact she'd been right about the actual modus operandi made her feel a little queasy. At least she could rule out a nasty new Covid variant. It was simply plain old poison.

Peering at Davey, it was like he'd turned to stone. One of them must be a Medusa as well. He finally moved, and then he was off, shouting at Isabel and then shouting at Ailsa. How must it feel to be faced with the fact that two close members of your family are murdering bitches? Probably not that good. She could sympathise with Jules. What would she have done in the same circumstances? The same, or with her background, possibly worse. Her mum had never been the same since that last horrific attack. Blinded in one eye but scarred deeply inside, she'd withdrawn inside herself. Blamed herself for not protecting her son. Hetty could never say what her father had done to her after that. Her mother would have never recovered. No parent should ever have to bury their child, and definitely, no mother should have to bury their child because their husband had beaten him to death. And then be told her beloved husband had raped her daughter. No. That couldn't happen. Ever.

The difference between her and Jules was that while she fantasised about the many ways to rid herself of her father, now serving life in prison (which in her mind was too good for the bastard as it meant he was still alive, while her dearly loved Paul was deep in the cold ground), Jules had got her hands dirty and carried out her revenge. She'd been judge and jury and, in the end, executioner. In a way, Hetty applauded her, admired her audacity. Revenge. Best served cold. In a way... Yet murder was murder, whichever way you looked at it. The taking of a life. Shit! A moral dilemma? Ambiguous at best. Reprehensible at worst.

How did she feel about Ailsa? She watched as Davey pulled her into his arms and, well, basically forgave her. Again, it should be taken into account that she was a terrified kid persuaded by her overbearing relatives to follow a particular course. Not the right course but one that had led to here. To now.

When Pierre tottered in, swigging wine from a bottle, Hetty held out her hand. He thrust the bottle at her, and she took a hefty gulp. Then another one. The liquid burned down her throat and hit her stomach. She stopped drinking as a thought hit her.

'Jules? You didn't poison any of the other bottles, did you?'

'Nah! You're okay, Hetty.'

Then the bombshell. Jules and Elias' brother Mattias were married. It seemed fate couldn't be twisted so easily, couldn't be bent to one person's will. Hetty saw Isabel's expression. What was that saying? *Quelle horreur?*

'What we need to do is we need to call the hospital and the police.' Pierre looked stricken. 'We can sort out all the other bits later, but we need to save my dad!'

Hetty thought she'd try again. 'It's called Prussian Blue,' she said. 'The antidote. Just thought I'd put that out there...'

'What the fuck is the matter with you all?' Pierre screamed. *'My father is dying, and we have to get him the fucking antidote!'*

'Your father is dying,' said Mattias, 'whereas my father is dead.'

'Oh, I think,' said Jules, 'you need to hear the next part of the story.' She glanced up at Mattias.

As far as Hetty could see, there would be a huge bill for counselling sessions after this.

THIRTY-FOUR

Mattias

REVENGE?

2016 - Mattias

THERE WERE a few times when the police had been so close, could have reached out with their long arms and snagged him, yet somehow, he'd wriggled and slipped through their fingers. Maybe Elias was watching over him, beside his ma in the afterlife. He'd slunk back in the dark of night and dug up the money. It was so much he was at a loss as to what to do with it, but leaving it here was dangerous for him. It was too close to the watchful eyes of Archie MacGregor and the police he had in his pocket. It was amazing what money could do, the evil it could buy, and the corruption it could engender. So he found different places dotted across the countryside and buried it all, taking only what he needed so as not to arouse suspicion.

Some part of him thought he should leave it all in the past and allow Juliette to move on, but another part of him baulked at that. It was her right to know the truth, wasn't it? She must have believed Elias just ran out on her, and he needed to make that right to at least let him get justice in her eyes. It was like a small explosion in his head. He knew now was the time to contact Juliette. A couple of months past her seventeenth birthday. Not quite an adult but old enough to make up her mind about what to do.

'Juliette? It's me, Mattias. I have something I need to show you.'

That blew her world to pieces. At eighteen, Juliette packed her things and moved to Manchester, finishing school up there with excellent grades while working in bars until she could apply for university.

Mattias and Juliette kept in contact, and when she got her passport, she met up with him in Lyon. She was nineteen, and he was eighteen. Then they met the year after and the year after that.

Mattias visited Juliette in Manchester, perfecting his English and falling ever-so-slowly in love with her. It was then they started to talk about revenge. It might have started as a joke, in bad taste, but it was still a joke at that point. Then, it bloomed like a rotten, stinking flower.

'She's engaged, you know.' Juliette let this piece of information slip after they'd made love. It was in the afternoon, though sometimes that was the best time.

'Who is?' Mattias wasn't paying attention, too drowsy and sated.

'Isabel. She's engaged to a fascist pig of an M.P. Maybe you've heard of him. Jean-Jacques D'Aramitz?'

It was like someone had dropped an Alka-Seltzer into his brain. It fizzed and popped. He sat up fast in bed, giving him a head rush.

'The guy who's got it in for us Roma?'

'Yep. One and the same.'

'Let me get this right. Isabel, who murdered my brother, will now live a long and happy life in the arms of a racist shit?'

'A very rich, racist shit,' said Juliette. 'I think we should look at changing the story here. I don't think she deserves to live a long and happy life. I think she deserves to feel what we felt, to feel that loss. I think we should do all we can to make sure she has a really shitty life.'

'How?' Mattias shook himself like a dog dunked in cold water. 'I've daydreamed of bashing her head in with a shovel—'

'I know, love. So have I. But think about it. That would be too quick and also super dangerous for us. I propose we work out how to do something to old Jacky boy that doesn't lead back to us.'

'That means us getting into close proximity to the man, and that won't be easy.'

'Let's see if I get an invite to the wedding.'

'MacGregor wouldn't risk you all being there again. I mean, both Ailsa and Pierre know his part in this.'

'I don't think they dare not invite us. We're close family. I expect they all think they got away with it.'

'They did.'

Juliette smiled. 'But not for much longer.'

THIRTY-FIVE

Ailsa

BLOOD MONEY

'So,' said Ailsa, leaning forward, 'what you're saying is Archie had your father killed?' She reared back. 'Is that what you're saying?'

'Oh,' said Mattias, 'I know he had my father rammed off the road at that ravine.'

'How do you know?' said Pierre. 'We heard your father was drunk and speeding, and he lost control of his car at the bend—'

'Convenient, eh?' Mattias tilted his head. 'Just after Archie had paid my dad off, he had a nasty accident, when we all know he never drove at night. He drank, but he never drank while driving. You all know that.'

'Because,' Davey nodded, 'his father drove while drunk and killed a young woman in the village. I remember the story. He swore he'd never do the same.'

'Why would he be up the mountain, drunk, when he always drank in the village bars and walked home? And trust me, at that time, he wouldn't have risked being drunk or not being in control. Not with what he was doing—'

'Yes,' Isabel pointed at Mattias, 'we need to come back to that. The fact he was blackmailing my father—'

It was like Mattias turned into something else in front of their eyes. His face morphed into a mask of rage and hate. 'Why do you think that might be, Isabel?' He moved so fast that he was practically a blur. Then he was inches from Isabel's face, his voice now so low it was like some sub-sonic reverberation that juddered Ailsa's rib cage. Like a tiger's roar. 'You snuffed out my brother's life. You named him something reprehensible, and your fucking pig of a father buried him like a bag of rubbish somewhere.' His eyes were glowing yellow, like a wolf's. Christ! Had he turned into a werewolf or something?

'Don't you touch me!' Isabel's mouth was a slit.

'I don't ever want to touch you, Isabel. My hands are dirty enough as it is.' He moved away from her as if she was a leper. 'If we'd gone to the police, they would have protected you, as they finally did by killing my pa. I managed to stay one step ahead of them, working for my family and keeping my head down. I was protected by the very thing you all hate about us. I could disappear, and you lot couldn't find me.'

'Except they tried, didn't they?' Jules also stared at Isabel. 'Your father did everything in his power to hunt Mattias down. Archie wanted his money back, and he wanted him dead.'

Mattias continued. 'My uncle Tobias tried to get justice. He was thwarted at every turn. He even sussed out what happened to Elias. Your family were shielded by the very people who should have protected *us*.'

'If you remember,' said Jules, 'I left home at eighteen. Went to do my degree in Manchester. By then, Mattias had told me what you all did. What you, my beloved cousin Isabel and your father did. I do believe we are even.'

'You can't prove any of this.' Isabel smiled her cat smile. 'Can you?'

'Apart from the film they have?' Hetty slapped her hand over her mouth. 'Sorry!'

'I meant about Mattias' dad.'

Ailsa stared at her cousin. 'Does it matter whether they have proof? Did Archie do all that? Get the police to do his dirty work for him? Kill for him to protect you lot,' she gulped, 'I mean us lot?'

'He got in our business.' Isabel made a face. 'They tried to blackmail us!'

'You sound so horrified, Izzy,' said Jules. 'It seems you can put a price on a life.'

'My uncle,' continued Mattias, 'found our family home ransacked. They must have found the phone and given it to your dad. He must have destroyed it and thought, no, believed that was the end of it. Each member of our family was hauled into the police station and, how do I say this, interrogated. And they weren't nice about it.'

'That was our money!' Isabel rose, but Mattias pushed her back down.

'It's blood money, true. We had no form of restitution. Not one of you could ever amend what you did. Except you all have to make a choice now. You can save Archie. He still has time, and then you can let us be on our way.'

'Because,' said Jules, 'if you don't, we'll take you all down with us.'

'What about us?' Davey motioned at himself and Hetty. 'We were nothing to do with any of this. You can't threaten us—'

'No,' agreed Jules, 'but we can ask you one simple question. Do you want your cousins and sisters to go to prison for murder or as an accessory to murder? Do you want Archie's name dragged through the courts? I'm afraid it will be all or none of us.'

'This is the most horrendous thing I've ever heard—'

'I think being told the man you loved beyond anything has been killed by your ever-loving family is actually the most horrendous thing you could ever hear. Mattias told me about a year later and sent the film to me. Told me he'd also lost his dad. And how. For a year, I thought Elias had abandoned me. I don't know what was worse, how that made me feel or then finding out he was always true to me. That he'd been killed because he wasn't acceptable to my family.'

'We didn't plan to be together,' said Mattias, glancing sweetly at Jules, 'but it happened so slowly, at first we weren't even aware of it—'

Isabel snarled, 'None of us cares about your little love story—'

'Er, I do,' said Hetty. 'A tragic romance.'

'Oh, do shut up!' Isabel waved her hand at Hetty as if she was an annoying fly.

'And there's that.' Jules motioned at Hetty. 'When would be the point when you lured poor, sweet Hetty into the barn to bump her off?'

'What?' said Hetty.

'*What?*' said Davey. 'What are you saying?'

'That's it. Just saying. You should watch your back, Hetty, in case someone stabs a great big knife into it.' She raised an eyebrow. 'What happened to Elias could quite easily happen to you.'

'What!' Hetty shrieked. '*What is wrong with this bloody family?*'

'It's okay, Hetty,' said Davey, pulling her into an embrace.

'Nothing like that is going to happen. We're out of here the moment we are allowed to go.'

'About that.' Mattias leaned forward and eyed them all one by one. 'We have Prussian Blue upstairs. We can give it to you. All you have to do is give a solution to Archie without anyone noticing. You mix it into a bottle of Evian or whatever.'

'In exchange for not saying anything?' Pierre looked so hopeful. 'We can save my dad if we keep our mouths shut?'

'Exactly. We slip off into the night, and you all carry on business as usual.'

'Just don't expect a card at Christmas,' said Jules. 'What do we say? We agree to a truce. We overlook what you did, and you give us the same respect. Oh, and we will give you a bonus. We let Archie live, but only in exchange for the whereabouts of Elias' body. Agreed?'

Looking around the room, Ailsa saw the wars in their minds. They were all complicit in some way, except Davey and Hetty, although would they lose their whole family for the sake of their morals?

'It's too late for Elias and J.J.,' she said.

'Don't forget my pa,' said Mattias, a heavy scowl across his face.

'And your dad, but it's not too late for us. Please,' she swivelled to look at Davey and Hetty, 'don't throw our lives away.'

'Looks like you've all managed that with no help from me.' Davey's voice was raspy with emotion.

'So how do we do this?' Ailsa wanted to chew off all her fingernails. 'Hands up? Secret ballot?'

'Hands up would be the clearer choice,' said Jules. 'No misunderstandings.'

'Okay then.' Mattias raised his hand. 'I vote to let bygones be bygones.'

'As do I.' Jules raised her hand.

'Me too,' said Ailsa. 'I don't want to ever experience the inside of a French prison, and, also, I can't say sorry enough for my part. I knew it was wrong, but I feared the repercussions if I told the truth. And I'm ashamed to say I didn't want to lose Isabel's friendship. She meant the world to me then.'

'She knew that,' said Jules, 'and she used your feelings against you.'

'Nor me,' said Pierre. 'I don't think I'd fare well in prison, and I need to get the blue stuff to my dad. No matter what you say, he must be running out of time.' He hesitated. 'I also want to say that I'm so sorry for what I did. In my defence, I didn't understand what I was doing, and Dad... and Dad and Izzy made it sound like he'd done something terrible.' He sank onto one of the easy chairs and lowered his head into his hands. Through sobs, he said again, 'I'm so sorry.'

'We know,' said Jules soothingly. 'You were a kid and were pushed into acting against your better judgement. Davey? What will you vote for?'

'Jesus! What choice do I have? I don't want to be visiting any of you in prison, with metal files secreted in a fruit cake. I'm having difficulty taking all of this in right now. Part of me thinks I'd be thrilled if I never see any of you ever again!' He made a guttural noise at the back of his throat like a growl. 'Then I vote for bygones and damn you all to hell!'

'Understood. Hetty? You have the least to lose here. How will you vote?'

'I think by now you know I love thrillers, but I wasn't expecting to be in one. I don't like it. Not one bit. You all terrify me, and I don't want to be forever looking over my shoulder to see if one of you is trying to kill me. So, I'm with Davey on the "never want to see any of you again", and I vote for bygones.'

'Isabel.' Jules' voice was icy like she'd just taken it out of the freezer. 'You have as much as I do to lose. Possibly more, if you count Archie. With us, and you get to save your scrawny little arse, or against us, and we all go down?'

Isabel tucked a lock of her long dark hair behind her ear. 'I'm not getting a centimo from J.J. because of the Prenup, and his fucking awful parents would fight me every step of the way.' She bit her lower lip, and unshed tears hung on her lashes. 'I'm his widow, and yet I get nothing. I suppose I have to work out what I want more. To have the satisfaction of seeing you fucktards go down but end up going down with you, or to remain free.' Wiping briskly at her face, she seemed to come to a conclusion. Ailsa held her breath. Her life hinged on this one moment in time.

'I love my freedom more. But I will never forgive you. I loved J.J. so much—'

'Touché,' whispered Juliette.

Mattias stirred, wet streaks down his cheeks. 'I gather from that, we are letting bygones be bygones. Just remember, all of you, we have copies of the film in very safe places. Unlike my pa, we do have a contingency plan that if anything should happen to us, it will immediately be released onto the internet and to the French authorities.'

Sobbing, Jules clapped her hands as if it was the end of an outstanding performance. 'All's well that ends well.'

'That blue stuff?' Pierre held out a shaking hand. '*Now!*'

Epilogue

'ARE YOU GOING TO CONTACT THEM?' Hetty handed Davey a hot chocolate. Cuddled on the sofa, they were ostensibly watching *Narcos* on Netflix, but even with all the violent death and machinations, it had been hard to keep reading the subtitles, and their minds had wandered back to what they'd endured in France. 'It's been over a year.'

'They could have contacted me. It works both ways.' He drank some cocoa, and Hetty smiled at his chocolatey moustache.

'They might think, considering what you yelled at them that last afternoon in the house, that you don't want to ever see them again?'

'I think they should make the first move. They're the ones in the wrong here.'

'Wrong is subjective, sometimes.'

'I know you want us all to be a family again...' He looked down at that. Hetty had told him about her past, about Paul and her mother. And her father. He'd been visibly stunned, and

Hetty thought maybe she had pushed him away with her revelations. That he couldn't cope.

'We seem to have a cemetery's worth of skeletons in our closets,' she'd joked.

He remained dazed. 'I'm so sorry. I have no idea what else to say except something like that should never happen to anyone. Let alone a child. I hope the bastard rots in hell.'

'Not as much as I do. You see, that's where I can empathise with Jules. I would have given my dear old dad a lovely cup of poison if I could have—'

'Would you, though?'

'If I'd been a stronger person, maybe.' She bit her lip. 'I looked it all up online. That's why I knew so much about thallium. I seriously contemplated giving it to my dad.'

'First. You're one of the strongest people I know. And second. *Really?*'

'Maybe, I don't know. Do you see what I'm getting at? There's a fine line between what you fantasise about and what you manifest in reality. It's a knife's edge. And Ailsa and Pierre were kids heavily influenced by an older kid they looked up to. And then there was Archie. An adult and a high court judge. Can you honestly say you wouldn't have done the same in those circumstances?'

'Pierre didn't know better. He blindly accepted what they told him, but Ailsa? She was there. She saw exactly what Isabel did—'

'I think Isabel couched it in terms of, if you tell on me, we'll both go to jail, or worse, I'll say it was you. I bet something like that happened.'

'Isabel was a nasty piece of work. I didn't see it when we were growing up, although it was always there. I think she also influenced Ailsa a lot.'

'Exactly. But Ailsa and Pierre? I'm pretty sure they would love to see you. I mean, maybe they really took what you said to heart. That you never wanted to see them again.'

'I still don't know if I *do* want to see them.' He shifted about on the sofa and took another swig of his chocolate. 'Ouch. That's hot.'

'Ailsa's your sister. I bet she misses you. Surely you miss her, too?'

Davey again shuffled around, as if he was uncomfortable and Hetty realised that he was. He was having trouble dealing with all the stuff that had happened.

'Do you want me to call you Becky?'

'You're changing the subject. I understand why. And, no, I'm not her anymore. I'm not Becky—' Hetty swallowed. 'But I do want you to meet my mum. Would that be okay? I need her to see I turned out all right.'

'I'd love to meet your mum.' Davey pulled her down and kissed her gently. 'Love you, Miss Hetty.'

'Love you, too, Mr Davey.'

'I love you more. Now let's stop talking about all this. It's giving me a headache.'

Even though she was expecting it, the doorbell ringing still made her jump. Hetty opened the door to their flat. She'd had to have a glass of red wine to steady her nerves.

'Hi, come in.' She gestured in. The people outside stamped their feet and bundled into the long corridor. 'Let me get your coats.' She hung them on the coat rail bolted to the wall. 'The lounge is just to the right. My mum's in there. Go in and make yourselves at home.'

'Thanks, Hetty.'

Hetty nodded and smoothed out their coat and jacket as they passed her and pushed into the living room. As it was Christmas Eve, all the decorations were up, and everything was twinkly and sparkly.

'Mum?' Hetty followed them in and motioned at the two people who stood awkwardly in the middle of the lounge. 'This is Ailsa, Davey's sister, and Pierre, his cousin.'

'Very pleased to meet you,' said her mum, trying to lever herself out of the sofa. One eye was a soft opaque, like a pearl. A visible reminder of Hetty's father.

'Please don't get up.' Ailsa bent over and gave Hetty's mum a hug and a warm kiss on the cheek. Hetty nearly fainted.

'Come and sit down on this side, else I won't be able to see you properly.' Her mum patted the sofa beside her. Pierre bounced onto it and kissed her mum on both cheeks. 'Oh, you're so French. How lovely.'

'Would you like a glass of wine, a G&T?' asked Hetty. 'Or maybe a coffee?' She smiled at Pierre, sitting on the sofa.

'Have you got rum? I'd love a coffee with a slosh of rum in it?'

'Sounds like Christmas is coming,' said her mum, with a wink of her good eye.

'It is indeed, Mrs Green.' Pierre winked back.

Hetty understood that 'brandy' wasn't on the cards now, after everything they'd all gone through, no matter how expensive it might be. 'Coming right up. Ailsa?'

'A red wine would be great. Thanks.' She sat beside Pierre, their knees touching. 'It all looks wonderful in here.'

'I love Christmas. Didn't always,' Hetty glanced at her mum, 'but now I do.'

'Davey used to love it too,' said Ailsa. 'I remember it was the best time of year for us all. We felt like a family, eating

Christmas breakfast at the table all together before we were allowed to open the presents.'

A little tree, twirled and bedecked with lights and baubles, and enough tinsel to fell an elephant, sat on a wooden table in front of the large bay window. Winter light streamed in through gauzy net curtains. Other decorations hung from the paintings and prints on the walls, and were precariously perched in front of the books on the bookshelves tucked into the alcoves on either side of the fireplace. Hetty had always bemoaned the fact that they couldn't risk an open wood fire, although it looked very pretty with a vase of dried flowers on the hearth.

'I'll get those drinks,' said Hetty, pushing a wayward curl back into her ponytail. 'Mum? A top up?'

'No, I'm fine, love.'

'Can I help?' Ailsa stood hesitantly.

'Sure.' Hetty led them down the long hallway. Paintings lined the white decorated wooden clad walls.

Ailsa stopped and leaned in close to one. She turned from examining it and smiled genuinely at Hetty. 'I love the artwork. Are they yours?'

'Yes, painting is my hobby.'

'Do you sell your work? I think they'd go like the proverbial hotcakes.'

'I sell locally, though I'm not that good at marketing.'

'Maybe I can help you? Do you have a website?'

'Not yet. It's on the list of things to do, which I never get around to doing.' She entered the kitchen, Ailsa on her heels.

'It's something I can do easily, and I'd love to get a website set up for you.' Ailsa peered out of the back door window into the backyard. 'If you'd like?'

'That would be brilliant. Thanks.'

'I can link you to Etsy and all the other platforms. Like I said, I think you'd do very well.'

Hetty knew she was blushing. 'Right, I'll get the coffee on for Pierre, and you can pour us the wine. Here's my glass, and there's a clean glass in the cupboard behind you.' She pointed.

'When will Davey get back?' Ailsa retrieved the glass.

'Maybe half an hour to an hour. I thought we could have a little bit of time to chat.'

'And if he blows his top?'

'You booked into a hotel, didn't you?'

'Yeah, some little boutique place in the Lanes. It's quite odd, but Pierre seems to like it.'

'How is he?' Hetty ladled coffee granules into the percolator and placed it on the gas. As Ailsa handed her the glass of wine, she turned fully to look at her.

'He's dealing. Not particularly well, though we've got through the worst of it. At least, I hope we have. The family, as you might imagine, is a mess.'

'I bet. How much has Romi been told?'

'She's been kept completely in the dark. Archie now knows the truth and knows that we know the truth. I gather he's keeping a low profile and has retired early from the judicial system.'

'As he should,' nodded Hetty.

'I also want to say,' said Ailsa, looking Hetty in the eye, 'I know you haven't had an easy time of it either.'

'No, I haven't.'

'If you want to talk about it?'

'No, I'm okay, thanks. Like we said on the phone, let the past stay in the past.'

'And your mum? How much does she know?'

'The bare bones. Simply, Davey's French side of the family

experienced some difficulties. It's not like she doesn't know that any family can experience trouble.' Hetty coloured at that. 'And Isabel?'

'Isabel has lost her golden touch as an influencer. She tried to wheedle money out of Archie, but he's pretty pissed off about everything. He lost five hundred thousand euros and his job, and only just about clung onto his prestige, but only because he felt forced to retire. And all based on a lie.'

'I think even if he'd known at the time, he would have still done the same. To protect his daughter.'

'Yeah, I suppose so. The thing is, Isabel has been forced to get a proper job—'

'You mean she's working for her money?' Hetty grinned widely. 'How funny is that?'

'I know. She's also lost her looks, so no catching a rich young bachelor. Well, not at the moment.'

'Poor Romi.' Hetty clinked glasses with Ailsa. 'She must wonder what the hell went on.'

'They are basically blaming it all on J.J.'s death. I expect she's perplexed about the change in dynamics, but she always just goes with the flow.'

'How did they explain Archie having the same symptoms?'

Ailsa looked up at the ceiling. 'Ah! Archie bribed one of the pathologists to say it was mushroom poisoning after all and that he must have got a micro dosage.'

'Wow! Money sure does get you what you need, doesn't it?' Holy shite! Bribed a pathologist? Things like that really happened? Hetty had presumed it was only in books.

'Seemingly so.'

'How do these people sleep at night?'

Ailsa raised an eyebrow. 'I asked Isabel that years ago. As far as I can work out, they sleep absolutely fine.'

'Unbelievable, though I suppose an infusion of cash into their lives helps.'

'Money talks, or in this case, money stopped them talking.'

The coffee was hissing and bubbling on the stove. Hetty made a coffee how Pierre enjoyed it. She could remember from her time in France how they all liked their teas and coffees, as she had made an inordinate number of them while the family crumbled.

Returning to the lounge, Hetty handed Pierre his coffee and a bottle of dark rum.

As he sloshed in a liberal amount, he looked up at them both. 'Merry Christmas, you guys.' Swivelling, he grinned at Hetty's mum. 'Merry Christmas, Mrs Green. Very pleased to have finally met you.'

'Merry Christmas.'

Hetty needed to broach the question. 'Has anyone heard from Jules and Mattias?'

'No.' Ailsa looked like she was struggling with her emotions. 'I don't think we'll see them again.'

'Even after the ghastly things she did,' Hetty took a gulp of her wine, 'I still liked her.'

'I know you did, and I'm sorry I was such an arse when I first met you.' Ailsa covered her mouth. 'Oh, sorry, Mrs Green.'

'Oh, I don't worry about things like that, dear.'

Ailsa looked over at Hetty. 'Am I forgiven?'

'Of course. The main thing is, will Davey forgive you?'

'We can but try.'

'Listen,' Pierre scratched at his ear, 'if he throws us out, will you still meet us for coffee tomorrow? We're only down the road.'

'Why would Davey throw you out?' Hetty's mum looked perplexed. 'Especially as it's Christmas.'

'Family problems, Mrs Green.' Ailsa shrugged. 'It's up to him.'

Hetty said, 'I've got Christmas dinner sorted for us all. I told him I had a couple of old mates down from London, and he accepted that. He's been torn, I can tell you. You're his family, and the fact that this all happened, and he knew nothing about it, made him feel a bit sickened. You know? Like he should have picked up on it. I also think he feels guilty he never caught up with Elias. That he accepted his disappearance too easily. It's made him question so many aspects of his life.'

'I hear you on that.' Pierre topped up the rum in his coffee.

Ailsa rolled her eyes. 'It's made me question, too. I would like to say I hope I'm a better person because of it all.'

Hetty refrained from saying that she couldn't be a worse one. She held her tongue. There was nothing like adversity in a person's life to highlight what was good and bad. And what to hang onto and what to throw away.

Pierre bounced up from the sofa. 'Someone is coming down the steps. Is that Davey?' He made a quick cross over his chest. 'I hope he can forgive us.'

'I'm sure it'll be fine, dear.' Mrs Green nodded. 'Davey has not got a mean bone in his body, thank the Lord!'

'I'll pre-empt him,' said Hetty. 'Let him know you're both here.' She trotted to the front door just as it opened.

'Boy,' said Davey,' it's cold out there. I wonder if it'll snow?' He shrugged out of his jacket and hung it over the other coats on the rack.

'A white Christmas? That would be magical. Listen, Davey. I don't want you to be angry, but we have a couple of guests—'

'Your friends from school? Why should I be angry?'

'They're not exactly my friends from school. Come in and meet them.'

'That sounds a bit ominous,' he whispered.

'Just come in.' She took his hand and led him into the lounge. '*Surprise!*'

'Hello, Davey,' said Ailsa. 'Merry Christmas.'

'Davey,' said Pierre.

There was a stretched-out moment of silence. Hetty held her breath.

'Merry Christmas.' Davey pulled Ailsa and Pierre into his arms. 'Merry bloody Christmas!'

Acknowledgments

I would like to thank my publishers, Hobeck Books and their dedicated team, for believing in me and my work. So, thanks to Rebecca and Adrian, and thanks to my hard-working editor, Sue, who has been brilliant and caught those inconsistencies. And thanks to Jayne for her fabulous cover.

My thanks are extended to my amazing beta readers, who include Cheryl Davison, Nigel Stubley, Caroline Fox, Jan Gibbs, Sarah Louise Green, Krystyna Rogerson, Pam Newman, and last but by no means least, Theresa Terry Hetherington. Thanks for all your invaluable insights.

Thanks to my partner Malk, to whom this book is dedicated.

Thanks also to Cornerstones Literary Consultancy, who have critiqued my work and taught me invaluable lessons along the way.

And last but by no means least, thanks to my mum and dad (who have now both passed on), as they never wanted me to let go of my dreams and told me to do whatever I wanted with my life.

I did, but I wish they were here to see it.

So again, thanks to everyone who has helped me on my journey to here.

Hilly Barmby

About the Author

Hilly attended Rochester College of Art to experience an excellent Foundation Course, which led to a degree course in Graphic Design at Central School of Art and Design in London. Here, she led a colourful life, which she has woven into many of her stories.

After her degree course, she went on a woodworking course to make furniture. Combining her art and woodworking skills, she got a stall at Covent Garden Craft Market to sell hand-made chess and backgammon sets.

She moved to Brighton, a fabulous city (where Hilly's first novel for Hobeck *Best Served Cold* is set). After teaching Design Technology for fifteen years, she gave it all up to relocate to Órgiva in southern Spain. She has been here for the last seven years, living happily in an old farmhouse on an organic fruit farm in the mountains, with her partner and two rescue dogs.

Hilly is also part of Artists' Network Alpujarra (ANA), a community of artists who have exhibited extensively in the region of the Alpujarra. She also makes ceramics, jewellery, and up-cycles anything not nailed down.

To connect with Hilly you can find her on a variety of platforms.

Website: www.hillybarmbyauthor.com

Instagram: https://www.instagram.com/hillyollie
Twitter: https://twitter.com/Hilly_Barmby
TikTok: https://www.tiktok.com/@hillybarmby387
Facebook: https://www.facebook.com/HillyOllieBarmby
BlueSky: https://bsky.app/profile/hilliebillie.bsky.social

Hobeck Books - the home of great stories

We hope you've enjoyed reading this novel by Hilly Barmby. To keep up to date on Hilly's fiction writing please do follow her on Twitter.

Hobeck Books offers a number of short stories and novellas, free for subscribers in the compilation *Crime Bites*.

- *Echo Rock* by Robert Daws

- *Old Dogs, Old Tricks* by AB Morgan
- *The Silence of the Rabbit* by Wendy Turbin
- *Never Mind the Baubles: An Anthology of Twisted Winter Tales* by the Hobeck Team (including many of the Hobeck authors and Hobeck's two publishers)
- *The Clarice Cliff Vase* by Linda Huber
- *Here She Lies* by Kerena Swan
- *The Macnab Principle* by R.D. Nixon
- *Fatal Beginnings* by Brian Price
- *A Defining Moment* by Lin Le Versha
- *Saviour* by Jennie Ensor
- *You Can't Trust Anyone These Days* by Maureen Myant

Also please visit the Hobeck Books website for details of our other superb authors and their books, and if you would like to get in touch, we would love to hear from you.

Hobeck Books also presents a weekly podcast, the Hobcast, where founders Adrian Hobart and Rebecca Collins discuss all things book related, key issues from each week, including the ups and downs of running a creative business. Each episode includes an interview with one of the people who make Hobeck possible: the editors, the authors, the cover designers. These are the people who help Hobeck bring great stories to life. Without them, Hobeck wouldn't exist. The Hobcast can be listened to from all the usual platforms but it can also be found on the Hobeck website: **www.hobeck.net/hobcast**.

Other Hobeck Books to Explore

Silenced

A teenage girl is murdered on her way home from school, stabbed through the heart. Her North London community is shocked, but no-one has the courage to help the police, not even her mother. DI Callum Waverley, in his first job as senior investigating officer, tries to break through the code of silence that shrouds the case.

This is a world where the notorious Skull Crew rules through fear. Everyone knows you keep your mouth shut or you'll be silenced – permanently.

This is Luke's world. Reeling from the loss of his mother to cancer, his step-father distant at best, violent at worst, he slides into the Skull Crew's grip.

This is Jez's world too. Her alcoholic mother neither knows nor cares that her 16-year-old daughter is being exploited by V, all-powerful leader of the gang.

Luke and Jez form a bond. Can Callum win their trust, or will his own demons sabotage his investigation? And can anyone stop the Skull Crew ensuring all witnesses are silenced?

Pact of Silence

A fresh start for a new life

Newly pregnant, Emma is startled when her husband Luke announces they're swapping homes with his parents, but the rural idyll where Luke grew up is a great place to start their family. Yet Luke's manner suggests something odd is afoot, something that Emma can't quite fathom.

Too many secrets, not enough truths

Emma works hard to settle into her new life in the Yorkshire countryside, but a chance discovery increases her suspicions. She decides to dig a little deeper...

Be careful what you uncover

Will Emma find out why the locals are behaving so oddly? Can she discover the truth behind Luke's disturbing behaviour? Will the pact of silence ever be broken?

Blood Notes

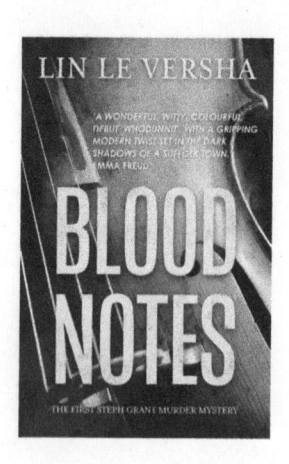

Winner of a 2022 Chill With A Book Premier Reader's Award!

'A wonderful, witty, colourful, debut 'Whodunnit', with a gripping modern twist set in the dark shadows of a Suffolk town.' EMMA FREUD

Edmund Fitzgerald is different.

Sheltered by an over-protective mother, he's a musical prodigy.

Now, against his mother's wishes, he's about to enter formal education for the first time aged sixteen.

Everything is alien to Edmund: teenage style, language and relationships are impossible to understand.

Then there's the searing jealousy his talent inspires, especially when the sixth form college's Head of Music, turns her back on her other students and begins to teach Edmund exclusively.

Observing events is Steph, a former police detective who is rebuilding her life following a bereavement as the college's receptionist. When a student is found dead in the music block, Steph's sleuthing skills help to unravel the dark events engulfing the college community.

Also by Hilly Barmby

Best Served Cold (Hobeck Books)

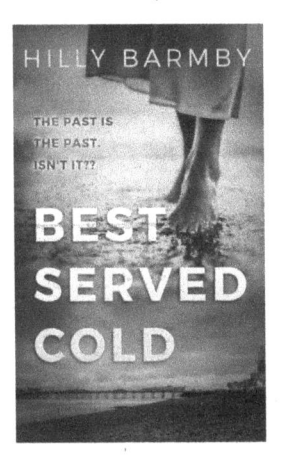

'terrific storytelling'
JENNIE ENSOR

A mystery woman enters Lily's life
At the launch for her latest children's book, a member of the

audience asks Lily for an strange inscription in her copy of the book. Why does this unnerve her?

Is Jack the answer to Lily's prayers?

Later, while celebrating in a local bar, Lily, and best friend Alice, spot the same woman. Her name is Rose. Putting aside earlier unease, a new friendship between the three is formed. Rose offers to help Lily re-enter the dating scene after a bad breakup and they come across Jack, Mr Perfect on Paper. Lily quickly falls for handsome Jack. Is he too good to be true?

The past is the past, or is it?

Soon after the pair start dating, bizarre things start to occur to Lily, things are moved or they go missing, and, what's worse, her precious artwork is damaged. Who did this to her? Surely it can't have been her new boyfriend, her new friend Rose, or even oldest friend Alice? They all have a motive. Perhaps Lily did this all herself. Who can she trust, in fact, can she trust herself? Or has a ghost from Lily's past come back to haunt her?

Available as ebook and paperback.

Also by Hilly Barmby

From My Cold Dead Hands (Bloodhound Books)

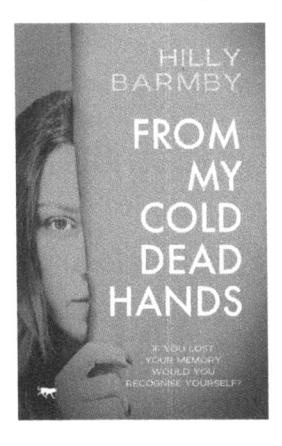

Little by little, Cassie, an amnesiac, pieces together the truth about her Southern family, her old life, and a friend's murder, in this engrossing novel of suspense.
https://geni.us/ColdDeadHands

The Pact (Bloodhound Books)

A get-together reveals dark secrets that tie old friends together—
and tear them apart—in a twisting new thriller.
A group of old friends caught up in a terrible tragedy.
https://geni.us/ThePactCover

Hilly also publishes YA fiction as **Billie Hill**.

Eazee Life (Spellbound Books)

What is it that makes you human?
The ability to pass your genes on into the future?
Or maybe it's how *rich* you are.
Could it be the fact that you were born and have the right to a soul? But what about Benedict? A clone. Not born but grown in a tank to fulfil a purpose not his own? Is it his capacity to care, to *love* that will make him human?
https://amzn.eu/d/aHax9Tv

Glimpse (coming soon)